"I'M NOT WEARING THAT."

Ty eyed the pair of red silk boxers, jingle bell suspenders, and the Santa hat that had been laid out for him on one of the tables at Darla's wine bar. When she'd called and said the Chamber of Commerce wanted to get an early start on the cowboy calendar, he had no idea what he was walking into.

"I already told you. I'll wear boots and jeans." Actually, he'd said *if* he did the calendar he'd wear boots and jeans. He never remembered officially agreeing to this baloney. How Darla had managed to convince eleven other rodeo stars to travel out here a few days early for this, he'd never know.

"But you're Mr. December." Darla held up the suspenders and shook them to make them jingle. "This is the wardrobe we've selected for Mr. December." She peered up at him from underneath those long sleek eyelashes, and it finally clicked. It was her eyes. That was what he found so captivating about her. They were persuasive as hell. No man had a shot at telling her no.

A Cowboy for
Christmas

PRAISE FOR THE ROCKY MOUNTAIN RIDERS SERIES

COLORADO COWBOY

"Readers who love tear-jerking small-town romances with minimal sex scenes and maximum emotional intimacy will quickly devour this charming installment."

—*Publishers Weekly*

TRUE-BLUE COWBOY

"Richardson takes readers on an emotionally satisfying, sometimes wrenching journey in her fourth Rocky Mountain Riders contemporary western."

—*Publishers Weekly*

RENEGADE COWBOY

"Top Pick! An amazing story about finding a second chance to be with the one that you love."

—*Harlequin Junkie*

"A beautifully honest and heartwarming tale about forgiveness and growing up that will win the hearts of fans and newcomers alike."

—*RT Book Reviews*

COMEBACK COWBOY

"Richardson beautifully illustrates the rocky road of love and the power of redemption in this emotionally charged tale. With a tight, compelling plot and expert characterization, she creates a warm, comfortable world readers will want to visit again and again."

—*Publishers Weekly*

"Richardson's empathy for her protagonists shines through every page of her second Rocky Mountain Riders novel, making their long-awaited reunion into a sweet tale that will easily win readers' hearts."

—*RT Book Reviews*

HOMETOWN COWBOY

"Filled with humor, heart, and love, this page-turner is one wild ride."

—Jennifer Ryan, *New York Times* bestselling author

"An emotional ride with characters that come alive on every single page. Sara brings real feelings to every scene she writes."

—Carolyn Brown, *New York Times* bestselling author

"[The] story is sensitive, charmingly funny, satisfyingly spicy, and dedicated to ensuring both protagonists grow to earn their lasting love. This will satisfy Richardson's fans while welcoming new readers to a sweeping land of mountains, cowboys, and romance."

—*Publishers Weekly*

A Cowboy for Christmas

A ROCKY MOUNTAIN RIDERS NOVEL

SARA RICHARDSON

FOREVER
New York Boston

Grand Central Publishing
Hachette Book Group
1290 Avenue of the Americas, New York, NY 10104
grandcentralpublishing.com
twitter.com/grandcentralpub

First Mass Market Edition: October 2019

Grand Central Publishing is a division of Hachette Book Group, Inc. The Grand Central Publishing name and logo is a trademark of Hachette Book Group, Inc.

The publisher is not responsible for websites (or their content) that are not owned by the publisher.

The Hachette Speakers Bureau provides a wide range of authors for speaking events. To find out more, go to www.hachettespeakersbureau.com or call (866) 376-6591.

ISBNs: 978-1-5387-1229-0 (mass market), 978-1-5387-1231-3 (ebook)

Printed in the United States of America

OPM

10 9 8 7 6 5 4 3 2 1

To Joni Leahy

Acknowledgments

It's hard to believe this is the last book in the Rocky Mountain Riders series! I have loved spending time with the colorful characters in Topaz Falls, Colorado, and am so grateful to everyone at Forever for allowing me to extend this series. To every editor I have worked with— Amy Pierpont, Alex Logan, and Lexi Smail, thank you for investing in this series and in these characters. Each of you contributed so much to making the Rocky Mountain Riders everything it has become, and I consider myself a better writer because of everything you have taught me.

A huge thank you to my wonderful agent Suzie Townsend for believing in this series and in me. I so appreciate your guidance and encouragement as I build my career. I couldn't ask for better representation!

If it weren't for my incredibly supportive husband and two amazing sons, I would never get any writing done. Will, AJ, and Kaleb, thank you for being my champions. You are my greatest blessing.

To my fabulous readers—it's been incredible to see how you have connected with the Topaz Falls community.

Thank you for all of your notes and reviews and comments on these characters and their stories. I have to say, out of all the characters, I have received the most questions about Darla. It seems so many of you have been anxiously awaiting her story. I hope you love it as much as I do.

Chapter One

Everyone had their dirty little secret, and Darla Michaels fully intended to keep hers under wraps.

She cinched the belt on her trench coat, pulled a long brunette wig over her short black hair, slipped on her Jackie O sunglasses, and climbed out of her cherry-red Mercedes roadster, which she'd parked across the street in case anyone she knew happened to drive by.

You'd think traveling two towns away from her home in Topaz Falls, Colorado, made for a pretty safe bet that none of her friends or acquaintances would find her out, but one could never be too careful. What if someone she knew back home had to make an impromptu Target run? Glenwood Springs would be the first place they'd come. They would likely take this very route, which meant they would inevitably recognize her car, because—hello—a cherry-red Mercedes roadster stuck out like a sore thumb among the burly, big-tired, four-wheel-drive SUVs and diesel pickup trucks that typically cruised these mountain roads. But that was okay because even if someone did happen to drive by and see her car, they wouldn't know where she'd gone.

For all they knew she could be shopping in one of the many boutiques right here along the main drag. They'd never in a million years suspect she'd gone into the dingy basement of the nondescript brick building across the street. And that was good because whatever she did, she had to make sure no one in Topaz Falls ever found out about her secret life here.

After a quick scan of the street, Darla made her way across and ducked into the building through the glass door, which had been splattered with slush from the last snowstorm that had hit, right after Thanksgiving.

Once she stepped inside, the space's familiar warmth brought a soothing comfort—the feel of the threadbare carpet beneath the soles of her boots, the hum of the old rickety furnace churning out heat. The first night she'd come here, she'd sworn it would only be a onetime thing. But somehow, eight years later, here she stood, getting ready to attend her eightieth meeting with her bereaved spouses support group.

Before going down the steps to join the others, Darla quickly removed the trench coat, then the wig, then the sunglasses. She balled up the coat and shoved it onto one of the cubby shelves the community center had built for children to store their belongings. The disguise was only for the outside world, not for this little community she'd become part of.

When her husband had died nearly ten years ago at the age of thirty, there were all these steps she felt she had to take. Step one: Make a ridiculously expensive and impractical purchase. Hello, Mercedes roadster. Step two:

Get a new job that would completely dominate all of her time and thoughts. Three weeks after Gray's funeral, she'd decided her job as pastry chef at an upscale restaurant in Denver wasn't nearly consuming enough, so she'd taken the insurance money, moved three hours away to Topaz Falls, and opened the Chocolate Therapist—a wine and chocolate bar on Main Street, which had indeed dominated all of her thoughts and time. Then there was Step three: Attend a support group for grieving spouses so she could talk about her feelings with people who understood.

She'd found the group two towns away, lest anyone in Topaz Falls get the idea that she was still a poor, grieving widow. Pretty much everyone in town knew her husband had died a long time ago, but after too many sympathetic glances and awkward *I'm so sorry*s, she'd made a habit of never discussing it with any of her friends. She gave them the basic facts, answered their questions, and made sure to always be the life of the party so they would all know she didn't need their pity.

She'd never planned on discussing Gray's death with anyone, actually. She had only attended that first bereavement support group meeting with the intention of crossing it off her list, a kind of *Look! I did it! I checked off all the boxes! I'm a healthy and happy widow.* But...well...for some reason she chose not to examine too closely, she hadn't quit coming yet.

"Darla? Is that you?" Josie Wilken lumbered up the concrete steps from the basement meeting room. "I thought I heard the door." Her smile went broad, the ends of her mouth accented with crescent-shaped dimples. Like everyone else in the group, Josie had gray hair, though she always wore it coiled on top of her head in a carefree knot that bobbed from one side to the other as she walked.

"You're late," Josie announced with a glance at her watch. As the group's fearless leader, she'd always been a stickler for time. "You missed refreshments."

Darla grinned at her and fluffed her hair back into shape. "I don't need refreshments. I make chocolate for a living."

"Speaking of…how'd the new recipe turn out?" Josie was always giving her ideas for new flavor combinations to try in her truffles. "For the lavender-infused variety?"

"They turned out unbelievable." Darla unearthed a small box of truffles from her purse. "Seriously. I never would've thought to try it, but once again, you're brilliant." She handed the box to Josie.

"I knew it would turn out!" The woman opened the box and popped a truffle into her mouth, closing her eyes in obvious rapture. "Damn, I'm good."

Darla laughed and linked their arms together, guiding her friend back down the steps to the basement. "So how've you been?" Seeing these friends only once a month meant there was always plenty of gossip to catch up on. In fact, that was really what the group had turned into—a place to talk about life with people who knew what it meant to go on living after someone you loved was gone.

"It's been a boring month," Josie complained. "The kids at school are doing all this crappy testing, so I haven't even been able to do any fun projects." As the art teacher at the local elementary school, fun projects were Josie's specialty. "What about you?" Her friend paused outside the door of the community meeting room. "How's your month been?"

Darla gave the same answer she usually did. "Good. Busy." Though she would've liked it to be busier. Topaz Falls didn't exactly see many tourists October through

November. Things didn't usually pick up until the ski season started, and even that had been slower with the warm, dry winters they'd had the last few years. "Hopefully we'll have a busy Christmas season this year." God knew the town needed it. They'd already lost three businesses over the previous several months.

"Yeah, I've been thinking about Christmas." Josie gave Darla's shoulder a compassionate squeeze. "You'll be comin' up on the big One Zero this year, huh?"

Darla was only half paying attention. Inside the room, she could hear Peter, Ralph, and Norman discussing Peter's latest date. "'One Zero'?" she asked, also trying to eavesdrop on the men's conversation.

"Yeah." Josie steered Darla's gaze back to hers. "You know, the ten-year anniversary."

The realization of what her friend meant sent her heart skidding. "Oh. Right." December 23. Ten years since Gray had died. "I guess I haven't thought about it too much," she lied. The closer the holiday got the more that familiar anxiety seemed to simmer. All those memories of trying to give Gray one last beautiful Christmas only to lose him days before.

"It's a tough one, that ten years," Josie said solemnly. She'd lost her partner twelve years before, so she always liked to keep Darla informed on what to expect as time went on. "I don't know why, but that one hit me the hardest. Almost had me a mental breakdown, I did. Made me reevaluate everything in my life." Josie and Karen had been together for almost twenty years, which was more than triple the time Darla had shared with Gray, but somehow that didn't seem to matter. A soul mate was a soul mate whether you'd spent six years with them or twenty.

"You got a plan for how you're gonna get through it?" Josie was big on plans.

"Like I said, I haven't thought about it too much," Darla said, brushing the whole thing off. "It's always such a busy time of year, and I don't usually mark the anniversary." In fact, she did everything she could to keep herself too occupied to think about it at all. That was her MO: avoidance through escapism. So far, it had worked pretty well for her. In fact, it could work for her right now. She peeked back into the meeting room. "We'd better get in there before we miss all the juicy details about Peter's date."

"What? I told him to wait until I got back!" Josie took the bait and charged into the room with Darla at her heels.

"Hello gentlemen." Darla dug into her purse and retrieved more boxes of truffles, handing one to each man.

"My God, I wish I was thirty years younger." Norman gave her a hug. At eighty, he was the oldest in the group—but also the most handsome, she'd say.

"Lookin' good, doll." Ralph took his turn next. "Thanks for the chocolate. You're my dream girl."

Darla smiled and placed a kiss on his cheek. Come to think of it, this could be why she hadn't left the group yet. It was good for her self-esteem.

"You'll have to fight me for her, Ralphie," Peter said, forgoing the hug completely to give her a quick smooch on the lips.

"You're all a bunch of playboys," Josie mumbled behind them.

"And I love them." Darla gave her friend a wink. These men were actually decent, kind, and loyal.

"What took so long?" Peter demanded, munching his way through his third truffle. "What were you two talking about in the hallway?" Chocolate crumbs sprinkled the gray scruff on his chin.

"Darla's coming up on her ten-year," Josie informed the others.

Groans went all around.

Seriously? It was that bad? Dread crammed itself tightly into her chest. "It's not a big deal."

Peter finished off the last truffle. "Oh it's a big deal all right."

"There's something about a decade that makes you re-think your whole life," Ralph added.

Josie's head bobbed in a self-important nod. "That's what I told her."

"And I'm telling you all, I'll be fine." She didn't want to hear any more about how hard it would be. This year was like any other. She had her business, she had her friends, and she would plan a whole lot of festive events to keep her moving from one thing to the next. Memories of the previous year crowded her mind. She'd attended at least five parties in the days leading up to Christmas, but that hadn't quite been enough to keep the loneliness at bay. She'd sat at home by herself on December 23 looking through old pictures of her first few Christmases with Gray. Not that she would share that with the rest of the group.

"Come on." Darla took Peter's hand and led the way over to the circle of chairs they typically sat in for their discussions. "I'm dying to hear how your date went last month."

For the next hour they discussed Peter's disastrous date. The woman he'd met online had brought her cat to the restaurant in her purse. The poor man had been caught unawares until the cat climbed up his leg and started to nibble on the mints he had in his pocket. When he'd jumped out of his chair, the entire table had flipped over.

"I wish *you'd* agree to go out with me," he said to Darla as the meeting was wrapping up.

"Sorry, Pete. You know I don't date." She went out with men—and sometimes hooked up with the very tempting specimens—but dating was off the table.

Josie sent a look to the others and at the exact same time, they all opened their mouths. "Ten years," they said in a chorus.

"Wow, did you practice that?" Darla stood and folded her chair. "Is that what you were doing before I came? Rehearsing?"

"Sorry, love." Norman swooped in and put her chair away for her. "We just don't want you caught off guard. It's better to be prepared."

"And anyway, I don't understand why you don't date," Josie said, while Norman took care of the rest of the chairs. "If your loss is no big deal and all."

Darla gave her a look. "Wow, it's such a bummer we're out of time tonight. Guess we'll have to save that topic for another time."

"Another time never comes," the woman muttered.

Darla pretended like she hadn't heard. "Can I give you a ride home, Ms. Josie?"

That perked up her friend's sullen expression. "Sure." She never could resist a ride in the roadster.

They all walked up the stairs together, filing out onto the street while they pulled on hats and gloves and coats. Darla went ahead and stuffed her wig and sunglasses into her purse since it was dark outside. Surely she wouldn't see anyone she knew at this hour.

Everyone exchanged more hugs, and after the hearty goodbyes, Darla and Josie crossed the street together.

"Poor Peter." Darla started to giggle again. "I was dying when he told us how the cat jumped the waiter." That had to be one of the best blind date stories Darla had ever heard.

"That's what you get when you use those online dating sites," Josie said. "You only meet a bunch of weirdos."

"And you wonder why I don't date—" A spray of ice-cold slush hit Darla's upper body. *Cold.* She gasped and sputtered, trying to mop her face with the sleeve of her coat, which had been soaked clean through. Oh God, it was freezing. She glanced at Josie, who by some miracle, had been spared. "Who the heck—?" A truck pulled over next to the curb ahead of them and stopped just behind her car.

It was a big truck. A black burly diesel extended cab with a familiar pro-rodeo bumper sticker.

Uh-oh…

"I'm so sorry." Ty Forrester got out and came jogging down the sidewalk. "I didn't even see you there until it was too late."

Darla stopped dead in her soggy tracks. *No.* Not Ty. Anyone but Ty. "It's fine," she called, lowering her voice so he wouldn't recognize it. "No worries." *Leave. Turn around and get into your truck.* But Ty was a cowboy, and if there was one thing a cowboy couldn't stand, it was leaving a damsel in distress.

"It's not fine," he said, making a fast approach. Of course he had to look good. Ty always looked good. He wasn't tall, but his upper body had a lot of brawn, which didn't seem to fit the classically handsome structure of his face. Maybe it was the flawless angle of his jaw or inviting curve of his mouth, or the magnetic energy in his deep-set blue eyes. Yes, those eyes. They happened to be the perfect contrast to his dark hair.

"You're soaked—" Ty's eyes went wide and he skidded to a stop two feet away. "*Darla?* Is that you?"

Leave it to her to try to hide right under a streetlight.

"Damn, it is you," he said when she remained silent. "I thought that looked like your car. What're you doing here?"

"Noth—" she started, but Josie butted in.

"We just finished our bereaved spouses support group meeting," her friend offered. "I'm Josie Wilken, by the way. And you are . . . ?"

"Ty. Ty Forrester. I'm a friend of Darla's. From Topaz Falls." He quickly wriggled out of his winter coat and wrapped it around Darla. "I'm sorry. Did you say *bereaved spouses* group?"

"Yep. As in dead spouses," Josie said helpfully.

"*Spouses?*" A look of pure shock bolted his gaze to Darla. "Wait. You were . . . ? You're a . . . ?"

"Yes," she huffed through a putout sigh. And that overly sympathetic look on his face, along with the awkward silence, was the exact reason she didn't talk about it with anyone back home.

"Wow." Ty diverted his disbelieving stare to the ground. "I'm so sorry. I had no idea."

"But you said you were a friend." Josie turned to Darla and crossed her arms. "Surely you tell your friends about your husband."

"'Friend' can mean a lot of different things." In her and Ty's case, it was supposed to be fun and casual. He was single, she was single—and it was slim pickin's in Topaz Falls—so of course certain things had happened between them. A few times. Isolated incidents, if you will. "I was married a long time ago," she informed Ty. "And I was a completely different person back then."

That didn't seem to alleviate the concern that pulled at his mouth. He was likely thinking back through their sexy encounters to figure out how he'd missed the fact that she was a widow.

"She's coming up on her ten-year anniversary," said Josie, aka the informant. "I was telling her that's one of the toughest."

Aaannd that was her cue. "Josie, why don't you go ahead and get into the car?" Darla found her keys and hit the Unlock button. "I'll be there in a minute."

"Right." Her friend suddenly seemed to realize she'd overstepped. "Nice to meet you, Ty," she mumbled before she scurried away.

"Yeah. Nice to meet you too." He didn't even look in Josie's direction. The man was obviously trying to wrap his head around the new information he'd learned, but Darla would stop him right there.

"You never said what you're doing here." Other than exposing a perfectly good secret.

"Oh." Ty seemed to shake himself out of his thoughts. "I had to get a part for my truck. The auto shop here was the only location that had it in stock."

Of course it was. The universe loved her like that. "So what's it going to take for you to keep this quiet?" she asked, getting down to business.

"Keep what quiet?"

"The support group. No one knows. And I'd like to keep it that way." If her friends found out, they'd realize she wasn't over her past. They'd be scheduling weekly coffees to try to counsel her about her unresolved grief. But none of them knew what it was like. They wouldn't understand the extra layers of protection she'd had to build around her fragile heart. They couldn't grasp the traces of fear and anxiety that still lingered even all these years later.

Ty continued to stare at her with that damned frown. "I won't tell anyone, Darla."

God, even the way he said her name had changed. It was so solemn. They used to joke around, poke fun at each other, banter back and forth, but now he obviously felt sorry for her.

"I know you're surprised, but it was a long time ago," she said.

"You still attend a support group," he pointed out.

"Because they're my friends." She didn't know why she even tried. There was obviously no talking him out of the sympathy he suddenly felt for her. She would simply have to work extra hard to convince him—and everyone else— she was *fine*.

Chapter Two

Darla Michaels was a widow. How the hell had he missed that?

During the entire drive back to Topaz Falls, Ty had analyzed every encounter he'd had with Darla over the past few years—there were plenty. And yet there hadn't been one single clue that she'd been married before. Married and widowed because...her husband had been killed in a car accident? Or he'd had a heart attack? Or he'd been an adrenaline junkie and had fallen off a cliff?

Their brief encounter on the street back in Glenwood Springs hadn't given him a chance to ask for the details. Scratch that. *Darla* hadn't given him a chance to ask. Right after she'd pleaded with him to keep his discovery about her group a secret, she'd shoved his coat back into his hands and then hotfooted it to her sports car and driven away, leaving him standing on the slushy sidewalk wondering what the heck had just happened.

He wondered the whole drive home.

Ty slowed the truck to navigate a glossy patch of ice that stretched across the highway on the outskirts of Topaz Falls. On both sides of the narrow, two-lane road, snow had piled up a good three feet already, and they weren't even through November. He was used to it, being from Montana. Snow didn't bother him any, but most people hated making the drive to Glenwood Springs in the wintertime. Even at nine o'clock, the road was pretty much deserted. Darla had to be cruising around somewhere nearby though. Driving back to Topaz Falls in her impractical roadster. Knowing the way she drove that sports car around, she'd likely beat him back to town by a good half hour. And there she was again, hijacking his thoughts. Had she made it home? Should he stop by her place to check on her?

For some reason after Darla had asked him to forget what he'd learned about her, he only wanted to know more. He felt like he *should* know more about her. He'd slept with her just over a month ago. They did that occasionally—hooked up after attending a party or an event in town. They never planned it, but it had become a regular occurrence. You'd think she would've mentioned a marriage. Even if it had been a long time—

Sirens whirred somewhere behind him—faint at first, but quickly gaining momentum. He checked the mirrors, noting a whole line of fire rescue vehicles from the volunteer fire department trucking up the highway at an alarming speed. Within seconds, their lights lit up the interior of his cab. Quickly, he eased a foot onto the brakes and nudged the truck over to the shoulder to let them pass. Man, looked like they had everyone out on the call. That couldn't be good. Worry reared up and kicked him in the chest. Was it Darla? Had her roadster slid on the ice and wrecked somewhere in front of him?

Nah. He couldn't think like that. He wasn't a worrier. Hell, he was a bull rider; he'd learned to ignore every worry and plow right through life taking risk after risk without considering the what-ifs. This whole widow thing was messing with his head, that's all. He'd never admit it to her, but it did change the way he saw her. He couldn't help but feel bad for her. Last year he'd watched his grandmother grieve for his grandfather, and even though they knew the cancer would take him, it had been hell saying goodbye.

Another rescue vehicle went clipping by, this one from the next town over. They were calling in the big guns. Ty let the truck pass, and then sped up to follow it—just to be sure there was nothing to worry about.

Right as he rounded the curve, the town of Topaz Falls lit up the sky. It seemed everyone in town went all out in the decorations department, putting up lights and wreaths and those cheesy inflated lawn ornaments that blinked and spun and played tone-deaf musical numbers. And he'd thought his hometown had been Christmas crazy.

His phone rang. It was his best friend, Levi, according to his Bluetooth. Ty hit the button to answer. "Did you know Darla was a widow?" he asked without even saying hello. Yeah, that shock wasn't going to wear off anytime soon.

"Huh?" His friend paused a second. "Yeah. She was married a long time ago. But we'll have to have the conversation another time. We need you at the Farm Café. There's a fire."

"A fire?" His stomach dropped. All those fire trucks... they were headed to Mateo and Everly's café? "I can be there in ten minutes," he said, stomping on the accelerator. "What happened? Is everyone okay?"

"They weren't there when it started," Levi said. "Mateo doesn't know what happened. They're thinking gas explosion. Fire department's on the way, but it sounds like we're gonna need all hands on deck."

"I'll meet you there." Ty hung up and focused on driving. Levi and Mateo were his two best friends. Years ago, they'd all trained together under famed rodeo champion Gunner Raines. They'd had each other's backs through injuries and crushing losses and all the drama that goes with traveling the circuit. But a fire? How could the café be on fire? Mateo and Everly had completely renovated it just over a year ago. It was an old farmhouse that Everly had converted into a restaurant, but they'd updated everything.

He sped through town, and it soon became obvious he wasn't the only one headed out to the café. A traffic jam clogged the road a few blocks away, so he parked his truck at the curb, got out, and slipped on his coat and hat and gloves. He jogged down the block and turned the corner.

The scene before him looked like something out of one of those TV dramas. Flames were devouring the modest building, shooting upward toward the black sky. Acrid smoke hung heavy and thick in the air. It took him a second to move—to remember this wasn't some terrible dream. His friends' place was on fire. Ty sprinted over to where the fire trucks were mobilizing. It was complete chaos. People were running and shouting. The flames were snapping and crackling and sizzling against the eerie music of a low roar. Ty moved close enough in that he could feel the heat of the flames.

He spotted his friend talking to a fireman nearby.

"Mateo? What can I do? How can I help?" Adrenaline spiked through him the same way it did when he climbed on the back of a bull.

"I don't know." Mateo stared at him blankly, dark soot tinging his jaw and forehead, as though he was stuck in his worst nightmare. "For right now, you all need to stay back. Let us do our job." The firefighter charged away to join his comrades, who were already pulling out hoses.

Ty laid a hand on Mateo's shoulder. An overwhelming sense of helplessness recoiled through him. He was used to doing things, not sitting back and watching while all hell broke loose. "Where's Everly?" he asked, searching the crowd that had gathered.

"She's with Darla. Checking on the animals."

If he hadn't had to pick up the part for his truck, he would've been back already too. Maybe he could've helped. Ty scanned the west side of the farm where they had stables and enclosures for the chickens and goats. Their brand-new farmhouse sat higher up on the hill. Thank God there was so much snow. It had likely prevented the fire from spreading to the other buildings.

"Everly's devastated." Mateo stared into the fire. "All that work we just did..."

Ty watched the firemen attack the flames with the water hoses. "Maybe they can save it." Maybe it wouldn't be as bad as it looked. Damn, he hoped that was the case. That café was their main source of income now that Mateo had scaled back on riding to settle into family life.

"They won't be able to save it. There won't be anything left," Mateo said, his voice hoarse. "I heard the explosion. That's why I ran over here. Everything's already gone."

Ty said nothing. *Sorry* wouldn't be enough. And he wasn't good with words anyway. He had to do something, take action. "I'll be back," he said, already trotting toward the front lines. "How can I help?" he asked one of the firemen who was calling out orders.

"You can't." The man pulled him away from the flames. "It's too dangerous. We need everyone to stay back."

Ty fought the instinct to push him out of the way. "I want to help." He had to help. He couldn't stand there and watch his friends' place go up in smoke.

"You really wanna help, go get some supplies. We're gonna be here awhile." The fireman walked away.

Ty hesitated a few more minutes before heading for his truck. His boots crunched through the snow, the sound competing with the fire's growl behind him. When he'd made it to the truck, he jumped in and drove around town, stopping at the gas station and the outdoor gear shop, which reopened to let him in. When he drove back to the café, the flames were still raging. He got out of the truck and made three trips over to the crowd with the various items he'd bought—blankets and bottled water and energy bars for the firemen. When he had everything unloaded he joined the growing support group clustered around Mateo. Everly and Darla had come back, and it seemed their entire group of friends had gathered to be with them. Charity and her sheriff's deputy husband, Dev; Levi and his two brothers, Lance and Lucas.

"You must be freezing." Ty wrapped one of the heavy fleece blankets he'd bought around Everly's shoulders.

Her surprised eyes lifted to his. "Thank you." Tears glistened on her cheeks, but she offered him a grateful smile. "I didn't realize how cold I was."

"I brought water too. And some food." He glanced at his friends. "You want to help me hand it out to the firefighters?"

"Yeah, let's go." Levi moved in, followed by Lance and Lucas, along with Dev. The four of them loaded their arms with supplies and hurried off, leaving Ty standing there with Mateo, Everly, and Darla. He noticed a controlled shudder in Darla's shoulders, so he found another blanket he'd laid on the pavement nearby. "You still haven't changed," he murmured as he wrapped the blanket around her shoulders. She had on the same jacket he'd splashed with muddy slush from the road back in Glenwood Springs. It seemed to have dried, but it still had splatters of grime everywhere.

"No time." Darla stared past him. "I got the call from Everly before I could make it home." She gathered the blanket tighter around her shoulders. Ty couldn't remember ever seeing her face so expressionless. Darla was the life of every party, the wind in everyone else's sails. She had this red-hot energy that always seemed to charge everyone and everything around her. But now her eyes were empty and her cheeks had hollowed.

Once again, Ty wondered how she'd lost her husband. Was this scene bringing up bad memories? Would she ever tell him?

"The firefighters said to tell you thanks." Levi jogged over, empty-handed. "It sounds like they're expecting to be here all night."

Ty shared a look with Darla. They didn't talk much when they were together. They laughed and joked and did crazy things like jump in the snow and then back into her hot tub. They had fun. But maybe it had solidified more of a connection between them than he'd realized. Because he knew exactly what she wanted to say but couldn't seem to get out. "Why don't we all go to the wine bar? Get out of the cold? There's nothing we can do here anyway." Except for watch their beloved café crumble.

"Yeah. I guess we should go somewhere warm." Mateo turned to his wife, taking both of her hands in his. "I'm so sorry, love. Everything you've worked for."

Fresh tears slipped down Everly's cheeks. "I'm not sorry," Everly murmured, stepping into her husband's embrace. "We may have lost the café, but I still have you. We have our home and our friends. That's all I need."

The intimacy of the moment pushed Ty back a step. He'd never been able to say that. If he ever lost his dream—everything he'd worked for—if he ever got injured and had to quit riding, what would he have? A few good friends. A crappy relationship with his family. But nothing intimate, nothing that bonded him to another person.

Everly turned to Darla. "Is it all right if we all head to your place?"

"Of course," she said. "Then you'll be close by in case the firemen need you. Everyone's welcome, actually."

That was Darla for you. She had a gift for bringing people together. Ty had never appreciated it more than he did right then.

"We'll get the coffee pots going and I can grab some muffins from the Butter Buns Bakery as soon as Ginny opens."

"I can run to the store," Ty offered. He had too much adrenaline going to go sit at some table all night.

"That'd be great." Darla smiled at him as the group dispersed. Mateo tucked Everly under his arm and led her down the driveway toward their truck.

"Come on." Darla nudged him. "Let's go warm up." She took a step and started to slip on the ice.

Ty reached for her hand to steady her and then held on, but after a few steps she pulled away from him and walked briskly to her car.

* * *

The charred skeleton of the Farm Café still smoldered, looking eerie in the early light of dawn. Darla walked the perimeter of the foundation, which had been reduced to a jagged concrete rectangle. Blackened debris filled the middle—fragments of stools and chairs and tables. There were melted Christmas garlands and the scorched artificial tree with Everly's huge collection of locally made festive ornaments baked to the branches in unrecognizable blobs. Even the sleek, stainless steel ovens and refrigerators Mateo and Everly had purchased during the renovations had been melted down, and were now misshapen and half their original size.

"There's nothing left." Everly paused next to her, gazing over the scarred remains with a look of wide-eyed bewilderment.

"There might be." Darla gave her friend's hand a squeeze. "We'll look. We'll search through the debris and maybe we'll find something." She did her best to sound hopeful.

"Most of it can be replaced. I know that." Everly wandered to the melted Christmas tree, tears streaming down her cheeks. "But I put my great-grandma's Christmas star on top of the tree. I shouldn't have. I should've kept it at home, but I loved her so much. And having it at the café made me feel like she was part of all this. The café. My life here…"

"Oh honey." Kneeling, Darla dug around the tree searching for anything that remotely resembled a star. Everything was too melted, too misshapen. "Maybe it got knocked off in the explosion." At least it wasn't melted to the tree like some of the other ornaments…

"When I was little, my great-grandmother used to tell me that star had magic powers," Everly sniffled. "That all you had to do was hold it and whisper your biggest Christmas wish and it would all come true."

"Then we'll find it." Darla stood and kicked through some of the ashes, but there were so many. A whole restaurant full of disintegrated furniture and knickknacks and tablecloths and dishes and silverware and supplies. It would take time to search through it all. Time and a whole army of people.

"Why? I don't understand." Everly turned to Darla. "We didn't deserve this. Did we?"

"God, no." No one earned tragedy. It had taken her years to accept that. Okay, maybe she was still moving toward accepting that. Whenever you were standing in the ashes of your life, it was the first question you asked. What could I have done differently? How could I have prevented this? Those were the kinds of questions that tended to haunt her, and Darla knew only one way to cope with them. "Look around at all these people who are here for you." She slipped her arm around her friend's shoulders, gathering her in close. "You lost a lot last night, and believe me, I know how hard it is to lose a dream." When she'd married Gray, she'd built all of her dreams on him. On them. They'd wanted to open a restaurant together. They'd wanted babies—he'd even been reading up on all of the superstitions about how you could guarantee twins. He was her future, her everything, and then he was gone. "When you lose a dream, you have to focus on what will hold you together instead of what will tear you apart," she told Everly, as if she had so much wisdom to share. She hadn't been able to follow her own advice. Gray's death had torn her apart. It had torn her whole life apart. The only way she could rebuild was by putting up protective walls to shield her from the pain and the risks and the possibility of ever building her world around someone else again.

But this wasn't about her. Inhaling deeply, Darla let the wave of lingering grief recede before she spoke. "Do you know why we're here?" She gestured to the group surrounding them. "Because we love you guys. And we'll carry you through this." She would do everything she could to make sure they had the support they needed.

Darla scanned the various groups of people who were sifting through the debris the firemen had piled up nearby. The Cortez brothers and their wives, Charity and Dev, and their nephew, Bodie. And Ty. She watched him work on his knees, meticulously sorting through soggy scraps of wood in search of anything meaningful they might be able to salvage. He hadn't slowed down all night. After they'd congregated at her wine bar, Darla had a hit a wall and had fallen asleep right at the bar. When she woke up, Ty was busily making coffee for people while he served the baked goods he'd picked up. He hadn't slept or taken any breaks. He hadn't said much to her all night either, but he'd kept looking at her with sad eyes every time he thought she wouldn't notice. She had though. She could read the pity and the concern in his expression, and she didn't need it. Didn't want it. Those looks he kept giving her only fortified her walls, made her want to prove she was bullet-proof. In fact, when she was done talking to Everly, she'd march right over there and set the man straight.

"You're right." Everly wiped tears from her cheeks. "I don't know what we'd do without you guys." She rested her head on Darla's shoulder. "Still can't help but feel awful. Mateo could've made so much money on this land after he bought it, and instead, he held on to the café for me. We have insurance, but it'll take so long to process everything, and we have no income now." A long sigh puffed out of her mouth, crystallizing in the cold air. "His mom and sisters rely on the money we send them every month, and there's something else too." She straightened, facing Darla directly. "I'm pregnant," she whispered.

"Oh, Everly." Darla threw her arms around her friend, squeezing as tight as she dared. "Sweetie, that's amazing!" Both Everly and Mateo were so good with kids. "That's the best news." A familiar sting hit her eyes. The best news, but hard to hear too. Why did it always have to remind her of the life she thought she'd have? As a mother, as Gray's wife? They were supposed to watch their kids grow up together. They were supposed to have years of happy family memories, and now she never would.

Everly swiped at the tears flowing steadily down her cheeks. "We haven't told anyone because I'm only about six weeks along, but the doctor confirmed it. Just last week. We were so excited, and now..." The words dissolved into a sob. "I don't know what we're going to do."

"Don't worry about that right now." There was no way this town would let two of their own struggle—especially during the upcoming holidays. It might take some work, but Darla would figure out how to replace the income they'd lost for the foreseeable future so Everly and Mateo could focus on rebuilding and planning for the baby. "A baby!"

It had been a while since their group of friends had welcomed a little one. Lucas and Naomi Cortez's daughter would be starting preschool soon. And Lance and Jessa's triplets were well into the toddler stage. "You and Mateo have to enjoy this, Everly. Even with the fire. Or maybe more because of the fire." Life was so short, so unpredictable. "You have to take every opportunity you can to soak in the joy."

"I know." Her friend reached into the pocket of her coat and found a Kleenex. "I wish I didn't feel the stress so much."

"It's okay to feel it, but try not to focus on it." Darla glanced over at Ty again, an idea formulating. "We're going to help you. All of us. Everything will work out." She had a plan and she knew exactly who would help her execute it. "I need to talk to Ty about something." She checked Everly's face. Her friend had stopped crying, but her eyes still held that look of desolation. "You going to be okay?"

"Yes," her friend said resolutely. "I'll be okay. I think I'll go see what Mateo is discussing with the fire chief."

"Sounds good." Darla had already started to walk. Well, more like jog. Whenever an idea this good hatched, she tended to let it carry her away. By the time she'd made it to Ty she was almost out of breath. She took a second to gather her thoughts. As the director for the Chamber of Commerce in town, she had her ways of bringing the businesses and shops together for a common cause. Lately, they'd been discussing ways to boost tourism this Christmas to pump more money into the town, and she'd just gotten the perfect idea for how they could combine that with a fund-raiser to help her friends.

She purposely crunched her boots into the snow to get the man's attention. Ty looked up. His eyes were tired but he held himself with a strength that never seemed to waver.

"Hey." He gazed at her the way someone might look at a wounded, matted, homeless puppy trotting down the street in the middle of a blizzard—sympathy and pity and hesitancy all wrapped into one complicated expression. And yet somehow he also still looked as handsome as ever, which didn't help matters.

"Hey." Darla shored up her shoulders and stared directly into his eyes so he'd know she was still the same uncomplicated, carefree woman he'd slept with. "Can I talk to you for a minute?"

"Sure." He rose and dusted off his heavy work gloves. "You holding up okay?" he asked, taking his gaze down the full length of her. Not in a way that checked her out but in a way that made it seem like he was afraid she might be falling apart piece by piece.

"I'm fine." How many times would she have to tell him that before he accepted it? "You're the one who hasn't stopped to take a breath all night," she reminded him with a stern look. If she gave him a healthy dose of sass, maybe he'd remember who he was really dealing with here. "Are *you* okay?"

He didn't pause. "Yeah." The man definitely wouldn't tell her if he wasn't. Maybe that was why they got along so well. From what she could tell, neither of them let themselves feel anything too deeply, and like her, he tended to take action—to find projects. Since he'd taken over as the head of the rodeo association, he'd already signed five new sponsors and had created a scholarship fund for young riders. Ty obviously wasn't the type of cowboy to sit around doing nothing, which she could use to her advantage.

"I haven't found much they can save." The heartfelt concern brewing in his eyes surprised her. She'd never realized he cared so deeply about his friends. Then again, she'd never looked that closely at his heart either.

"Well, I know they appreciate you trying." She couldn't help but appreciate it herself.

"I hate it," Ty said. "Seeing stuff like this happen to good people. Not being able to do anything about it. I hate seeing people suffer."

She'd never seen him so solemn. From the way he was looking at her, she knew he wasn't only talking about Everly and Mateo. *I'm not suffering anymore*, she wanted to tell him. But she hadn't come over to talk about herself. About her past. About her loss. None of that was any of Ty's business. "I hate it too, but I think there's something we can do to help." She looked around until she located Mateo and Everly, still safely out of range. "I mean, I think we can do more than sift through the remains of their business. They're going to need money to stay afloat while they rebuild." The insurance might give them a little cushion, but it wouldn't be enough to live on, enough for his entire family back in Mexico to live on.

"What did you have in mind?" Ty asked with a degree of wariness.

She got it. She'd built a reputation for crazy ideas that usually involved her male friends having to dress up. She had a thing for theme parties—the Roaring Twenties, the disco seventies, and a couple of months ago, she'd done a Casablanca party that every man in their friend group had complained about. But what could she say? She had a knack for event planning, and the event she was envisioning for Mateo and Everly...well, it just might be the craziest thing she'd ever come up with. Especially since they'd only have a few weeks to pull it together.

Instead of leaving him in suspense any longer, she came out with it. "What if we put together a Cowboy Christmas Festival to raise money for them?" Excitement sparked her voice. "It would be perfect. It could draw more tourists to town so they'd spend money in our stores and restaurants, and we could do a couple of special events specifically to raise money."

The wariness she'd detected in his voice earlier had migrated to his narrowed eyes. "What kind of events?"

"A rodeo for starters." As head of the town's rodeo association, surely Ty would see the benefits of a big event to bring everyone together. The proceeds could all go to Mateo and Everly, but it would also draw more tourists to town, which meant all of the businesses would benefit too. And it would be great publicity for the Rodeo Association. "Oh! And maybe a cowboy bachelor auction!" Of course they had to do an auction. Those things always raised a ton of money.

"I'm sorry. What was that?" Ty's jaw had clenched the slightest bit tighter.

Darla put on her sweetest smile. "Hear me out," she said before he could reject the idea. "This is a rodeo town and we're known for cowboys. You've seen all of the females who show up to our events hoping to snag a cowboy. Think how many would show up for the chance to spend an evening with one of you."

"Most single cowboys I know don't want to be put up for auction." Ty's deadpan expression made it clear that meant him included.

Well, at least he'd stopped looking at her like he wanted to fix her. With a common focus, maybe he would stop seeing her as the wounded widow and things could go back to normal between them.

"The auction would be for a good cause." She batted her eyelashes at him. "Not only will it help the town draw in tourists, it could potentially raise a lot of money for our friends."

Based on his tireless work all night, Ty was obviously

a fixer, which explained his hesitation. He didn't want to be auctioned off, but he also wanted to help. She could read it in his eyes. So she basically had him right where she wanted him. "We could also do a cowboy calendar," she suggested while she had his attention. Why quit when she was on a roll? "All you cowboys could dress up in seasonal costumes." She smirked and wriggled her eyebrows. "In fact, with a little tinsel and a Santa hat, I think you'd make the perfect Mr. December."

A hint of his signature grin shadowed his lips. "That so?"

"Oh yeah. You'd make a great stocking stuffer." She poked him in the shoulder, baiting him. "I betcha those babies would sell like hotcakes." Without meaning to, her gaze slipped below his neck. He had the body to pull off a sexy tinsel costume, she knew that for sure.

Ty stared her down. "Maybe we should do a business owners calendar instead," he suggested. "You could wear a chocolate bikini."

"Ha!" She eased a step closer, drawn in by their familiar flirtatious vibe. "And what would Ginny Eckles wear? Hmmm? A skimpy little apron and nothing else?"

Ty squeezed his eyes shut as though the image pained him. "How about a snowsuit instead? She'd make the perfect Ms. January."

Darla shook her head at him. "It has to be cowboys and you know it. We could sell a fund-raiser calendar for a good twenty bucks a pop. From the talk I hear during girls' nights at my wine bar, I'm pretty sure every female in Topaz Falls from ages eighteen to ninety-seven would be making that purchase. Not to mention any out-of-town tourists we manage to attract." With her old marketing contacts from her restaurant days in Denver, she could have the calendars made for next to nothing. "I'd guess that'd be at least five thousand dollars right there." And the auction…that could bring in thousands more. Especially if Ty invited his brother. She didn't know much about Rhett Forrester—only that he played in the NFL—but that was enough. If they could auction off an NFL star, they'd definitely raise some serious money. Now might not be the best time to bring up Rhett though. Ty and his brother didn't seem exactly close. So she could save that conversation for another time.

Ty didn't say anything. Instead, he looked past her to where Everly and Mateo stood locked in an intimate embrace. Everly had her forehead nestled into her husband's chest, and he was rubbing his hands up and down her back while she sobbed.

Sympathy for her friend bubbled up again, and Darla could see that Ty was just as affected. How could he say no now? "So do we have a deal?"

"You're unbelievable," he said, turning away from the spectacle like he couldn't stand to watch their friend cry.

Darla decided to take that as a compliment. "And you're not going to say no."

"Oh yeah?" The man turned back to her and leaned down, bringing his face in line with hers. "No." He straightened back up. "I could get on board with a rodeo, but no calendar. No auction. You may be a master at getting your way, but it's not gonna happen this—"

"She's pregnant," Darla blurted. "They haven't told anyone yet, but she's pregnant."

Ty snapped his mouth shut.

"I'm not telling you that to manipulate you." She'd already given that her best effort and he'd shot her down. Now she had to resort to honesty. Everly and Mateo having a baby was the best news ever, and she knew it would matter to him. It would make a difference. He and Mateo had been best friends since they were eighteen years old. They'd traveled and competed together, and based on Ty's actions all night, both Mateo and Everly mattered to him a whole lot. "I'm telling you that because they need our help."

"Fine." His lengthy sigh could've blown down what was left of the Farm Café. "We can *talk* about a calendar and an auction. But I'm not making any promises."

"Of course not. We can discuss it later. Tomorrow night, actually. At the Chamber meeting." They didn't have one on the books, but she'd put out an emergency meeting request earlier tonight.

Once some of the other women on the board caught wind of a cowboy calendar, Darla had a feeling she wouldn't be the only one trying to convince Ty to dress up in a Santa costume. He had plenty of admirers who wouldn't take no for an answer.

Chapter Three

I think a calendar is a *wonderful* idea." Ginny Eckles, the owner of the Butter Buns Bakery flicked her bifocals down and gazed at Ty from across the large table in Darla's wine bar. "In fact, maybe each of the cowboys could pose at a different business in town to give us a little publicity, hmmm?" She fluffed her frizzy gray curls and winked at him. "I have a few aprons you could wear for the pictures. Oh! And you could lay on the counter holding one of my buns."

Darla snorted next to him, but quickly covered the sound with a cough.

Ty tried his darnedest not to grimace. *Yeah. Real funny.* How was it that he'd gotten roped into showing up at the Topaz Falls Chamber of Commerce meeting when none of the male business owners were able to make it? That was more than a little fishy, if you asked him. Bruce—the guy who owned the hardware store—likely wouldn't have voted for a sexy cowboy calendar. Or maybe he would have, considering that everyone in town loved the Farm Café. As much as he disliked the idea of wearing tinsel, unfortunately, Ty hadn't come up with any better ideas for how to make that kind of money. "If I do the calendar— and that's a hearty *if*—I'm wearing jeans and my boots," he informed the females in the room.

"That's fine," Ginny purred, dragging her gaze down to his chest. "As long as you don't wear a shirt. We need these puppies to sell, if you know what I mean."

Oh, he knew. They wanted the equivalent of one of those firefighter calendars where the poor schmucks were all greased up and flexing their muscles. "I haven't committed to anything yet," he said for at least the tenth time during the course of the hour-long meeting. Mostly because he had no clue how he was going to convince his friends to cooperate. Serious riders competed for the thrill, the status, the grit of competition. Hell, that was why he'd gotten roped in. He didn't take too kindly to being used as a sex symbol, and his friends likely wouldn't either.

It's a good cause though, he reminded himself. And they'd likely all agree solely because this was Mateo they were helping out. One of their own. A brother who'd lost his business and had a baby on the way. Damn it. There was no way he was gonna get out of this.

"Well, at least I think we've all agreed on the benefit rodeo." Darla flipped through some of her notes. "We just need to make a final decision on the bachelor auction and the calendar. It's not like we have much time."

Ty noticed she wasn't looking in his direction. She knew exactly what he thought of her ideas.

"All in favor of the calendar?" Darla called out before he could put in his two cents.

"Aye!" Ginny Eckles waved her hand in the air. The

other ladies at the table were shyer about it, but they all agreed. Of course. Ty remained silent. He didn't have a vote anyway since he wasn't an official member of the Chamber.

"And all in favor of the bachelor auction event?" Darla rushed on, still refusing to look directly at him.

Another round of hearty ayes came at him.

A sigh grumbled out. He might not have a vote, but he could still voice his opinion. "I'm not excited about it, but I'll do my best to make it happen." He tried to relax his jaw so he didn't sound so irritated. "Just so you all know, I'm gonna have a hell of a time convincing the guys to do this."

"Remind them what a good cause it is." For the first time during the meeting, Darla looked him in the eyes. She raised her eyebrows and he could practically hear her whisper, *Baby. They're having a baby.*

Yeah, yeah, yeah. It wasn't like he could tell the rest of their friends that. Couldn't ruin Mateo and Everly's chance to make an announcement when they were ready. So he'd likely have to get creative…

"We'll need at least twelve cowboys," Darla said, all businesslike again. "And we definitely need your brother to attend the bachelor auction."

Whoa. Hold on a second. "My *brother*?" Ty gaped at her. How did Darla know about his brother? He'd never mentioned Rhett to her. Though he shouldn't be surprised she knew about him. His brother had made a name for himself in the NFL. Even on injured reserve with the Dallas Cowboys, Rhett got more attention than most of the players out on the field.

"Rhett absolutely has to come," Darla said. Her eyes were always so emphatic—deep and dark and lit with whatever emotion she happened to be feeling at the moment. He recognized this one as stubbornness. "Everyone knows who he is. Think of the publicity he'll get us."

It wasn't meant as a slight, and yet Ty flinched anyway. Blame it on years of conditioning. Even with all his experience competing and winning some nice prizes, no one knew who he was, but everyone knew Rhett Forrester. His brother had been a star linebacker practically his whole life. First at their high school, then at the University of Idaho, and now for the Dallas Cowboys.

"It shouldn't be a problem for him to travel out here since he's on injured reserve the rest of the season, right?" Darla asked, giving him a coy smile. She was buttering him up, but it would not work this time.

"My brother is not coming. You can get that idea out of your head right now."

Everyone sitting at the table trapped him in curious stares, but he was not about to discuss his issues with Rhett. He didn't discuss them at all. As long as he didn't see Rhett, he didn't even have to think about their issues.

"Why not?" Darla demanded.

Ty considered the best response. "He already has plans for the holiday." The whole Forrester family had plans, and if Ty invited Rhett out here, then he'd have to invite everyone, and he'd already given them an excuse for why he wouldn't be able to come home for Christmas this year. An excuse that might have involved the woman sitting next to him wearing that familiar glare.

"Well, you could at least ask him to come," Ginny suggested. "Maybe he'll want to change his plans. You should let him decide."

Forget playing nice. He gave them all a stern frown so they'd drop it. "I'm not asking."

First of all, he'd had enough of living in the golden boy's shadow. Second, he might have led his parents to think he and Darla were engaged... and that she was unable to travel for the holidays because of her very successful and very busy wine bar.

When they'd called and told him they expected him home for a good old-fashioned family Christmas, it had caught him off guard. It happened to be the day after he and Darla had hooked up, and the lie tumbled right out. He figured after the holidays he'd simply tell them they'd broken up and that would be that. Simple. He wasn't about to complicate everything by inviting them to Topaz Falls.

"Well if you won't ask him, I will. I follow him on Instagram, you know." Darla pulled out her phone as if she wanted to prove it was more than a threat. He wouldn't put it past her. Darla could be about as persistent as a bull in the bucking chute when it came to getting her way. But this was one argument she couldn't win.

"You're not asking him either." Ty set his jaw so she'd know he was serious. "You ask him and my cooperation with this whole festival thing is over."

Darla didn't seem to know what to say to that.

"We don't need your brother," Ginny offered, nudging his boot with her foot. "You're enough of a man."

Ty wasn't sure if he should thank her or run away.

"Of course we need him." Darla started tapping on her phone. "The guy has over a million Instagram followers." She waved the screen in front of Ty's face, as if he didn't already know how popular his brother was.

"We don't have much time to generate publicity," she went on. "But if he posts something, women are going to flock up here for this event. Isn't that the point? To raise as much money as possible?"

Murmurs of agreement went around the room, but Ty had had enough. He pushed back from the table and stood. "If you want my help organizing the rodeo, my brother is not invited. Let me know what you decide."

Before Darla could try again, he walked out of the building.

* * *

"Wait!" Darla frantically zipped up her coat and darted down the sidewalk after Ty. Typically, she didn't resort to chasing after men—especially in her over-the-knee leather heeled boots—but this was an emergency. If she couldn't convince him to get his brother involved, they had absolutely no shot of attracting the kinds of numbers they'd need to make this event successful. "Hey! Hold on," she called to his retreating back.

At the end of the block, Ty stopped to wait for her, his left shoulder sagging with obvious impatience.

Darla jogged all the way to him, her heels skidding on a patch of ice right before she got there. She screeched a little and tried to balance herself, but he ended up catching her in his arms.

"You're not going to seduce me into changing my mind," he said, securing his hands on her upper arms and standing her back up straight. His physical strength combined with that playful grin proved to be a lethal combination. It never failed to turn her insides gooey.

"I'm not trying to seduce you." Darla straightened her coat and gazed up at him. Light from a streetlamp poured down on them in a soft glow. Romantic, some might have said. Especially this time of year. Topaz Falls had one of those storybook town centers—cobblestone sidewalks, mismatched brick buildings with large storefront windows and charming striped awnings. Garlands were strung from lamppost to lamppost, adorned with red velvet bows and twinkling with white lights that seemed to make everything sparkle. Fat snowflakes floated down, getting stuck on Ty's eyelashes. He had nice eyelashes. Nice eyes. A dreamy sigh broke loose in her chest, but she locked it down before he could notice. What was the matter with her? She didn't look at Ty like that. It had to be the seasonal ambience.

A-hem. Get it together. Before her eyes started twinkling like the Christmas lights. She was on a mission here. "I'm only trying to understand," she said in a soft, placating tone. "I know you want to help Everly and Mateo as much as I do, so what's the problem with your brother?" Talking about personal things happened to be a line they had never crossed, but she had to get to the bottom of this if they had any hope of making the festival a success.

"I already told you." Ty's hardened stare grazed hers. "He has plans for the holidays. Since it's the first year he hasn't had to play football, my family is having this huge Christmas celebration up in Montana."

A tension in his voice made the words sound brittle. It was a tone Darla had never heard from him. Ty joked around a lot. He laughed. He got along with everyone. But it seemed he had an issue with his brother. Curiosity drew her eyes back to him, but she bolted her hands on her hips to make it seem like irritation. "Well, why aren't you going back to Montana then? If it's a family celebration and all?"

Ty turned his head from hers and watched a car roll past. When he looked at her again he wore a smirk. "Why aren't *you* traveling to be with your family over the holidays?"

And there was the cowboy she knew. Deflecting every question that went deeper than *What would you like to drink?* At least she had a good answer though. "I can't leave town because of the bar." Christmas was one of her busiest seasons, and she had some pretty great employees, but that didn't mean she wasn't a total control freak. "Besides that, my dad will be in France with his new wife, and my mom is going on a trip to Mexico with her crazy sisters, so..." The holidays had never meant anything to either one of her parents. There were no big family gatherings or turkey dinners or gift exchanges. They both had always viewed Christmas as an opportunity to get out of town, and that was fine with her. After all these years she'd made her peace with it. Besides, she loved Christmas in Topaz Falls.

The quaint holiday spirit was one reason besides the bar that she never left town this time of year. It offered the kind of magical Christmas she'd always dreamed about, complete with the thick layer of snow frosting everything from the granite mountain peaks surrounding them to beautiful evergreen trees to the quaint buildings to the festive Christmas light displays that popped up all over town. She swore there was nothing more beautiful in the world than the glow of colorful lights buried beneath a powdery snow.

Ty didn't seem to know what to say at the mention of her own parents. This was new territory for them. "Listen..." She eased a step closer. "I don't like my family much either. That's totally normal. But if I had a famous brother who could help rake in the cash for one of my best friends, I would suck it up and invite him to come be a part of the festival." Of course, if she had a famous brother who played in the NFL, she might've tried hitting him up to buy her an island in the South Pacific so she wouldn't be here right now, but she was getting off track. "Having to tolerate your family for a week seems like a small price to pay. That's all I'm saying."

According to the pained look on Ty's face, it wasn't that simple. "I can't suck it up. I told my parents I couldn't come home because I had other plans. And if I invite my brother out here, they'll all know I lied."

So? She didn't say it. Hard to believe Ty was that worried about disappointing his parents—but then again that was easy for her to say, since her parents had exactly zero expectations for her. "What did you tell them you were doing?" she asked.

"Spending the holidays with my fiancée."

"I'm sorry, what? Did you say 'fiancée'?"

Ty raised his head. "I told them I couldn't come home because I got engaged and my fiancée is too busy to travel during Christmas," he said loud and clear. And yet she still wasn't getting it.

"Your fiancée?"

"My fake fiancée," he corrected. "It worked like a charm. They were so ecstatic I was in a relationship with someone they didn't even give me a guilt trip about missing the family celebration."

It was actually pretty brilliant. And incredibly amusing. "Who did you tell them you were engaged to?"

Ty immediately dropped his gaze to his boots and shook his head.

Darla ran through all of the possibilities. It didn't take

long. "*Me?* You told your parents we're engaged?" She busted out a laugh. If that didn't beat all. Her and Ty Forrester—the two most commitment-shy people in Topaz Falls—engaged!

"It just came out." His voice got louder, defensive. "It was that Sunday after we'd..." The words trailed off, leaving behind a small smile.

Oh, she didn't need to be reminded. She remembered exactly what they'd done that Saturday night. Ty had taken her home from a party at the Cortez Ranch, and of course she'd invited him in. Not that she'd ever admit it to anyone, but after spending so much time with all the married people, she sometimes felt a little lonely. Maybe he did too. They'd turned on some music and she'd opened a bottle of wine exactly like they had a few times before. Things always started out innocently enough, but when Ty kissed her, it was all over. He happened to be a very good kisser. That particular evening, they'd ended up naked in her kitchen. Throw in some canned whipped cream and chocolate sauce from her refrigerator, and it had definitely been a memorable night.

Whew, was it hot out here? Suddenly her down jacket felt like the inside of a volcano. She could feel the snow-flakes melting on her cheeks on contact.

"Anyway..." Was it just her, or did Ty's face suddenly seemed to have a shade more color to is as well? "Yes, my parents and my brother think we're engaged. But don't worry. A few weeks after the holidays, I'll tell them things didn't work out and life will go on."

Oh no, he wouldn't. This was perfect. Perfect! "We can pretend to be engaged."

The man's eyebrows nudged his hairline. "Say what?"

"I'll pretend to be your fiancée." The answer to this

whole dilemma was so obvious. "We'll pretend that we're planning to get married, and that'll solve everything. You can still invite them out, we can still raise a ton of money for Mateo and Everly." Problem. Solved. In the process, she could remind him she wasn't some poor fragile widow who needed to be handled with care. "Of course, we'll have to convince the rest of the town before your parents arrive so no one accidentally ruins the secret." She knew how people talked in Topaz Falls. Visitors were welcomed right into the local gossip scene. "But that shouldn't be a problem." They had enough time to go on a few public dates and then rush into an engagement.

For some reason Ty still had his jaw hinged open with a dumbfounded look. "You want to pretend we're engaged? To be married?"

"It wouldn't be that hard for people to believe." She could no longer hold off the impatience. While the rest of her still felt toasty, her toes were starting to freeze. "We already know each other. I'm sure there've been rumors about us. My neighbors have to have noticed your truck parked in front of my house more than once. We'll hardly have to lie at all. We can go out on a big public date to that town cookie-decorating event next week, and news about us will be all over by the time your family comes for the festival." Their closest friends would never buy it, but none of them would rat them out to Ty's parents and brother either.

"You really think we can pull it off?"

"I think we have to." He didn't get it. Topaz Falls wasn't Vail or Aspen. If they wanted to get visibility they needed a major draw. Enter Rhett Forrester. "I know people around here will support the cause, but we need tourists. We need to make this thing Colorado's Christmas celebration of the year."

And the only way to do that was to convince Ty's family that the two of them were headed for a happily ever after.

Chapter Four

Ty tossed a charred and splintered two-by-four into the dumpster that had been parked at the edge of the Farm Café's parking lot. He and Mateo had been working on clearing the debris since the sun had risen over Topaz Mountain, and they'd hardly made a dent in the massive pile of rubble. It would likely take weeks to clear it out. Mateo had hired a salvage company to come in after Christmas, but he'd wanted to do some of the work himself so they could watch for anything of significance that could be recovered. So far, they'd found nothing.

Ty adjusted the mask he wore over his nose and mouth. Digging through someone else's ruined livelihood really put things in perspective. Crazy how fast everything could change, how something could be taken away without warning.

He tromped back to what had once been the kitchen to help Mateo lift what was left of an oven. The once pristine stainless steel bore the black scars of a hot fire, and yet somehow the appliance had retained its original shape.

"So Everly mentioned something about a cowboy calendar?" His friend grimaced under the weight of the oven as they carried it toward the dumpster.

"Yeah." Ty hadn't mentioned it to anyone yet. He hadn't quite figured out how to pitch it to the guys. Somehow he'd have to convince all his contacts in the rodeo world to travel to Topaz Falls so they could humiliate themselves with a festive photo shoot and then be auctioned off like cattle. If that wasn't a pitch, he didn't know what was.

Mateo paused and readjusted his grip on the oven's door. "You don't have to organize a whole rodeo and pose for calendar pictures, you know. Everly and I can figure stuff out. We have some savings we can fall back on."

"But you're gonna need your savings later." He stopped himself before saying *when the baby comes*. Until Mateo offered him that information personally, he wouldn't talk about it.

Mateo's grin turned wry. "Darla told you about the baby, didn't she?"

Busted. Ty stepped over a wrecked bar stool. "How'd you know?"

Mateo stopped again, and they set down the oven. "I figure you never would've agreed to a calendar and bachelor auction without some serious motivation. Everly told me she accidentally spilled the beans to Darla, so I figured she used that to coerce you into this whole thing."

"Not exactly to coerce. More like to encourage." She was good at that encouragement stuff. Ty scrubbed his gloves together to warm up his hands. He'd be surprised if the temperature hit twenty today. "It's great news. I'm happy for you guys." Those two deserved something good in the midst of all this. Something to hold on to even when they were clearing away the ashes of their business.

"We're thrilled," Mateo said, leaning against the oven. "It's just tough timing is all."

That was an understatement. Getting news like that should've meant anticipation, celebration, excitement. Hell, Ty didn't know what he'd do if he found out he was gonna be a dad. Probably a couple of backflips. He'd always wanted kids, but children tended to require commitment, and that had never been his strong suit. "Well, you're not gonna have to worry about a thing. Darla's the best at putting events like this together. I have a feeling we'll raise enough cash for you to rebuild this place twice as a big. I just hope I get to wear clothes during the photo shoot."

"You and me both." His friend moved to pick up the oven again, so Ty lifted the other side.

"Everly said something about Rhett coming?" Mateo gritted his teeth as they navigated the edge of the charred foundation.

"Yeah," Ty grunted. They hoisted the oven up and tossed it in the dumpster. It made a satisfying crash when it hit the metal floor.

"You're on board with that?" Mateo dusted off his work gloves.

Ha. His friend knew better. "I didn't have a choice. You know how Darla is when she gets an idea in her head." The second he'd seen her chasing him down the street, he'd known it was all over. "Darla wants him here, so I'll get him here." That was another thing he hadn't done yet—called his brother and parents to invite them out for a good old-fashioned cowboy Christmas. He'd put off that phone call as long as he could. But he couldn't put off telling his friends about his and Darla's engagement plan. He had to prep everyone. Might as well start getting the word out. "Speaking of the cowboy festival, now that my family is coming, Darla and I will have to pretend to be engaged."

Mateo spun to face him, his jaw dropped. "You're not serious."

"Does it look like I'm joking?" he asked, sporting a blatant frown. Darla had acted casual about the whole thing. They'd joked around and flirted like usual, but...he couldn't help it. He wondered about her past, about her husband, about how that loss had affected her...

"You and Darla?" Mateo laughed. It was the first time he'd seen his friend crack a smile since before the fire. He guessed that made his predicament worthwhile.

"Why not me and Darla?"

Mateo looked him over. "Won't that be...complicated?"

Ty had purposely been not thinking about how compli-cated it could be. Not that he minded spending time with Darla, but they'd have to act like they were in love. Still, he didn't know what Mateo was getting at. "Why would it be hard?"

"I guess I always thought you really had a thing for her." Mateo tromped back to the remnants of the kitchen. "It would suck to spend all that time with her just pretending if you really felt something."

"I don't feel anything." A niggle in his chest counter-acted the statement, but he couldn't pinpoint the emotion. Needing to busy his hands, he started to sift through what looked to be half a cabinet.

"Really? You don't feel anything for Darla?" His friend came closer and got in his face like he could see right through him. "I could've sworn you did."

Ty kept digging through blackened pots and pans and dishes. "Why would you think that?" He found a plate fully intact and pulled it out, carefully setting it aside.

"Because I recognize what it looks like. You watch her a lot when we're all together. In fact, I was under the impression the feeling was mutual."

That gave him pause. "Darla doesn't have feelings for me." Neither one of them did real feelings. That was what had made their thing work. But for some reason it felt like something had shifted when he'd stood on that sidewalk and learned that she'd been widowed. Maybe because he'd seen pain in her eyes before she'd masked it—real, raw pain. Ty stood. "Did you know she was married once?" He still couldn't get over that. She had this whole other life he knew nothing about. No one seemed to know anything about it.

"Really?" His friend obviously didn't find it any easier to believe than Ty had. "Darla was married?"

"Yeah. I didn't know either, but Levi did. He doesn't know details. Just that she was married a long time ago and her husband died. That's why she moved here." That was all anyone seemed to know. The night of the fire, Levi had told him Darla didn't talk about it, not even with her best friends.

"Damn." Mateo kicked through some snow and reached down to pick up a ceramic teakettle. "He passed away? That's harsh. I guess it explains a lot."

"What d'you mean?"

His friend shrugged. "You know how Darla is. She doesn't seem to get too attached to anyone."

"Exactly." And neither did he. "So this whole engagement thing shouldn't be too tough. It's only for a couple of weeks." Maybe he'd even stage a breakup while his parents were here. That would save him the trouble of having to break the news to them later.

Mateo carted the teakettle and the plate over to a box he had sitting nearby. "Man, that's a lot. For you to have to bring your family out when I know you didn't want to be around them for the holidays." His friend gave him a guilty look. "I can talk to Darla if you want. Tell her we don't need Rhett out here."

"Absolutely not." Ty grinned. He was doing this for his friend whether Mateo wanted him to or not. "Your wife does more good for people than I could ever do in my lifetime."

Everly fed people. She brought them meals when they were sick or struggling with finances. He happened to know she and Mateo gave out plenty of free meals at the café—pretty much to anyone who couldn't pay. This was one small thing Ty could do to help them. "I can suck it up and spend a week with my brother. I can pose for a couple of pictures and take some random woman out on a date after the auction." He clapped Mateo on the back. "Showing a woman a good time happens to be one of my specialties."

"Uh-huh." His friend leaned over and lifted a scorched tabletop, searching underneath. "And how good of a time are you planning to show Darla during your pretend engagement?"

Ty wandered to where the dining room used to stand, pretending he hadn't heard the question. He had no idea how to answer that. There was no denying the physical chemistry between him and Darla, but what was a fake engagement supposed to look like?

Searching for a distraction, he focused on scanning the wreckage, moving his gaze over soggy chunks of wood and metal and...wait. What was that? About ten feet away from his boots, something gold glinted in the sun. He walked over and knelt to pick it up.

"Either you didn't hear me or you're ignoring me." Mateo approached just as Ty pulled a large gold-and-red-beaded star out from under the back of a melted metal chair. Somehow it had come through the fire unscathed. There wasn't a mark on it. He held it up. "Looks like there was one survivor."

Mateo stopped abruptly. "Holy smokes. You found it. I can't believe you found it." He said it like Ty had just unearthed the Holy Grail.

Ty looked it over again. "It's just a star." An old, beaded star that looked like it belonged on top of a Christmas tree.

"That's not just a star." Mateo carefully took it out of his hands and inspected it. "It belonged to Everly's grandma. It was the one thing in the café that we couldn't replace. You have no idea how much this'll mean to her."

"Really?" The day suddenly seemed warmer. "Glad I could help."

"Yeah. This is gonna be the perfect Christmas gift for her." Mateo found one of the towels they'd brought with them and carefully wrapped up the star. "Her grandma used to tell her the star granted Christmas wishes." He shot Ty a grin. "Anything you want to wish for this year?"

There were plenty of things Ty would have liked to wish his way out of—spending the holidays with his brother, complicating his casual arrangement with Darla by faking an engagement—but he simply grinned back. "Sure. I've got a wish. Please let the women in charge of this calendar come to their senses and let us wear actual clothes."

Mateo laughed. "Amen to that."

* * *

She couldn't wear the red heels...could she? *Should* she?

Before making a final decision, Darla carefully examined the shoes one more time. They were one of her favorite pairs—three inches high with spiraling straps all the way down the ankle and across the foot.

No. She definitely couldn't wear them. Those shoes meant business. They begged for a hot night of uncomplicated fun, but for some reason her impending date with Ty had started to feel very complicated. They were supposed to make an appearance at the town cookie-decorating party and then go out to dinner where Ty would pop the question in a very public proposal. But would they really look like a couple? What would they have to do to sell their relationship to everyone? The whole thing had started to unnerve her.

On the bright side, she'd been more motivated to focus her energy entirely on the Cowboy Christmas Festival. For the last week, she'd thrown herself deep into planning. The events were already scheduled and staffed, and the marketing materials should arrive any day. Now she would have nothing to focus on except for Ty and their alleged engagement. She would simply have to handle it like another project. Oh! Maybe she could make spreadsheets with facts about each of them so they could study and make the ruse even more convincing.

Feeling better at the thought of spreadsheets, she tossed the red heels back into her closet and scrutinized the other shoes she'd laid out beside her bed. There were the silvery booties, fun but a bit more conservative. Or the leopard print wedges with exactly the right amount of sass. Or maybe she should go with the more sensible black pumps with only a hint of sparkle. Any of the above would be a perfect compliment to her little black dress, but she wasn't sure exactly what message she wanted to send to Ty.

Make sure to dress up so we can go out to dinner after the cookies, he'd texted an hour before. For some reason it had put her on edge. She and Ty had never been on a real date. Heck, she hadn't been on a real date with anyone since...

Her empty stomach clenched. After their last grief group meeting her stomach had done the clenchy thing a lot. Like anxiety had threaded itself into the fibers of her muscles, tying them up in knots.

The ten-year anniversary is the hardest...

Nope. She couldn't think about Gray. Couldn't think about how he'd sneak her away in the broom closet of the restaurant where they worked to steal a kiss. Couldn't remember how he used to surprise her with reservations at all the best restaurants in town. Couldn't think about how much she'd loved getting dressed up for him—the way his entire face would break out into a grin when she'd walk out of their bedroom, and how he'd tease her that he'd changed his mind about dinner and wanted to take her to bed instead. She'd laugh and put an extra sway in her hips as she gathered her purse and coat just to torture him.

"Definitely the sensible black pumps." Tearing herself out of the memory, Darla reached for the shoes and shoved them onto her feet. Rationality. That was what she'd hold on to in this whole charade with Ty. She would be sensible about keeping the boundaries they'd always managed to maintain, even as they tried to convince the rest of the town and his family they were in love.

Those knots in her stomach pulled tighter, so she marched straight into the bathroom, opened the medicine cabinet, and quickly popped two Tums. "Get ahold of yourself," she muttered. It wasn't even a real date. It was a fake date. An acting gig, if you will, and she'd gotten good at acting over the years. This would be nothing.

Checking her makeup one more time, she added a fresh coat of red lipstick—something she never left the house without—and raised her shoulders, taking one last glance in the mirror. Over the years, she'd made sure she looked nothing like Gray's wife. Back then, she'd always worn her dark hair long and in waves. The year after he passed away, she'd cut it all off—wearing it in a pixie style before growing it out to be more shoulder-length this past year. She had more wrinkles now—the start of crow's-feet lining her eyes, and delicate creases bordering the corners of her mouth—but when she looked hard enough, she still saw the happy-go-lucky girl in her twenties who'd put all her faith in love only to have it ripped away.

The doorbell rang, earning a curse word she used only on special occasions. Ty was early. What kind of man showed up for a date early she wondered, cruising down the hallway of her small bungalow before crossing the living room and throwing open the door. "I thought we said—"

The package delivery guy's confused expression cut her off. "Excuse me?"

"Never mind." Darla smiled at him. "I thought you were someone else." She quickly took the package from his hands and signed the electronic device he held out before bidding him a quick goodbye and happy holidays, even though Christmas was still three weeks away.

As soon as she closed the door, she glanced at the

address on the box. It was from Nora Michaels, her mother-in-law. That incomprehensible mix of joy and pain washed over her at the sight of Nora's scrawled writing. She'd always loved the woman—in some ways Nora had been more of a mother to her than her own mom. After Gray had died, they'd stayed in close touch, and Darla still saw Nora and Larry a few times a year when she'd make trips down to Denver.

Checking the time, Darla carted the package into the kitchen and quickly ripped it open. In addition to several festively wrapped presents, there was a large manila envelope. Smoothing out the creases, she parked herself on a stool at the kitchen island and read Nora's note, which was scrawled on the outside.

Dearest Darla,

Happy Christmas! I know the package is early this year, but I wanted to send it as soon as possible. By the time you get it, Larry and I will be on our cruise around the Hawaiian islands, and I didn't want to wait. There's something else included this year. Something I promised Gray I would give to you when ten years had passed...

Something from Gray? Those knots in her stomach turned sharp, cutting into her. Nearly breathless, Darla swallowed the dread that had risen into her throat and continued reading.

I debated about sending this to you. I know you've done your best to move on. We've all done our best. But he made me promise I would give this to you, and he specifically asked me to wait ten years. I haven't read it, but I know how important it was to him. So here it is. I'm so sorry if this causes you pain. That is not my intention, and I know it wasn't his either. He loved you so much. And we love you too. Remember that always. As soon as we return from our trip, we'll come up for a visit.

Much love,
Nora

The words blurred into thick black smudges. Ten years. It had been ten years since she'd spoken to Gray. And now he had a message for her? The envelope shook in her hands, but somehow she managed to open it and pull out a letter written in his handwriting. Oh, that blocky, messy handwriting...

Tears flashed a searing heat across her eyes. Darla furiously blinked them back and held her breath so the wave of pain wouldn't drag her under. She stared at the words, written by her beloved husband's hand.

DD,

God, I love you. More than anything. I hope you know that. I hope I showed you that. I didn't want to leave. I would've given anything to stay with you, to build the future we dreamed about. But I know I'm running out of time. This is so much harder to write than I thought it would be. But I have to write this because I know you. I know who you were before you let me in—before you let me love you, and I'm worried about you.

Tears flowed steadily down her cheeks and dripped onto the collar of her dress. She couldn't move to wipe them away. Her hands were too stiff with grief. A cold hollowness shivered through her, but she forced herself to keep reading.

Before we met, I know you didn't have anyone. To love you. To protect you. To believe in you. Those first few dates we went on...you were so closed off. But then you started to trust me. You started to open up. And I saw the most beautiful heart I've ever known. It kills me to think that me leaving you has broken your heart. It kills me to think that you won't let yourself love someone else. That worry keeps me awake at night. I keep wondering what your life will look like in ten years. I want it to be full. And beautiful. And meaningful. Maybe it is. Maybe you have everything you've dreamed of. I hope so. But if not, DD, I just wanted to remind you...you can't keep that big beautiful heart hidden away, my love. I was so lucky to have you. To know you. To love you. And I want you to love someone else. To love deeply and selflessly and fully the way you loved me. Even more than that, I want you to let yourself be loved again. I know how strong you are—you proved that often. You've taken care of me. These last few months, you've taken on the weight of the world and you've done it all with such grace. If you haven't found it yet, promise me you'll look for love. It will give you life and purpose and strength when yours starts to run out. You have faithfully given me all of those things. Be brave enough to give them again. To give someone your heart. Please my love. Do it for me.

Love forever and always,
Gray

A heaving sob rose up in her throat and gagged her. She moved in front of the sink waiting to empty her stomach, but nothing came. No vomit, no tears, no sounds. She stood there hunched over, holding herself up with her palms jammed into the countertop, somehow still breathing even with the shock jarring her lungs.

How was it possible for her stomach to feel so empty and so painfully full all at once? *I want you to love some-one else.* No. No! He couldn't ask that of her. It was too much. She couldn't. Not when it hurt like this. Gray was wrong about her. She wasn't strong. That was the problem. Her heart had broken, and it was still in pieces.

The doorbell chimed. *Oh, God.* Ty could not see her like this. She quickly shoved the package into a cabinet and snatched a paper towel to dab at the mascara that had to have run down her cheeks. Pain hammered in her heart, sending an ache through her ribs, but she quickly jogged to the bathroom and touched up her face.

How could Gray intrude on her life like this? *I keep wondering what your life will look like in ten years. I want it to be full. And beautiful. And meaningful.* Didn't he know that was impossible when there was a part of her missing?

The doorbell rang again, followed by a steady knock. "Darla? Hello?" Ty called.

"Coming!" If only she could cancel. But then Ty would know something was wrong.

She put another few dabs of powder under her reddened eyes and applied more lipstick before scampering back out to the living room in a rush to get to the front door. It took her a full minute of fumbling with the lock before she could pull it open. "Sorry," she gasped, stepping aside so he could come in. "I'm running late."

"No apology necessary." Ty held a bouquet of colorful gerbera daisies in his hand. He'd dressed up too. In sleek gray pants and a white button-down shirt instead of his usual jeans and flannel. He gazed at her for a few seconds. "Are you okay?" he finally asked.

"Of course." Without making eye contact she closed the door. She'd been okay. She'd been just fine before Gray's letter. *Maybe you have everything you've dreamed of.* Didn't he know he'd taken her dreams with him?

"I brought you flowers." Ty held out the bouquet, looking at her carefully, as though he knew something wasn't right but couldn't figure out exactly what.

"Thanks." She took the flowers and bustled away from him, into the kitchen where she filled a vase with water.

He followed, still eyeing her. "Are you sure you're okay? You look...upset."

"It's a cold." She set the flowers on the counter and slipped past him to find her coat. She had to keep moving forward. She couldn't stop to think about that letter. About Gray. She had things to do. Important things. Things that proved her life wasn't pathetic. "I'm just a little stuffy right now," she said, forcing a smile. "But I'll be fine."

"You sure?" Ty helped her into her coat. "Because we don't have to go. If you're not feeling good..."

Darla stepped away from him and did her own suspicious staring. Did he not want to go? Why was he hesitating? "Of course we have to go." She snatched her purse off the console in the entryway. They had a plan and they were sticking to it. "Your parents will be here in a few days. If we're going to convince them we're a couple, first we need to convince everyone else in town." She pulled open the door and shooed Ty outside. "So buckle up, Buttercup. We're about to get engaged."

Chapter Five

Darla stared out the passenger's window of Ty's truck, watching the blur of Christmas lights pass. For once she didn't feel like talking. Too much simmered inside of her: a tangle of sadness and anger against the cards she was dealt and, the worst of them all—defeat. Gray knew. He knew in ten years she'd be alone. He knew that she would be hiding in plain sight, and he'd called her out on it.

"Soooo...what should this look like?" Ty asked as they turned into the parking lot of the Topaz Falls Community Center. The square, one-story building was entirely outlined with colorful globe lights set on a mismatched twinkle pattern, making the display look as chaotic as her current mood.

"What should what look like?" Darla asked, still distracted by the emotions trying to claw their way out of her chest.

"This. Us. The...*relationship* we're starting tonight." Ty kept the engine running and turned to face her. "This isn't something I've had a ton of practice with. The whole serious relationship thing. What do we do?"

He was nervous. Her jaw nearly dropped. Ty was so nervous that his knee was pumping and his face had flushed. Amusement pressed in against her sadness. Ty Forrester rode bulls for a living, but he was nervous about being her pretend boyfriend.

"You can start by taking a deep breath," she told him, allowing herself to do the same. The pause brought some semblance of clarity. This was what the two of them did. They were the life of the party. They had fun. They flirted. And tonight, they'd simply turn that up a couple of notches. "What do you like best about hanging out with me?"

The question seemed to sit him up straighter. "Uh. Well. You know..."

"Besides the sex." Darla scolded him with a look. Though she had to admit that was one of her favorite parts about hanging out with him too.

Ty finally grinned. "Okay. If I have to pick something else..." His gaze moved slowly down her body.

"Butt, boobs, and legs don't qualify for an answer either," she said, reading his mind.

"That's not what I was going to say." Ty shrugged defensively. "But for the record, you are hot, Darla. That's not *my* fault." He straightened the collar of his shirt. "What I was going to say, though, is you make me laugh. I like hanging out with you because you make me feel...happier."

Now she was the one sitting straighter. That wasn't exactly what she'd expected him to say. "I do?"

"Yeah." His expression took on a more serious tone. "We have fun together. And not just in your kitchen. I can be at the most boring event—like, say, a cookie-decorating extravaganza—and when I see you walk in, I know I'm gonna have fun."

"Oh." A stirring warmth brewed low in her stomach. She could say the same about him, but they usually didn't do this. Talk about deeper things. Darla shrugged off the compliment. "Then that's what you focus on when we're in front of all those people. Having fun. I'll make you laugh. I promise." It would be better for him to laugh than it would be for him to keep looking at her the way he was now—steady and sure, like he'd started to see past their boundaries. She moved to get out of the truck, but Ty caught her arm.

"Wait. What about you? What do you like best about hanging out with me?"

"The sex." She tried for the same playful tone she'd always used on him, but there was a catch in her throat. "Definitely."

"You said that didn't count." He narrowed his eyes into a naughty look. "And I already know how much you like the sex. Last time, I believe your exact words were—"

"You're really thoughtful," she said quickly, cutting him off. She didn't need him to remind her how she'd begged him not to stop. "Which is surprising given that you're a bachelor bull rider."

Ty seemed taken aback. "I'm thoughtful?"

"Yes." And the fact that he didn't realize it made it even more genuine. "You always seem to know when I need a drink or something to eat or...a distraction." Like tonight. Sitting here with him had already eased the pain Gray's letter had brought. "And you gave me gerbera daisies."

"I did." He nodded, looking rather proud of himself. "I

brought you those flowers because I remembered you said they were your favorite."

"Exactly. You remembered." And that said a lot about him.

"Damn, I'm a pretty good pretend boyfriend." His grin turned sly. "You're one lucky woman."

She laughed. "I see your confidence is back."

"It wasn't really gone. I just wanted to hear you admit you liked something about me." Ty cut the engine. "Let's do this." He got out and before Darla could open her door, there he was being the perfect gentleman.

He helped her out of the car, and she had no choice but to hold on to him as they navigated the icy parking lot. He paused outside the main entrance. "You think people are really going to buy this?"

"Depends how well we sell it." Something told her Ty would be an incredible salesman.

"Here goes nothing." He took her hand and led her through the doors. Right away, Darla stopped. It seemed the whole town had crammed into the large room, talking and laughing above the low hum of Christmas carols. Festive plastic tablecloths covered the long tables, which had been set up in rows.

"Wow." Darla had never seen so many sugar cookies in her entire life. Her teeth hurt just looking at the full platters and cans of frosting and enough different kinds of sprinkles to fill a swimming pool.

"Welcome! I'm so glad you made it!" Ginny Eckles rushed over. She was dressed in red and green from head to toe. "Wait." She looked at the two of them suspiciously. "Did you two come together?"

Ty slipped his arm smoothly around Darla. "Of course." He gazed down at her. "We've been spending a lot of time together lately. Haven't we?"

Darla leaned in to him and put on a mysterious smile. "We sure have."

"*Really?*" Ginny's eyes went wide behind her glasses. "So you two are an item now, huh?"

"You could say that." Ty moved his hand up and down Darla's arm in an affectionate caress. He was really good at this...

"Oh, how wonderful!" Despite her enthusiasm, Ginny seemed the slightest bit disappointed. She did have a sweet spot for Ty. "And just in time for Christmas too. How long has this been going on?"

"Um, well—"

"Hey, we saved you a seat!" Thankfully, Charity waved them over to a table where their friends had gathered. They were all in on the ruse and had pledged to help them however they could.

"We'd better get over there." Darla gave Ginny a little wave. "We'll see you later." She and Ty hustled away from the potential for any more questions.

"Well if it isn't the happy couple." Mateo elbowed Everly and they both grinned.

Darla sent him a warning look. "We *are* happy." She looked at Ty for confirmation.

"I'll be happier once I get my hands on one of those cookies," he said, eyeing Everly's professionally decorated Christmas trees.

"We're not eating them," her friend informed Ty. "They're for the auction. To keep people happy during the intermissions."

"Got it." Ty shrugged off his coat and rolled up his sleeves. "So what do we do? I've never been to a cookie-decorating party before."

"Pick your cookie and give it your best shot," Darla told

him, taking her place at the table. "Ginny said the ten best cookies will win a prize." Though it looked like Everly already had that one in the bag.

The contest seemed to appeal to Ty's competitive side. He took his time picking out a Santa-shaped cookie, while Darla selected a reindeer. They got to work decorating, and Darla was grateful for something else to focus on. She slathered on the brown frosting, detailing a few wisps of white bordering the tail and the ears. All around them, she could feel people watching her and Ty with curiosity— the rest of the Chamber members, some of her regulars at the wine bar.

"What are you, a professional?" Ty demanded when she put the finishing touches on the reindeer. "Are you hoping they'll put your cookie in a museum or something?"

She looked at his creation and laughed. She couldn't help it. There were blobs of red and white frosting where Santa's hat and beard were supposed to be, but the colors had smeared together. And he'd added big chocolate chips for a pair of creepy eyes.

"Are you laughing at mine?" The man asked with mock outrage.

That only made her laugh harder. "Don't worry," she managed. "I'm sure they'd love to display that in the kindergarten room."

Ty gasped as if the insult had shocked him. But he was laughing too. Giving her a mischievous look, he swiped a finger across her perfect reindeer, getting a glob of the frosting on his finger, and then he smeared it over her lips.

"You did not just do that." She came at him with a spoonful of frosting but he caught her hand and pulled her to him. "I only did it so I could do this." Lowering his head, he pressed his lips to hers, sealing them in a sweet, sugary kiss.

A fluttering sensation traveled up from Darla's toes until it engulfed her fully. Ty's arms came around her, easing her in closer as his lips teased hers. She teetered forward, resting her hands on his chest, letting herself fully embrace the rush it brought. *Yes, yes, yes.* It made her forget. That physical contact, that explosive desire, made her forget every hurt.

Ty pulled back, his thumb skimming her cheek. "How was that for selling it?" he murmured so only she could hear.

"Very convincing," she whispered, her lungs still shuddering from the lack of oxygen. It seemed she'd forgotten how to breathe properly. How to think. How to move. Sparks were still zinging around inside of her, and she couldn't quite get them to shut off. Hence the reason she'd brought Ty home with her more than once. That mouth of his...

"Sorry I messed up your cookie," the man said, his eyes ridiculously repentant. He reached over to the table and picked up the now-smeared reindeer. "I bet it still tastes good though." He took a bite and then offered her one.

She could feel everyone in the place staring at them, so Darla bit into the soft sugary frosting too. "Mmmm. Still good," she agreed.

"Awww." A few teen girls at the table next to them swooned.

Ty leaned in closer. "How am I doing?"

Darla finished chewing before she answered. "I would say you're exceeding expectations." In more ways than one.

* * *

Mission accomplished. Ty put the finishing touches on his Christmas tree cookie and added it to the platter sitting in the middle of the table. Sure, his cookies looked like they'd been frosted by a three-year-old, but over the last hour, he and Darla had managed to become the center of everyone's attention, and that was the point, right? As far as he could tell, everyone in this place believed they were a couple. And it hadn't been half bad. Being someone's boyfriend happened to be a lot more fun than he would've guessed.

"What'd you think of my tree cookie?" he asked Darla, waiting for her to look at it and laugh. But she didn't respond. In fact, she hadn't seemed to hear him. Her head was bent and her eyes were focused on the table.

Whoa. She didn't look so good. "Hey." He scooted closer and put his arm around her. "What's up?"

"I don't know. All of a sudden I'm not feeling so hot." Her face seemed a lot paler than it had been ten minutes ago.

"Is it your cold?" Though he hadn't noticed her sniffling at all...

She shook her head and wrapped an arm around her middle. "I have to get out of here. Like now."

"Okay. Sure." He hopped up from the table and draped her coat over her shoulders. "We're gonna head out," he called to their friends. Darla was already making her way slowly to the door.

"Now?" Everly shot him a concerned frown.

"Yeah. I'm gonna take her home. She's not feeling good." What had changed? All evening they'd been flirting and laughing...

"You'll make sure she's okay?" Everly whispered. "That's what a boyfriend would do. Take her home and make her feel better."

"I can do that." Probably. Maybe. Hell, he'd figure it out. Before anyone could see the doubt on his face, he hurried to catch up with Darla. She leaned in to him as he opened the door for her, and they stepped out into the snowy evening.

"Do you want to get something to eat?" he asked, not sure what else to say.

"No. Definitely not." Darla stopped abruptly and turned away from him, hunching over to throw up into the snow bank that flanked the sidewalk.

Uh-oh. That couldn't be good. Ty wrapped his arm around her, holding her up. She eased in a few deep breaths and closed her eyes with a groan. "I'm so sorry."

"Sorry?" He smoothed her hair away from her face. "You're sick. You don't have to be sorry."

"I don't know what's wrong with me. I feel awful." She swayed, and that was all Ty needed to see. He swept her up into his arms.

"What're you doing?" she asked, her legs flailing. "No one's watching us now."

"I know." He started across the parking lot, careful not to jostle her. "But you're not steady on your feet and there's a lot of ice."

Surprisingly, Darla didn't argue or demand he put her down. He carried her all the way to his truck and then helped her climb in. On the drive back to her house, she rested her head against the seatback and closed her eyes. When he parked in her driveway, Ty cut the engine.

Darla raised her head but it seemed she could hardly hold it up. "You don't have to walk me in." She suddenly seemed weak and tired.

"Sure I do. I don't want you to slip on the ice." He

got out of the truck and opened her door to help her climb out.

"I'll be okay." She held on to his arm as they made their way to her front door. "Really, Ty. You don't have to make such a fuss over me."

"I promised Everly I'd keep an eye on you. She informed me that's what boyfriends do." He held out his hand, and she gave him her house key along with a weak smile. Obviously she was too sick to argue.

Once they got inside, Ty helped her slip off her coat and then hung it up in her closet. Tea. That was supposed to be good when a woman didn't feel well, right? He shed his own coat and tossed it onto a nearby chair before rolling up his shirtsleeves and undoing the top button on the collar from hell. "Why don't you sit down?" He caught Darla's arm and led her to the couch. Her face had gotten so pale that it had changed her eyes. They were usually sharp and vibrant, but now they had a dullness to them. Even her posture had wilted during the few minutes she'd been standing by the door.

"You don't have to stay." She sunk to the couch and rested her head back, gazing up at him with a stubborn frown. "I don't need anyone to take care of me."

"I know you don't." Hell, Darla Michaels had to be the lowest-maintenance woman he'd ever met. "But like I said, I promised Everly." And what kind of person would let someone sit and suffer by themselves? What if she wasn't okay? Knowing Darla, she'd keel over before she called someone and asked for help.

"Do you think you have a fever?" He snatched a blanket off the back of the couch and tucked it in around her.

Her shoulders slumped. "I don't know. Don't think so. I just feel queasy."

Ty nodded. Must be a stomach bug, he thought. He'd have to make sure to give her a wide berth. "Do you have any ginger root?" he asked, cruising into her open-concept kitchen. "And lemon? And honey?"

"Why, are you going to make a stir fry?" She might be sick, but her grin still brought out his.

"No. I'm going to make you ginger tea. It's good for your stomach."

Darla raised her eyebrows.

"My grandma used to make it for me," he explained, searching her cabinets. "So I'll make it for you. As long as you don't tell the guys." He'd never hear the end of it from them.

"Ginger and lemon are in the fridge," Darla half groaned, wrapping an arm around her middle. "Honey is in the pantry."

"Got it." Before collecting the ingredients, Ty filled the teakettle and set it back on the stove. Darla's kitchen bordered on pristine. There was no clutter, and everything seemed to be organized with Type A precision. He supposed that was how it was when you ran a restaurant of sorts. But still, for some reason it surprised him. Darla had such a laid-back, easygoing personality. He never would've pegged her for a perfectionist.

"When did you start feeling sick?" he asked, rifling through a drawer until he found a zester.

"I don't know," she mumbled. "It's been a few days off and on, I guess. But it hit me hard tonight." Those last words wavered as though she was trying to hold back tears.

Ty glanced at her from across the expansive kitchen island. She'd closed her eyes and leaned her head back and seemed to be breathing deeply.

"Well, from what I remember, this tea is some ancient remedy or something." At least that was what his grandma had claimed. Of course, she'd also claimed that she'd once kissed John Wayne, so who knew?

Darla didn't respond, so he let the silence settle as he grated the ginger and some lemon zest into a small pile on the cutting board. When the teakettle screeched, he poured the steaming water into a mug and added in the ginger, lemon zest, and a generous tablespoon of honey. Damn, it smelled even better than he remembered—spicy from the ginger, but also citrusy and sweet. He gave the tea a stir, and then carried the mug over to the couch where Darla still sat with her head back. Trying to be quiet, he set the tea on the coffee table in front of her, but she startled and opened her eyes like she'd forgotten he was there.

"Supposedly ginger is a good for an upset stomach," he said, settling into the chair off to the side of the couch. Her living room had always reminded him of a Victorian-era parlor with rich velvety furniture and solid wood accents.

"Thanks." Darla scooted forward and picked up the mug with both hands, inhaling deeply before she took a sip.

Ty watched her lips on the mug, aware of some low, stirring hunger. He'd enjoyed kissing her earlier, more than he probably should've given the pretend nature of their relationship.

"Wow. That's good tea." Her obvious surprise made him laugh.

"Told you." Of course, Darla never seemed to take anyone's word for anything. She had her own ideas, an independence he respected.

"I'm sorry I threw up on our date." She set down the mug and drew the blanket tighter around her shoulders.

"It was that bad, huh?" he teased.

"It wasn't bad. Actually, I think it was quite successful. You sure had people talking." Color came back to her cheeks. "I don't think we'll have any problem convincing your family we're an item."

His family. He had exactly one week before he had to pick them up from the airport. When he'd called and asked his brother to be part of the festival, his parents had jumped on the chance to get them all together. Now they were all coming to stay with him for the better part of three weeks—all the way through New Year's. That meant he'd get three weeks of competing with his brother for the best son award. He didn't know why he still tried. Rhett won every time.

Darla picked up the mug again. "Ginny Eckles seemed sorely disappointed to learn that you're off the market, you know."

"Don't remind me." He grinned. "We need to get engaged ASAP. Then maybe she'll stop undressing me with her eyes all the time. It'll be against the rules."

"Rules." Darla sat up a little straighter. "Yes, rules." She obviously had something on her mind, given the way her gaze shifted up to the ceiling, but he didn't push her.

"We need to talk about the rules," she finally said. "In fact, we need to write a list of rules."

"Uh…" This wasn't making sense. Maybe she had a fever or something. "What do we need rules for?"

Darla snatched her iPad off the coffee table and started to type. "You know, like boundaries. Faking an engagement is kind of a big thing—especially with the whole town watching. Every good con needs rules."

What did she know about cons? "Okay." He'd never been much of a rule follower, but Ty leaned over and rested his elbows on his knees to hear her out. "What have you got?"

"First rule, no sex."

"But we've already had sex," he reminded her. More than once. And it had been good sex. Good sex worth repeating.

"I know we have, but we don't need to confuse things. This is a ruse, and we don't want things to get complicated."

In his opinion, sex was one of those things that didn't have to be complicated, but if it meant that much to her he could compromise. "Fine. No sex." Though that wouldn't stop him from thinking about it. "You must be really worried that I'm going to seduce you." He shouldn't be giving her a hard time when she wasn't feeling well, but he couldn't resist.

"Ha." She raised her chin and looked down on him. "I just don't want to get distracted, that's all. We both have a lot to do. I want to be focused."

So she found him as tempting as he found her. "But maybe after we're done pretending I can go back to distracting you?"

Darla shook her head at him, but she didn't say no. "Rule number two, we should definitely ease up on the PDA."

Ty laughed until Darla's serious expression cut him off. "Seriously?" he asked as nicely as he could. "Just tonight you said we had to play that up. To sell our relationship."

"Well it doesn't have to be so over-the-top." Her eyes avoided his. "Anyway, it's your turn. Do you have any rules you'd like to add?" she asked, holding out the iPad in his direction.

"Yeah, now that you mention it, I do." He reached over

and pushed the device back into her lap. "Don't talk to my brother alone. Without me around."

She dropped her chin and stared at him. "Seriously?"

He put on his most serious expression. He'd sat there and listened to all of her ridiculous rules. She owed him one. "Rhett twists things around. And he'll take any opportunity he can find to make me look bad." He'd been doing it since they were kids. "Trust me."

"Okay, fine," she muttered, throwing in a roll of her eyes. "I won't talk to him alone. Anything else?"

"Nope. That's it for me." He eyed her. "I've never been a big rule guy."

"Okay then." She set the iPad back on the coffee table. "We should probably talk about our backstory. How we met, how we got engaged and all that."

Ty shrugged. "We met when I moved here, started hanging out, fell in love, and I asked you to marry me." As long as they kept it simple, it shouldn't be too hard to keep their story straight. "Isn't that the way it happens for most people?"

Darla lifted her mug again, holding it tightly in her hands. The shadows had come back to her eyes, darkening them as she stared at the floor.

Was that how it had happened with her first husband? He wanted to ask, but something told him he shouldn't. Darla seemed lost in her own thoughts. Or maybe *lost* wasn't the right word. More like consumed. She looked as sick as she had back at the community center. The longer they sat in silence, the more uncomfortable he got. Something was bothering her, and he didn't know how to help.

Maybe she wasn't comfortable with their arrangement. "Look, if you don't want to do this—"

"I'm fine with it." She raised her head. "It's no big deal."

Then why all the rules? Why was she acting so weird?

"I'm just not feeling well," she said, slipping off her shoes and resting her feet on the coffee table. "That's all. You've been a great pretend boyfriend, but you can go now. I'm really not in the mood to talk anymore tonight."

"We don't have to talk." Ty leaned over and picked up the remote. "Why don't we just watch a movie? Hang out?" He still didn't feel right about leaving her to fend for herself. Before she could protest, he started flipping through the saved movies on her DVR. "Oh, *White Christmas*. I haven't seen that in years."

Darla smirked. "You've seen it before?"

"Heck yeah. My mom used to make us watch it with her every year. It's actually not half bad." He clicked the Play button. Darla stared at him a few more minutes, but then she lay down on the couch and seemed to get comfortable. Twenty minutes into the movie, she fell asleep. Ty hauled himself out of the chair and quietly and carefully pried the almost-empty mug of ginger tea out of her hands. He gazed down at her, struck by how peaceful she looked when she was asleep and wasn't guarding herself so closely. Her hair had fallen across her cheek, and he lightly brushed it away.

He'd told Mateo he didn't have feelings for her, but he couldn't deny that something stirred when he looked at her. When he touched her. When he kissed her. Something definitely stirred and it made him want more.

Chapter Six

Darla sat straight up in her bed. A warm cozy feeling from the dream she'd been having still enveloped her. *Oh. Dear. God.* She shoved her hair back from her forehead, recounting what exactly had been going on in her subconscious. She'd dreamed about Ty. And it hadn't been a sex dream either. It had been...nostalgic. The two of them were standing at her kitchen counter. She'd been mixing up a batch of chocolate truffles and he'd come up behind her, wrapped his arms around her, and kissed her neck while she giggled. Giggled!

It had been a scene straight out of a sappy engagement ring commercial. A scene that she'd experienced with Gray plenty of times. But Ty...*Ty?* Nope. Nuh uh. She didn't think of him like that. She *couldn't* think of him like that.

Darla threw off the covers and scrambled out of her bed. This was because of last night, that's all. The emotional rollercoaster Gray's letter had put her on. She'd been so upset when Ty had shown up that she hadn't kept her wits about her. Of course she'd dreamed about him after his stellar acting job last night. The scenes flickered through her mind. Of course she'd dreamed about him when he'd gone and smeared frosting across her lips and kissed her. Oh! And he'd made her that delicious tea, which really had soothed her stomach somehow. Then they'd watched *White Christmas*—her favorite Christmas movie of all time.

Wait. She glanced around, trying to get her balance and her bearings. How'd she get in her bed? She had no memory of walking into her bedroom. But Ty wasn't in here with her. And, though she stood on her wood floor barefoot, she was still wearing her dress from last night. If she didn't walk in her room on her own, then...Darla bolted out the bedroom door and careened down the hall into the living room.

Sure enough, Ty was still there, passed out on the couch. The sight of him made her pause. He lay flat on his back, his hair and clothes rumpled. Another few buttons on his shirt had come undone so that the very top of his muscular pecs peeked through. He looked peaceful and relaxed and too sexy for his own good. Or for her own good, for that matter.

She had to stop looking. That dream had messed with her. Ty was a friend she'd had some fun with. That was all.

"Wake up." She leaned over and shook his shoulder. "Come on, Ty. Wake up."

His eyelids fluttered, but he simply groaned and turned onto his side. "Few more minutes..."

"No. Not a few more minutes." Darla tugged on his arm, trying to sit him up. "Come on. Time to get up." Time for him to go home so she could clear her head.

Ty yawned and opened his eyes fully, then squinted at her. "What time is it?"

Good question. Darla glanced at the kitchen clock. "Almost eight." Embarrassed, she tried to smooth her wrinkled dress, which was ridiculous because this was only Ty. Ty who'd already seen her naked on numerous occasions. Ty who'd touched her almost everywhere.

Okay, this wasn't helping.

"Why are you still here?" she demanded, images from that dream playing in the back of her mind.

He sat up and moved his head as though trying to get a crick out of his neck. "I thought I'd stay in case you needed anything."

"I don't." Darla crossed her arms tightly over her chest, feeling too exposed. "I don't need anything. Do you know how many times I've been sick and on my own? Plenty. I can take care of myself. I've been taking care of myself for a long time." And she'd been fine. Her life had been very manageable up until last week. Until she'd agreed to be Ty's fiancée. But none of that was his fault. "I'm sorry. I'm just tired. Still not feeling great." She must have the stomach flu. Or maybe she'd eaten something that didn't agree with her. Yes, that had to be it. She didn't have time to be sick right now. "Did you really carry me to bed?"

"You were conked out." His sleepy tone would've been adorable if she wasn't so desperate to get him out of her house.

"I thought you'd sleep better in your bed. I was only going to hang out for a while to make sure you didn't need anything, but I guess I fell asleep." He pushed himself off the couch, his eyes brighter and more awake. "How are you feeling?"

Worse. She was feeling worse. Her stomach sloshed

and gurgled. "I'll be right back," she wheezed, running to the bathroom. She got there just in time to throw up in the toilet, and then she quickly splashed water on her face. She had to get herself together. This was ridiculous. As if having some weird stomach bug wasn't bad enough, now she had all of these emotions to contend with—a deep yawning sadness, confusion, and that other one she usually kept in check. Fear. She hadn't dreamed about anyone but Gray since he'd died, and she couldn't start now. Faking an engagement was one thing, but real feelings? No. She couldn't. She *wouldn't*.

When she came out of the bathroom, Ty stood at the end of the hall waiting for her. "Are you sure you're all right?"

"I'm fine." Or she would be if she could just go about her usual routine, her normal life, and forget all of this for a few hours. Forget that Gray had asked her to risk her heart again. Forget about this fake engagement that had seemed like such a good idea at the time. She needed to go to work. She needed to plan and prepare for the festival. "Thanks for keeping an eye on me, but I have to go."

Ty leaned his broad shoulder into the wall and stared at her, tilting his head slightly. "You sure that's a good idea? Maybe you need some rest."

Rest was the exact opposite of what she needed. "I have too much to do. The festival starts next week, and I still have to finalize the details." She needed to call the county and make sure the permit was approved and confirm with all the vendors who would be selling food during the rodeo. "I'm great. Feeling much better now, actually." Or at least she would feel better when she got her mind off of everything.

"Okay." Ty still didn't look convinced, but he

straightened and moseyed back to the living room. "You're still coming with me to pick up my parents from the airport, right?" He sat on the couch and pulled on his boots.

"Yep." Darla hurried over to the chair and grabbed his coat, holding it out for him. "Just text me and tell me when you want to leave."

"They get in late Monday, so maybe we'll head down in the early evening." Ty took his coat from her and slipped it on. He paused in the entryway and patted his pocket. "I almost forgot. I have to give you the engagement ring. You still want to tell people I popped the question last night, right?"

"Oh." Right. That had been the plan. "I think we should. That way everyone will know before your parents get here." Hopefully the town's shock would wear off by then.

"Here." He pulled out a small box and popped it open.

The single solitaire diamond set in an intricate gold band made her gasp. "That's a real ring." A beautiful real ring.

"It was my grandma's." He carefully took it out of the box and slid it onto Darla's left ring finger. "She gave it to me after my grandpa passed. Said she wanted me to be ready when I found the right woman."

But she wasn't the right woman. "I can't wear this." She traced the diamond with her finger and then went to pull off the ring. "We can find a fake one. What if I lose it? What if—"

"My family won't believe us unless you're wearing *this* ring." He slid it back up her finger. "Trust me. I know you won't lose it. It actually fits you pretty well," he said, admiring it.

"Mm-hmm." Darla's heart had gone haywire with

conflicting emotions again. The ring was very elegant, but it sat heavy on her finger. It had taken her five years to stop wearing the ring Gray had given her. And even then she'd only taken it off because customers at the bar would ask about her husband. She'd gotten tired of the horrified expressions she'd see on their faces when she would tell them he passed away, so she'd tucked the ring into a box and kept it in her bedside table.

Ty seemed to be watching for her reaction, so she gave a nod of approval. "It'll work. For the plan. And I'll give it back right after they leave." A few weeks. That was all it would be. And then everything would go back to normal. There wouldn't be any confusing emotions or crazy dreams. "Okay, well, I guess you should get going." Darla nudged him toward the door. "See you soon."

He said a quick goodbye, and she all but shoved him outside. As soon as the door closed, she flew around the house, showering and getting herself ready for work in record time. Once she looked presentable enough, she pulled on her wool pea coat and walked out of her house. The crisp, cold air seemed to calm her stomach, so she decided to walk the few blocks to the wine bar. It would do her good—help her sort out all the nervous energy that Gray's letter and that dream and the ring had trapped inside of her.

She started off down the sidewalk, and it was like stepping into a magic snow globe. The frosted lawns of her neighbors glistened with incandescent sparkles in the early-morning sun. Overhead, the royal sky hung like a giant banner—the purest blue. There was no name for that color. It showed itself only on perfect winter days.

Darla inhaled it all, and something inside of her settled. She could handle this. All of this. She could process Gray's dying wish for her and Ty's nonnegotiable presence in her life for a couple of weeks. She'd handled so much more in the past. As long as she kept everything under control, things would be fine. She could raise money for Mateo and Everly. She could be strong and supportive for her friends.

"Darla! Yoo hoo!" Ginny Eckles rushed up the sidewalk. She was dressed for the weather in all wool from her shawl to her pants to the cap on her head. "I didn't expect to see you out here this early." She leaned in. "Not after I happened to drive by your house early this morning and saw Ty's truck parked out front."

It was the opening she needed. Darla bent her lips into a sheepish smile. "Yeah. We were actually supposed to go to dinner after the cookie-decorating party, but we went back to my place instead." She didn't mention she hadn't been feeling well. Only their friends knew, and they wouldn't have spread the word. "Ty actually proposed last night." The ring sat like a weight on her finger, but she held it out, the diamond catching the sun's sparkle.

"What!" The woman darted in front of her and inspected the ring. "Oh lordy! Look at that rock! You and Ty are getting married? Already?"

"Mm-hmm." Darla was glad she'd slipped on her sunglasses so her eyes wouldn't give her away. She pulled back her hand. "I mean, he just asked, so no one really knows about it yet." But they would now. Give Ginny two hours and everyone in town would know.

"That's marvelous news! Just marvelous." The woman linked her arm with Darla's and all but pulled her in the direction of their storefronts. The bakery was only a few doors down from her wine bar. "I've always thought he was sweet on you. I definitely picked up on it over these last few months."

Darla stumbled on a curb. Picked up on what? The harmless flirting between them? "Really?" The dream haunted her again. She could almost feel Ty's arms sliding around her, holding her close. And that kiss at the cookie-decorating party... it had felt about five steps past harmless. Her pulse quickened, but she couldn't tell if it was from anticipation or fear.

"Of course," Ginny chirped. "You can just tell whenever the two of you are in the same room. Like at the Tumble Inn a couple months ago. And at that Chamber meeting last week. He couldn't keep his eyes off of you."

She tried to think back, to remember if he'd been staring at her at the Chamber meeting, but she'd been so focused on the festival. Ginny had to be mistaken. Ty's feelings for her didn't go any deeper than their occasional fling. But that kiss last night...

"There's always been something between you two, hasn't there?" the woman prompted.

"I guess so." Her face got hot enough to melt her makeup. "But lately it's become something more." Something that wasn't feeling nearly as safe.

"Well, trust me." Ginny let go of her and veered toward the door to the Butter Buns Bakery. "I've been around a long time. I know how to recognize a man in love."

"I'm sure you do," Darla said, even though Ginny clearly did not. Ty didn't love her.

"I have to say, I'm quite surprised the feeling is mutual," she went on. "You must be very good at hiding your feelings."

Ten years of practice had made her a professional. "Well, you know. I'm kind of a private person when it comes to my love life." Or lack thereof.

"Oh, I can't wait to attend the wedding." The woman went about unlocking the door to her bakery.

"We haven't set a date yet," Darla said quickly. "We'll probably wait a year. Or two. You know how long it takes to plan a wedding," she babbled. The key to this whole ruse would be remaining vague about pretty much everything, including the wedding that would never be.

* * *

"I'm not wearing that." Ty eyed the pair of red silk boxers, jingle bell suspenders, and the Santa hat that had been laid out for him on one of the tables at Darla's wine bar. When she'd called and said the Chamber wanted to get an early start on the cowboy calendar, he had no idea what he was walking into.

"I already told you. I'll wear boots and jeans." Actually, he'd said *if* he did the calendar he'd wear boots and jeans. He never remembered officially agreeing to this baloney. How Darla had managed to convince eleven other rodeo stars to travel out here a few days early for this, he'd never know.

"But you're Mr. December." Darla held up the suspenders and shook them to make them jingle. "This is the wardrobe we've selected for Mr. December." She peered up at him from underneath those long, sleek eyelashes, and it finally clicked. It was her eyes. That was what he found so captivating about her. They were persuasive as hell. No man had a shot at telling her no.

Of course that wouldn't stop him from trying. "I'm not wearing boxers and suspenders." That was ridiculous.

"It's either this or we assign you Mr. September and you go to Ginny's bakery for the pictures." Darla's expression turned as innocent as an angel with a bent halo. "I seem to recall her offering to let you hold on to one of her buns."

Ty held up the boxers and studied them. "You know, actually these aren't so bad."

"Good." The woman handed over the suspenders. "Everyone will be expecting my fiancé to happily represent the Chocolate Therapist."

Her fiancé. That wouldn't get less weird for him to hear. Hopefully none of the people milling about had noticed his obvious flinch. "So you think everyone's buying it?" he whispered with a glance around. A few other Main Street business owners hovered on the other end of the table, getting their cowboys all rigged up with costumes and props.

"So far so good," Darla murmured. "But if you keep looking so shocked every time I call you my fiancé, people are going to start catching on."

"Sorry. It's just..." He didn't even know how to describe it. Weird? Appealing? Unsettling?

"I'm not wearing this." Levi stomped over, holding up what looked to be white jeans and a USA muscle shirt. "White jeans?" he demanded. "*White?* News flash: Cowboys don't wear white pants. And that hat is out of the question." He pointed to a nearby table, and Ty busted out laughing. It was a bedazzled Uncle Sam hat full of red, white, and blue sequins.

"Let me guess, you're Mr. July?" he asked, suddenly appreciating the chance to be Mr. December.

Levi flipped Ty off.

"Hey, at least you get to do your photo shoot at the ice cream shop," Darla offered. "If you're really good, maybe you'll score a double-decker cone."

Levi's scowl tightened. "This is not what I signed up for—"

"You?" Lance asked his brother, walking over to join them.

This time Ty about doubled over with laughter. "Hold on. I gotta get a picture of this." Before Lance could run or sock him, he snapped a shot on his phone. Mr. February was wearing jeans with a white fur vest—no shirt underneath, of course—and a white fur trapper hat on his head.

"I swear, whoever came up with the idea that cowboys walk around shirtless all the time has never met a real cowboy," Lance grumbled. "And seriously? Fur? I'd rather wear nothing."

"Maybe that could be arranged," Ginny called over.

Laughing, Ty eyed his red silk boxers again. Maybe he didn't have it so bad after all.

"Man, I never thought cowboys were such whiners either," Darla commented, somehow staring down on the lot of them even though she stood much shorter. "Let's all try to remember why we're doing this, shall we? You don't hear Mateo complaining."

That was true, and their poor comrade currently stood on the other side of the room wearing leather pants and a leather vest with a hell of a lot of fringe. The owners of the flower shop were already oiling up his chest, the two happily married middle-aged women giggling like a couple of kindergarteners.

"This calendar had better raise a shit ton of money," Levi muttered.

"We're never gonna live this down out on the circuit," Lance added, itching around his midsection.

"Half hour, boys." Darla gave them each a pat. "That's all we need."

Ty's friends walked away, but he could still hear them grumbling.

"So what were you saying about flinching when I call you my fiancé?" Darla asked, handing him the silk boxer shorts. Her expression was distant. "Because I could call you something else if you'd prefer. 'Honey'? 'Dear'? 'Schmookie poo'?"

"Very funny." He set the boxers and suspenders back down on the table. He wasn't about to put them on until he absolutely had to. " 'Fiancé' is fine. I'm just not used to—"

"There're the love birds!" Ginny Eckles dashed over to them. "Congratulations!" She snatched Ty's hand and pumped it up and down. "I couldn't believe it when Darla told me you two were already getting hitched!"

He slid a glance to his fiancée. "Yeah, I think it caught us both by surprise." In more ways than one.

"Well, we simply have to get a picture of the happy couple for the Chamber's Facebook page!" Ginny patted her pockets until she located her smartphone. "Everyone is dying to see you two pose together!"

Darla broke away from him. "Actually, everyone's so busy right now—"

"I'm not," Ginny said. "I'll take it!"

"Great." Ty moved in next to Darla and slipped his arm around her. Her shoulder seemed to stiffen against his. Talk about people catching on to their ruse. Would she turn to stone every time he touched her?

"Could you get a little closer?" Ginny held up her phone. "Oh! Maybe give her a kiss, huh? That would be *adorable*."

This time Darla stepped away from him. "I don't think the whole town needs to see us kissing. We're not into PDA," she said.

"Why ever not?" the baker demanded. "You're in love! It's Christmas time. A sweet couple smooching is exactly the kind of lovely thing people want to see this time of year."

Ty turned to Darla and shrugged. "She's right, schmookie poo." He eased his arms around her rigid shoulders. Wow, she really didn't want to do this. "How about if I sneak a kiss on her cheek?" he asked Ginny. "I'll be real sly about it." Everyone would go crazy for that, and maybe Darla would loosen up too.

"Aw that'd be so sweet." Ginny aimed the phone's camera, and Ty leaned in, pressing his lips lightly against Darla's cheek with a grin.

"That's perfect!" Ginny studied the phone screen with a wide grin. "You two make the cutest couple," she gushed. As soon as she walked away, Ty faced Darla.

"If I can't flinch when you call me your fiancé, then you definitely can't turn to stone whenever I touch you. We're supposed to be newly engaged. We're going to have to hug. And kiss. And hold hands. If that'll be a problem—"

"It's not going to be a problem," Darla insisted. "Sorry. I'm just . . . tired today. It's been a busy week."

Ty grinned at her. "All the more reason to live a little." He winked. "This engagement doesn't have to be another thing that stresses you out. I promise I'll make it fun."

Chapter Seven

This was going to be a problem. Good lord, every time Ty got within five inches of touching her, her stomach flipped and her palms got clammy and sparks of heat brought on a wave of perspiration that tingled on her face.

Combine that with the lingering nausea she couldn't seem to shake since the cookie-decorating party, and Darla felt like she was right back in junior high, nervous and awkward. Completely unlike herself.

"You okay?" Everly studied her from a few tables over, where she was glancing through the calendars Darla had ordered for inspiration.

"Never been better," she sang, keeping an eye out for Ty. He'd disappeared into the back room to get his costume on—complaining about it the whole way. As far as she was concerned, he could take his time getting dressed. At least she could think straight when he wasn't standing next to her, when Ginny wasn't forcing them to kiss.

Everly walked over. "I can't believe you organized all of this."

"It gave me something to do." Something to focus on other than her and Ty's fake relationship debut.

"So how's it going with Ty?" Everly asked. "When are his parents coming?"

Rather than answer the first loaded question, she went straight for answering the second. "We're going to pick them up at the airport tomorrow night." And from then on they would have to play the part of the happy couple. Lord help her, her stomach might not hold up for the next three weeks.

Everly pulled out a chair and sat at the table. She seemed more tired than normal, but Darla supposed that was to be expected. "Everyone around here seems to have bought the whole engagement story, huh?" her friend asked.

What could she say? Ginny had really sold it for them. "Seems like it." She hoped so anyway. The last thing they needed was for someone in town to blow their cover with Ty's family.

"Well, I know you've taken on a lot of extra stress for us managing all these event details." Everly's eyes got teary. "We really appreciate everything you're doing, Darla. I don't even know how to thank you." She dabbed at her eyes with her shirtsleeve.

"No thanks necessary." Everly would do the same—or more—for her. "We're happy to help." Well, for the most part. Ty would be happier when he didn't have to wear the red silk boxers and suspenders. But she had a feeling he'd look good in them. Really good...

Darla decided to change the subject. "Have you heard anything from your insurance company yet?"

Her friend slumped with a heartsick sigh. "It's going to be a process. I don't know that we'll be able to start rebuilding until the spring. And with the baby coming..." The words trailed off as if she was too overwhelmed to finish.

That was to be expected too. It was overwhelming enough to have a baby, but then to have your livelihood up in the air...Darla couldn't even imagine. "Don't worry about that. We can do more fund-raisers. We'll all pitch in and help to get the café open again. And of course, as soon as you're ready to go back to work I can help out with the baby. You know how much I love babies."

"Yes I do." Everly's expression perked up. "Everyone's kids love you too. You're their favorite aunt. I know the baby will love you."

"I'll make sure he or she loves me." Darla had her methods. Sometimes it was fun being the one who never had to discipline them—the one who could spoil them and love on them and then hand them back to their parents. And other times...well, she couldn't go there. At this point in her life, she'd have to settle for loving other people's kids.

"Well, how do I look?" Ty strolled over to the table, jingling the whole way.

Darla fumbled with her phone and accidentally dropped it onto the floor. Oh, yeah. Ty Forrester definitely fit the perfect profile for Mr. December. From that sexy, naughty look with the Santa hat crooked on his head to his lean, muscled torso, Ty just might sell out the calendars all by himself. She stooped to pick up her phone and was suddenly so hot she wanted to take off her sweater. When she stood back up, Darla narrowed an eye as she looked him over, hopefully giving the impression she was simply analyzing the outfit for the calendar. "It'll do," she finally said, angling her body back to Everly and away from Ty. Why did the sight of him have to stir that greedy hunger?

Her friend gave her a thoughtful look. "Well, I know I'm married to his friend and all, but he looks pretty hot to me." Everly raised her eyebrows as though expecting Darla to agree.

"Yeah, sure." She gave the man another quick glance. "It'll work."

Ty's head dropped to the side. "It had better work. I'm not humiliating myself for nothing here."

"Well, we appreciate it, Ty," Everly offered. "Really. I know none of you are exactly excited about the calendar, but it's so nice of you to do this for us."

At that, his entire demeanor softened. "You know we'd do anything for you guys. We've got your back."

Exactly what Darla would've said if she wasn't having a hard time speaking at the moment. Or breathing.

"Well, well, well, Mr. December." Ginny Eckles hurried over carrying a small basket. "It looks like you're ready for the tanning lotion."

Darla spun to face the woman. "Tanning lotion? What tanning lotion?"

"Some of the other members and I thought they might need a little glow for the pictures." She pulled a bottle of tinted lotion out of the basket and held it up. "I guess I should let your fiancée do the honors?"

Darla backed up a step. "Is that really necessary?" If they weren't careful, these cowboys were going to revolt and they wouldn't have any calendars to sell. "They don't have to look bronze in the pictures."

"We're simply giving them an extra glow," Ginny

corrected. She thrust the lotion into Darla's hands. "Lay it on thick," she instructed with a grin.

Darla could feel everyone in the room watching her. So now she had to give Ty a very public oily massage? Wonderful. And to think this whole calendar thing had been her idea in the first place. She internalized a hefty groan.

"No one said a word about tanning lotion." Ty glanced at the door as though trying to calculate how long it would take to run through it.

"Well you do want the pictures to turn out good, don't you?" Ginny sniped. "Really, these models think it's all about them."

Oh sure. It was all for the greater good. Darla rolled her eyes. She would bet her bar that the other women on the committee had simply wanted to see Ty all oiled up and bronze.

"The better the pictures look, the more calendars we sell," the woman insisted.

"Fine." With his jaw tensed that way it was a wonder Ty could speak at all. He looked at Darla. "You want to start with my back?"

No. Avoiding his gaze, she glanced at Ginny. "I've never used tanning lotion. Maybe you should do it."

"Oh no. Nuh-uh." Ty marched over to Darla and turned his back to her. "This is your job, schmookie poo. Now oil me up."

"Of course." Wearing a tight smile, Darla dumped some of the goop into her hands.

"Make sure you don't get any on your clothes," Ginny called helpfully. "It'll definitely stain."

"Thanks for the tip." She brought her hands to Ty's back and lightly spread the lotion against his smooth, taut skin.

"Ahhh." He stretched his neck to one side. "Do you mind putting a little more oomph into it? For some reason I'm very tense right there."

For some reason. Darla wanted to smack him, but seeing as how they had an audience, she simply moved her hands in circular motions around the knots embedded between his shoulder blades. "Is that better?" she asked doing her best to sound patient and supportive.

"Nope." Ty snuck a sly peek over his shoulder. "And I think you missed some spots lower."

Did he have to have so much muscle? There was a lot of ground to cover, and her hands had gotten shaky. As a matter of principle, she did her best not to enjoy the feel of his brawn beneath her hands, but she was only human. She glided her hands down to his lower back, her fingers grazing beneath the boxer's elastic waistband. *Stop there*, she reminded herself, *before you take things too far*. The fact that she was tempted brought on a shot of panic. Quickly, Darla worked the lotion into his skin and then pulled her hands back. "There we go. All done." She went to put the bottle back in Ginny's basket so she could escape to the restroom and collect herself, but the woman moved it out of reach. "Not so fast. You haven't done the front of him yet."

"Right." The hard lump in her throat made it impossible to swallow. Ty simply grinned down at her as if reminding her this whole thing had been her idea. He seemed to enjoy that she had to share in some of the pain.

Ha. That smirk of his was all she needed to see to reclaim her dignity. He obviously loved teasing her. *We can have fun with this.* He was right. Why was she letting this stress her out? So she'd had a dream about him. So he made her feel a little hot and bothered. It didn't mean anything. And she could easily make him just as hot.

She squirted a generous amount of lotion into her hand and then set the bottle on the table. If Ty wanted a massage, she'd give him a massage. Rubbing her hands together, she started up at his shoulders and moved her hands slowly down his arms, caressing suggestively with her fingers the whole way.

Ty's grin disappeared. Yeah he was as uncomfortable with this as she was. Somehow seeing that made her grow bolder. She walked her hands back up his arms and then smoothed them over his pecs, rubbing the lotion in as she moved her hands down over his ribs, then his carved abs, all the way to the waistband of his silk boxers.

Ty's breath hitched and he closed his eyes for a brief second before opening them wide and aiming an unreadable glare at her.

"How was that, schmookie poo?" she asked innocently.

Out of the corner of her eye, she noticed Everly watching the two of them with interest.

"You two are adorable!" Ginny aimed her camera at them again. "Give her a real kiss this time," she clucked. "Our Instagram followers are going to eat this up! Think of the publicity we'll get for the calendars."

"Yeah. The publicity." Ty lowered his gaze to Darla's. She swore his eyes were bluer than they had been a few minutes ago. A smoldering blue, and they were locked on hers. Before she had time to brace herself for the kiss, he brought his hand to the back of her head and guided her face to his. For a split second he seemed to hesitate, pausing just before their lips met, but then he let go a small sigh and brushed his lips against hers.

The touch hit her like a seismic wave, filling her with

a rush of energy that seemed to pulse through her in rhythmic beats. She inhaled sharply and slipped her arms around his waist to steady the sudden sense of vertigo that knocked her off balance. She had kissed Ty before, but this was something different entirely. It was slower, wrapped in tenderness. His lips guided her mouth to open and the heat of his tongue weakened her knees.

"Whew! It's getting hot in here," Ginny sang somewhere nearby. Darla couldn't be sure where the woman was because Ty was still kissing her, still holding her, and she had completely melted into him.

"There," he said when he pulled away and let her go. "Everyone happy now?" He seemed to wait especially for Darla's response.

It was hard to say much when he had completely stolen her breath.

"I'm happy! That was a humdinger of a kiss." Ginny madly tapped on her phone screen as she walked away.

Ty and Darla still stood face-to-face. It seemed he had temporally frozen too. An awkward silence stretched between them until he finally seemed to shake himself out of it. "I should go talk to the photographer," he murmured, still eyeing Darla like he couldn't tell what she was thinking.

She wasn't thinking. He'd stolen her thoughts along with her breath. "Yeah. I think he's about ready to get started," she managed.

Their eyes locked for a beat longer, and then Ty was gone.

The second he walked away, Everly moved in. "Are you sure you're faking those feelings for Ty? Because it seemed to me there were all kinds of things happening beneath the surface with you two just now. And, girl—" her friend shook her head slowly "—that was some kiss."

It had been some kiss all right. A kiss that could seriously mess with her if it kept happening. "I don't have feelings for Ty. Not real feelings." Her body might desire him, but not her heart. It was still broken. Over the years, she'd managed to gingerly weave the pieces back together, but it wouldn't take much for those delicate threads to fray. She couldn't let that happen. She couldn't offer her heart, her dreams, her life, to someone else and risk losing it all again.

Chapter Eight

Here goes nothing. Ty pulled up in front of Darla's house and let his truck idle. In less than three hours he and Darla would pick up his parents and brother from the airport, and he had no idea how it would go. Up until the calendar photo shoot, this whole thing had been fun and games, but the joke had been on him. During the calendar shoot, he'd been teasing Darla when she made it obvious she didn't want to touch him, but the tables had turned fast when she'd started to massage his chest. And damn that Ginny Eckles for making him kiss her. He'd been under the false impression that he had things under control, but that notion had quickly gone up in smoke when his lips touched Darla's.

It had been different than when he'd kissed her at the cookie party. Then it had been for show. When he'd kissed her at the calendar shoot, he'd ached for it—for the feel of her lips and her hands on his chest again. Everything else had disappeared and he'd forgotten where he was, who else was there. That wasn't entirely true. He hadn't forgotten; he just hadn't cared. The second he'd kissed Darla, she was all that mattered, and that was a new feeling for him. A new feeling that had thrown him.

Not that he had time to dwell on feelings right now. They had a high mountain pass to get over before the impending blizzard started. He climbed out of the truck, but before he could make it to the front door, Darla emerged with a large duffel bag slung over her shoulder. "I have snacks and a playlist and a few audio books," she announced, locking up her house. "And my pillow. I may have to take a nap. I've been so tired lately." The woman slipped past him without a glance and got into the passenger's seat.

So much for a hello.

Ty climbed into the driver's seat next to her and eyed the bag that now sat at her feet. "We're only going to be gone for six hours, you know." At least, that was the hope. He looked up at the sky. It had darkened in the last half hour, and the low-hanging clouds had started to spit out fat snowflakes—the kind that liked to stick to the roads. With any luck, they'd be able to clear Vail Pass before conditions deteriorated too much.

"I know it's only going to be a six-hour drive, but I never pack light." Darla settled into her seat, clicked in her belt, and pulled a foodie magazine out of her bag.

"Why don't you pack light?" Ty backed down the driveway and headed for the highway. It was crazy how much he didn't know about her, and yet they were supposed to be engaged. That could potentially be a problem. His parents would assume he knew everything about the woman he was going to marry. Knowing his mom, she would have all kinds of questions he'd better be able to answer. Ty reached over and tilted down Darla's magazine so she would look at him. "I should know more about you. If we're going to make this whole engagement thing look convincing, then I need to know more about your past." Hell, he didn't even know where she'd grown up.

Darla lowered the magazine to her lap, but she didn't put it away. "My past has nothing to do with this."

He begged to differ. Her past had everything to do with this dynamic between them. Ty pulled the truck out onto the highway. A dusting of snow already covered the asphalt, so he took it easy. "You don't think it's important that you've been married before?" Wasn't that kind of a big deal? "My parents are going to wonder about you. It won't look good if I know nothing about your previous marriage."

"We don't have to tell them I was married." She turned to stare out the window. "They don't need to know anything about my first marriage." *And you don't either*, her rigid tone seemed to add.

"Given the circumstances, I think it's best that we lie as little as possible." It would already be hard enough to keep their stories straight. "What if they hear someone mention you were married before?" He could see that happening with all the buzz about their engagement. Ginny had even said something about how wonderful it was that Darla had found love again. "We have to be prepared for that possibility."

"Fine." Darla kept her head turned toward the window. "We'll tell them I was married before but that my husband passed away ten years ago."

"How long were you married?" he asked gently.

"Three years."

The last thing he wanted was to bring her pain, but he had to ask. "How did he ... pass away?"

"Cancer."

She said nothing more, but she didn't have to. That word always put him in a chokehold. Dying from cancer meant suffering. He knew that from when his grandfather had fought for his life for three long, painstaking years. "That must've been hard." There was no way to make those words sound less trivial. Hard was likely a serious understatement. "How old was he?"

Darla sighed and tucked her magazine back into her bag as though she'd finally given into her fate. "He was thirty when they discovered the brain tumor. He was the healthiest person I knew. Worked out every day, ate organic food, and he got a brain tumor before he'd even had the chance to live most of his life." She rushed on before he could respond. "What about you? Any other significant relationships I should know about? Past girlfriends your parents loved? Or hated?" She was done talking about her husband. He might not have the best intuition, but he knew that much. Rather than push to know more, he let it go.

"Nah. No significant relationships." That sounded bad, so he quickly explained. "I moved to Gunner Raines's ranch in Oklahoma when I was seventeen. My parents kind of stopped showing much interest in my life after that." They hadn't met many of his girlfriends. He hadn't kept any around long enough to bring them home for a visit either, but Darla likely already knew that. She knew he preferred the no-strings-attached approach to relationships.

She shifted to face him. "So you're not close to your parents?"

"I wouldn't say that. It's complicated." Ty stared out at the road stretching in front of them. The clouds had shrouded the peaks in the distance with a heavy gray fog. "I think they would say we're close, but I don't see them much. Not unless I go there." He'd leave it at that. His whole career, he'd invited them to come to his events. He'd even offered to pay their way, but they weren't interested. They did, however, fly out to most of his brother's football games.

"What about your brother?" Darla asked. "He seems like a nice guy. At least on social media."

Everyone seemed nice on social media. "Sure. Rhett's okay."

"You two aren't close?"

Looked like it was his turn to withstand an interrogation. At least he had an excuse to stare out the windshield instead of look at her. Had to keep his eyes on the road. "When I'm with my brother, everything feels like a competition." And Ty always lost. Rhett had to be better, stronger, bigger, smarter, faster. There was a reason his brother had made a name for himself in the NFL. "Rhett loves the spotlight, and I feel like I'm always standing in the shadows." He'd never admitted that to anyone else, but Darla was so easy to talk to. Somehow he knew the admission wouldn't change they way she saw him.

Darla shifted so her body faced him. "You might feel like you're in the shadows, but that's another thing I like about you," she said thoughtfully. "You're a good rider. You're pretty well known in that world. But you'd never know it just meeting you on the street. You don't play it up—your skills or your notoriety. You're genuine."

The words roused the same longing that had gripped him during that kiss yesterday. "Thanks. I've never looked at it like that." But she made it sound like she preferred someone who didn't try too hard to impress people.

"Judging from his social media, your brother seems a bit obnoxious." Darla's soft smile made her mouth look so inviting, but he couldn't pull over on the side of the road and kiss her.

"'Obnoxious' is a good description for Rhett." The next few weeks should be a blast, he thought. Pulling a Darla, he turned the question back on her. "What about you? Any siblings?"

"Nope." She seemed more at ease. "My parents divorced when I was three and went their separate ways. Neither one of them has ever had any other kids."

"I used to wish I was an only child," he admitted. He used to think his parents would pay more attention to him if they'd only had one kid, but maybe that wasn't true.

"It can be really lonely being an only child." Darla said. "I used to wish that I was adopted and my real family was the Brady Brunch. I would've given anything to have five brothers and sisters. I always thought I would have a bunch of kids." She looked down suddenly, as though she hadn't meant to admit that.

He waited for her to continue, but instead she dug her pillow out of her bag. "I really am tired," she said through a yawn. "Sorry. I think I'll take a nap. Wake me up if you want me to drive."

"It's fine." He didn't need her to drive. At least the snowy roads would give him a distraction. He definitely had to stop focusing on her. Wondering about her. Wanting her. The more time he spent with her, the harder it got to remember they were supposed to be pretending.

* * *

Darla woke up to wheels skidding and Ty swearing. Instinctively, she reached for the dash to steady herself while the truck fishtailed. "Everything okay?" she asked as soon as they'd evened out.

"It's getting bad out there." Ty gazed out the windshield, his mouth bent into a grim frown. With the blur of sleep still hazing over everything, she couldn't see much—only the snowflakes flying at them in the glow of their headlights. "Where are we?" Man, it felt like she'd slept for hours...

"About to head up Vail Pass." He had both hands firmly attached to the steering wheel, and they were crawling along at a measly twenty miles per hour.

"Sorry I slept so long." She had to have been out for at least an hour. Seriously. First the stomachaches, now she was so tired she could hardly keep her eyes open. These weird symptoms were starting to freak her out. It had been a while since she'd been to the doctor. Maybe something was wrong. She'd never been someone who could take naps. In fact, the whole reason she'd gotten out her pillow was so she could bail on their conversation, on his question about Gray, on reliving the past. She'd gotten so caught up in the memories of her childhood, she'd actually told Ty how much she'd wanted children. At that point, it had seemed safer to sleep than to continue down that road, so she'd rested her head back and bam, she'd fallen right to sleep.

"You must've been tired." Ty continued to stare straight ahead, squinting like he could hardly see. "I heard from my parents a few minutes ago. Their flight is delayed because of the weather."

"That figures." Flying into Denver in the winter was never a guarantee. "You think we should turn around?" There sure didn't seem to be anyone else out on the roads, which was actually a good thing. Less chance for an accident that way.

"Nah." Ty adjusted his posture as though his shoulders had gotten stiff. "My mom thought they'd only be delayed a few hours, and at the rate we're moving it'll take an extra five or six hours to get to Denver anyway."

Darla peered out the windshield again. Everything she could see in the beam of their headlights was covered with a thick layer of snow. Not even the lines on the highway were visible. "I hate driving in the snow," she commented, rifling through her bag to find something to settle the hunger that seemed to gnaw at her stomach. She pulled out the trail mix and opened the bag, offering some to Ty.

"Snow doesn't bother me." He took a handful. "The winters in Montana were worse than this." He dumped the trail mix into his mouth.

Darla munched on the raisins and peanuts and saved the chocolates she'd made herself for last. "Did you like growing up there?"

"Didn't appreciate it enough at the time, but yeah. It was a nice place to grow up. I got to run wild, ride horses, work outside. As much as I hated it sometimes, it was good for me." He stole a glance at her. "What about you? Where'd you grow up?"

Now that she could talk about. As long as it didn't lead to Gray. "In Arizona. But I came out to Colorado for college and never left." She'd fallen in love with the mountains and Denver's laid-back vibe. And Gray. Sorrow expanded in her chest, forcing a sigh. That letter he'd written her was still stashed away in the cabinet. She couldn't seem to make herself take it out and read it again. But that wasn't something she could talk about with Ty. She wanted to forget about it. "I love having four distinct seasons in the year instead of just hot and lukewarm," she said, popping some of the chocolates into her mouth.

"Yeah. I could never live where it's summer all the time..." Ty's gaze narrowed as he stared up ahead of them. "Uh-oh."

Darla leaned forward and squinted. Not too far in front of them, red and blue lights flashed in the center of the highway.

He let out a groan. "I know what that means. They closed the pass."

"That's great." It was just her luck they'd get stuck on the highway. Yesterday it was sunny and beautiful, and today they were in the middle of a blizzard.

Ty brought the truck to a sliding stop, and a police officer walked over to the window. "We've got a twenty-car pileup near the top of the pass," he informed them. "Had to close it down for now. You're gonna have to sit tight."

"Got it. Thanks." Ty buzzed the window back up and slipped the truck into park. "Looks like we'll have to hunker down for a while."

He seemed completely calm about it, but a tendril of panic curled through Darla's stomach. "Like spend the night here? In your truck on the side of a mountain?" While snow piled up all around them? Anxiety squeezed her heart, making it pump harder. She would never reveal it to anyone else, but since Gray had died her thoughts had tended to jump right into the pool of worst-case scenarios. They could freeze to death out here. Or get buried under the snow. She'd once read a story about a couple whose car had gotten stranded in the mountains and the man had gone to find help, but had died of hypothermia before he found anyone.

"There's nothing to worry about." Ty turned up the heat. "We might not have to be out here the whole night.

My guess is they'll be able to reopen the pass in a few hours."

Even with the heat blasting on her, Darla shuddered. In her head, she knew the anxiety was ridiculous, but the rest of her body couldn't seem to relax. "We'll freeze." They couldn't let the truck idle for hours without running out of gas. "And what about food? I don't know if my snacks are going to last all night."

Ty laughed like he thought she was joking. "We can ration out the trail mix." He eyed her with humor. "As long as you stop eating all the chocolate."

She was too nervous to look offended. "How much gas do we have?"

"We'll have to ration that out too." Ty unbuckled his seat belt. "I keep an emergency kit in the back of the truck. It's got bottled water, sleeping bags, flashlights, and a shovel in case we have to dig ourselves out."

"Dig ourselves out?" Darla put away the trail mix and sat on her hands so they'd stop trembling. "We could turn around and try again tomorrow morning." That sounded much safer.

"Actually, I don't think we should drive more than necessary in this weather." Ty leaned closer to her, watching her carefully. "Are you worried?"

"A little." A little? Blood raged through her veins hot and cold at the same time.

He put his hand on her shoulder. "You have nothing to worry about. I promise. I'll take care of you. Everything'll be fine."

The touch, the gentle drawl of his voice stilled something inside of her. Of course she'd never given in that easily. "How do you know everything'll be fine?"

"I'm fully prepared to spend a night in my truck. I grew

up in Montana," he reminded her. "I've ridden out more than one winter storm."

"Okay." So they were doing this. They were spending the night in his truck. Together. One day after he'd given her a kiss that still produced hot flashes if she let herself think too much about it. She couldn't think about it. Darla defiantly reached for the trail mix and shoved more chocolate in her mouth.

"We'll run the engine for a few more minutes," Ty said, reaching out to blast the heat. "You can stay warm while I grab everything we'll need from the back."

Before she could respond, he'd climbed out of the truck and disappeared in the dark snowy night.

Sitting all by her lonesome, she let out the breath she hadn't realized she'd been holding. *Perfect.* She had a few minutes to pull herself together. *Everything will be fine. Everything will be fine.* As long as she didn't kiss him again, everything would be fine. It was only seven o'clock, so with any luck, they could get going again before it got too late. She and Ty had spent plenty of time together. Though a lot of those times they'd been doing things she wanted to avoid now. They'd simply have to find other ways to pass the time when they were alone.

The memories of their hot nights together burned through her. It was hard to forget how he'd touched her, how he'd managed to bring her outside of herself on more than one occasion. But those times hadn't been like the night he'd made her tea, or the kiss yesterday. She'd been able to emotionally detach—and so had he. Something had shifted since then, and it made her want to run scared.

The back door was flung open, and Ty thrust a large bin onto the backseat of the cab. "This should do it." He closed the door and then climbed in next to Darla. Snow covered his hat and coat. "It's freezing out there." He pulled off the hat, which made his hair stick up in a very sexy, disheveled look.

Stop it, she reminded herself.

"You're warm enough?" he asked, looking her over.

Warm didn't begin to describe it. "Nice and toasty."

"Good." Ty twisted and rose to his knees in his seat, reaching for the bin in the back. "Before I turn off the truck, why don't you get settled?" He tossed her a compact downy sleeping bag. "Need a water or anything?"

"Nope. I'm good." She pulled the sleeping bag out of its cover and maneuvered the opening down to her feet, pulling it up her legs until she was fully nestled inside the fabric.

Ty did the same with the other sleeping bag, and she couldn't help but laugh at how they both must have looked, stuffed into sleeping bags in the cab of his truck.

He turned off the engine, which made things seem too quiet. Quiet and too intimate and dark. "What else do I need to know about your family before I meet them?" It was easier to talk to him when they could only see a shadow of each other in the darkness.

"Hmmm." Ty seemed to think for a moment. "My parents are ranchers, so they're tough as nails," he finally said. "They say what's on their minds, but my mom talks about three times as much as my dad."

That made her smile. "Good. Then she can do most of the talking for all of us."

"She'll definitely do most of the talking." He maneuvered to face her, but it was too dark for Darla to read his expression. "You don't have to worry much about them. They're good people."

She didn't even try to disguise her confusion. "If

they're good people, and you had a good childhood, why don't you see them much?" She liked to think that if she had fond memories of her childhood, she'd stay close to her parents.

"I guess I got tired of trying so hard." The words were subdued. Almost defeated. "My first competition after I went to train at Gunner's place, I asked them to come." A humorless laugh interrupted the words. "And back then I really thought they might. I bought them plane tickets and made hotel reservations for them. They said they'd be there, but when I looked up in the stands before my ride, their seats were empty."

"That's horrible." Sympathy gave her heart a good tug. It definitely hurt when the people you counted on weren't there for you, but surely his parents had a good explanation, especially with all the money he'd spent. "Did they tell you why they didn't make it?"

"Rhett came home for the weekend, so they decided to stay with him." The words weren't bitter, more like...resigned. "All my friends had someone there to cheer them on—Levi's dad and brother came. Mateo's sister. But I had no one."

"I didn't know that." She never would've guessed pain and disappointment had isolated Ty the same way it had isolated her.

It got so quiet she could almost hear the snow falling, the flakes landing softly on the windshield, sealing them into a safe cozy space.

"I tried to get them to come a few more times," Ty finally said. "But they always had an excuse. They couldn't get away from the ranch, or Rhett really needed them at his game. So eventually I quit trying. I got tired of the disappointment."

On some level, she'd felt the same thing growing up. That desire to make her parents love her the way she wanted to be loved. Instead, they were distant. More like guardians than real parents. She'd always been an after-thought. That was why she'd fallen so hard for Gray. He'd loved her like no one else ever had. He'd put her first. And then he'd been taken away and she'd spent ten years making sure she didn't need anyone else. Maybe Ty had been doing the same thing. Partying and traveling and keeping himself ridiculously busy enough to avoid building any deep connections.

"After Gray's funeral, I didn't get out of bed for five weeks." She'd never told anyone that. Not even her best friends knew. But Ty had shared so much, and she wanted him to know she understood what it felt like to be lonely. "Even then I wouldn't have gotten out of bed if the fire alarm hadn't gone off in my building. My neighbor finally broke down my door and carried me out." When Mr. Reed had come in, she'd begged him to leave her there. Without Gray, her life hadn't mattered.

"I can't even imagine how hard that must've been." It was the perfect thing for Ty to say. It wasn't *I'm so sorry*. It wasn't a question she had to answer. It was an acknowledgment of her pain and nothing more.

"Six months. That's all it was from the time he was diagnosed until he died." She'd tried to take care of Gray the best she could. To make him smile. To ease his pain. But during those six months she'd learned how powerless she really was. "I think he was the only person who's ever loved me." He'd taught her how to love, how to be loved, and when he died he'd taken all her love with him.

Ty eased closer to her. "Do you think you'll ever let anyone else love you?"

"I don't think I can." She'd done a stellar job of convincing everyone around her that she was strong and independent and fearless, but underneath all of that, there was still this terrifying sense of fragility.

"Gray must've been a great guy," Ty murmured.

"He was the best." She used to think Gray had been too good to be true, and in some ways he had been.

The sleeping bag swished softly as Ty moved to rest against the driver's side door again. Even in the dim light she could see the sad twinge of a frown on his lips. "Are you sure you want to do this, Darla?" he asked. Something that sounded like disappointment edged into his tone. "Are you sure you want to pretend to be engaged to me? Because I can tell my parents things didn't work out between us after all. I don't want to bring up any hard memories for you."

She stayed quiet for a few seconds, searching out his face, reading his feelings. Something she said had hurt him. She hadn't meant to, but it was better to get this conversation out of the way now. "Pretending isn't hard." It was the real feelings she had to avoid at all costs.

Chapter Nine

Ty should've learned by now to be careful what he asked for. He'd asked Darla if she could ever love someone again, and he'd gotten his answer. Then he'd had to stare at her for the last several hours wanting something he knew he could never have.

He rubbed his eyes, which were sticky with fatigue from a sleepless night, and tried to focus on the highway in front of him. Leave it to him to let himself feel something for her right before she told him she could never let anyone else love her.

His desire to wrap his arms around her and take away her pain had brought a deep, physical ache, but he forced himself to stay still, to keep his hands in his own sleeping bag while he thought about the hell the next couple of weeks and their fake engagement would bring. Touching her, probably kissing her, spending time with her, all the while wanting it to be real but also knowing he'd never be enough to help her heal.

She was still grieving, and he might be good at giving her a physical escape every now and then, but he didn't know how to reach deeper into her pain—how to help pull her through it—and she needed someone who did.

At first he'd thought she told him about Gray because she was opening up to him, but then he realized the truth. She'd told him about her pain so he wouldn't pursue her. It had been so obvious. After Darla had told him she'd never let anyone else love her, she'd seemed to relax. They'd talked more about his family—mainly going over details like relative's names and pets and significant happenings in his childhood before Darla had fallen asleep. Ty had spent most of the night turning the truck on and off occasionally to keep them warm, and finally, just before five, the trooper had knocked on the window to tell them they'd reopened the highway.

Darla had only made it a half hour before nodding off again, and she'd slept the whole way down, which had been fine with him. He had plenty on his mind with the impending show they were about to put on during his family reunion. He hadn't seen his parents since the early spring, when he'd gone home for a quick week to help his dad with some work on the ranch. And he hadn't even talked to his brother in person in well over a year. Should make for a fun afternoon. He'd best get it started.

"Hey." Ty gently rocked Darla's shoulder. "Time to wake up. We're almost to the airport."

She stirred, yawned, and sat upright, pulling the pillow that had been propped against the window into her lap. "Wow. That's quite a sunrise." She looked ahead of them in a daze, and Ty had to remind himself to steer his gaze back to the road. Yeah, the sunrise was impressive— the far edges of the eastern sky were fringed with deep reds and pinks, but that didn't hold his attention nearly as much as Darla did. How could the woman look even better when she'd just woken up? It was that unguarded happiness lighting her eyes. Like she'd forgotten to pick up her shield and wedge it between them.

Ty steered his gaze back to the road. He had to stop looking at her, had to get it through his mind that she wasn't available.

"Whew." In the seat next to him, Darla pulled down the visor mirror. "Sheesh, I have no idea why I'm so tired." She patted her cheeks and smoothed her hair, though Ty preferred the bedraggled look.

"So it's Robert and Maureen," she recited. "And your brother, of course, is Rhett."

Of course. No one ever forgot his name, his brother made sure of that. "Sounds like you've got it all down." He changed lanes to exit off the highway onto Pena Boulevard. If only he had it all down. The rules. The dos and don'ts. The handle on his own feelings. This was all new to him. He'd never wanted to complicate a relationship with a bunch of emotions on either side. He was so wrong for Darla, and yet that didn't seem to make him want her any less.

"I hope they like me." She moved her head from side to side as though inspecting every angle of her face in the mirror.

"They'll like you." He wanted to tell her she looked fine too. Better than fine. She looked beautiful in the soft light of morning, but he'd best keep that thought to himself. "Who doesn't like you?" he asked instead.

"Plenty of people don't like me," she insisted, though she didn't offer him any names. Most likely because she couldn't think of any.

Ty pulled up along the pick-up curb that ran the length of the airport's ridiculously long terminal, scanning the people standing on the sidewalk. Nerves clenched his stomach.

"Is that them?" Darla pointed farther down. Sure enough, there was his mother, standing at the edge of the walkway waving both arms in the air like she was trying to land a jet.

Here we go. "Yep." He eased the truck up the curb to where they were standing and braced himself for the greeting. After he slipped the truck into park, he quickly climbed out. "Hey Mom and Dad," he called, taking long strides to Darla's door. He opened it for her, and she gave him a wide smile before stepping out to meet them.

"Darla!" His mother sidestepped him and went right for his supposed fiancée, seizing her in a hug that nearly knocked her off balance. His mom wasn't a small woman—she was a rancher, strong and sturdy and nearly as tall as he was.

"So nice to meet you, Mrs. Forrester." His mother's shoulder muffled Darla's voice.

"You'd better call me Maureen. Or Mom! Better yet, call me Mom." She finally released Darla so she could get a look at her. "Oh my lord, you're a pretty one. It's a crying shame that Ty hasn't sent any pictures of you two. I've been dying to get a look at you. I knew you'd be pretty, of course. Ty likes the pretty ones."

Ty gave his mom a look meant to quiet her down and turned to present Darla to his dad. "This is my old man—"

"Call me Dad." His father jutted out his hand for a firm shake.

Darla seemed to take the awkwardness in stride. Ty

had to hand it to her—that smile on her face sure looked genuine.

"I can see where Ty gets his good looks," Darla said, looking back and forth between his parents.

"It's mostly from me," his mom joked. His dad only blushed.

"Or maybe it's from me." Rhett sauntered over. Who knew where he'd been, probably signing autographs for some kids or something. "He learned *everything* from me." Ty didn't like the way his brother appraised Darla. He didn't like the smirk on his brother's face either.

Darla's eyebrows pointed. "And you are...?" She was obviously giving his brother a hard time, and Ty loved her for it.

His brother shot him a degrading look. "You know who I am. I'm the main attraction for your auction."

Darla gave him a repentant grin. "Oh that's right. It's nice to meet you, Rhett. Thanks for making the trip."

"I couldn't say no when I heard I'd get to meet my little brother's fiancée." Rhett let his gaze linger on her, likely only to piss Ty off. "I have to admit, you're not exactly what I pictured."

The muscles at the back of Ty's neck bunched. It was a veiled dig, but he hadn't missed Rhett's meaning. He might as well have come out and asked how a lowly bull rider like Ty had scored someone as beautiful as Darla.

"What, exactly, did you picture?" Darla asked, crossing her arms in that intimidating way women had.

Unfortunately, no woman had ever intimidated Rhett. "Someone less...captivating," he said, turning on the charm.

And there it was. Let the insults began.

"Actually, I'm the lucky one." Darla walked over

to Ty, swinging her hips in a way that commanded attention. She slid her hands across his shoulders and drew him close. "I can hardly believe I found such a captivating guy." With a wink, she brushed her lips across his and it took everything in him to not hold her there so he could bring the kiss deeper. It was an act. He had to remember that.

"Well I guess I was wrong then. Welcome to the family." Clearly amused, his brother somehow managed to pick up three of the suitcases that were strewn around the group.

"Wow," Ty said, looking at the other four suitcases. "Did you pack up the whole house?"

"I had to bring presents." His mother rolled one of the suitcases to the back of the truck. "We have so much to celebrate! Be careful with this one."

Ty collected the other suitcases and started to load everything into the back of the truck while Darla chatted easily with his parents.

"She's hot," Rhett said, handing him a suitcase. "Still wondering how you managed to close the deal."

"Guess I lucked out." He concentrated all of his attention on fitting the suitcases into the truck bed so they wouldn't slide around. Before his brother could say anything else, he closed up the tailgate and went back to where Darla stood. "Ready? Maybe we could grab breakfast or something."

"Yes, we need to do breakfast." His mom beamed at Darla. "We can order mimosas and toast your engagement! I can't wait to learn everything about you."

Oh boy. Ty moved to open the front passenger's door for Darla, but she shuffled to the other door. "It's okay. I can sit in back with your parents."

"Oh." He did his best to conceal his disappointment. That meant his brother would be riding shotgun. Peachy.

They all climbed into the truck and belted in. Ty kept his eyes focused on the road. At least he didn't have to worry about awkward silence. Darla and his mom chatted like they were long-lost best friends.

"Nice ride." Next to him, his brother was busy looking around the truck, likely finding its inadequacies. "Two thousand ten, huh?"

"Yeah." Unlike Rhett, he didn't buy himself a new rig every year.

"I brought all the family photo albums in my suitcase," his mom was telling Darla behind them. "All the way from Ty's baby years through high school."

"Yeah, barely had room for my underwear," his dad muttered.

"I can't wait to see them," Darla gushed. She was really good at this pretending stuff. Although he should've seen that coming. Darla was personable and outgoing and genuinely friendly. His mom would likely be attached before they'd even ordered their meals.

He saw a sign for a diner and pulled off the highway, a whole new set of worries flooding in.

Everyone piled out of the truck and walked toward the entrance, but Ty held Darla back.

"You don't have to be so nice to them." He didn't need his mother devastated when he told her they broke up.

"Of course I do," she said, giving his parents a wave before they disappeared inside the restaurant. "I'm supposed to be your fiancée."

"Yeah, well you're not." He didn't care if she picked up on his frustration. If he wanted to keep his head on straight during this whole thing, he'd better keep reminding himself she wasn't his. "How do you think it's going to make them feel when we break up?" It would only give them something else to be disappointed in him about.

"I'm a nice person. I'm going to be myself. That's the only way this is going to work." She nudged a playful elbow into his ribs. "Come on. I know you're not thrilled that your family's here, but you're the one who said we could have fun with this. I'll do my best to make the whole three weeks a lot less painful for you." She gave his chest a pat. "I promise."

He didn't bother mentioning that was one promise she would not be able to keep.

* * *

If she didn't quit eating, Ty's parents would probably think she was a glutton, but wow, this stuffed French toast was *divine*. Not that Darla hadn't enjoyed Everly's breakfast selection at the Farm Café, but this was a real diner with unhealthy, inorganic, greasy food, and for some reason, right now, it was the best thing she'd ever tasted.

"You going to finish those home fries?" she asked Ty, eyeing his plate from across the table. He shook his head and slid his plate over to her, remaining as quiet as he had the rest of the breakfast. No one else had seemed to notice his subdued glower. His parents weren't exactly what she'd expected. First off, they were younger than she'd been picturing. Or at least they seemed younger. Ty's dad still had dark hair, and his mom had only a few gray streaks in her reddish ponytail. For some reason, she'd expected them to be closed off and uptight, but they were actually easy to talk to. Especially Maureen, who asked a lot of questions and seemed very personable.

Of course, neither of his parents had said more than two words to Ty since they'd gotten to the restaurant. They were too busy talking to her and listening to Rhett's stories. She could see why his brother drove Ty crazy. He was your stereotypical egotistical jock—flirting with the young waitresses, sliding in digs against his brother every chance he got, commanding all the attention in the room with loud talk about his football team. He even signed autographs for people seated nearby. All the while, Ty sat in the figurative shadows, sipping his black coffee.

"So when is the wedding?" Maureen asked, withdrawing a small calendar from her purse. "It should be in the summer, don't you think? Preferably late August—"

"Summer's bad for Darla," Ty interrupted. "And we just got engaged, Ma. We don't need a date yet." Everything about the man seemed tense, and Darla wasn't quite sure what to do. They were supposed to be looking at each other with stars in their eyes, and he hadn't looked at her once all during breakfast.

"Well surely you don't want a winter wedding," his mother persisted. "And you're going to wait a whole year and a half?"

The corners of Ty's mouth pinched, so it seemed like a good time for Darla to jump in. "We have a while to decide. I'm not planning on a huge, grand affair. Something small and intimate. Simple." That was what she and Gray had done. They'd eloped, and then a few weeks later they had the best party she'd ever been to. She smiled against the welling sorrow. *You can't keep that big beautiful heart hidden away, my love.* She didn't know how to stop hiding. Last night she'd felt this emotional connection to Ty, and it scared her so much she was actually relieved when they picked up his parents and Rhett. Relieved because it wasn't just the two of the anymore, relieved because she could act and pretend and be someone else.

"A small and intimate wedding sounds lovely," Ty's mom said.

Darla kept on smiling and let her role pull her away from her thoughts. "We can talk more details after the holidays. This Christmas festival has really been consuming our time." She shared a look with Ty, silently telling him to relax. *Breathe. Inhale, exhale.* He shifted his stony gaze to the windows.

"Speaking of the Christmas festival…" She glanced at Rhett. "I saw your posts on Instagram. Thank you so much. I think most of the inns and hotels are completely booked for the entire weekend. The ski resort sold out the first week we started promoting." Once Ty saw how much money they were going to raise, hopefully he would agree inviting his brother had been a small price to pay.

"No problem." Rhett brushed off her gratitude with a sly shrug. "Maybe you can fix the auction results so I end up going out with one of your hot single friends."

Ha! Most women might be reduced to giggles when he talked to them but she saw right through him. "I know you're not asking me to cheat."

"Cheating's not always a bad thing," he said with a confident smirk. Wow. He really was used to getting his way.

"You won't need my help getting a hot date." He clearly didn't need anyone's help hooking up with women. "I'm sure you'll have plenty of your single fan girls there to bid on you." Darla redirected her attention on Ty. After all, she'd promised to make this fun for him, and right now he looked like he could use some amusement. "The word on the street in Topaz Falls is that you two are going to bring the highest bids."

Ty glared at her from across the table. "Me? I'm not doing the auction."

"Of course you are." He'd already agreed to help…

"But we're engaged," he argued stubbornly. "I'm officially off the market." His grin turned smug.

Poor man. He had no idea who he was up against. "We're not married yet," Darla said sweetly. "And it's such a good cause, schmookie poo. I'm willing to let you go out on one last date if it means helping our friends. I'll make sure whoever wins you will behave herself."

"Both of my boys on one stage?" Maureen clapped her hands together. "I can't wait to see that. Of course they'll bring in the highest bids."

Rhett smirked at his younger brother. "We all know I'm going to come away with the highest bid."

"How do you figure?" Ty asked, his eyes narrowing.

Oh geez. Darla should've realized they'd turn this into a competition. "I think what's most important is that we raise as much money as we can for Mateo and Everly." *Remember them?* she wanted to ask Ty. "Let's not forget why we're doing this."

Neither of the brothers said a word, but they did continue glaring at each other.

"I can't wait to take pictures!" Maureen smiled proudly. "I never thought I'd see you two onstage together again. It's been years."

"Together onstage?" Darla nudged Ty's boot with her own. "This sounds like a story I need to hear."

"Never mind." He started to put on his coat.

"Yeah we should probably get going." Rhett glanced

around like he was searching for their waitress, probably so he could impress them all by paying the bill.

Lucky for Darla, the wait staff seemed to be taking a break in the back. She scooted her chair closer to Maureen's. "When were these two onstage together?"

"Ty never told you about the play they were in?" his mother asked, reprimanding him with a disappointed gaze.

"No," she answered for him. "He left out that childhood tidbit."

"I can't imagine why." Maureen dug her wallet out of her purse and rummaged through it until she found a picture.

Darla slapped a hand over her mouth so she wouldn't disturb the peace in the restaurant. "They were in a production of *Grease*?" It was impossible not to laugh. The picture had to have been taken early in high school. Ty was dressed up like a rebel greaser and Rhett like a jock.

"You're darn right they were in a production of *Grease*." Their mom admired the tattered photograph. "Ty had the lead role—Danny."

"Really?" She eyed her fiancé—*fake* fiancé—picturing what he would look like as a bad-boy greaser now. It was kinda hot.

"I could've had the main part," Rhett said, flagging down a waitress. "I didn't want it."

"Whatever." Ty stood abruptly. "You couldn't sing. That's why you didn't want the part. You knew you'd make a fool of yourself up there."

"And you *could* sing?" his brother shot back. "You *did* make a fool of yourself—"

That was Darla's cue. "Why don't we go get the truck started?" she asked Ty cheerfully. Before these two started to throw punches. "That way it'll be nice and toasty when everyone comes outside."

"Wonderful idea," their mom agreed. "We'll be out in a few minutes."

"After I pay the bill," Rhett added. "I *always* pay the bill."

Darla noticed Ty's fists clench. "Come on, schmookie poo." She linked their arms together and dragged him away from the table before Rhett baited him into an all-out brawl.

Chapter Ten

If he had to listen to his brother detail one more of his legendary defensive plays, Ty thought, he just might pull the truck over and make Rhett walk the rest of the way to Topaz Falls, like his dad had constantly threatened to do to them when they were kids.

Not much had changed since those days when they'd try to one-up each other in the backseat of their dad's old Ford. Only difference now was Ty had gotten smart, and he simply didn't respond to Rhett's constant attempts to draw him into a pissing match. Unfortunately, that only seemed to make his brother try harder.

It had been more than twenty-four hours since he and Darla had left to pick up his family from the airport, and yet the drive home seemed to have taken years. All the way up the highway, his parents and brother had wanted to stop at every point of interest, and had then insisted on eating lunch in Georgetown and dinner in Glenwood Springs. There would be no more stopping, though, since they were almost home.

"Then there was that time I got that strip sack against Tom Brady." Rhett couldn't seem to quit.

"I remember that!" Their mother bounced excitedly in the backseat. "It was in all the highlights. Oh, you should've seen Brady's face!"

Robert laughed. "Looked like he was about to cry."

Ty glanced in the rearview mirror and caught Darla rolling her eyes. "I bet you guys are pretty proud of Ty too," she said sweetly. "I know everyone in Topaz Falls is. Wait until you see him ride at the benefit rodeo."

There was a long pause before his mother cleared her throat. "Oh. I don't think we're going to make it to the rodeo."

Why didn't that surprise him?

"Really?" Darla's voice sharpened. "I thought that's part of the reason you came out. To watch him."

"Well, sure. Yes," his mom said quickly. "I mean, we really wanted to, but the theater in Vail is doing a production of *A Christmas Carol* that afternoon, and that's one of our favorites."

By now it shouldn't have bothered him, but Ty took it like a kick in the gut.

"Aren't they doing the play another day too?" Darla now had a definite edge in her tone.

Ty shot her a small smile in the rearview mirror. It was nice of her to try, but they obviously didn't want to come. She might as well let it go.

"We already have tickets, I'm afraid," his mother said. "But I can't wait for the auction! And maybe after the play we can all go out for a big family dinner." She patted Ty's shoulder. "How would that be?"

He didn't have a chance to answer before Rhett chimed in. "I've heard of a few good restaurants in Vail. I'd be happy to take everyone out for a five-star dinner. We can meet up after the play and rodeo."

How many more times would they have to hear about how wealthy his brother was? Ty applied more pressure to the gas pedal, inching up the speedometer.

"That would be wonderful, Rhett." Ty's mom turned to Darla. "Wouldn't that be wonderful?"

"Sure. I guess." Darla yawned loudly. "Sorry," she said quickly before yawning again.

Ty checked on her in the rearview mirror. Her unwavering enthusiasm must've worn her out. All day she'd played the part of the perfect Colorado tour guide. He'd had no idea she was so knowledgeable about the area, but it had worked out well. She'd been so busy wowing his brother and parents with facts about the scenery that she and Ty didn't have to interact much. Between his mother and Darla, no one had to interact much.

"No need to apologize. Of course you're tired," his mother said, giving Darla's shoulder a pat. "You two had such an ordeal being stuck on the highway all night."

"Well everything turned out all right, since Ty was so prepared." Darla reached forward from the backseat and laid her hand on his shoulder. "He's the one who's probably tired. At least I slept."

That was the other thing Darla had done all day—she'd tried to show him in the best possible light every chance she got. And while he appreciated the effort, it didn't help him keep his feelings for her in check.

"I'm fine." Instead of relaxing under Darla's touch, his shoulders tensed.

As they drove down Main Street in Topaz Falls, Darla pointed out everything of interest. "There's the town hall, and the library and the bakery. Ginny Eckles makes the best cinnamon buns you'll ever eat," she chatted. "And there's my chocolate confectionary and wine bar."

"The Chocolate Therapist," his mom read from the sign. "I love that name! How clever."

"Looks like the nicest establishment on the block," Rhett said. "Do you need investors?"

Ty tightened his grip on the steering wheel. With Rhett, everything always came down to status and money.

"I'm good on the investors front," Darla said.

"Well I'd love to check it out more." Rhett glanced back at their parents. "What about you two? Maybe we should head over later this evening."

"Great idea," Darla said before Ty could shut down the conversation. If his family was wearing on him, they definitely had to be wearing on her.

"I thought you were tired." He found her in the rear-view mirror and widened his eyes with a subtle cue to get them both out of more family time, but she didn't seem to get it.

"I have to be there anyway. I'd love to show it off. We can all head over as soon as you get settled."

"Wonderful idea," his mom exclaimed. "I can't wait to try the chocolates. Homemade is so much better than that store-bought nonsense."

"How'd you get the idea to start a wine-and-chocolate bar?" Ty's dad asked.

"Well, I've always loved both." Darla went on to tell them more about her business, and Ty was happy to listen to her talk for a while instead of his brother.

He turned onto his street and pulled the truck in the driveway of his rental house. Like most of the older homes in town, it was a simple log cabin—square and compact, but at least it had three bedrooms and an acre of land.

He glanced in the rearview mirror at Darla. Though she'd kept that smile intact all day, she really did look tired. This pretending stuff was exhausting. "I figure we can drop them off and get them settled here, and then I'll take you home," he told her.

"Home?" His brother angled his head to look back and forth between Ty and Darla. "Why would you take her home? Don't tell me you two aren't living together."

His mother harrumphed. "They don't have to be living together."

"Your mother and I didn't live together until after the wedding," his dad added.

"Yeah, that was forty years ago." His brother eyed him with suspicion. "Things are different now. Everyone moves in together before they get married. It makes more sense."

His tone implied that nothing about Ty and Darla made sense. Ty had to hand it to him—Rhett was smarter than he gave him credit for. He unclicked the locks so his family could get out of the truck. "We're not living together." *Deal with it.*

"Not yet anyway," Darla rushed to explain. "We have to figure out what do with our houses, and there're so many logistics to take care of. We haven't had the time."

"I get that, but you don't have to stay at your place just because we're here." His brother had never been one to let things go. "No one cares if you're shacking up."

"Leave them alone," their mother said, swatting Rhett over the seat. "I think it's nice to be old-fashioned about things like that."

Yeah. Old-fashioned. That was one way to describe him and Darla. Ty should've known Rhett would make a big deal out of their living arrangement. "Here's the key." He handed it back to his dad. "Why don't you head on inside? I'll grab the suitcases and be right in."

"You got it son." His dad climbed out of the truck before helping his mom out. Rhett gave Ty one more scrutinizing look, and then he got out too.

After the door slammed, Darla moved to the middle of the backseat where Ty could see her.

"You sure you're up for having them all at the bar tonight?" Was he the only one who wanted to go to bed early? "We've hardly slept."

Darla's smile disappeared. "I have to be up for this. Your brother's not buying the engagement. He's suspicious."

"So?" Of course Rhett was suspicious. Mostly because he didn't buy that Ty was good enough to be with someone like Darla. "It's probably jealousy. He's not used to Mom and Dad giving me—and my fiancée—so much attention. It's overshadowing him for once." If it wasn't all fake, Ty might be gloating.

"We can't afford to lose him right now. We've based our whole marketing campaign on him. He's the star attraction." Darla peered out the window. Rhett was standing farther up the driveway, watching them with interest. "If he finds out we're lying, he'll be pissed, and we can't risk him leaving. You have to start selling this."

"I don't know how to sell this," he shot back. How was he supposed to act? He was fake-engaged to a woman he was falling for. A woman who was still grieving for her dead husband. And Gray had sounded pretty damn perfect, by the way. That meant this was one more competition Ty wouldn't win. "What'd you want me to do?"

"Act like we're engaged. Like we're in love. Like we're happy." Darla moved her face within kissing range and put on a coy smile, likely for Rhett's benefit. "The last thing

I need right now is for you two to get into some big fight that sends him packing."

Acting. Rhett was right about one thing. Ty had sucked at acting ever since that lead role in *Grease*. "I'll do my best." The way his heart pounded when she got this close, he might not have to act at all. "I have to take their suitcases in, then I'll drive you home."

"Sounds perfect, schmookie poo." Darla gave him a quick peck on the lips and then waved at his brother.

Leaving the engine running, Ty got out and moseyed to the back of the truck with a grin on his face. Rhett met him at the tailgate. "Trouble in paradise?"

"No. There's no trouble." Ty slid out the suitcases one by one and set them on the driveway.

"Darla didn't look too happy when you two were talking just now," Rhett pressed.

Okay, that was it. Enough veiled questions. Ty faced his brother directly. "Why is it so hard for you to believe I found someone like her?"

"It's just weird." His brother stared him down. "Mom said you never mentioned a girlfriend until she called to invite you home for Christmas, and all of a sudden you're engaged?"

"Darla and I have known each other for a long time, but I wasn't about to tell Mom until I knew for sure it was serious." That shouldn't have come as a surprise. As far as Ty knew, Rhett had never brought home a woman to meet their mother.

His brother's eyes narrowed. "And you know for sure now?"

He knew for sure he wanted her. He knew for sure he could never have her. Not all of her. "We're getting married aren't we?" he growled. Before his brother could see the mounting frustration, he snatched as many suitcases as he could carry and headed into the house.

* * *

Nothing like an impromptu Christmas party to get the blood pumping.

Darla careened around the bar, making sure the truffles and wines were all set out and easily identifiable. Thankfully she'd already dressed up the place with various Christmas decorations—garlands draping the bar, white snowflake lights dangling from the ceiling, and a festive Christmas tree in each corner of the space. To complete the ambience, she'd put country Christmas hits on the Bluetooth, and as if by magic, light snow had started falling outside, shimmering in the glow of the streetlamps.

Given Rhett's obvious suspicions about her and Ty, the worst thing they could do right now was spend time alone with Ty's parents and brother. That was why she'd invited all of their friends for free wine and chocolate at the last minute. If she was going to make it through this fake engagement, she'd need some serious moral support. Miraculously, everyone had made it. Everly and Mateo, Lucas and Naomi Cortez, Levi and Cassidy, Dev and Charity.

She suspected most of their friends were here out of sheer curiosity to see her and Ty masquerade as a couple, but she'd take it. If she and Ty were going to pull this off, they needed their friends' help.

"Okay, everyone!" She gave off a shrill whistle to quiet the crowd. "Ty's family will be here in a few minutes, so I wanted to go over this again." She climbed up on a chair so everyone could see her. "Ty and I met when he moved out here and became friends. Eventually the friendship developed into something more and you were all ecstatic when we got engaged. Keep it short and simple if it happens to come up while you're talking to his parents."

"What if they ask us about the wedding?" Mateo yelled out from the back of the crowd. "When are you two finally getting hitched?"

Laughter went around the room, but Darla silenced it with a wave of her hand. This was serious. They didn't have time for jokes. "Let me remind you how important it is to welcome Rhett Forrester to town and to keep him here so our benefit auction goes off without a hitch."

Mateo gave her a repentant nod, but he was still grinning.

"Are there any other questions?" She kept an eye on the storefront windows in case Ty happened to drive by.

"Yeah." Never one to be upstaged by his colleague, Levi stepped forward. "What about that picture of you two kissing on the town's Chamber of Commerce *Instagram* page?" he asked slyly.

Oh. Yeah. That. She'd caught a glimpse of the well-liked photo on the drive home from Denver. Seeing it had brought back the rush Ty had given her. *Thinking* about it threatened to bring back that rush. "What about it?" she asked as though it hadn't meant anything.

Levi elbowed Dev. "It sure didn't look fake to me."

Darla rolled her eyes at the murmurs of agreement. "That kiss—and the others that will probably follow—are simply for the purposes of selling our engagement. We all know what's at stake here if we screw this up. Keep that in mind tonight." Before they could ask any more questions, she climbed down from the chair and hit the Play button on her phone. Right on cue, the speakers filled the room with Dolly's effervescent voice singing "I'll Be Home for Christmas."

"Everything looks perfect." Everly came up behind her. "But you seem stressed. Can I pour you a drink?"

"No thanks." Lately, wine hadn't sounded good at all. Just the thought of it seemed to turn her stomach sour. "I'm not stressed. I'm just not sure how Ty is handling having his family here." If the first twenty-four hours had been this rough, they weren't going to make it another week, let alone the whole duration of his family's extended stay.

Her friend walked the length of the bar, selecting a few of her favorite truffles. "Mateo said he and his brother don't get along."

"That's putting it mildly." That was exactly why they had to step up their game. "If you get the chance to talk to Rhett, make sure you tell him how right we are for each other," Darla instructed.

"Oh I will." Everly's wry smile poked fun at her, but before Darla could ask her what was so funny, Rhett sauntered in, followed by Ty's parents.

"Welcome to the Chocolate Therapist." Darla waltzed over to greet them. "I invited some of our friends to celebrate with us tonight. I hope that's okay."

"Okay?" Ty's mom hugged her tight. "It's perfect," she said, pulling away to marvel at the space. "This is a beautiful place. And it smells absolutely divine."

"Pretty impressive," Rhett agreed, giving the bar an obvious appraisal. "I like the vibe."

"Thank you." Coming from him, she assumed that was a big compliment. "Where's Ty?"

"He's parking the truck," his dad said. "I told him we've got two good legs for walking, but he insisted on dropping us off at the door."

"It was so considerate." Ty's mom wore a proud smile. "I think you've changed him for the better, my dear."

"Oh no. It has nothing to do with me. He's always been considerate." Why did his mother not recognize that? "That's one of the things I've always loved most about him." As she said it, Darla realized it was the truth.

"Yes, of course," Maureen agreed.

"Oh please," Rhett muttered.

Before he could say more, Darla jumped in. "Let me introduce you to some of our friends." She led them over to the group of women first, all of whom were warm and friendly—not to mention completely trustworthy and great at keeping secrets. Next, she gave short introductions to the men, who immediately pulled Rhett into a football discussion.

"Well then." She turned back to his parents. "Can I get you a glass of wine?" She pointed out the bar. "All of the wines are paired with truffles meant to enhance the flavors." She could spend hours talking about all of the different combinations and ingredients, but most people found that boring, and she wanted Robert and Maureen to mingle.

"You don't have to wait on us," his mother said, tugging her husband away. "We'll help ourselves so you can spend time with Ty."

The door opened and Ty walked in. Something about him had changed. He held up his head, kept his shoulders back, and strode right to her purposeful and confident, his eyes locked on hers the whole way. "Hey darlin'." He pulled her in and slid his hands down her sides to her waist. "I missed you."

Her heart seemed to start a slow descent, sinking like the setting sun. "Mm-hmm." She took him in, the clean look of his freshly shaven jaw, the dark button-up he'd paired with those tight cowboy jeans. If that wasn't enough, the scent of him alone had her captivated. He smelled like cold air and traces of pine—like Christmas wrapped up in the sexiest package she'd ever had her hands on.

"Does that mean you missed me too?" His hands melted into her lower back, filling the entire region with tingles.

She was suddenly aware of everyone watching them. "Yep. Uh-huh. Sure did."

A slow smile overtook his eyes. "Come here." He lowered his lips to hers, and instead of shying away from her like he had done all the way home, Ty went for it—claiming her lips, seeking out her tongue, wrapping her tightly in his arms. The kiss seemed to raise her up until she was soaring. She couldn't help but kiss him back. *Really* kiss him back, clinging to him while he held her close.

"Aw, you two." Maureen broke up the moment by taking a picture of them. Darla pulled away from Ty and smiled while his mother snapped another picture.

"I can't wait to share this with everyone back home," she chirped, slipping her phone back into her purse. "I hope you can come for a visit in the spring. So we can introduce you to the rest of the family."

"Of course we'll come. Right, darlin'?" Ty slipped his arm around her, resting his hand comfortably on her hip. "Maybe during the off-season when the bar isn't so busy." He glanced down at her. All of the tension that had knitted his brows together during the drive home was gone. He looked comfortable and relaxed.

"That's a great idea." Aware of Rhett watching them from across the room, Darla snuggled into his side, her heart still struggling to find a regular beat.

"Hey..." Ty pulled her in closer. "You want to dance?"

Darla glanced around them. Everyone was talking and mingling, but no one was dancing. "Um. Right now?"

"Yeah. This is a great song."

The whooshing in her ears had finally subsided enough that she could hear Kelly Clarkson's "Underneath the Tree" playing. She almost laughed. She'd never pegged Ty as a Kelly Clarkson fan.

"Come on." Before she could tell him he was crazy, Ty grasped her hand and started to pull her away. "You don't mind if we dance, do you, Mom?"

"Mind?" Maureen nudged her husband forward. "We'll join you. Won't we, Robert?"

The poor man couldn't answer because he had a mouthful of truffles.

They drifted away from the crowd, and Ty pulled her in close against him. He moved his hips against hers as he led her in a surprisingly good two-step.

Darla smoothed her hand over his broad shoulder, peering up at him with a sassy smirk so he wouldn't notice she'd gotten a little shaky. "What are you doing?"

Ty's grin went broader. "I'm selling it." He nudged her away from his body and twirled her into a spin before reeling her back to him, all the while staying perfectly in step with the music.

Despite the dizzying sensation, Darla laughed. "I'll say you're selling it." She did her best to keep up with his movements. She wasn't one to be upstaged on the dance floor.

They two-stepped and twirled and spun until she could hardly stand up straight. At some point, most of the other couples joined in—but everyone else seemed to be a blur. She kept her focus on Ty until the song ended and she was light-headed and warm and out of breath.

"Mind if I take the next dance?" Rhett appeared next to them, and she expected Ty to bristle like he did whenever his brother looked at her, but instead he clapped Rhett on the shoulder.

"Sure. I'll go grab a drink." Ty let his gaze linger on her for a minute. "Be right back, darlin'." He brushed a kiss over her lips and then walked away. She watched him all the way to the bar.

"I might not be as good of a dancer as my brother." Rhett offered his hand and Darla took it, feigning a shocked expression.

"I thought you did everything better than Ty," she joked.

He grinned. "Not everything. Just most things." A slower song played on the speaker, so they swayed back and forth, with Rhett thankfully keeping a respectable distance.

"I was wrong before," he said. "Based on the drive home, I assumed he didn't know how to treat you, but he's clearly head over heels."

"What makes you say that?" Her dance with Ty had been fun and spirited and they'd laughed, but it hadn't been overly romantic. At least it hadn't seemed that way. The kiss on the other hand…

"I can tell how much he loves you." Rhett changed their direction. "It's obvious when he looks at you. He looks at you like he still can't believe he found you."

This was exactly what she wanted—for Rhett to believe they were together and happy and in love. But Ty wasn't really falling for her, was he? It was only an act. She'd told him on the way to Denver that she'd never be able to give her heart to someone else.

Ty's brother stopped moving and stared down at her. "Do me a favor. Don't hurt him."

"What?" She couldn't hide her shock. Rhett was actually concerned about Ty?

"I don't want to see him get hurt."

Darla found it hard hold his gaze. "I don't want to hurt him." But would she? Was he really simply selling their relationship, or did he want it to go somewhere else? "I mean, I won't hurt him. He's such a good person." She searched the room for Ty, and finally spotted him over by the bar with Lance and Lucas.

"He's one of the best," his brother said, starting up their dance again. "But don't you dare tell him I said that."

Her smile grew weighted. "Maybe *you* should tell him."

"And ruin our perfectly good brotherly competition? Not a chance." Rhett lost the cocky grin. "I know I've always been tough on him, but I'm happy for you two. Really. Ty deserves someone who'll treat him right."

"He does. He deserves the best." And she already knew the best wasn't her.

Chapter Eleven

T y always made it a point to look a bull directly in the eyes. It was a practice he'd started after his first ride when he'd been all of seventeen years old—a cocky kid who was about to learn a little respect for those bovine athletes. That ride, he'd only made it two seconds before the bull had launched him face-first into the dirt.

You have to learn to respect the animal, Gunner had told him afterward. *You don't stare them down to intimidate them, you do it so you learn to read them. You look 'em in the eyes so you can build a connection before the ride.*

"What'd you think, Primo?" From outside the chute, Ty kept his gaze steady with the champion bull he'd be riding for his training run.

Primo watched him, his eyes still placidly black for now, glassy and serene. But when he tore out into the arena, they'd get wider—so wide you'd be able to see the whites of them.

"Whenever you're ready, Forrester." Tucker McGrath,

who they'd contracted to distract the bulls after the rider is thrown, stood on the other side of the chute ready to lead Primo to the gate.

Ha. Ty was never ready. In his humble opinion, climbing aboard a 1,500-pound animal and holding on with one hand knowing you'll eventually get tossed required as little logical thought as possible. There was no preparation. It was best to go with instinct and adrenaline instead.

"You two clowns want to run my time?" he called to Levi and Mateo. They stood outside the arena, getting loose for their own training runs. The main event wasn't until the end of the weekend, but given that it was the off-season, none of them had been training as regularly as they did spring through fall. They figured they'd better get a few rides in so they could give the crowd a good show.

"I've got it." Mateo pulled out his phone and leaned in to the fence standing at the ready.

"All right." Ty gave Tucker a nod, and the bullfighter led Primo to the gate. That small signal was all it took to change the bull's eyes. They widened slightly and shifted, searching out that space beyond the gate. Almost looked like the bull was visualizing what special brand of torture he could inflict on Ty today.

Oh, yeah. This was gonna be one wild ride. Ty double-checked to make sure his helmet was secure and then climbed up the fence. At Tucker's count he slid onto the bull and the gate swung open. The empty stands whizzed past and then started to spin in circles. Ty picked a focal point and held his form—keeping that left hand raised above his head.

Beneath him, Primo bucked and wrenched his powerful body, flinging Ty back and forth with a series of forceful kicks. Pain calcified the knuckles on Ty's right hand, which only made him reinforce his grip. Some riders said time moved faster when they rode, but for Ty it always seemed to slow—or maybe he existed outside of time for those few seconds when all he could do was hold on. *Hold on...*

And then that moment came when his grip always weakened. When the flesh and sinew in his hand started to give out.

"Eight!" Mateo was yelling, letting him know he'd made it, giving him permission to embrace the dismount he'd fought so hard to avoid.

Primo reared up again, Ty felt the kick coming. He loosened his grip and flung his body off to the side just as the bull's back end rose. His boots hit the ground first, skidding and stumbling, but he managed to stick the landing, earning hoots and whistles from his friends.

Tucker was already luring Primo back to the chute, so Ty took his time sauntering over to Mateo and Levi.

"What a ride," Mateo said, pocketing his phone. "You pull that off at the rodeo, and you'll be crowned the king."

Ty brushed the dust from his jeans. "That's the plan." Even if his parents refused to watch him ride, maybe they'd clear their busy schedule so they could make it to the award ceremony. Maybe they'd finally realize what he did was worthwhile. Maybe he wasn't out there tackling wide receivers and saving touchdowns on television, but he was good at what he did, and he could use that to raise money to help a friend. That meant more than his brother's multi-million-dollar paychecks. Besides all of that, Darla would be there for him. Watching him. Last night he'd done what she asked. He'd sold their engagement. Darla had laughed while they'd danced, and she'd kissed him back every time his lips touched hers. Maybe he was wrong, but it hadn't felt much like pretending.

"Does that grin have anything to do with how you were dancing with Darla last night?" Levi asked with a smirk.

Was he grinning? Huh. He hadn't noticed. Apparently that was his natural response when he thought about Darla.

"*Dancing*?" Mateo snorted out a laugh. "The two of them were tongue-wrestling every time I looked over at them."

"Not every time." They'd talked too. He'd eaten some truffles while she'd told him about how she melded the different flavors. She'd even paired a truffle with an IPA for him. "We're supposed to be engaged," he reminded his friends.

"Uh-huh." Mateo shot him a skeptical look. "So on a scale of one to ten—one being completely bogus—how fake is this relationship?"

"I don't know." But maybe he didn't have to know right now.

"Okay, how fake do you want it to be?" Levi never knew when to let anything drop.

"She doesn't want anything real." She didn't want anything that would involve her heart. That was the truth of it. But for the first time in his life, he did.

* * *

Darla scrubbed the rag over the bar top for what had to be the five hundredth time that morning. She'd already wiped down every shelf and cabinet, done all of the inventory, and polished every spot off her expansive collection of wineglasses, and it wasn't even noon. When Maureen had invited her to go out to breakfast and Christmas shopping, she'd politely declined, saying she had gotten behind on things at work. But truthfully, she couldn't spend the morning with Ty's mom. Darla liked her too much. She liked all of them, actually—even Rhett, ever since he'd revealed that he did have a heart underneath all that ego.

And she liked Ty. She liked dancing with him. She liked kissing him. She liked the way he made her forget her pain for a while. But after she'd gotten home last night, the spell had broken and she'd sat down on her couch and cried. She might forget Gray for a few hours, but truthfully, the fear of losing someone was always there, simmering beneath the surface of every emotion, every thought. And it wasn't fair to lead Ty to believe she could ever love anyone so deeply again.

Darla sank her elbows down to the bar, watching out the window. Josie appeared from across the street and headed for the Chocolate Therapist's main door. It had been a few weeks since their last bereavement group meeting, and she'd never invited any of her Glenwood friends to town, but this happened to be an emergency.

Darla rushed to open the door for her.

"What's going on?" her friend asked with no greeting. "You said on your message you had a crisis, and I nearly got myself arrested speeding all the way over here."

"Sorry. Did anyone see you come in?" Darla scanned the mostly empty street and locked the door. Thankfully she didn't have to open the bar for another three hours.

"How should I know if anyone saw me?" Josie shed her coat and shook off the snowflakes. "Maybe the lady working at the bakery. She kind of looked at me funny as I walked past."

"Ginny Eckles?" Oh great. No stranger ever passed

through Topaz Falls without answering to Ginny. For all they teased her, the woman really did care about the town. If you asked anyone, they would say Ginny held things together. Most days Darla appreciated it, but today she didn't feel like explaining she'd been part of a secret grief group for ten years. "Come on." Darla tugged on Josie's arm and led her to the back room where she had something of a living room configuration—a couch, a couple of overstuffed chairs and lamps.

"When you invited me to come to your bar, I about had a heart attack. All these years and I've never been here." Josie looked around. "You don't live here too, do you?"

"No. This is my event room. I host meetings here." This was where she hosted book club and the chamber meetings, and sometimes she did special wine-tasting events. "I don't want Ginny to see us chatting."

"So this is like a secret rendezvous." Her friend pronounced the word with a French accent, the smart aleck.

"Sure. It's a secret." Right now she had a lot of secrets and it was getting harder to keep them all straight. "I put out some truffles for you." She gestured to the coffee table in front of the couch. "Thought you'd like to try the new gingerbread and eggnog recipes." That ought to make up for her asking Josie to drive all the way here. Darla had hated to ask, but most of her staff had the day off, so she had to work. She didn't have an extra three hours to spend in the car.

"Well why didn't you say there'd be truffles?" Josie tossed her coat onto a chair and made a beeline for the couch. "I would've led the cop who pulled me over on a high-speed chase. At least he didn't give me a ticket. Must've been my charm." She picked up one of the eggnog truffles. "Did you add a splash of dark rum like I suggested?"

"Taste it and see for yourself." Darla happened to know they were melt-in-your-mouth-and-all-the-way-down-to-your-toes delicious. She'd eaten half the batch for breakfast.

Josie popped the whole thing in her mouth and flung herself back onto the couch. "Mmmm. Enough of these and I won't be able to drive home."

"I'll box some up so you can take them with you," Darla promised, sitting in the chair across from her friend.

"So it's a truffle emergency?" Josie straightened herself up and snatched a gingerbread truffle. "That's why you called me out here? Were you afraid you were going to eat them all yourself?"

"I might've, but that's not why I asked you to come." She'd been desperate to talk to someone about Ty— someone who didn't know him, who didn't have any vested interest in the two of them. She knew her Topaz Falls friends would love it if she and Ty were an item in real life, and she needed an objective opinion. "I have a situation. A dilemma, if you will, and I'm not sure what to do about it."

Josie finished chewing the truffle and blotted her mouth with a napkin. "Well this sounds intriguing."

"I can't talk to my other friends." Because they wouldn't understand. They'd all experienced loss in some form or another, but Josie shared the loss of widowhood. Their loss wasn't necessarily more painful than any other kind of loss, but it did seem to be more consuming. Gray was the only one she'd ever shared her life with, the one who she still shared her life with in some ways.

"You okay?" Josie's face had sobered, and she set down her half-eaten truffle on the coffee table.

Much to Darla's horror, fat tears formed, transforming

the room into a watery blur. *No.* She sniffed them away. She didn't cry in front of people. "I'm pretending to be engaged to Ty. That guy you met on the street a few weeks ago. It's a long story, but his family is here and he needed a fake fiancée and so I volunteered..."

With each word she spoke, Josie's eyebrows inched farther and farther toward her hairline.

"But now I think Ty has feelings for me. I mean, I'm pretty sure he has feelings for me. Last night, I had a party for his family and we danced and kissed and laughed." Exactly the way a loving couple would.

"And that's bad because...?" Josie waited for her to fill in the blank.

"His brother told me Ty has never looked at anyone the way he looks at me. He said he thinks he's head over heels." And then Ty had gone on to prove it all night. He'd been the perfect fiancé—chivalrous and attentive and fun. But..."I don't want him to fall for me. He *can't* fall for me." An expanding emptiness rumbled her stomach. She leaned forward and picked up a truffle, taking a tiny nibble at one of the corners.

Meanwhile, Josie seemed to take her time assessing the situation. She tapped her fingers against her knee, letting her gaze drift up to the ceiling. "So let me get this straight. You volunteered to act like the man's fiancée, but now when he treats you like his fiancée you're freaking out."

Leave it to Josie to say things like they were. "Yeah, but I didn't think it through. I didn't think he'd develop real feelings for me. We've always just been friends with benefits."

The woman's laugh seemed to come straight up from her belly. "This gets better and better. You're telling me you and Ty have hooked up?"

"Only a few times." She devoured another truffle.

"And you didn't think there was any danger in agreeing to be his fiancée?" the woman demanded. "After you'd already slept with him?"

A defensive energy flushed her face. "It's for a good cause. His brother Rhett is a famous football player, and we needed him to come out for our bachelor auction. So we could raise money for our friends who lost everything in a fire." At the time it had seemed like the best solution, but that was before. Before Ty had smeared frosting over her lips so he could kiss her. Before he'd made her tea to help her feel better. Before he'd kissed her senseless while wearing that Santa hat. Before she'd felt that kindling in her heart when he touched her—something warm and stirring and at the same time terrifying. It was the awakening of a need she'd buried a long time ago.

Josie sat back and studied her in only the way she alone could—somehow seeing right through everything. "What are you afraid of, Darla?"

Her friend never failed to ask the tough questions either. "I'm afraid he's falling in love with me." Like his brother had said.

"Are you sure that's what you're worried about? Or are you more afraid you'll fall in love with him?"

"I can't fall in love with him." She might have feelings for him, she might love being *with* him, but she wasn't capable of loving *him*. She wasn't capable of loving anyone.

"It wouldn't be cheating on Gray," Josie said gently. "Falling in love with someone else can't hurt him, honey."

"I know that." But it could hurt her. She'd been lost after Gray had died—lost and stumbling and blind, and she would never ever admit it to anyone else, but there were even days she'd wished she'd never met him. Because then she wouldn't have known. She wouldn't have known how empty life was without him. Since then, she'd rebuilt her entire world to guarantee she didn't need anyone. That way she would never have to risk losing everything again. "Gray knew I would hide." She took the letter out of her pocket, unfolded it, and laid it on the table for Josie to read.

Her friend read the words silently, tears welling in her eyes. "He knew you well."

"Better than anyone has ever known me."

Josie pushed the letter back across the table. "Maybe it's time to let someone know you again."

"Ty needs more than I can ever give him. I'm too afraid." She could never admit that to anyone else, but Josie already knew.

"I'm afraid too." Empathy softened Josie's face. "I fear putting everything into a relationship that might not work out. I fear losing another person I love." She took a deep breath as though choosing her next words carefully. "But do you want to know what scares me more than that?"

No. She didn't. Those were Darla's deepest fears. "What?"

"Letting those fears push me away from someone who could change my life. Someone who could help me heal. Someone who needs me to love them too." Josie reached for her hand and gave it a squeeze. "It's not up to you to decide what Ty deserves. He can do that all by himself," she said gently. "What you have to decide is what *you* deserve. It's been ten years since you lost your husband, and look how far you've come."

A familiar pain wedged itself tightly beneath her ribs. She had come far, but it had cost so much.

"The question you have to ask yourself is: What do you want your life to look like in another ten years?" Josie went on. "Or even in five? Do you want everything to be exactly the same as it is now? Will this always be enough for you?" She looked steadily into Darla's eyes. "Or is there something better waiting on the other side of your fear?"

Something better. Yes, she wanted something better. Of course she did. But… "I don't know how to get past it." Those fears were shackled around her ankles, and she wasn't strong enough to drag them forward. Keeping everything the same meant keeping control. It was predictable and safe.

"Then I suggest you figure that out first." Josie carefully selected another truffle and savored it before she spoke again. "Stop focusing on what Ty needs and focus on finding your freedom from the fear that's holding you back."

Freedom. That word was like a dust mote floating in front of her. Darla wanted so badly to grab it, but how could she hold on? True freedom didn't seem possible. "Have you found yours?" she asked hopefully.

Josie took her time with the question. "I've found moments," she finally said. "Glimpses. It's not something that happens all at once, honey. It's something you move toward one step at a time, one day at a time. The key is to quit pretending the fear isn't there."

"That might be the hardest part." If she stopped pretending, people would see every wound she'd so carefully guarded. It would mean admitting she wasn't as strong as she wanted everyone to believe. It would mean admitting she did need people. She did need love. It would mean putting her heart out there, exposed and raw.

"Hard?" Josie chuckled. "Acknowledging that fear is excruciating. But it's also worth it. After a while you'll notice the fear is a little further behind you. Still there maybe, but not holding on to you as tightly as it did before. And then you're more open to new possibilities." Her sassy smirk returned. "Who knows? Maybe you'll even be open to a new possibility wrapped up in a cowboy package."

Chapter Twelve

So far so good.

Darla dropped her napkin onto her empty plate and sat back in the chair. During her dinner with Ty's parents, she'd made it a point to tell as much truth as possible—mainly answering questions about the wine bar and being a business owner. That seemed to be a safe topic of conversation, and they were very interested in how she ran her business. She asked them questions too—about the ranch and about Montana, and she'd actually enjoyed hearing the answers. Even Ty had seemed to enjoy himself, likely because his brother was out at the Tumble Inn for the evening. When Rhett had heard it was ladies' night, he'd bailed on dinner with them.

At first when Ty's mom insisted Darla join them for dinner, she'd tried to decline, but the woman hadn't given her a choice. And she'd felt bad for avoiding them all—especially Ty—for the better part of two days. After her talk with Josie, she'd needed some space, some time. She'd forced herself to read Gray's letter again, to appreciate his reason for writing it, even though it brought her pain. She hadn't figured anything out—like Josie had said, it didn't happen all at once—but she so desperately wanted to be open to something new.

Darla sipped the last of her water and set down her glass. "What a delicious meal, Maureen." She'd been so hungry, she'd eaten two helpings of everything.

Ty's mom had seemed to sparkle with happiness the whole evening. "Why, thank you. That roast is an old family recipe that my grandma passed down to my mom. And don't you worry. Before the wedding, I'll pass it down to you too."

Tension worked its way back into her neck. The wedding. If only they could go on avoiding that topic. "That would be great." Hopefully no one else noticed the hollow ring in her voice. They'd managed to make it through the entire dinner without one mention of the wedding, but now she braced herself for the questions and happy exclamations about how excited they were for the big day.

"Have you thought about keeping your maiden name and hyphenating?" Maureen asked. "That's all the rage these days. Darla Michaels-Forrester has a nice ring to it."

It did, but that wasn't her maiden name. She didn't want to talk about her past, but it would also likely curb the wedding talk. At least for a while. "Actually, Griffin was my maiden name. Michaels was my first husband's last name." And it had been her identity. When she'd taken Gray's last name, she'd become part of a real family for the first time.

"Oh." Maureen shared an unreadable look with her husband. "I guess I didn't realize you'd been married before."

"Yeah." Ty sat up a little straighter in a protective

stance. "This will be her second marriage. The other one was a long time ago." Darla knew he was trying to rescue her, to gloss over her first marriage so she didn't have to talk about it, but she wanted to tell them. Gray still deserved to be known. And wasn't this part of what Josie said she had to do? Acknowledge the pain?

"I got married in my twenties," she explained. "But my husband passed away. Ten years ago."

"What?" Ty's mom gasped the same way everyone else did when they found out she was a widow. "Oh sweetheart…"

"You shoulda said something." His father scolded Ty with a deep frown.

"It's okay." She gave them both a practiced smile. "I don't mind talking about it." She didn't want to mind. "He died of cancer. A brain tumor."

Maureen covered her mouth with her hand. "That's just plain awful," she said, getting all teary. "You brave, brave girl."

She wasn't brave. She was simply hiding. "It was a long time ago, and yes it was very difficult, but I've put it behind me." The lie seemed to catch in her throat, leaving a bad taste. This was exactly what Josie had been talking about. She wouldn't find freedom until she could be honest. Why was it so hard for her to admit the loss still tormented her?

Ty angled his face to hers, studying her as though trying to determine what was true and what was part of their lie. She wasn't sure she knew anymore.

"Well I'm so happy you two have found each other, then." Ty's mom held her husband's hand. "There's nothing better in this world than having someone to share your life with. Even if they drive you nuts sometimes."

Darla nodded, a growing heaviness in her heart weighting her to the chair. She knew the truth of Maureen's words because she lived with a hole in her life, a missing piece. And God, it was so lonely sometimes.

"We feel pretty lucky." Ty eased his arm around her, stroking his fingers across the back of her hand. It was a tender gesture, meant to comfort, and she leaned in to him, letting his touch temporarily soothe the wound like she'd done so many times before.

"Oh, goodness." Maureen dabbed at her eyes with her napkin. "I feel terrible. Here we are taking up all of Ty's time lately, and you two have hardly even been able to talk." She dropped her napkin onto the table and started to stack the plates. "You should stay tonight. Then you two can have a nice romantic evening and we'll make ourselves scarce."

The candles flickering in the center of the table suddenly seemed to put off more heat. She probably shouldn't stay with Ty, given that it was so easy for her to end up in bed with the man. Things were already confusing enough. "That's okay. We're both busy preparing for the festival. And I've been pretty tired." *Bone-weary tired* would be a more accurate explanation. She really needed to make that doctor's appointment as soon as the holidays were over.

"Well, I insist you stay tonight." Maureen rose from the table holding the stack of plates. "You poor dear. Doing all of this for other people at such a busy time of year. You need a night off. Robert and I were going to call it an early night anyway, so you two can snuggle up on the couch and watch a movie or something."

They were going to bed already? Darla glanced at the clock. It was all of eight. "You two don't have to do that. I really should go home." Alone. "I haven't been feeling all that well lately." When she'd gotten to Ty's house, she'd been starving, but after eating all of that rich food, nausea had started to set in again.

"All the more reason for you to stay." Maureen brought the dishes to the sink and Robert quickly got up to help her.

"You shouldn't be alone when you're not feeling good. Right, Ty?" his father said in a leading question.

"Right." Ty seemed to watch her face for a reaction. "Yeah. Why don't you stay? I'll make you some tea and we can watch that other Christmas movie you've been wanting to see." He said it so smoothly, like they snuggled up on the couch for Hallmark Christmas movie marathons on a regular basis.

"Wonderful idea!" Maureen turned on the water and started to rinse the plates. "I'll finish up these dishes and then we'll be out of your hair."

Another protest teetered on the tip of her tongue, but she let it die. What would be the harm in staying one night? If she went home, she'd only sit there and stew about everything—details for the festival, Josie's haunting question. *What if there's something better waiting on the other side of your fear?* And she did love that tea Ty made. "Okay. Sure. I think I'll stay." She gauged Ty's expression.

He smiled softly at her and she smiled back. Maybe for one night she would try not to overanalyze everything. She would acknowledge she was afraid, and she would stay anyway. How else would she ever move forward? Darla rose from her chair and joined Ty's parents in the kitchen. "I can help with the dishes."

"Absolutely not." Robert steered her toward the living room. "You've had a full day. Go get comfortable on the couch. Let us take care of the mess."

"He's right." Ty appeared next to her and rubbed her shoulder. "You get comfortable and I'll make your tea."

"Are you sure?" She wasn't used to letting everyone else take care of her. That definitely didn't feel comfortable. "I don't mind—"

"We've got it." Ty took her hand and led her to the couch. "Relax."

"Right. Relax." She could do that. While Ty and his parents worked in the kitchen, Darla settled herself on the couch. Surprisingly, Ty had a nice place for a bachelor cowboy. The house wasn't large, but everything had been updated. A beautiful stone fireplace provided the focal point of the room, almost taking up one entire wall. Of course, he had a gigantic television mounted above the mantel, but it wasn't overly obnoxious. The leather couch and matching chairs were oversized and cushy, perfect for sinking into. And he even had a wall of bookshelves filled with actual books instead of trinkets or memorabilia. Darla smiled as she admired the Christmas decorations he'd added. She never would've pegged him as the nostalgic type, but he'd definitely put some effort into making the place look festive. In the corner sat a beautiful blue spruce covered in colorful lights but no ornaments. And garlands wound around the stair banisters that led to the second floor. Those small touches added such a cozy feel to the space.

In the kitchen, Robert and Maureen worked swiftly, as though they couldn't wait to give her and Ty some alone time.

"Oh, I'm so happy you'll be staying!" Ty's mom called. "I'll make us all a big breakfast in the morning. If you thought that roast was good, wait until you try my grandmother's quiche. She was half French, you know."

"I can't wait." Breakfast happened to be her favorite meal of the day. "But tomorrow I'm doing the dishes." She couldn't let them wait on her hand and foot, though she had to admit it was kind of nice.

"Here's your tea." Ty set it on a coaster on the coffee table in front of her. "Need anything else?"

"No. Thanks. I'm fine." She moved over so he could join her on the couch. When he sat beside her, she leaned her shoulder in to his, letting his solid weight hold her up.

Ty tucked her in under his arm. "What was that movie you wanted to watch again?"

They hadn't discussed any of her other favorite Christmas movies, so she went with one of her tried-and-true selections. "*Miracle on 34th Street.*" It had been one of her favorites since she was a little girl. She and Gray used to watch it every Christmas Eve. But now she was with Ty. On his couch, at his house, spending the night. Her heart skipped a couple of beats, and once again she couldn't tell if it was anticipation or panic.

Darla lifted the mug of tea to her lips and sipped. The warm, calming aroma of ginger seemed to envelop her senses. Spicy with a hint of sweetness and the perfect temperature to soothe.

"How is it?" Ty picked up the remote and searched for the movie.

"It's good." Perfect. Exactly what she needed. She took another sip and set down the mug.

Maureen traipsed into the room, followed by Robert. "Just one more picture of you two lovebirds before we turn in." She unearthed her phone from her large purse, which was hanging by the door. "Scooch over now," Ty's mom instructed. "A little bit closer, you two."

Darla wasn't sure they could get closer, but Ty seemed

to try. He smelled good. She could only get hints above the scent of ginger, but it was that woodsy scent, clean and virile. And...it actually felt comfy to lean against him, warm and safe. Or maybe that was the calming effects of the ginger tea.

"Say cheese." His mom snapped pictures, the flash making Darla see spots.

"Okay, Ma. I think you captured the perfect shot." Ty kicked his feet up onto the coffee table and leaned back into the cushions, but he kept his arm around her. Sitting there like that, nestled in against him, his shoulder the perfect height to rest her head on, Darla realized how sleepy she was.

"Okay, okay." His mom slipped the camera back into her purse. "You two make such a beautiful couple, that's all. But we're going to bed now. Not to worry. You'll have the whole downstairs to yourself. We can't hear anything up in that guest room." She winked and Darla felt Ty's groan.

"Good night," he mumbled, giving his parents a disgruntled look.

"'Night." His father obviously took the hint and all but dragged Maureen up the staircase.

As soon as they'd disappeared, Ty brought his arm back to his side and scooted away from her. "Sorry about that."

"It's okay." A tinge of disappointment suddenly made her feel chilled. "I don't mind your parents. I think they're great, actually." Maybe that wasn't the right thing to say given his issues with them, but she couldn't help herself. "I wish my parents were that interested in my life."

"They're not interested in my life." His tone was too quiet to sound bitter. "They're interested in you. In the potential for grandchildren. But they haven't taken an interest in my life since I was a kid. It's like when I left home they stopped caring."

"Have you ever asked them why they didn't come to watch you compete?" Maureen might not talk about Ty's riding career, but she obviously loved her son.

"I didn't have to ask." Ty clicked Play on the movie, but it didn't distract Darla. She continued staring at him expectantly.

He sighed as though resigned that she wasn't about to give up on this line of questioning. "They always went to Rhett's games instead," he muttered. "That's my answer. They'd rather see him play than watch me compete."

"Maybe there's another reason," Darla suggested. "Maybe they couldn't afford to travel—"

"It's not money." Ty stared at the television, but she could still see the hurt in his eyes. "I paid for their tickets. That's how much I wanted them there. I was willing to do whatever it took to remove the barriers so they'd come. And they didn't. They haven't. Ever. This weekend wouldn't have been the first time they saw me ride, and I've been competing for fifteen years."

"That's a lot of competitions for them to miss," she acknowledged. Between that and the fact that they never seemed to talk about his riding, she could understand why he felt like they didn't care. She knew what that was like. She covered his hand with hers. "I like watching you compete."

He paused the movie and turned his face to hers. "Really?"

"Yeah. You're different than a lot of those other cowboys."

"Different." He didn't seem to know if that was good or bad.

"You're really good," she clarified. "Great technical ability, solid strength, but you're not showy about it. You're confident." She'd spent plenty of time studying the riders who came through town. "Your parents are really missing out not seeing you do something you love."

"Thanks." He looked down at her hand, which was still attached to his.

"Maybe you should talk to them about it," she said softly. "Give them a chance to explain."

"We don't do that in my family. Talk about how we really feel." Ty shrugged like it didn't matter, but disappointment laced his voice. "We put our heads down and power through."

"I get that." Life was definitely easier that way. Ignoring feelings exactly like the ones that were stirring in the uncharted realms of her heart. Ignore them and they'd go away. But Ty's eyes held her so intensely it made those feelings much harder to ignore. "Sometimes talking is overrated."

"Yeah." His hungry gaze lowered to her mouth. "Movies are overrated too. Don't you think?"

Heat rolled through her. "Sometimes."

"Remember that night in your kitchen?" His forehead rested against hers.

"Yes," she whispered, anticipation flickering through her the same way it had then.

Ty's lips hinted at a grin. "That was fun."

"Mm-hmm." She hadn't had that much fun since then...

"If you think about it, sex has never complicated things for us," he said with an adorable shrug. "We're still friends."

"Of course we are." And she was working on her fears, trying to be open...

"Being friends has its benefits," he murmured. "And since you're staying the ni—"

Darla shut him up with a kiss, just a teasing brush of her lips over his before she pulled back. "I thought you said talking was overrated." Talking allowed her to think too much, and she didn't want to think.

"Talking is definitely overrated." Ty guided her lips back to his, rekindling a fierce desire to give herself over to him. She brought her hands to his shoulders and moved to her knees so she could inch to his lap. He moaned, his hand pressing into her lower back guiding her to straddle his hips.

His hands lowered to her butt, caressing as she grinded against him. Oh yeah. It had been way too long. "Bedroom," she gasped, not caring that she sounded desperate.

Answering with a kiss, Ty somehow stood up and carried her back to his bedroom. He set her feet on the floor and closed the door, backing her up against the wall, gliding his lips down her neck until her breaths turned ragged.

Darla rifled her hands through his hair as he kissed her neck, nibbling up to her ear.

"You sure?" he asked her, fingering the hem of her sweater.

In response, she pushed his shirt off his shoulders and ran her hands over his muscled chest, tracing her fingertips lightly over the bends and curves. "Why are you still talking?" she asked him.

"I'll shut up now." Ty whisked her sweater over her head and spun her toward the bed. Laughing, she held on to him as they teetered and then fell onto his mattress. Impulse took over then, obliterating all thought as Ty greedily undressed her.

She tore open the button fly on his pants and shimmied

them down his hips along with his boxers. Ty kicked them off the rest of the way and reached for the drawer in the bedside table. Before Darla even knew what was happening, he had a condom on and he'd flipped onto his back, pulling her to lie over him.

Reaching up, Ty gently smoothed her hair away from her face and looked into her eyes as though he was seeing her for the first time. *Be brave.* Before, Darla would've looked away, searching for something to distract her from the ache he put into her heart, but she kept her eyes on his, looking back, letting him see more of her.

An intensity passed between them, driving a sense of need deeper into her. Ty guided her lips to his, and her eyes fell closed. For the first time in so long, she let herself feel the intimate connection ignited by a kiss. Darla threaded her hands into his hair, kissing him back, letting those pieces of armor she'd surrounded herself with fall away. This was different. He was different. *She* was different. Open and wanting him with a fierceness that seemed to trample her fears.

Ty slid his hand up her inner thigh and parted her legs to tease her with his fingers, but she pinned his arms against the mattress and slid onto him, abandoning herself to the feel of his skin against hers, the fluid motions, the heightening sensations. He seemed to know her body, her need. He held her tightly to him and he kissed her again and again. She moved with him, arching and thrusting to bring him deeper until they were both gasping and the orgasm broke her apart, giving her the release she'd been craving. Ty shuddered beneath her, holding her tight, keeping much quieter than he usually did, which made her smile.

Darla fell over him in a heap. "Your parents said they wouldn't be able to hear anything, you know."

"It's still weird." He lay like he was dead, with both arms spread out to his sides. "I'm just going to pretend they're not here."

Darla laughed. "Won't be a problem for me." A cavernous yawn interrupted. "I have a feeling I'll be out cold within minutes." She turned onto her side and faced him. "I never realized how comfortable your bed was."

"That's because you've never spent the night." His fingertips drifted up her bare hip. "But I'm glad you're staying tonight." His eyes searched hers.

"I am too," she almost whispered. A deep peace settled over her, making the fears she'd had before seem so far away. Was it a glimpse of the freedom Josie was talking about? She hoped so.

Another yawn took her by surprise. Dear God. What time was it? Nine o'clock? She was pathetic. "I'm so tired I don't know if I could drive home anyway."

Ty's grin turned naughty. "It was that good, huh?"

She inched closer and brushed a kiss over his lips. "It was amazing." So freeing and hopeful it made her want to be brave again.

Chapter Thirteen

What was that sound? Ty forced open his eyes and turned his head to the side, blinking until he could make out the source of the quiet snoring noises in the dim light.

Darla lay on her side facing him, her hair in total disarray and covering most of her face. She was sawing logs—snoring in the cutest way possible, and looking so peaceful and unguarded he had to take his time studying her. *Beautiful* wasn't quite the right word to describe Darla. He wasn't sure there was a way to describe her, but as he watched her in the early-morning light, lying there all wrapped up in his shirt with her hair in tangles, she took his breath away.

Trying not to disturb her, Ty glanced at the clock. It was already past seven, so his mom would likely be in the kitchen making breakfast, just like she used to do when he was a teenager. Except back then he hadn't had a girl in his room. Well, not that his parents had known about anyway.

He'd been shocked that Darla had wanted to stay, but

then again, she'd been different last night. More relaxed. Less guarded.

The events of last night replayed again, but he wouldn't let himself touch Darla. Wouldn't wake her up. He'd let her sleep in and surprise her with breakfast before he had to head out for a training ride with Mateo and Levi.

Inch by inch, Ty moved to the edge of the bed and slipped out from underneath the covers. He quietly stumbled around and pulled on some sweats. Darla stirred, turning to her stomach and snoring louder. Grinning, he carefully pulled the covers up to her shoulders before slowly opening the door and maneuvering into the hallway. For a few seconds he paused to listen outside the door, but it didn't sound like he'd woken her.

He walked down the hall and into the kitchen where his mother worked busily frying potatoes on the stove. "What're you doing up so early?" she demanded.

"I have to head out for a training run later, so I thought I would bring Darla breakfast in bed."

"What a marvelous idea!" His mom wiped her hands on the Christmassy apron she must've brought with her in one of her ten suitcases. "The quiche will be coming out of the oven in a few minutes." She started opening cabinets. "Do you have a tray anywhere? We could dress up the plate with a sprig of some fresh holly from the fireplace mantel."

"No tray, I'm afraid." He didn't exactly do breakfast in bed on a regular basis. In fact, this was a first.

"Hmmm." His mom spun in a slow circle, eyeing what seemed to be every inch of the kitchen. "Ah-ha." She snatched up a cookie sheet sitting on the counter. "It's not fancy but it will do."

Ty stood back and watched her work. There seemed to

be no limit to her energy. She rifled through cabinets until she'd found plates, a mug, a full set of silverware, and a small vase he'd forgotten he even had.

"There." She added a sprig of holly to the vase and stood back. "Now we'll just wait for the quiche."

Wait. That was the hard part. Impatience flared as he thought about getting back to Darla, but he poured himself a mug of coffee and forced himself to sit on a stool at the island. "What are you doing tod—"

A familiar whistling cut him off. Rhett came sauntering into the kitchen with a smug look on his face.

"There you are." Their mother gave him a once-over. "What time did you get in last night?"

"It was actually sometime this morning," his brother said, stealing some potatoes out of the skillet.

Ty knew what that meant. "Just tell me you didn't end up with anyone I know," he said, draining a third of his coffee. He didn't need his brother causing any drama in town.

"She's not a local, don't worry." Rhett pulled out the stool next to Ty and took a seat. "She's from Steamboat, actually. And she's a rodeo queen."

Of course she was.

"You didn't want to invite her over for breakfast?" His mother seemed disappointed. She probably thought they were simply out dancing all night.

"She's staying at the ski resort," Rhett said, popping another potato into his mouth. "They have free breakfast there."

Ty was tempted to roll his eyes, but the truth was, he couldn't judge Rhett. Hooking up had been his MO once too. But now...he thought about Darla snuggled up in his bed. He felt ready for something else.

"I noticed Darla's car is out there," Rhett said, shoving an elbow into Ty's ribs.

"Yeah. She's still in bed." If he didn't need to get in another training run before the rodeo, he'd spend the whole day in bed with her.

"Speaking of..." His mom slid the quiche out of the oven. "It's perfect." She quickly set it on the stovetop and ran a knife through the soft layers. The aroma had Ty's mouth watering. After placing a slice of quiche onto the plate, his mom added a heaping pile of the breakfast potatoes and a garnish of fruit.

"Hurry up and take it to her." She shoved the cookie sheet into Ty's hands. "Before it gets too cold."

"Damn." Rhett eyed the tray. "I'd definitely marry you if you brought that to me in bed."

"He's not trying to win her over, silly." Their mother eyed the vase and then quickly added another sprig of holly. "She's already marrying him. Because he treats her like a woman deserves to be treated." Her eyes gave Ty's brother a stern reprimand. "You could learn a thing or two from watching Ty."

Well, well, well, would you listen to that? His mom had paid him a compliment, and judging from the stony look on his brother's face it had pissed him off. He couldn't help but gloat as he filled up a glass of orange juice to take to his fiancée.

* * *

It was going to be a beautiful day. Darla sat up against the pillows in Ty's bed and admired the view through the crack between the curtains. The morning sunshine made the fresh snow gleam brilliantly all the way to the peaks off in the distance. Against those white mountains, the sky had a crystalline-blue glow. It was as perfect as last night had been. She'd forgotten how it felt to let herself go, to stop analyzing and controlling every emotion. But Ty had made it easy for her. Easy and safe. Now if he would just get back in bed with her, the morning would be even better. Where'd he go anyway?

She slipped out from under the covers and quickly redressed in the clothes she'd been wearing the day before. Peeking in the mirror that hung over Ty's dresser, Darla fluffed her hair as best she could without her full arsenal of products and walked out of his room. She followed the sound of voices to the kitchen, where she spotted Rhett and Maureen and Ty, who was holding a tray of breakfast.

She went right to Ty. "Morning."

"Well, hello." He set down the tray and wrapped her in a hug. Ty happened to be one handsome cowboy, but it seemed he was especially sexy in the mornings with his hair tousled and a little wild and more stubble than usual shading his jaw.

"What's all that?" she asked, nodding toward the beautiful tray of assorted breakfast foods. A sudden hunger pang rumbled through her stomach.

"I was going to bring you breakfast in bed." Ty replied, running his eyes down the full length of her body.

"That's sweet." She raised up to her tiptoes so she could kiss his cheek. Two days ago that would've been for the benefit of his family, but now she simply kissed him because she wanted to. "But we don't have to eat in bed. We can have breakfast with your family."

"Great idea." Rhett swiped a slice of bacon off the tray and ate it on his way to the dining room table.

"I'd love to, but I have to go wake up your father." Maureen untied her Christmas apron and pulled it off, hanging it up on a cabinet nob. "And we still have so many presents to wrap upstairs." Before Darla could jump in and help, Maureen quickly carried the food and a few more plates to the dining room table. "But you kids sit down and enjoy your breakfast."

"Oh, we will." Rhett flashed what Darla had come to think of as his camera-ready smile.

Ty didn't smile, but he followed her to the breakfast table and they sat with his brother.

Rhett piled food onto his plate. "So what do you two lovebirds have planned before the auction today?"

Darla glanced at Ty. She couldn't seem to stop smiling. Maybe she should've let him bring her breakfast into the bedroom. What would it be like to spend a whole day with him? Someday soon she might like to find out. "I have an appointment in Glenwood Springs around eleven." Every year she looked forward to their support group's Christmas party, but for the first time, she wondered if she could skip out to be with Ty. She took a bite of quiche and savored the salty taste. Maureen wasn't kidding. It was the best quiche she'd ever tasted.

"And I'm meeting Levi and Mateo." Ty looked as disappointed as she felt. "We've got to get in a few more training runs before the main event." He slipped his hand onto Darla's thigh. "But maybe we can meet up this afternoon?"

That simple touch brought waves of desire rolling through her. "Hopefully."

Rhett poured himself a glass of orange juice. "Speaking of training, I just read an article about a bull rider from Texas. Blane Fuller."

Darla didn't know anyone named Blane Fuller, but Ty immediately set down his fork.

"Did you know him?" his brother asked.

The answer was obvious. Ty's eyes had narrowed into a glare. "Yeah. Why?"

"Just wondering." Rhett glared back at his brother. "He was killed during a training run this fall, wasn't he?"

Ty didn't answer. Instead, he held his coffee mug against his lips and took a sip.

"Was he a friend?" Darla asked. She vaguely remembered Ty, Mateo, and Levi traveling down to Texas for a funeral in October, but Ty had never said much about it.

"Yes." Ty set down his mug, his jaw tightening. "He was a friend."

He obviously didn't want to talk about it, but she couldn't stop herself from asking, "What happened?"

"The article said it was just a routine training run, but the bull bucked him and then stepped on his chest," Rhett answered for his brother.

Ty's gaze got even stormier.

"I don't get it," Rhett went on. "Bull riding makes no sense to me. Why would you want to risk your life to ride around on the back of a lethal animal?"

Darla could feel an argument brewing between them, but she was still stuck on the fact that Ty's friend had died. During a normal training ride. Probably a training ride a lot like the one he was getting ready to take. A tremor ran through her stomach, killing her appetite.

"Same reason you run around tackling a bunch of grown men," Ty shot back. "For the challenge. The competition. The discipline."

Rhett raised his hands as though surrendering. "All I'm saying is, it doesn't seem worth the risk."

For the first time, Darla had to agree with Rhett. Thinking about Ty getting on a bull had never bothered her before. She'd seen him ride plenty of times, but then he'd only been a friend, someone she hooked up with occasionally. She hadn't let him get to her heart. Not before last night.

Even though he hadn't finished his food, Ty pushed away his plate. "Football has its fair share of risks too."

"Sure. But it's nothing like bull riding." Rhett pushed away his food too, staring down his brother. "You should look up the statistics sometime."

"What statistics?" Darla's throat had weakened.

"About how bull riding is the most dangerous sport in the world," Rhett said with his typical self-importance. "About how many deaths and catastrophic injuries have happened on the rodeo circuit. More than any other sport, that's for sure."

Judging from Ty's expression, he already knew the statistics, but she'd never even considered them. How many deaths? How many catastrophic injuries? She couldn't make herself ask. *Don't analyze. Don't think. Don't fear.* Too late. She could already feel herself freezing up again. How could she have ignored the fact that Ty competed in the most dangerous sport in the world? "You don't have to train today, do you?" She slipped her hand in his and held on, desperate to find the same courage she'd felt when they'd made love last night.

"I'd rather not." Ty lifted her hands his lips and kissed her knuckles, his eyes softening. "Trust me. I'd much rather hang out with you, but I have to be ready for the competition." He refocused on his brother, his face turning stony again. "I know the statistics. And I know sometimes things go wrong out there. But we don't focus on that."

Why, Darla wanted to ask. Why didn't they focus on that? Because she was sure starting to. What had she been thinking searching for freedom from her fears with Ty of all people? Ty who rode bulls for a living. Oh God. One wrong step from the bull was all it would take to rip him away from her.

Heart pounding hard, Darla suddenly stood up. "Will you excuse me?" she half whispered before making a fast escape down the hall to Ty's bedroom. She moved to shut the door behind her but Ty was there.

"Are you feeling okay?"

"I feel fine." She paused midstep and turned back to him. That was a lie. She wasn't fine. Her stomach had clenched and her heart raced. This whole thing had gotten out of hand. She'd let herself get swept away in hope and desire, but Ty was not right for her. They weren't right for each other.

"Actually, we need to talk." She needed an out. A firm plan for how they would end their supposed engagement. This couldn't happen again. They couldn't keep growing closer when she wanted nothing to do with his life as a bull rider. She couldn't walk that road with him. She couldn't be part of that. The engagement was going to end anyway, but it would be best to do it as soon as they could.

"Sure, we can talk." Ty walked over to her. "What's wrong?"

"This whole engagement thing has gone way too far. I think we should stage a breakup before your family goes back to Montana."

"A breakup?" His gaze darkened. She quickly looked away. She'd messed this up. Ty had feelings for her. And she had feelings for him, but she hadn't thought any of this through. She didn't want a future with him, a future filled with anxiety and dread every time he left for a training ride or competition.

"It's not fair for us to lie to your parents," she went on. "They're so excited about the wedding and everything. We can't keep doing this to them."

He stared at her for what felt like a month. "This isn't about my parents," he finally said. "You were happy last night. I saw it in your face. And this morning before we had breakfast with my brother." His jaw locked. "What happened?"

"Nothing happened." She held her arms against her chest like a shield. "But I shouldn't have spent the night with you." Because this couldn't go anywhere.

"We don't have to keep lying," Ty said. "We can tell my parents and Rhett the truth. I don't care. But I'm not pretending, Darla. I have feelings for you. You have to know that by now."

Her racing pulse thumped in her temples making her cheeks alternate between hot and cold. "I'm sorry." She didn't even try to hold back the tears. "Gray died, Ty. And he didn't take nearly the kind of risks you take every time you go to work."

"I'm not Gray," he said firmly. "You can't compare me to him. This is different. *We're* different."

"I'm not different." She wanted to be, but she wasn't. Not yet. "I'm still a woman who lost the love of her life. And I can't do it again. I won't do it again."

"How did you feel last night?" he demanded.

"It doesn't matter." She started to turn away so she could run from him, go back to hiding. But before she could, Ty gently turned her shoulders to face him.

"It *does* matter. You feel the same connection I do. I know it. I saw it last night." He dropped his arms to his sides. "When are you going to stop running from it, Darla?" Color tinged his cheeks, and it seemed all those muscles in his upper body had tensed.

She'd never seen him this passionate about anything except for riding. That was why she had to do this. She couldn't give him everything, knowing the risks. And riding was so much a part of him. "I didn't mean to hurt you. I'm sorry." She held back the tears. "But I can't do this. Spending all this time together is too much." It was messing with her—making her feel things she didn't want to feel. "We need to break up."

She expected him to argue, but instead he gave her a stiff nod. "Fine. How?"

"We'll have to wait until after the auction." She paused, trying to get her thoughts in order. "We can stage it Sunday afternoon. You could bring your family to the bar and I'll tell you we need to talk in the back room."

When Ty said nothing, she went on. "I'll make it all about me. I'll explain to them that I'm not ready for a commitment. That you're a great guy, but it's not going to work out."

"You don't want it to work out," he corrected. The words weren't angry, only subdued, but that was worse.

Darla slipped past him and sat on the bed, unable to face the disappointment in his eyes. "After the auction, Rhett can cut his vacation short and go back to Dallas. He can hate me. You can all hate me."

"They're not going to hate you. That's not possible." He walked over and knelt in front of her. "And I definitely will never hate you. I'll always care about you." Brushing his fingers across her cheek, he gave her a sad smile. Then he stood and walked out of the room.

Chapter Fourteen

Darla pulled up across from the community center in Glenwood Springs and let the engine idle. She leaned her forehead onto the steering wheel with a sigh. Her body had felt as heavy as her heart since her confrontation with Ty that morning. She'd been thinking about him ever since. Had his training ride gone okay? Should she call him? But what else could she say? *Sorry* wasn't enough.

A knock clunked against the driver's side window of her car. She jerked up her head and found herself staring into Josie's eyes.

"You look like you could use a drink," her friend yelled through the glass.

Darla gathered up her purse and got out of the car. "I don't need a drink. I'd rather have a do-over." She'd rather go back to that moment she'd offered to be Ty's fiancée so she could undo everything that had happened up until this point.

"This have anything to do with your real friend slash

fake fiancé who's falling for you?" Josie asked as if she already knew the answer.

"I spent the night with him last night." Defeat slumped her shoulders. She'd thought she was being brave, moving toward freedom, but she clearly didn't have the strength. One breakfast conversation had sent her spiraling right back into fear.

"What'd you mean you slept with him?" Josie linked their arms together and led her across the street.

"I was trying to let go, to lose myself in the moment. Like you said." But if she would've thought about it, she would've realized Ty was the wrong man to find freedom with.

"I didn't tell you to sleep with him again." Her friend yanked her to a stop when they reached the sidewalk. "I only said move toward freedom. Not jump right into it. There's nothing wrong with baby steps, sister."

"Don't worry. I'm not blaming you. I messed up." She could own her mistake. "I had this wonderful night with him, but then this morning I lost it. Again." Darla trudged to the door. "It scares me too much. He's a bull rider, Josie. I could lose him so easily. So I told him we have to stage a breakup before his parents leave." If she would've simply kept boundaries in place, things wouldn't have gotten so out of control.

"Oh boy," Josie said, holding open the door for her. "We'll continue this conversation later. After the party. I swear. Right now your life has more drama than *The Bachelorette*."

"Well, this is new for me, I'll tell you that." She'd done everything she could to remain drama free for the last ten years.

She stepped fully into the community center's reception

area and felt another hot flash coming on. Hormones. That had to be it. That had to be the source of her troubles lately. She hadn't anticipated going through *the change* for at least another ten years or more, but she supposed it could be early.

Darla's stomach rolled as she shrugged out of her coat. Ever since she'd moved to Topaz Falls, she'd gotten to witness everyone else's drama. She hadn't had even a smidgeon of her own. That's why life was easier without romantic relationships. She had no obligations, no expectations.

Yes, but is that really fulfilling?

Whew. Another heat wave crashed over her, making her head feel funny. Great. Now her own subconscious was turning on her. Probably from the morning's stress. Once she got downstairs for their Christmas lunch, she'd feel better.

"You look a little flushed." Josie studied her with those astute, beady eyes. "Are you feeling okay?"

"I'll be fine. I haven't eaten much." Not since she'd freaked out and rushed out of Ty's house where she'd left a perfectly good breakfast sitting on his dining room table. It was that fight or flight thing. On her way out, she'd apologized to his mother, saying she'd forgotten she had an appointment. Of course, Maureen had been as gracious as always, which only made her feel worse.

"Come on." Josie beckoned her down the stairs. "Let's get you something to eat. I picked up the food from that new diner outside of town. Fried chicken with mashed potatoes and creamed corn."

The thought of all that grease turned her stomach upside down. "Sounds fabulous." Maybe she would be able to get away with not eating anything.

They walked into the meeting room just in time to witness an argument between Norman and Peter about which side of the plate they were supposed to set the forks and spoons.

As usual, Josie took control. "Oh just give it to me."

"Hey there Darla." Ralph greeted her with a hug. "You did bring dessert, didn't you?"

"Of course I did. But I forgot it in the car." She'd been so distracted, and this strange fog had settled over her brain. Fighting the wooziness, she greeted Norman and Peter and admired the table they'd put together. "Everything looks amazing." They'd gone to the trouble of setting the table with real china and crystal glasses and even a festive red tablecloth. A lovely white-and-red poinsettia plant sat in the middle.

"Only the best for you," Peter said, giving her hand a squeeze. "Do you want me to run out to your car and get the dessert?"

"No, that's okay. I can—"

The room spun around her. Darla reached out a hand to steady herself against the table, but her body swayed.

There were noises around her—voices, but everything seemed to fade to gray. Dark, dark gray. Her body tipped backward. Someone caught her before she crashed to the floor. Blackness flickered all around her before the world came back into view.

"Call nine-one-one!" Josie squealed.

Darla blinked a few times.

"I can't get my damn phone to turn on," Norman grumbled next to her.

Some of the haze had started to lift. Darla took in her surroundings. She was sitting in a chair with her four friends gathered around, all of them trying to get their phones to work. "Don't call nine-one-one," she said, straightening herself up.

"You passed out!"

Ow. Her head. She really wished Josie didn't have to yell right in her ear.

"You almost keeled over!" the woman went on. "If Peter and Ralph hadn't been standing right there, you would've gone down."

"I'm *fine*." But she was also too smart to stand up unassisted. She would simply sit for a few minutes and take some deep breaths. Everything would be fine. Even with the mental pep talk, anxiety lurked on the edges of her rationality. Was something seriously wrong?

"It's either an ambulance ride or I drive you to that urgent care place down the street," Josie said in her take-no-prisoners tone Darla knew well. There'd be no talking her out of it.

"But our lunch—"

"The boys will stay here and hold down the fort." Josie adopted a gentler tone. "They can start, and we'll come back after we make sure everything's okay." She held up her phone. "Or I can call an ambulance. Up to you."

"Fine." Darla started to stand, and Peter and Norman positioned themselves on either side of her while Ralph brought up the rear. He followed behind as they moved across the room and walked up the steps, keeping his arms outstretched like he was ready to catch her.

Despite the headache and the sloshing in her stomach, Darla had to laugh. They were quite the spectacle.

When they reached her car, Darla opened the back door and pulled out the chocolate torte. "Here. You can take this inside." She handed it to Peter.

"But don't you dare eat it until we get back," Josie instructed.

"We won't," Norman promised. He gave Darla a kiss on the cheek. "You'll be all right. Everything'll be all right."

"Of course it will." She did her best to cover the doubt. She'd had weeks of weird symptoms and now this. Something was definitely wrong.

Darla went to open the driver's door, but Josie swiped the keys out of her hand. "You're not driving."

"Yes I am." She made a grab to get her keys back but her friend held them out of reach.

"Then I'm calling nine-one-one."

"Fine. You can drive." Making sure to scowl, she climbed into the passenger's seat and tried to massage the ache out of her temples. "I'm sure it's nothing," she said as Josie peeled out onto the road. "I'm probably just hungry."

"You don't pass out from hunger." Josie whipped the roadster around a corner.

Darla eyed the speedometer. "Seriously? You don't have to speed."

"This is a medical emergency." And Josie seemed determined to make the most of the opportunity.

After Darla's life flashed before her eyes at least three times, Josie pulled the car into a parking lot and hustled Darla into a nondescript building at the end of a strip mall. The place seemed completely deserted until a scrub-clad nurse finally walked out from the back. "Oh hi!" She seemed excited to have something to do. "Can I help you?"

Josie pointed at Darla. "She passed out."

"I was feeling a little light-headed," she corrected. "But

I'm guessing everything is fine. We just wanted to come in and make sure." That she wasn't dying? That she was simply going through a *very* early menopause?

"Of course!" The woman reached into a drawer and pulled out a clipboard. "You're in luck. There's no wait today. If you'll just fill out this paperwork, we'll be able to get you right back."

Though she still felt a bit wobbly, Darla took long strides to sit in a chair and started to fill out every detail of her health history while Josie looked over her shoulder.

"I didn't know your mom was a cancer survivor," her friend commented.

"Breast cancer. A few years ago." Of course she only heard about it all in an email six months after the fact. "They caught it at the earliest stage." So according to her mom, it had been no big deal. But maybe it was a big deal. Maybe Darla had the gene…

"And your dad has diabetes, huh?" Josie asked, still reading over her shoulder.

Darla gave her a look.

"Sheesh. I was just curious," her friend muttered.

Curious was not helping her current state of mind. Darla brought the clipboard back to the desk and the nurse happily took it out of her hands. "Why don't you come on back?" She gestured to a door off to their left. Darla started to walk through and Josie followed right behind. "You're coming with me?"

"Of course. I was there. I can tell them what happened."

"I can tell them what happened too." But really it was sweet of her to be so concerned, so Darla let it go.

"Right this way." The happy nurse led them into a small, sterile room. "Okay, so it looks like you're in pretty good health overall." She flipped through Darla's paperwork. "What did you say your symptoms were again?"

"Light-headedness," Josie answered for her. "Oh, and she looked really red a few minutes before she passed out."

It seemed Darla wouldn't have to say a word throughout this whole ordeal.

"Did you lose consciousness?" Nurse Happy asked.

"No," Darla said at the same time Josie said, "Yes."

"Maybe for a second, but I sat in a chair and felt much better." In fact, she was feeling fine now. Well, almost fine.

"Okay, why don't we take a look at your vitals before I send in the doctor?" The nurse pointed to the small bed gurney thing in the corner. Wearing a disgruntled frown, Darla sat herself up there, feeling like a little kid.

The nurse went about her business, taking her temperature, which was normal. She listened to her pulse. Also normal. Darla took a second to gloat at Josie as she held out her arm for the nurse to take her blood pressure.

"It's a little lower than it should be." She jotted something on the chart. "Have you been dehydrated lately?"

"No." She always carried a water bottle wherever she went. "Actually, I've been drinking more water than normal." She was always so thirsty.

"Hmmm." Nurse Happy made another note on the chart. "I think the doctor's going to want a urine sample. Just to rule out some things."

Darla's heart beat faster. "What things?"

"Oh you know..." The nurse waved her hand nonchalantly. "Diabetes, pregnancy..."

"Pregnancy? No." Darla laughed. "It's probably early menopause or something. There's no chance I'm pregnant."

"But you *are* sexually active," Josie pointed out.

"Kind of, but…" She'd only slept with Ty twice in the last two months. It wasn't like she was out there hooking up with men all the time. Besides, they'd always used protection.

"I just had a baby last year." The nurse pulled out a urine sample kit from the cabinet behind her and handed it over. "I'll tell you what, pregnancy sure does mess with you. I was like a different person. Nauseous one minute and starving the next. And emotional. Oh my, I was so emotional."

Suddenly Darla found it harder to swallow. Those symptoms sounded a little too familiar. "I'll be right back." She escaped the room before Josie and the nurse could detect her suspicions.

"Bathroom's to the right," the nurse called behind her. "You can leave the sample in the cabinet."

She quickly went about the task, her hands shaky. She and Gray had never used any preventative measures and she'd never gotten pregnant. If he hadn't gotten sick, they would've sought out fertility help, but after his diagnosis she hadn't even thought about getting tested. She simply thought it wasn't possible. She'd never wanted a baby with anyone besides him.

After leaving the sample in the cabinet, Darla staggered back to the room where the nurse and Josie were still chatting.

"When's the last time you had your period?" Josie demanded.

"I don't know." Panic jumbled her thoughts. "The older I get the more sporadic it is."

The nurse paused abruptly. "So you don't remember the last time you had your period?"

"A few months ago, I guess." She was forty, for crying out loud. The baby train had long since passed her by.

The nurse shared a wide-eyed look with Josie, who must've spent the last three minutes becoming her new best friend. "Oh, yeah, we'll definitely run a pregnancy test on that sample."

Darla's knees buckled. *Whoa.* There was that light-headedness again. She made her way back to the table and sat, bracing her hands on either side of her for more stability.

"I'll go run the tests and tell the doctor you're waiting," the nurse said before slipping out the door.

It hadn't even latched shut before Josie started in. "Do you want to talk about this?"

Darla fanned her face. Wow, it was hot in here. "About what?"

Josie tipped down her chin and widened her eyes in a you-know-very-well-about-what expression. "The fact that you might be pregnant?"

"I'm not." There was no way. Of course she'd wanted kids when she'd been married. She hadn't known such heartbreak back then. She hadn't been forced to shut down a part of her heart and soul.

Tears scalded her eyes. A baby. Could a baby change her? Could a baby open her heart back up? Tiny tendrils of hope unfurled inside of her, but she stamped them down. At forty, the odds for a baby—or a healthy pregnancy—weren't in her favor.

"How long ago did you sleep with Ty?" Josie asked.

"A month and a half ago." Back in early November. That one wild, fun night before she'd felt an emotional connection with him. Before she'd tried to be brave and had only ended up proving she was a coward. "That was the last time. Until last night." The tears fell. Last night. Ty had been so sweet to her. He was always so good.

"And there hasn't been anyone else?" her friend asked quietly.

"No." If she was pregnant, Ty had to be the father.

Josie blew out a sigh. "Sooooo you might be having a real baby with the fake fiancé you're about to fake break up with? Woweee!" She smacked her hand against her thigh. "I told you this was better than *The Bachelorette*."

Darla couldn't muster any amusement. The very foundation of her life was shaking. "I'm not having a baby." She couldn't. She had to keep those hopes where they belonged.

"Would it be such a terrible thing if you were?"

"No. It wouldn't be terrible at all." Just completely unexpected. A baby? With Ty? "It wouldn't have to change anything." Even she could hear the desperation in her words. She couldn't let it change anything. Everything she'd told him that morning was true. She didn't know how to build a life with him—with both him and the baby—when Ty risked his life every time he went to work. How would she do it? Kiss him goodbye, watch him kiss their son or daughter goodbye not knowing if he'd come back? Thinking about it made her stomach churn.

"How do you think he would take the news?" Josie asked.

"I have no idea." But if that doctor came back in and told her she was pregnant, she couldn't tell Ty. Not now. Not when his family was in town. Not when she needed to put space between them. Darla lay back on the small bed and inhaled deep, meditative breaths. Her mind raced through all the reasons it wasn't possible, but her heart pounded harder and harder and she already knew.

The door creaked open and she shot to a sitting position. "Hi there, Darla. I'm Doctor Leigh."

"Nice to meet you." Her voice squeaked.

"It's nice to meet you too. And it seems congratulations are in order. According to the tests we ran, you are officially expecting a baby."

Chapter Fifteen

Ty was running out of ways to avoid spending time with his family. After his training ride, his mother insisted they all go Christmas shopping together, but he'd told them he'd promised the Cortez brothers he'd help out with some work on their ranch.

After Darla ran out on him this morning, he couldn't pretend to be in a festive mood. He leaned in to the fence and kicked the snow off his boots. This December had been even colder than the last, making everything—from the pine trees at the edge of the meadow to the stark white peaks in the distance—look frozen solid. He'd been out here a good hour, checking on the bulls out in the pasture and cleaning up the stables, and now he was about frozen solid too. But he wasn't ready to go back home just yet.

His parents and brother had likely arrived home already. That meant he'd get to spend a whole afternoon in yet another pissing match with his brother and he wasn't in the mood. Might as well save that for the bachelor auction later tonight.

An engine gunned off in the distance and within minutes, Everly's truck came barreling up and over the hill. She parked near the fence and got out. "Hey, didn't expect to see you here today. How are things going with your family?"

"Great." He offered no additional explanation for why he'd rather stand in the snow than hang out with his family. He figured he didn't need to. From what Mateo had told him, Everly's parents weren't exactly easygoing.

Sure enough, she nodded. "I get it."

"What're you doing here?"

"I'm here to bring Jessa dinner. The triplets have been sick this week, and I know she's struggling. But then I saw your truck and I wanted to talk to you."

"You wanted to talk to me?" That was different. He and Everly chatted when Mateo was around, but they'd never exactly had a heart-to-heart.

"Yeah." Everly pulled a stocking cap out of her coat pocket and yanked it onto her head. "Does Darla seem off to you lately?"

"What'd you mean?" He'd noticed Darla hadn't been herself, but then again, before their fake engagement they hadn't exactly spent a lot of time talking about what was going on in their personal lives.

"She seems ... different. I don't know. I keep wondering if something's wrong with her."

Her obvious concern dropped his stomach. "Like what?"

"I don't know." Everly looked out on the bulls in the pasture. "Every time I've asked her, she says she's fine. But I've noticed she hasn't been eating much, and she seems so worn out."

"Yeah, I've noticed that too." It went past worn out. Darla had always had enough energy to light up a room, but lately she'd seemed to be missing her spark.

"I'm surprised she hasn't talked to you about it," Everly said, her eyes searching his face. "You two have been spending so much time together with the engagement and all."

"We're not really engaged." Maybe in a real engagement the couple would talk about things that were bothering them, but Darla seemed hell-bent on keeping him out of her life. "It's all fake. Part of a big show. In fact, she wants to stage a breakup." That ought to be a fun family gathering. Rhett was going to love every minute of it.

"Really? She wants to break up?" Everly frowned. "I guess I was wrong then."

"What'd you mean?"

She hesitated and then sighed. "I thought this fake engagement was a good thing. That it would bring you two together. *Finally.* I thought she would see how perfect you two are for each other."

"Yeah, that's not what happened." Instead, Darla had decided he was all wrong for her, that he took too many risks or whatever. It shouldn't bother him so much. He'd had no intention of wanting things to work out between them, of wanting her. Though that was what had ended up happening. "It's for the best."

"For the best?" Everly's face flushed with what seemed to be frustration. "But you care about her. I can tell. It's so obvious."

Caring about her wasn't enough. "I'm not gonna fight to be with someone who doesn't want me."

"But…" Everly seemed determined to argue. "I think she's terrified. Maybe that's why she's been acting so different. You two have been dancing around a commitment since you moved here." Her eyes brightened. "Of course that's why she's breaking up with you before your family leaves! Spending time with you is totally freaking her out. If she didn't have feelings for you, I'll bet she wouldn't be breaking up with you." The woman grinned. "Trust me, this is a good thing."

"No it's not." It wasn't good for Darla and it wasn't good for him. He had no desire to do a repeat of last night and this morning. It was like being on a damn seesaw. One minute she wanted him and the next she booted him out of her life. He didn't need to be jerked around. "It's fine. We'll break up. Everything'll go back to being the way it was before."

Everly stared at him with those disturbingly perceptive eyes. "Can everything really go back to the way it was, Ty? After you two have spent all this time together? After you've gotten a glimpse of what it would be like to be with her?"

"It has to go back." Simple as that.

Before Everly could argue again, Rhett drove up in Ty's spare Jeep—the car he usually used in the summer— and parked next to her truck. His brother cut the engine and got out.

"Great." Looked like his brother had gotten tired of hanging out with their parents.

"This conversation is not over," Everly whispered.

"I thought you were working today," his brother said as he sauntered over to meet them.

"I am. Was." Ty tried not to look too guilty. "How was Christmas shopping?"

"I'm not even gonna answer that." His brother turned to Everly. "Hey. I'm Rhett. Ty's older and much better-looking brother."

"I know who you are. We briefly met the other night." And she clearly wasn't impressed. "I'd better head down to Jessa's house." She flipped her long brown hair over her shoulder when she spun away from them. "See you tonight at the auction, gentlemen. I'm looking forward to it."

Rhett's eyes followed Everly all the way to the barn. "Too bad she's married."

Ty laughed. "Don't let her husband hear you say that." Mateo wouldn't hesitate to put Rhett in his place. "So what're you doing here?"

Rhett zipped up his coat. "We ran into Levi at the grocery store. I may have mentioned how bored I was and he offered to let us take out his snowmobiles for a few hours."

Rhett wanted to take out the snowmobiles? Together? "Why?"

"Like I said, I'm bored as hell hanging out with Mom and Dad. And we need some bro time."

"Bro time?" They hadn't had bro time for years. Call him crazy, but they'd sailed way past brother bonding activities. Besides that: "The auction starts in two and a half hours." Darla would have his head if they weren't there on time.

"So?" His brother mocked him with a wry grin. "What're you planning to do? Go to the spa and get your nails done first?" He whacked Ty's shoulder. "Come on. We'll go out for an hour and still have plenty of time for you to get all pretty for tonight. Not that it'll help. I'm still gonna kick your ass with the bidding."

"Actually, a snowmobile trip sounds great." Maybe he'd leave Rhett on the side of the mountain...

"I knew you wouldn't be able to pass it up. Levi said they're in the outbuilding behind the barn." His brother slung an arm around Ty's shoulders and started walking. "This is gonna be great."

"Yeah." A whole hour alone with his brother. At least they wouldn't have to talk much.

"Darla sure left in a hurry this morning," his brother commented casually as they slipped inside the outbuilding.

"She was running late." He wasn't about to share any details for what had gone down between them in his room after Rhett had gone on and on about the dangers of his career. Why did his brother think everyone always wanted to hear his opinion?

"What'd she have going on in Glenwood Springs?" his brother asked, pulling two helmets off a nearby shelf.

"She had an appointment." Likely with her support group, though she hadn't mentioned it to him. According to her he wasn't supposed to care what she did, but that was proving to be easier said than done. Especially after his conversation with Everly. *Can things really go back to the way they were?* He'd best not answer that. "So how're you liking Topaz Falls?" he asked to steer the subject away from Darla.

"I like it here." Rhett raised the outbuilding's garage door so they could drive the sleds into the snow. "It's a great town. Not a lot of excitement, but you can always go to Denver if you want some nightlife."

"Yeah." Ty rarely made the trip down there. He preferred the mountains. The space. The down-to-earth vibe. "This is a good place. Good people." Out of all the places he'd been it reminded him the most of his hometown. He never thought he'd miss Montana, but getting older had a way of making you nostalgic.

"Gotta admit, when I heard you were putting down roots, I was surprised." His brother strapped on one of the helmets. "But I can see why you like it here. Hell, I could see myself living in a place like this after I retire from football."

That set off all of Ty's internal warning sirens. Rhett coming to Topaz Falls? Heck no. This town wasn't big enough for the both of them. "Retirement has to be what? Another five years or so?" That might be stretching it, but a guy could hope.

"I don't know, man." His brother climbed onto one of the sleds. "The injuries are getting tougher to deal with."

"But you'll come back. You always have." Rhett had been lucky to only have a few minor injuries before the ACL tear. "A few more months, you'll be as good as new." And he'd continue on with his life the way it was—partying in Dallas, far away from Topaz Falls.

"We'll see," his brother said, a little too cryptically for comfort. "An injury's not gonna slow me down today though. I'll kick your ass up that mountain." He moved the goggles from the top of the helmet over his eyes.

Looked like it was go time. Ty put on his own helmet and climbed onto the other sled. "One hour, max," he called to his brother, but Rhett had already started the engine.

"Take it easy out th—" Without heeding the warning, Rhett cranked the throttle and flew out of the garage, disappearing from sight.

Ty got the engine on his sled started and took off after him. He should've known that's how this was gonna go. Rhett didn't want bro time. He wanted to make him look like a dumbass. It had been, what, twenty-four hours since he'd insulted him last? He was probably going through withdrawals.

Ty coasted past the corrals and pushed his speed across the flat meadow, following the tracks Rhett's sled had cut into the freshly fallen snow. Further ahead, he spotted his brother, stopped and waiting for him at the edge of the woods. Back when they were kids, they'd gone snowmobiling all the time in the mountains, and Ty went out with Lance and Levi all the time, but it had likely been a while for his brother. "Watch the trees," he yelled as he approached Rhett.

"I know how to drive these things," his brother yelled back. "You're the one who's driving like Grandma Betty."

"I'd rather not wreck my friend's sled," Ty ground out. "So let's take it easy up the mountain." All he saw was a grin on his brother's face before Rhett took off again, weaving in and around the trees like they were on some crazy obstacle course. Once again, he followed his brother, dodging the massive pine trees and cranking the throttle in an effort to keep up.

Fresh powder sprayed into the face shield of his helmet and speed blurred everything. The fast pound of his heart stoked the adrenaline rush, heightening it until he felt like he was flying. An embankment came into view up ahead and Ty saw his opportunity to pass Rhett if he made his move now. Gunning the engine, he came at the embankment at an angle and shot past his brother's sled, catching some air as he came over the top. When looked back to gloat, Rhett's sled sped up and swerved in to cut him off. Ty cranked the handlebars to avoid a collision and went barreling into a wind-whipped snowbank. The engine stalled out, and Ty flew off to the side, landing on his back with a thud.

Rhett drove his sled up next to him and pulled off his helmet. "Sweet wipeout, man. Told you you drive like Grandma Betty."

Ty scrambled off the ground, red-hot molten anger

erupting inside of him. He'd had enough of his brother's shit. "You cut me off," he accused, blocking Rhett from driving away. "I had you beat and then you cut me off."

"Quit whining." Rhett plunked his helmet back onto his head. "It's no big deal. You're fine."

"I'm fine, but the damn sled is stalled." It likely had snow all the way up the tailpipe. "There's no way it'll run." He walked over and tried to start it a few times, but it wouldn't even turn over. "This is so typical." He marched back to his brother. "You always have to be better than me. Faster. Stronger. More popular. And you know what? You're already all of those things. So you can stop trying."

His brother got off the sled. "What the hell are you talking about?"

"You know what I'm talking about." Ty moved to get in his face. "Mom and Dad have been to almost every game you've ever played. And they've never seen me compete once. You've always demanded their attention. Everyone's attention. And now look at you. You're a famous football player. So why can't you leave me alone?"

Rhett shook his head, his eyes dangerously narrow. "You think Mom and Dad didn't come watch you compete because they like me better?"

"I think it's because you've always demanded their attention. It's always been a competition. I gave up a long time ago."

"If that's really how you feel, then why did you invite me out here? You could've found another celebrity. Someone you like better." He'd heard that warning growl in Rhett's voice before, but he wouldn't let it stop him.

"Oh trust me. I would've, but Darla's the one who made me invite you. She thought a football player would bring in the most cash." Even as he said it, he knew he'd likely just blown that. They could lose all the extra money they'd get for having Rhett Forrester there. But he couldn't make himself care. "As far as I'm concerned, you can go on back to Dallas."

He expected a retaliation, but instead, Rhett turned his back and stomped through the snow. His brother climbed onto the working snowmobile and took off, leaving Ty there to fend for himself.

Chapter Sixteen

The show must go on. For the last ten years, Darla had lived by that philosophy. Somewhere along the way, the show had become her reality, but she didn't know how much longer she could play a part. Not with a baby coming.

A strange anticipatory sensation sent her heart seesawing again—soaring with a breathtaking exhilaration and then crashing back down into a space of raw cold fear.

All around her, cowboys milled about, preparing for their moments up on the stage, but Darla felt like she'd been transported into her own world, someplace foreign and removed. Isolated. Separated by the secret she carried.

She'd gathered everyone into the backroom of the banquet hall at the rodeo grounds, and she was supposed to be running things—getting everyone organized, giving out instructions—but she couldn't seem to think clearly. Her hand rested on the low bulge of her abdomen. The one she'd blamed on too much chocolate. A baby. What would that look like? Her being a mom? Ty being a father? Their already tangled relationship?

"You okay?" Everly placed a hand on her shoulder, bringing Darla back to the room, back to the show.

"Of course." She quickly dropped her arm to her side. "Just thinking through the details." If only she could tell her friend the truth. But she couldn't risk anyone finding out while Ty's family was in town. She was supposed to break up with him tomorrow.

"Where are Ty and Rhett?" Everly had offered to help keep things moving behind the scenes while Darla MC'd the event. Her friend glanced at her clipboard. "They're the only two we're missing."

"They should be here." Though she had no idea how she would face Ty when she had to keep something like this from him. That was why she hadn't exactly gone looking for him.

"Well, the seats are getting full out there. We'll have to get started in about twenty minutes," Everly reminded her. "I saw them out at the Cortez place earlier this afternoon, and they said they'd be here."

"They have to be here somewhere." Ty wouldn't be late. He wouldn't let Rhett be late. Darla shook off the worry building in her stomach. "Let me see if I can find out where they are." She hurried to the main banquet hall where the crowd was filling in seats. Some of their friends had clustered in the back of the room near the doors. She headed right for them, determined to stay business-like. "Have any of you seen Ty and Rhett?" she asked, trying not to sound frantic. This was a problem. Rhett was supposed to be their main attraction. Based on the number of young, decked-out females packing the room, he *was* the attraction.

That was what had her hands shaking. Not the fact that Ty hadn't called to tell her he'd be late. Not the fact that he was usually so reliable, almost always punctual. He'd always followed through on his promises.

"I haven't seen them recently, but I think they took the snowmobiles out a few hours ago," Levi said.

"A few hours ago?" Why would Ty decide to go snowmobiling right before a huge event like this? Had something happened to him? Every winter she saw plenty of news stories about snowmobilers who were killed in avalanches. "What were they thinking?"

Levi shrugged like it was no big deal. "I ran into Rhett at the store. He asked if they could go for a ride this afternoon."

"And you told him yes?" Darla demanded. The sudden anxiety fueled an absurd anger. As if this was all Levi's fault. But she couldn't seem to rein in her emotions. "Knowing the auction was tonight?"

He glanced around the room. "I figured they'd be back by now. They should be back by now. It's not a good idea to be tearing around the backcountry on a snowmobile after dark."

This time the fear caught in her throat. Before anyone could notice the trembling in her hands, Darla whirled away from them. "If you see Ty or Rhett anywhere, tell them they'd better get their asses into that back room." She marched to the door, trying to drown out the worst-case scenarios by focusing on the details. In twenty minutes she had to get up on that stage and somehow hold herself together. She didn't have time to worry about Ty. To think about how he might've crashed somewhere on the mountain. No, no, no. She wandered back into the prep room feeling light-headed.

"Ty and Rhett went snowmobiling," she informed Everly. A scowl pinched at her mouth, but it was only there to cover up the nauseating drum of her heart. They'd left a few hours ago. It had been dark for at least a half hour. Anything could've happened to them out there—they could've crashed. Or there could've been an avalanche...

"I'm sure they're okay," Everly said as though she detected the concern Darla was trying so hard to hide. "They probably lost track of time."

"That's my guess." More like that was her hope. And yet the anxiety gained momentum, squeezing her heart. "Maybe we should tell Dev to send out a search party." Just in case. In case Ty was hurt...

"Let's give it a few more minutes." Everly checked her watch. "I'm sure they'll be here any time now."

"Right. They'll be here in a few minutes." Tears welling in her eyes, Darla brushed past her. "I'm going to the bathroom to freshen up. Be right back." She weaved through the assortment of cowboys without really seeing any of them. Finally, she escaped into the bathroom just as her face broke out into a sweat. *Breathe.* She inhaled deeply against the rising panic, but her stomach lurched, sending her to the toilet where she threw up.

"I knew you weren't okay." Everly stepped into the stall, concern rounding her eyes. "You're sick. You should go home and rest. We can take over."

Darla stood and leaned her back against the stall, her knees threatening to give. "I'm not sick." Tears sliced through her vision. "I'm pregnant."

Everly gasped. "Pregnant?" Her eyes widened. "Oh god, I feel so selfish. Here I've just been talking about myself—my baby—and you're pregnant too! We're pregnant together!" She hugged her arms around Darla's neck, but that only made Darla cry harder.

"I just found out," she blubbered. "I think I'm still in shock."

Everly led her out of the stall and they sat on the small bench by the door. "Ty's the father, right?"

"Yes, but he doesn't know. And you can't tell him. *I* can't tell him. Not yet. Not until his parents leave."

"Why not?" Her friend squeezed her hands tight. "They'll be ecstatic. So will Ty. I know he will. He loves kids. He's always so good with them at the rodeos."

"But we're not together. In fact, I told him last night that we should stage a breakup." They had to. She couldn't keep spending time with him. Especially knowing about the baby. How in the world would she be able to keep that from him?

"How are you going to break up?" Everly looked almost as disappointed as Ty had.

"His family is supposed to come to the bar tomorrow. That's why I asked you to cater the lunch." She hadn't given much detail when she'd texted Everly the order. "We're going to tell them then. We'll say things aren't working between us anymore." Something told her the whole thing wouldn't be nearly as simple as she made it sound. "I don't want his parents to know about the baby until he and I have sorted everything out." That could be a while. She didn't even know where to start. "After they leave, I'll tell him and we can decide what to do before we have to tell everyone else." They could come up with a plan.

"What do you want to do?" Everly asked carefully.

Darla didn't even hesitate. "I'm having the baby." Saying it out loud was terrifying in the best possible way. "I never thought I'd have the chance, and there's nothing

I want more." She might not have everything figured out, but she was already in love with this baby.

Everly gave another excited squeal. "I know things are a little complicated, but I'm so happy for you. You'll be such a great mom, Darla. That is one lucky baby."

"Really?" She sniffled. At some point you'd think she'd run out of tears, but that didn't seem to be happening yet. "You think so?"

"Your heart is gold. Look at you. Everything you're doing for us. Putting this event together, raising all of this money while you get nothing out of it. And you've overcome so much. That compassion and strength is all you need to raise a child."

Strength? Darla slumped against the wall. She obviously had Everly fooled. "I'm not strong." The hoarse whisper ached in her throat. "It's been ten years since Gray died, and I'm still scared." She turned her face to Everly's, letting her see all of it. "I'm so worried about Ty right now. I know it sounds crazy, but I'm sick with worry. That he's hurt. Or…dead." God, she hated hearing herself say those words. They were so weak. And yet she was helpless against the panic. It devoured her. She felt far more for him than was safe, and it was wrecking her.

"It doesn't sound crazy." Everly steadied Darla's shaky hands. "I know how much you care about him. I sent Mateo out to find him, and everything'll be okay." Her friend pulled her into a hug and smoothed Darla's hair the way a mother would for a child. "Everything'll be okay," she murmured over and over.

Darla wanted so much to believe her, but she didn't know how.

* * *

Oh boy. He was in for it. Ty watched Mateo's truck speed straight for the corral fences at the Cortez Ranch. He'd finally finished up fixing the snowmobile and had left both of the sleds in the outbuilding as good as new. But he was late. Very late.

His friend jumped out of the truck sporting a grim frown. "Dude, where have you been?"

"It's a long story." Ty walked over to meet him. "And not a great one." He'd rather not recount what had happened between him and his brother.

"Did you forget about the auction?" his friend asked. "You were supposed to be there over an hour ago."

And he would have been there on time if Rhett hadn't abandoned him out in the woods. "I didn't forget. Levi's snowmobile stalled way out at the base of Topaz Mountain and Rhett took off, so I had to walk back."

The explanation didn't change Mateo's cloudy expression. "Trust me. Darla is not happy you didn't show."

"I figured Rhett would tell her what happened." At first, he'd been worried his brother might skip town, but that wasn't Rhett. He liked the attention too much, and he knew the spotlight would be on him tonight. He'd definitely make it a point to be at the auction. Or at least that was what Ty had assumed.

"Rhett didn't show either," his friend informed him.

"That's great." The heavy weight of guilt sunk his heart. His brother must've skipped the auction because of what Ty had said to him. He started to head to his truck, which was parked on the other side of the barn. "I'll go find him."

"There's no time," Mateo called behind him. "The auction already started. Everly sent me out to find you. I just got a text from her and she said Darla is worried sick."

That stopped Ty in his tracks. "Like I said, I figured Rhett would tell her I was going to be late." It was the least his brother could do after making him walk a good four miles back to the ranch.

"Well since he didn't show up, no one told her you were going to be late."

Ty swallowed another heaping tablespoon of guilt. Damn. He'd messed everything up. He glanced at his watch. If the auction was starting, they had plenty of other cowboys to sell off. "I should go home and clean up." No one in their right mind would bid on him looking like this. "That'll give me a chance to find Rhett too."

"Nope. I have strict instructions to bring you straight to the auction." Mateo opened his truck's passenger door. "You can text Rhett on the way over. Tell him he'd better get his ass over there if he knows what's good for him. Darla will find a way to make him regret it if he doesn't."

"Fine." Ty was too exhausted and freezing to argue. He climbed into the truck, which was nice and toasty, and pushed the toes of his boots up against the floor heater. With any luck, his feet would thaw out before he had to walk on the stage so he could somehow make this up to Darla. And everyone else who'd been counting on him. He looked down at his wet jeans and his wrinkled coat. He'd have to get real creative in finding ways to bring in the bids...

Mateo climbed in next to him, already on the phone. "Is she okay?" he asked, flicking the gear into reverse.

Ty tuned in and tried to listen to the conversation, but there was a long pause. "Is who okay?" he finally asked. Were they talking about Darla?

Mateo shushed him with a wave of his hand. "Right. Okay. Got it. I'll have him there in ten minutes."

"What's up?" Based on Mateo's dark expression, it wasn't anything good.

"I guess Darla wasn't feeling well. Everly said they'd been in the bathroom for the last thirty minutes, but now Darla's up on the stage running the show."

"Not feeling well how?" He didn't like how often Darla seemed to be sick lately. Something wasn't right.

"She threw up. That's all I know." His friend grimaced like he'd rather not know. "After losing her husband the way she did, I'd guess she worries a lot."

"Yeah." He'd figured that out this morning when she'd told him she could never be with him because of what he did for a living. "I tried to call her but I couldn't get service out there." He'd make it up to her though. "I have to text Rhett." Not only had he failed to put Darla's mind at ease, he'd also run off his brother—the auction's main draw—and Darla would be the one to take the heat if Rhett didn't show.

He fired off a quick text.

Hey, sorry about what I said earlier. We still need you at the auction. You don't have to come for me. Do it for Darla.

Satisfied, he pulled off the stocking cap he'd been wearing for a good four hours and messed with his hair, trying to smooth it down. "Not sure who's gonna bid on me looking like this."

"Ginny Eckles?" Mateo guessed.

"That'd be fine by me. At least she'd know better than to get any fancy ideas about the two of us hooking up."

When they arrived at the rodeo grounds, Mateo parked the truck at the edge of the packed parking lot, and they both jogged to the entrance. Once inside, Ty peeled off his snowy coat and tossed it onto a nearby coatrack. He undid his belt and the button fly of his jeans so he could tuck in his shirt as they walked to the main banquet hall. Outside the doors he could hear Darla speaking into the microphone. He peered inside and saw his buddy Jake Phillips from Oklahoma parading around the stage all decked out in a suit and a Christmas tie like he was part of some pageant. Ty recognized the Santa hat Jake was wearing from his own calendar shoot.

"She did a great job decking the place out." Mateo nodded toward Darla, who stood off to the side of a few intricately decorated Christmas trees. White lights and glittery snowflakes hung down from the ceiling, giving the whole stage a surreal glow.

"It looks amazing," Ty murmured. *She* looked amazing.

"So we've got Jake 'Wild Man' Phillips going for two thousand dollars," Darla said, sweeping out her arm. "Going once...going twice..." She waited but no other bids came forward. "Sold to this fine young woman in the front row!"

The mostly female crowd cheered and whooped. Jake, who was no stranger to attention, swaggered down the steps and gave the brunette who'd won him a flashy kiss.

"Aww. It's a match made in Heaven," Darla purred into the microphone. She sure didn't seem upset. She stood up there wearing that sexy smile of hers, her black hair shining under the lights. The sight of her legs in that soft tan suede skirt and those tall thigh-high boots nearly brought him to his knees.

"Damn," Mateo muttered beside him. "Jake went for two thousand dollars? Wonder what I'd go for?"

"You're lucky you don't have to find out," Ty muttered

back. He was dreading this. What if he stood up there and no one wanted to bid on him? Surely most of the women were waiting for Rhett to appear. They'd likely save all their pennies trying to win his brother. If Rhett decided to make an appearance, that was.

Darla gave off a whistle to quiet the rowdy crowd noise. "We're going to take a short intermission, and when we come back, we'll have the remaining cowboys ready to auction. Trust me, ladies. You won't want to miss them." She teased the crowd with a wink.

"Come on." Mateo tugged on his shoulder. "We'd better get you back to the staging room." They walked briskly down the hall and veered into a smaller room near the end.

"There you are!" Everly came blitzing over from across the room. "Oh geez, Ty. Look at you. You're a mess."

"Yeah. Sorry about that. I ran into some car trouble." Snowmobile trouble. Brother trouble. Whatever you wanted to call it. This whole day had been trouble from start to finish. He had a feeling it wasn't about to get better.

"Well at least you're not dead somewhere," Everly whispered. "Poor Darla was so worried. But you didn't hear that from me."

"Actually, I heard it from Mateo first." And guilt had sat like a hunk of metal in his gut ever since.

"Well you can't say a word to her." Everly's narrowed eyes were likely supposed to look stern, but they sparkled too much for that. "Got it? As far as you know, she's been great. No problems at all."

"Right." Darla must've have asked Everly not to tell him how upset she was. Once again she wanted to shut him out.

"Here she comes." Everly shot a desperate look over Ty's shoulder.

"Good luck, bro," Mateo said, and they both walked away.

Ty watched Darla cross the room. She looked like a woman on a mission, but once her eyes landed on him, she stopped cold.

Before she could turn her back to him, he hurried over. "I'm sorry," he said, making sure his eyes told her he meant it. "The snowmobile stalled and I didn't have cell service."

"It's no big deal." For some reason, Darla seemed to be having trouble looking him in the eyes.

"Are you ready to go onstage?" she asked, giving his attire a critical once-over.

"As ready as I'm gonna be." He was glad he looked like he'd just spent the week winter camping. Maybe no one would bid on him and he'd get out of this whole thing. There was only one woman he wanted to be with, and she'd already shut him out.

"Where's your brother?" Darla scanned the room.

He really wished he had an answer for her. "I'm not sure he's coming."

"You can't be serious." According to her tone, he'd better not be serious.

"We got into a fight. I said some things I probably shouldn't have." Things he'd wanted to say for years, but there could have been a better time and place.

Darla finally met his eyes. "I've seen how he treats you, so I understand. But you couldn't have waited one more day to tell him off? This is going to be a disaster."

As the one who had to be onstage, it would make Darla look bad. "I can go find him—"

"Hey, let's get this party started." His brother paraded into the room—with impeccable timing, as usual. It seemed he'd had plenty of time to shower and spruce himself up too.

"Over here," Ty called. He'd never been so glad to see his brother. Except for maybe the time the school bully had started following him home in fifth grade. One look at his football player brother and the kid had taken off.

"You look worried," Rhett said to Darla in a charming voice. "Did you really think I wouldn't show?"

"Of course not." Her smile seemed forced. "I wasn't worried at all. I knew you'd both show up and everything would work out."

Ty might've believed her if Everly hadn't told him the truth.

"Here." Darla threw some silver tinsel at them. "Make yourselves look a little more festive."

"You ready for this?" Rhett asked, wrapping the tinsel around his neck like a scarf with that cutthroat gleam in his eyes.

He was obviously trying to bait Ty into another war. This time though, he wouldn't let his brother's drive for competition pull him in. He'd had enough rivalry for one day. "Sure I'm ready." He draped the tinsel over his shoulders. "Let the bidding war began."

Chapter Seventeen

Wow. Pregnancy was really messing with her. Darla had never experienced conflicting emotions quite this extreme. How could she want to throw her arms around Ty while at the same time wanting to smack him? This emotional roller coaster was new territory for her.

Some internal thermostat suddenly kicked on, sending a rush of heat flowing through her. She didn't have time for emotions right now. She had to get these two up on that stage and auction them off to the highest bidder. "All right. Here's the deal." She looked down at the notes on her clipboard. "Ty will go first." She fully expected Ginny to offer a decent amount of money to spend the evening ogling Ty. "Then I'll call Rhett up—"

"Why can't we go up together?" Rhett interrupted. "Make it more of a bidding war between the two of us?"

"A bidding war?" That definitely wasn't in the script.

"Yeah." If it was possible, Rhett's grin turned even cockier. "Bring us both up onstage at the same time. Let the women go crazy. It'll be fun. I bet you'll raise a heck of a lot more money that way."

Darla could only glare at him. Let the women go crazy? He thought Ty was engaged. Sure they were on the verge of a breakup, but—for appearances—they were still engaged. "I don't know..."

"Let's do it." Ty locked his gaze on his brother. "I'm up for whatever makes this thing move faster. Let's get it over with."

That sounded good to her. Get it over with. Then she could go home and deal with her emotions alone. "Fine. But you two know you can't start throwing punches, right?" Maybe she should bring Maureen up on the stage too. That way their mom could keep them in line.

"We won't throw punches," Rhett assured her. "We'll let the ladies decide who the best man is."

Oh yeah. There was some serious tension sitting between those two. She was dying to ask Ty what happened out on that mountain, but the audience was waiting. "I'm game as long as you promise to behave yourselves."

They were glaring at each other, but they both nodded, so she went with it. "Okay, I'll do all the talking. You just—"

"The crowd is getting wild in there," Everly reported from a few feet away. "You'd best get going."

"Right." Darla reorganized her notes and led Ty and his brother out into the hall.

The three of them silently made their way to the banquet room. The second they walked in the whole space erupted in applause. Women whooped and catcalled while Rhett strutted his stuff all the way up the stage steps.

Oh brother. No wonder Rhett got to Ty so much. He was downright obnoxious. So opposite to Ty, who had this humble authenticity about him. She couldn't be annoyed with Rhett though. He was why most of these women had come. And if he wanted to play himself up, she'd let him. His bravado would likely bring in more money for Mateo and Everly.

Darla followed Ty up to the stage and grabbed the mic. "All right ladies. We have two more cowboys available for bidding tonight. Ty 'the Wanted' Forrester and Rhett 'the Outlaw' Forrester."

"Do we get a package deal?" a woman in the second row yelled out.

"Nope. Sorry. Each cowboy will be bid on individually." Darla sought out Ginny Eckles, who was sitting near the back of the room. "Being the competitors they are, they want the best man to win, so they're going head to head in a battle for the highest bid." She waited for the incessant cheering to die down before she continued. "We'll start the bidding at a hundred dollars. When you make your bid, call out the dollar amount and the name of the cowboy you want and we'll go from there."

"Five hundred dollars on Rhett Forrester," a woman called from somewhere in the middle of the room.

"I've got a thousand," countered another woman seated on the left side.

"Okay. A thousand dollars on Rhett." Darla squinted out at the crowd. "What about Ty Forrester?" She glanced in Ginny Eckles's direction.

"Fifteen hundred for Ty," the woman called, holding up a wad of cash like this was a strip club.

"Ohhhh." Darla played that up. "Fifteen hundred, huh? It seems Ty is currently in the lead."

Rhett snatched the mic out of her hands. "Come on, ladies. I know we can do better for Mateo and Everly.

I promise to show you a real good time. I'll make it worth your while." He handed the mic back to Darla and inched up his shirtsleeve, rolling it until his massive biceps showed. "There's more where that came from," he called, flexing.

"Yeah baby!"

"Work it!"

Not caring who saw, Darla rolled her eyes.

"Two thousand dollars for Rhett," a blonde called from the back.

"That's more like it," Ty's brother mumbled. He was doing all he could to draw attention to himself. In contrast, Ty simply stood off to the side watching it all unfold. "Okay, we've got fifteen hundred for Ty and two thousand for Rhett—"

"Three!" A middle-aged woman yelled from the front row. "Three thousand for Rhett!"

Wow. This seemed to be working. "Three thousand—"

"Six thousand dollars."

A collective gasp silenced the room.

Even Darla had to give off a low whistle. That was three times more than any of the other bids all night. "All righty, folks. We have a bid on Rhett for six—"

"Not on Rhett," the woman sitting on the side aisle interrupted. "I want the other one. I'd like to place my bid on Ty Forrester. Six thousand dollars."

Darla whipped her head to gauge Ty's reaction. He looked just as dumbfounded as the rest of the room.

Who was she? Darla squinted, but it was hard to see much with all of the bright lights shining in her eyes. "Um. Wow." She'd forgotten to bring the mic back to her mouth. She quickly raised it so the audience could hear her. "Okay. Six thousand on Ty Forrester. Going once..."

She frantically scanned the room. No one moved. "Going twice..." Darla sent what she hoped was a subtle plea to Ginny Eckles, who was on the edge of her seat.

In response, Ginny shook her head and raised her hands in surrender. She was out.

Some rogue emotion that might have a distant relation to jealousy formed a tight knot in her throat, but Darla put on her biggest, brightest smile and let the announcement rip. "Sold to that woman right there." The gorgeous young brunette stood and waved.

"What about me?" Rhett demanded.

"My offer for three grand is still on the table," the middle-aged woman reminded them.

"Seriously?" Ty's brother walked to the edge of the stage. "Come on, ladies. We can do better than three grand."

No one else seemed to agree. The audience sat there awkwardly quiet, and Darla had no choice but to end everyone's misery. "Okay. Three thousand for Rhett Forrester. Going once..."

Rhett paced across the stage, obviously trying to work some kind of magic, but this time his showmanship didn't help him out.

"Going twice..." Darla only let a few beats pass before she ended it. "Sold to that lovely woman right there for three thousand dollars."

"Woo-hoo!" The woman bounced up and down, clapping her hands.

"Okay, well I guess that does it," Darla said into the mic. "Thank you all for coming." Her eyes landed on Ty's very generous bidder again. She was definitely younger than Darla. A lot younger. And beautiful. Did Ty know her?

She realized the audience was waiting for their dismissal,

so she put a quick end to the evening. "Winners, you can pay your donation to my friends Dev and Charity at the back of the room. Merry Christmas, everyone! We hope to see you all at the gala after the rodeo!" She quickly switched off the mic.

The crowd got to their feet and started to make their way to the exit, but Darla walked straight over to where Ty stood on the side of the stage. "Six thousand dollars? What was that about?" she asked, trying to sound curious instead of possessive. It shouldn't bother her. He was free to go out with whomever he wanted.

Ty gave her a wide-eyed shrug. "I have no idea."

"I know what that was about," his brother grumbled.

The woman who'd won Ty was headed their way, and suddenly Rhett looked like he wanted to crawl under the table next to them.

The woman flounced up the steps to join them all right there on the stage. "Hiya, Rhett. How are you?"

He definitely avoided any kind of eye contact with her. "I'm good. How are you, Sierra?"

"Great," she chirped with a flip of her long hair. "I'm really looking forward to my date tonight." She shifted her teasing gaze to Ty before glaring at Rhett again. "You really shouldn't have left my hotel room without a good-bye this morning. And no phone call?" Her lips formed a disappointed frown. "Obviously you're not the man I thought you were."

Ohhhh. Darla almost laughed. Now it all made sense. The woman had been on a mission to publicly humiliate Rhett.

"So I forgot to call," Ty's brother whined. "You didn't have to go and spend six grand on my brother."

"He seems like the kind of guy who'll call the next

day." The woman—Sierra—gave Ty a nice, long appraisal. "Oh, and I may have let word get out to the others about what kind of guy you really are," she said in an overly guilty tenor. "Most of them prefer a decent cowboy."

So she'd gone and told the other women not to bid on Rhett either. Darla had to hand it to her. She was cold.

"He's engaged," Rhett shot back. "Did you know that? Ty is actually engaged to Darla here."

"Oh, how nice." Sierra turned her calculating gaze on Darla and then back to Ty. "When's the wedding?"

"Uh…"

Ty didn't seem to know what to say, so Darla jumped in. "We're not sure yet."

"Perfect." Miss Six Grand wrapped her arm through Ty's. "I guess we'll be off on our date then." She tugged him down the steps. "Y'all have a lovely night. We sure will."

Darla watched them walk away. Ty glanced back at her with desperation on his face, but there was nothing either of them could do about it. No matter how much Darla wanted to chase them down and give that woman hell, she'd won Ty fair and square.

"Wow." Rhett moved to stand next to Darla. "She's a piece of work, huh?"

That was one way to describe it. Though she couldn't blame the woman for wanting to publicly humiliate him. "Did you tell her you would call today?" she asked Rhett pointedly.

His silence told her everything.

"Then it's your own fault, buddy." In her estimation, Sierra and Rhett were a great fit. "What'd you think she meant by *perfect* after I told her we don't have a date for the wedding?"

"Based on the little I know about her from last night, I'd say other people's fiancées aren't exactly off-limits." Rhett seemed to brush it off. "But you can trust Ty. He won't cheat on you."

Maybe not if they were really together, but they weren't. He was free to do whatever he wanted with whichever woman he chose. She should've been glad it ended up this way. She'd wanted space from Ty, especially with the baby news, but...

Nope. But nothing. This was a good thing. Maybe Miss Six Grand would make Ty forget about his feelings for her. He could fall in love with someone who wasn't afraid to love him back, and then he and Darla could simply raise the baby together as friends. For some reason that thought brought her zero comfort.

Next to her, Rhett heaved a disgruntled sigh. "I guess I'd better go face the music and find my date."

"Good luck." She managed to muster some sympathy for him. Something about the way he'd looked at Sierra had hinted he'd rather be spending the evening with her. Darla could relate. Was it just last night she'd been on the couch with Ty? He'd made her that tea, and she'd felt warm and safe up against him. And the sex...it had been so much more than a physical release. It had been intimate and wonderful. She'd woken up so happy. Happy never lasted long though. Fear always managed to overtake it.

She'd gone back and found the article Rhett had mentioned at breakfast. She'd read about Blane's wife and the two young children he'd left behind. She'd stared at the family picture that accompanied the article for a long time. "I don't know what I'm going to do without him," his wife was quoted as saying. Darla knew that feeling. She knew and she couldn't go there again. Before the tears could start, Darla walked briskly down the stage steps. She had to clean up and make sure all the money had been collected and—

"Wow! That was a huge success." Everly caught up to her at the door. "I can't believe how much money you raised."

"Not me. All of us." She owed Ty. Not only for getting up on the stage even though he didn't want to, but also for organizing and convincing all of the cowboys to help out. "Ty deserves most of the credit." Figuring out the details was easy. He'd done the hard work. He'd convinced his colleagues to participate. He'd brought his family out, even though that wasn't how he'd wanted to spend Christmas.

"Speaking of Ty, do you know anything about the woman who bid on him?"

"Only that she had a one-night stand with Rhett. And she's gorgeous." And flirtatious. And bold. "She sure didn't seem to think his engagement was an issue."

Concern filled Everly's eyes. "Yeah, I overhead someone talking about her. It sounds like she's a rodeo queen from Steamboat Springs. Her dad owns some huge, profitable ranch out there. Along with half the town. She's probably used to getting what she wants."

Well she'd sure seemed to want Ty. And something told Darla Sierra could be very persuasive when she wanted to be. This conversation was not helping the small jealousy issue she was having. It might help if she saw them together. Then she could get a read on how Ty really felt about the woman. "Hey, do you feel like going over to the Tumble Inn after we're done here?" she asked Everly innocently.

"Why?" Based on her friend's amusement, Everly already knew why.

Darla continued to play dumb. "Just for a drink. I'm dying for some ginger ale."

"You? Ginger ale?" Everly gave her a look.

"Fine. I want to spy on them," Darla admitted. "I want to see what Miss Six Grand is up to."

"I don't think I've ever seen you jealous," her friend teased.

"I'm not *jealous*." Nope, not jealous. Just crazy. Not like she could keep that a secret. "Ty is going to be my baby's father. I think it's prudent that I find out more about potential women he might be bringing into this child's life, that's all."

That was her story and she was sticking to it.

Chapter Eighteen

Sierra DeYoung had told Ty almost nothing about herself before they'd parted ways at her car and agreed to meet at the Tumble Inn, but in that few minutes he'd walked alongside her, he had learned plenty.

She came from money, as evidenced by the bid she'd dished out to prove a point. Well, that and her shiny, brand-new Lexus SUV. She was quite a bit younger than him, based on the song she used for the ringtone on her phone—some pop number he'd never heard—which seemed to ring about every five seconds. And she was most definitely using him to get back at his brother for a botched hookup—something he wanted no part of.

And yet, she'd paid six grand to help fund Mateo and Everly's recovery and spend an evening with him, so instead of rolling past the Tumble Inn and continuing on home like he was tempted to do, he parked at the edge of the lot and waited until he saw her swerve into a spot near the doors.

By the time he walked over to her SUV, Sierra still hadn't gotten out. Instead, she sat in the driver's seat gabbing on the phone while at the same time reapplying her lipstick. He hoped that wasn't for his benefit.

He politely tapped on the window but she held up a finger and then proceeded to pull a compact out of her purse so she could powder her nose.

Ty stood back and watched. Huh. He had no idea powdering your nose was really a thing.

Sierra checked her face in the rearview mirror one more time and then slid the compact back into her purse. Still on the phone, she pushed open the door and got out of the car, giving Ty a dazzling smile that somehow both apologized for the delays and promised she'd be worth the wait. Only he wasn't waiting for anything. She was pretty, he couldn't deny that, but her whole look came off too manufactured for his taste—the styled hair, the heavy amount of makeup, the expensive clothes and car, and that horrible perfume. Once again, his thoughts drifted to Darla. Her preferred a woman who didn't have to try that hard.

"I know. It was hilarious. You should've seen it!" She switched the phone to her other ear and beckoned him to the Tumble Inn's main entrance. "I wish I would've recorded the expression on his face. I'll bet someone else did. I'll try to track down a video and send it over."

Being the gentleman that he was, Ty held the door open for her and let her go inside first. Too bad he had to follow her.

The Tumble Inn was packed, given that there weren't many other places to take your date in Topaz Falls on a Saturday night. There had to be at least half of the thirty or so bachelors they'd auctioned off tonight milling around with their dates. Darla had closed the Chocolate Therapist for the auction, so that left a choice between the country and western bar in town or one of the more intimate restaurants on Main Street. He had to admit, he was glad Sierra hadn't opted for one of those places where it would be just him and her in a quiet romantic atmosphere. Talk about awkward.

"Thanks, Suze," Sierra sang into the phone. "Make sure you tell Daddy it was money well spent. A charitable contribution, if you will. I'll talk to you soon." She clicked off the phone and dropped it into her bottomless purse. "Sorry about that. I had to talk to my finance manager about the donation."

Or about the way she'd snubbed his brother up onstage. He was surprised to realize it had bothered him to see Rhett get smeared like that. Maybe he did have a soft spot for his older brother after all. "You really went all out to make a point didn't you?" Ty asked, leading her to one of the only open tables near the bar.

"Men like Rhett need to learn a little respect." She slung her purse down on the table—it took up half the surface area—and settled herself on a stool. "I don't expect much. But I do expect a mutual consideration and respect. Your brother didn't offer either."

Ty had to grin at that. "I wouldn't say that's Rhett's strength." He took the seat across from her and signaled a waiter.

Chris, one of the younger riders in town who also moonlighted as a waiter, hurried over. "Hey Ty. What can I get you two?"

He pretty much ordered the same thing every time he came, but he gestured to Sierra. "Ladies first."

"I'll take a strawberry margarita on the rocks." She seemed to appraise Chris. In fact, she seemed to do that with every man who walked by. "Extra sugar on the rim, pretty please," she said with a bat of her eyelashes.

It took a Herculean effort for Ty not to roll his eyes. Extra sugar. Why wasn't he surprised? "I'll take a Corona."

Chris gave them a nod—and gave Sierra a grin—before disappearing.

As soon as he walked away, the woman leaned in to the table and refocused on Ty. "Your fiancée is super pretty," Sierra said. Her earnest blue eyes put a genuine stamp on the words. "I hope she knows that I'm not out to get between you two."

Would it even matter to Darla if Sierra did want to get between them? Probably not. "I doubt she's worried."

Chris swooped in and plunked down Ty's beer on the table before presenting Sierra's strawberry margarita with a bow. "Hope you enjoy," he said, backing away.

"Oh, I definitely will," she cooed.

Ty tried to hide his expression behind his beer bottle. There'd been a time he'd flirted that way too, so it wasn't like he could judge.

"How'd you know Darla was the one?" Sierra stirred the straw around her drink.

It was the natural question for her to ask, but for some reason it caught him off guard. The one. He took his time thinking through their history so he could pinpoint the exact moment he'd fallen for Darla. It didn't take long. "I knew after I kissed her."

But it hadn't been their first kiss. The first time they'd kissed they'd both had too much to drink and Ty had walked her home from a party at Lucas and Naomi's place. That time he'd kissed her once on her doorstep and they'd ended up inside, but it had been strictly physical. He'd sensed she'd needed a release as much as he had, so he hadn't hesitated to take her to bed. Those kisses hadn't reached deeper. Not like the one at the calendar photo shoot. The one that was supposed to be fake, but somehow turned into the most real expression of what he felt for her.

"We'd kissed before, but this kiss…it hit me like a shock wave." He hadn't expected the rush it had brought, especially because he'd been so irritated with Ginny. But when he'd touched his lips to Darla's everyone else—every*thing* else—faded except for her. And that was when he knew. She was the only thing that really mattered. For a few brief seconds, she'd wrapped her arms around him and it felt so right. Complete.

Ty blinked Sierra back into focus, but she was staring at something over his shoulder, her eyes narrowed. He turned around and looked toward the doors. Oh. It seemed Rhett and his date had gotten the same idea they had.

"Why would he come here?" Sierra demanded, rifling through her purse until she found her lipstick.

"There aren't many other places to go," Ty reminded her, nursing his beer while the woman desperately applied at least five coats of bright red lipstick.

"No that's not why." She stashed the makeup back into her purse. "He came to spy on us. Look, he's staring right at us."

His brother did seem to be interested in what was happening at their table, but he and his date went straight to the bar instead of heading over. "I wouldn't worry about it. He knows I'm engaged." Rhett was probably just pissed that Ty won something for once. That he'd raised more money than an NFL football player.

"We have to dance." Sierra hopped off her stool and rushed over to his side of the table.

Ty set down his beer. "Huh?"

"We have to dance." She pulled on his arm. "Right now. We have to dance."

He pulled away. "Dancing's not really my thing." Unless it was with a certain chocolatier...

Sierra went all diva on him, posting her hands on her hips and tossing her hair over her shoulder. "Darla promised us all that our dates—which we paid a ton for— would show us a good time." She grabbed his hand. "That means we dance."

Damn, Mateo owed him for this. After one more swig of beer, he allowed himself to be dragged over to the dance floor where only a few couples two-stepped to some older Garth Brooks song he'd never liked.

Trying not to scowl, Ty assumed the position—his hand very lightly on her hip and their hands clasped together. He started to move—not gracefully—but at least he could keep the beat. "Why it so important for him to see you having a good time with me?" he asked, watching Sierra watch Rhett.

"Because it'll drive him crazy." She inched herself closer to him. "The same way it drove me crazy waiting all day for him to call."

Ah. "So you like him." That's why she'd gotten flustered when Rhett walked in. It wasn't that she wanted to teach his brother a lesson. She wanted to make him jealous so he'd be interested in her again.

"I guess I do," she said angrily. "Unfortunately."

Ty two-stepped her around so she couldn't see Rhett anymore. He'd never been one for giving advice, but his current predicament had given him a fair amount of wisdom. "If you like him, why don't you just tell him?"

"I can't tell him." Sierra moved her head as though trying to see past Ty. "What if he doesn't feel the same way?"

That outcome sucked. He knew that for a fact.

"Oh no!" Sierra squealed. "He's coming over here. Rhett is coming over here."

"Well what did you expect?" Ty muttered. His brother never backed down when he was being provoked.

"I need to use the bathroom." She let go of his hand and disappeared into the crowd, leaving him to deal with Rhett by himself.

This ought to be fun.

"Are you trying to piss me off?" his brother demanded, shoulders raised, chest all puffed out. "You shouldn't be dancing with another woman like that when you're engaged."

"Try telling Sierra that." Though they hadn't done anything inappropriate. Ty had managed to keep at least a foot of space between them the entire time. "Trust me, I'm definitely not the one who's trying to piss you off." That goal belonged only to Sierra. He was simply lucky enough to find himself stuck in the middle. "I'm engaged. Remember?"

"How could I forget? That's all Mom has been talking about. The wedding and someday having grandkids. You'd better get on that, by the way. She won't be happy until you have a whole basketball team."

"Darla and I haven't talked about having kids yet." Ty took in the anger on his brother's face. So Sierra wasn't the only thing Ty had won recently. He'd also won their parents' favor, and Rhett hated it. "You can't handle that I'm the one getting attention for once."

"For once?" His brother got in his face. "What a crock. You want to know why they've never gone to watch you ride? Probably because it terrifies them, genius."

Oh, sure. Like he was supposed to believe that? His parents were ranchers—nothing terrified them. His mom had once shot at a grizzly bear in the yard to scare it away. "You play football and they're not afraid to watch you." Rhett had battled multiple injuries. He'd even had to be carted off the turf more than once.

"I get pushed around and beat up," Rhett said. "And a lot of times I do the beating up, but watching me tackle someone is a hell of a lot different than watching you get whipped around and bucked off by a bull. Every time you go out and compete there's a chance you could die in that arena." He looked at Ty, his face sober. "Football isn't like that."

Ty stood stock still, couples still dancing around them. Was his brother saying their *mom* worried about him or that *he* worried about him?

"She's always been more protective over you, being the youngest and all," Rhett continued. "And she knows she can't protect you out there. None of us can." For once his brother actually had some emotion in his voice. "Hell, I bet if Darla were honest about it, she'd say the same thing. Especially after losing her first husband and all."

The words cut into him. "Yeah. I know she worries." So much so that she wouldn't consider a real future with him. But his parents? He found it hard to believe they'd never come to one of competitions because they were worried. "I guess I've forgotten how much of a risk it is." He thought of riding like a job. Something he worked at and prepared for day in and day out, and sometimes it was easy to forget that he was competing in the most dangerous and extreme sport in the world.

"Maybe you should start thinking about it," his brother said quietly. "Especially now that you're getting married."

"Maybe I should." He'd never considered retiring early. The rodeo world was the only place he'd ever felt like he fit. It was his life—his community.

Rhett squinted at him in disbelief. "You'd think about giving it all up if Darla wanted you to?"

"Yes." The answer came straight from his gut. He didn't even have to think about it. If he thought it would make a difference, he'd make this rodeo his last ride.

"I figured you were the one who'd lucked out by finding her," his brother said. "But I guess she's pretty lucky to have you too." Before Ty could thank him for the rare compliment, Rhett eyed his date, who still stood over by the bar with her arms crossed and her right foot tapping. "I'd better get back to Kelly. Have fun with Sierra," he muttered.

Ty grabbed his shoulder before he could walk away. "I'd rather not have fun with her, and she likes you, by the way."

"Is that your idea of a joke?" His brother shook off Ty's hand. "You saw what she did to me up there. She definitely doesn't like me."

"That's why she did it." For being such a ladies' man, Rhett also seemed clueless when it came to women. "If you stop being an idiot, I'll bet you could easily make this up to her."

Sudden interest lit his brother's eyes. It seemed Rhett liked Sierra too. "Really? You think?"

"Sure. Why didn't you call her?" he asked, even though he likely knew the answer.

"You know how it is." The mask of confidence fell off his brother's face. "Can't seem too eager. You gotta play the game."

"Playing games doesn't seem to be working out for

you." Mainly because Sierra seemed to be better at it than Rhett. "Just get to know her. Don't analyze anything. Why don't you bring your date over here? The four of us can hang out. I can help distract her while you and Sierra talk."

"Seriously?" Rhett studied him as though searching for an ulterior motive, but Ty didn't have one. He simply wanted to hang out with his brother.

"Seriously. You'd better hurry up and invite your date over. She looks a little steamed."

Rhett grinned. "Sorry for leaving you out in the woods earlier. You're not so bad."

Ty smiled back. It was the closest they'd ever come to a bonding moment. "Sorry for telling you I didn't want you here," he said, reaching out for a handshake.

Rhett stared at his outstretched hand. "That was true though."

"Yeah, but I shouldn't have said it." Instead of a handshake he pulled his brother in for a man hug and gave him a noogie on the head. "And it's not true anymore. I'm actually really glad you're here."

Chapter Nineteen

Darla climbed into the front seat of Everly's SUV and let her shoulders slouch. It had been a day. Truthfully, the last ten hours had felt more like a year. Finding out she was pregnant, and then freaking out when Ty was late, and having to stand up on the stage like everything in her life was smooth sailing had scrubbed the energy clean out of her.

"Ready to go spy on Ty?" Everly asked next to her. Why was it that pregnancy seemed to give her friend a lovely glow and a charismatic energy while Darla only felt dog tired, on the verge of nausea, and a little fatter than normal? "I guess, but you might have to keep kicking me under the table so I stay awake."

"Oh I know." Her friend steered the SUV out of the nearly empty parking lot. "I'm so tired all the time. And I have to pee a lot too. Are you having that problem?"

Darla tried to think, but a fog had settled over her mind. "I don't know. I mean, I had no idea I was pregnant, so I wasn't exactly looking out for the symptoms." She'd blamed the tiredness and stomachaches on the stress of throwing together a huge event in only a few weeks.

"I know you're still in shock." Everly gave her hand a pat. "But I'm so excited. We're going to be able to go through pregnancy together! It seems less terrifying going through it with someone else."

"Definitely." Except Darla wouldn't call herself terrified. Surprised and overwhelmed for sure, but that glow in her heart could only mean it had been a desire she'd suppressed for a long time. A dream she'd let die with Gray that was now coming back to life.

Everly turned into the parking lot at the Tumble Inn. It was so crowded they had to park in the dirt overflow lot, which was covered with snow. "I'm sure it'll be hard keeping the news from Ty," her friend said as she cut the engine.

Darla inhaled a deep, silent breath. "It's not for much longer. And we're breaking up tomorrow, so I won't have to spend time with him." Or his family. The thought of hurting them made her heart ache, but it was for the best. This whole charade had already gone too far. When she told Ty about the baby, she would also tell him to make sure his parents knew they could see the baby whenever they wanted. No matter what her and Ty's relationship looked like, she would keep them involved. They would be the best grandparents.

Darla and Everly climbed out of the SUV and clung to each other as they navigated the icy parking lot. Once inside, they shed their coats and found a small table for two on the outskirts of the crowd.

"I'll go grab us a couple of ginger ales." Everly laughed. "How silly is that? Ordering two ginger ales at the bar."

Darla had to laugh too. "I guess I should start stocking ginger ale at the wine bar." It would be a long time before she'd drink wine again.

"At least we can still eat chocolate." Everly looked relieved. "I'd give up wine over chocolate any day."

"Yes." Thank God for chocolate.

Everly scurried away to the bar, which gave Darla the chance to scan the rest of the place in search of Ty. She spotted him on the dance floor, but he wasn't with Miss Six Grand. Instead, Ty was dancing with Rhett's date and Rhett was dancing with Sierra—and it looked like the two of them were getting pretty close.

Darla watched the four of them, staying near each other, occasionally chatting and laughing about something. It seemed like something had changed between him and his brother. They smiled easily at each other, and even the two women looked friendly. They looked like two couples on a double date—a fun double date with everyone enjoying themselves, and Darla had never felt more like an outsider.

"One straight-up ginger ale." Everly set down a glass in front of her and took her place on the other side of the table. She glanced over to where Darla had been staring. "He's dancing with Rhett's date."

Darla sipped her ginger ale. "Yeah. I'm guessing there's something between Rhett and Sierra after all." And being the good man that he was, Ty had decided to help out his brother.

"Have you decided how you're going to tell him about the baby yet?" Everly asked in her gentle way.

"No. I have no idea." There would be no easy way to spring that on him. It was likely the last thing he expected to hear from her. "I guess I'll meet him at a restaurant or something." If they were in public, her emotions wouldn't get away from her. She could simply tell him she was having the baby, and he could be as involved or uninvolved as he wanted. "I don't expect anything from him. Nothing has to change." She and Ty had always gotten along well. They'd been great friends, which would be good for the baby. Darla nestled her hand onto her lower stomach. It was crazy, but she swore she could feel the little peanut in there, growing and getting ready to change her whole life.

Everly quietly sipped her drink. She had something on her mind, Darla could tell, but her friend was always careful with her words. "What if he wants to be more than co-parents? What if he wants a real relationship?"

A heaviness cloaked her heart. That was something she couldn't give him. There was too much fear, too much insecurity. "He'll find it with someone else." Somehow she managed to hold off the tears. "Eventually." And she would have to be okay with that. With seeing him fall in love with another woman. Tonight she didn't have to be okay with it though. Tonight it could hurt a little. Weariness wrapped itself tightly around her temples, warning of a headache. Suddenly it seemed like a good night to wallow. She let out a long, dramatic sigh. "Ugh. I'm not feeling well. It's my stomach again. Can you take me home?"

Based on Everly's sympathetic smile, she knew exactly why Darla wanted to leave. "Of course."

They abandoned their ginger ales and walked out into the cold night, and it sure felt like she was walking away from something she desperately wanted. Staying mostly silent the whole way to her house, Darla thanked Everly with a hug when they pulled in the driveway and got out of the car. She trudged up her front walk and let herself in, feeling those sorrowful emotions rise. She used to wonder if she would ever get over missing the life she once thought she'd have, and then one day she realized she wouldn't. That sorrow would always be there, but she'd learned to soothe it with other things. Her job and her friends and, of course, chocolate. There was always chocolate.

Sighing, she slumped down to the couch and turned on another one of those romantic happy Christmas movies where everything always worked out in the end. Before she'd even made it to the first kiss-in-the-snow scene, there was a knock at her door. Being that it was almost ten o'clock, this knock was likely an urgent matter, so she dragged herself off the couch and peeked out the window.

The sight of Ty standing on her front stoop set her eyes ablaze with tears.

She hurried to the door and pulled it open. "Hey," she murmured, tugging her sweater in tighter around her shoulders. "What're you doing here so late?"

He took a minute to simply look at her, his eyes and mouth soft and tender. "I just wanted to come by and tell you nothing happened. On the date."

"Oh. Okay." Of course he did. He was thoughtful like that. Thoughtful and kind and sexy. And she could not invite him in. Darla held on to the door. "Something could've happened, you know. If you'd wanted it to. We're not really together. You don't owe me anything." He wouldn't owe her anything even when it came to the baby. Lord, it was hard to keep this secret from him. But she wasn't ready to tell him. She couldn't face his family tomorrow and break up with him if they all knew she was pregnant. It was best to wait until they could deal with it alone.

"I know we're not together." Ty's jaw tensed. "But I didn't want anything to happen with Sierra." His stare made it clear why. Because he wanted her. Only her, but she couldn't go there with him. They couldn't have this conversation again.

"Well, we're breaking up tomorrow, so then you'll be free anyway." No matter what, she couldn't let her fears hold him back.

"I won't be free," Ty said. The glow of her porch light haloed his head. "Not really. I get that we need to stop lying to my parents, so I'm fine with the breakup. But you need to know it won't change how I feel about you. You also need to know I'm not going anywhere. I understand you've lost a lot, but you won't lose me, Darla." Before she could respond, he walked away, down the sidewalk and got into his truck. Darla wrapped her arm around her middle, cradling their baby in there. She wanted so badly to let herself believe him.

* * *

Darla walked the length of the bar at the Chocolate Therapist, straightening the food that she'd had Everly cater for her lunch with the Forresters. She'd set out her fancy Christmas dishes and had decorated the bar with fresh red and white poinsettias. The food was perfect— French dip sandwiches and sweet potato fries and a huge spread of veggies with a fiery ranch dip. But the sight of it made her want to double over and throw up. Again. She'd already thrown up twice that morning. Once while she was brushing her teeth and again on the drive over to the bar. It seemed nerves didn't exactly help morning sickness.

Originally, she'd planned to call Ty this morning so they could put together a solid breakup script, but after he stopped by last night, she doubted he'd want to help write the words that would end their fake relationship. It was up to her, and she had no idea how to go about breaking all of their hearts.

It's not you, it's me. The old adage rang truer than Ty would ever know. More than anything else, she wanted his parents and brother to know the responsibility for this failed relationship rested solely on her shoulders. Her issues weren't his fault.

Outside the storefront windows, Ty's truck rolled past her bar and parked along the street. She quickly unlocked the door and watched Ty help his mom climb out of the truck. It didn't matter what day it was, Maureen always seemed to dress so festively. Today she wore a navy blue sweatshirt covered with silver snowflakes layered over a matching turtleneck. She was so motherly and nurturing—the perfect grandma for the baby. Darla rested her hand on her tummy, something that had become a habit even though she couldn't feel much yet. So many people were going to love this baby—a whole family, a whole community. She would make sure of that. Even if Robert and Maureen would be upset with her and Ty for breaking up, she didn't doubt that they would revel in their roles as grandparents.

Ty led the way inside the doors, where he greeted her with a lingering kiss.

Warmth wrapped around her, enveloping her into the safety of its glow, but she broke out of his hold to welcome his parents before she changed her mind about going through with the reason for this lunch. "So glad you could come."

"Me too." Maureen gave her a hug. "I feel like we've hardly seen you at all these last couple of days."

That was because it had been too hard to face them. Before she'd met his family, she hadn't planned on liking them so much, but the more time she spent with them, the more their quirkiness and warmth drew her in. "I know. I'm sorry. It's been crazy with the fund-raisers and all." And the pregnancy. The magnitude of her secret chipped away at her composure. Her stomach churned, making her throat burn. Uugggh. She could not throw up again.

"Thanks for lending me your fiancé last night," Rhett said, also leaning in for a quick brotherly hug. "He was surprisingly helpful as my wingman."

Yes, she'd noticed that, but she didn't say anything. Ty couldn't find out she'd been spying on him.

"Rhett here has a thing for Miss Sierra DeYoung." Ty pronounced the name with flair, earning a punch in the shoulder from his brother.

"Who's Sierra DeYoung?" their mother demanded. "And why haven't we met her?"

"I *just* met her," Rhett replied, all huffy. "We haven't achieved meet-the-parents status yet."

"Well I'd say Miss DeYoung has a thing for you too, based on how far she went to prove a point last night," Ty said.

"Oh." Their father grinned. He had the same grin as both Ty and Rhett, Darla noticed. She wondered if the baby would take after them too. She hoped so.

"That's the girl who paid six thousand for your brother." Robert whistled low. "Six grand. You could buy a brand-new steer and then some with that kind of money."

"Or you could take a trip to Hawaii," Maureen chimed in. "A whole family trip! Hey, maybe we should do that next Christmas." She turned to Darla, excitement evident in her eyes. "Wouldn't that be fun? Robert and me, you and Ty, and Rhett and Sierra?"

"Whoa." Rhett raised his hands like a shield. "I don't even know if we're going out next week, let alone next year."

Unable to face the hopefulness in Maureen's eyes, Darla stared at the floor. After the breakup, she wouldn't be going on any family trips with them.

"Well if it's not Sierra, then we'll bring whoever you're dating at the time," his mother insisted, taking off her coat and handing it to Robert. He walked over and hung it on a coatrack at the end of the bar.

"Is that beef I smell?" Ty's father eyed the spread of food, offering Darla the perfect distraction from talk of the big family Hawaii trip.

"Yes. Everly made us French dip sandwiches." She started to remove the plastic coverings from the platters Everly had arranged, but Ty swooped in and took over.

"Everyone can grab a plate," Darla said, carefully avoiding his long, steady gazes. She had to power through this lunch and do what had to be done. Then maybe she wouldn't feel so conflicted.

"I can't eat much." Rhett took a sandwich and a few veggies.

"He's taking Sierra to the restaurant up at the ski resort tonight." Ty helped himself to double the amount of food.

"What time?" Maureen asked, carefully selecting her veggies from the tray. "Maybe we'll go up there for dessert. We'd love to meet her!"

Rhett shot his brother a pained grimace.

"Yeah, probably let them get to know each other better before you and Dad ambush the poor woman." Ty gave both of his parents an affectionate smile. "Better make sure she's interested first."

"What's that supposed to mean?" Robert grumbled, already biting into his sandwich.

"We're not going to scare her away." Maureen took her plate and sat by her husband. "We're not scary, are we, Darla?"

"No." Oh lord. She was getting choked up. Man, those pregnancy hormones were powerful. "You're not scary at all," she managed. Before the tears slipped out, Darla grabbed a napkin.

"Are you okay, honey?" Maureen set down her fork and studied her. Darla made the mistake of looking the woman directly in the eyes. Something unspoken passed between them, and it was as if his mom could see what she'd tried so hard to hide.

"Um. Actually..." She darted her gaze away. *Whoa.* Heat rose to her cheeks. "Sorry." She pressed a hand into her abdomen and leaned in to the bar to inhale a deep breath.

Ty rushed to her side. "What's wrong?"

"I'm not feeling well." It wasn't like she could hide that from them all. "Sorry." She tried to stand strong. "It's my stomach."

"Your stomach?" Ty steadied his arm around her waist. "Again? Have you been to the doctor?"

"What do you mean, 'again'?" Maureen asked. She was still staring intensely at Darla, but Darla couldn't let her see. She couldn't—

"She's been sick on and off for the last few weeks," Ty told his family.

Darla wanted to shush him, but another wave of nausea crashed over her. "Um…"

"Oh, dear heavens." Maureen's stare turned into a gape and then an open-mouthed grin. "Oh!" She clasped her hands tightly together. "You're pregnant! Aren't you? I wondered. You just have this lovely glow, and I thought to myself, I wonder if she's going to have a baby. And you are!"

"Come on, Mom." Concern tinged Ty's expression. "That's crazy. Of course she's not pregnant." He turned his attention back to Darla. "Sorry. She *wishes* you were pregnant. But we're not even married yet," he called over to his parents. "So why don't you slow it down. We don't need that kind of pressure—"

"Actually." Darla tugged on his shoulder so he would look at her. It was too much. The secret. Keeping it from them on top of everything else. There had already been too many lies. She couldn't handle more. Besides that, Maureen knew.

Darla cast a wide-eyed gaze up at Ty to indicate her current level of panic. "I am. We are. Having a baby."

The room erupted around them—Maureen and Robert both hopped out of their seats.

"Wow. That's awesome." Ty's brother rushed over and gave them both hugs. "Congrats, guys. I can't wait to be an uncle."

Darla tried to smile and celebrate with them, but Ty's silence distracted her. He simply stood there and stared at her. "You're not serious." He seemed to be searching for evidence that it was all a joke.

This was not the way he was supposed to find out. In front of everyone else. "I literally just found out. Took a test." She didn't mention that it was at an urgent care center because she'd fainted. He likely wouldn't appreciate her keeping that detail from him.

"Wait a minute." Rhett steered his gaze back and forth between them. "Ty didn't even know?"

She continued to look at Ty. Only at Ty. He had to be shocked right now. "I was trying to figure out how to tell you. Without...complicating things."

"Complicating things?" Robert joined them by the bar. "Are you kidding? This is the best news I've ever heard! I'm gonna be a granddad!"

Maureen rifled through her purse, tossing out receipts and Kleenex until she found her phone. "I need to get a picture!" She shooed Rhett to the side. "Put your hands on her tummy," she instructed Ty.

Poor Ty. He hadn't even blinked.

Maureen held the camera up to her face. "Get closer. For the love of Pete, son, put your arm around your fiancée!"

He did what he was told, but his movements seemed robotic.

The flash went off at least half a dozen times, leaving Darla mostly blind.

"Oh, this is wonderful! Just wonderful!" Maureen somehow managed to wrap her arms around them both. "Wait until your grandma hears about this! She's going to be thrilled! Her first great-grandchild."

No one else seemed to notice that Ty hadn't said a word. He simply kept looking at Darla with bewilderment on his face. She had to get him out of there so she could explain everything and they could come up with a new plan.

Chapter Twenty

If the room would stop spinning for one damn minute, maybe Ty could think straight. It didn't help that his mom had trapped him and Darla in a death-grip hug.

"When are you due? Have you been to the doctor?" His mom peppered Darla with questions, not even giving her a chance to answer. "Have you seen the baby on the ultrasound yet?"

Baby. There went the spinning again. A baby? They'd gone from being on the verge of a breakup to having a baby?

"I'm so sorry." Darla politely shuffled away from his mom and grabbed his hand. "Ty and I should take a minute. I know this is all a bit of a surprise."

"It's a wonderful surprise!" His mom started to cry. "Oh, I have to call everyone back home and tell them right away."

"Sounds good! We'll only be a few minutes." Darla prodded him down the hall and all but shoved him into the back room.

The quiet brought him some sense of clarity. He looked at the woman standing across from him. "Is this part of the act?" He had to know now. Right now. Because if it wasn't . . .

"No." Tears glowed in Darla's eyes, making them even more compelling. "It's not part of the act at all. It's not even part of the plan. Remember in November when we—"

"I remember." He remembered every second of being with her. Every detail down to how it felt when he ran his fingers along the bend of her hip.

Tears slipped down her cheeks as she wrung her hands out in front of her waist. "This doesn't have to change anything though. We'll still be friends. We can be co-parents and—"

"What're you talking about?" A laugh slipped out even though emotion burned in his eyes too. "This changes everything." He gathered her hands in his. "This is amazing. A baby. We're having a baby?"

Darla nodded slowly, her expression suddenly guarded. He wanted to take her in his arms and spin her around, sweep her feet off the floor. He wanted to kiss her sense-less and then he wanted to fall on his knees and kiss that beautiful rounded part of her stomach. But the wary distance in her eyes held him off. He recognized it. This wasn't the first time he'd seen it. She didn't want him to touch her right now and she definitely didn't want him to love her.

"Are you okay?" Ty asked. She'd obviously been dealing with a lot . . . more than he'd known.

"I'm . . . good." She hesitated. "I mean, physically it's hard. I'm nauseous all the time and overly emotional, but I'm happy. I didn't think I'd have children, so it feels like a gift. The best most beautiful most important gift I've ever been given."

Relief flooded through him. "I feel the same way." He held his arms out to her and she walked into them, resting her head on his chest right above his heart. "We could get married. For real. We could give the baby a family..."

Darla noticeably stiffened.

Bracing himself, he let her go.

"We don't have to get married to give the baby a family." She walked away from him and sat on the couch.

No, that was true. They didn't have to get married. They didn't have to be together. But he loved her. "I'll quit riding."

Darla jerked her head to stare at him. "What?"

"I'll retire early." He sat in the chair across from her. "For you. For the baby." For them.

"No. That's not what I want, Ty." Tears slipped down her cheeks. "I'm sorry. I don't want to fall in love."

With him. She didn't have to say it. He'd offered to give up everything for her, and she still didn't want him. "What do you want then?"

She stared at her hands. "I want us to co-parent this baby the best we can," she finally said. "I want us to be good friends who are both there for the baby."

"Okay." What else could he say? He had his answer. "We'll be the best co-parents we can be then," he assured her. But he would never stop wanting her. His chest tightened painfully at the thought of raising a baby with her while living two separate lives. He had to get out of here. "I guess we should figure out what to do about my parents."

"Yeah. It's complicated." A sigh pushed Darla's back against the couch cushions. "For now we should keep the facade going," Darla said. "Until after they go home. And then you can tell them we broke up, but that we're still going to be great friends and we'll raise the baby together. We want them to be involved in the baby's life."

Ty considered that. It would be easier on all of them to let his parents continue believing they were engaged, but he couldn't do it. "I can't tell them that. It's not true." They deserved the truth. He never should've lied to them in the first place. For as long as he could remember he'd avoided dealing with anything real. With his parents, his brother. Since he'd left home he'd only built superficial relationships so he wouldn't have to risk feeling the rejection from someone he loved. But he was going to have a baby. And that would change everything. It would change him. Starting now.

Ty stood. "I'm done pretending. I have to tell my family we're not together."

"Wait." She pushed off the couch. "I'll come too. You shouldn't have to handle this alone."

"I need to. It's time for me to talk to my parents. Not only about the engagement." He wanted everything on the table. He had to ask them if Rhett was right, if they'd always been too afraid to watch him ride. "Call me if you need anything. Anytime. I don't care if it's four o'clock in the morning and you get some weird craving for French fries and ice cream."

"I will." It sure sounded like a shaky promise to him, but it was better than nothing. "Oh. I should give this back to you then." Darla raised her left hand and seemed to admire his grandmother's engagement ring before carefully sliding it off her finger. "I really think this is for the best." It almost sounded like a question instead of a statement.

Ty took the ring from her, the disappointment dragging down his heart. He'd liked seeing that ring on her finger. He'd liked spending time with her. He'd liked kissing her good night. He might never have wanted to work too hard at a relationship before, but he'd be willing to work at it with her. First though, he had to work at it with his parents. His brother. It was time to step up, to be honest, to acknowledge his own mistakes and forgive them for theirs.

He tucked the ring into his pocket. "I guess it's time to face the music. I'll let you know how it goes." He started to walk past her, but she grabbed his arm.

"I've seen you with kids. You're going to be such a good dad, Ty."

A dad. Man, hearing those words brought a bigger rush than a ride on Ball Buster. "I'll do my best every day. For both of you." And he'd start by making things right with his family.

When Ty walked back into the main bar area, Rhett and his parents were still eating their lunch.

"There you are!" His mom popped out of her seat the second she saw him. "Is everything okay? I'm so worried about Darla. Is she sick? Should we take her to the doctor?"

Oh, boy. Ty had no idea what to say, but he knew he couldn't say anything here. Darla shouldn't have to deal with the fallout from his decision to avoid his family. He grabbed his coat. "She's okay, but we have to go."

"Go?" His dad stole another sandwich from the platter. "We haven't even finished lunch yet."

"Bring it with you then." He waved them all to the door. "We need to have a talk."

His mother didn't budge from her seat. "What about Darla? We can't just leave her when she's sick! Someone should take care of—"

"She's not sick," Ty interrupted. "And she's going to

stay here and relax for a while. But we're all getting in my truck. Now."

The gravity in his tone seemed to get all of them moving. His dad put on his coat and picked up his plate, carrying it to the door.

His mom moved much slower, but finally she got her coat on too. "Ty, you need to tell us what's going on."

"I will. But not here." He held open the door, and on the way out, Rhett gave him a questioning glance. He pretended not to notice and simply led them to the truck, waiting until they'd all piled in before breaking the news. "Darla and I were never together. Not really." He started the engine, but let it idle and turned around to face his parents.

"What're you talking about?" his dad asked around a mouthful of French dip.

"When you called to ask if I would come home for Christmas, I didn't want to. So I made up a fiancée as an excuse. Darla and I have hung out occasionally over the last year, and when we started talking about the fundraiser, she asked me to invite Rhett. We pretended to be engaged so you wouldn't find out I'd lied." It sounded even worse when he said it out loud.

"But she's pregnant," his mother said through a gasp. "Is that a lie too?"

"No." Ty found it hard to look her in the eyes. "Like I said, we've hung out but there's never been any kind of commitment between us and—"

"That's bullshit," his brother interrupted. "You love her. I can tell."

Anyone who'd been watching them could tell, but loving her wasn't enough. "I don't know if the feeling is mutual." He'd like to think it was, or hope that it could be, but Darla would have to make that choice.

"What about the baby?" Tears were running down his mom's cheeks.

"Both of us want the baby to have a huge, loving family, even if it's not in the traditional sense of the word," he assured her. "You guys will be the perfect grandparents, and we'll make sure you see the baby as often as possible."

"What about me?" Rhett demanded. "I get to be an uncle. I want to see the baby too."

"You are all welcome to come out and visit anytime." He never thought he'd say that, but it felt good to want it, to welcome his family back into his life. "And I'll come home more too. Bring the baby to see where his dad grew up." He would teach the little bambino how to fish and ride horses and swim in the same pond he'd swum in growing up. He couldn't picture it without Darla being by his side though.

"I don't understand." His mom dug around her purse and found a Kleenex. "Why didn't you want to come home for Christmas? Why did you have to lie in the first place?"

Damn, he thought the initial part of this conversation was hard. "I guess I was tired of feeling like I was second-best." He looked at his brother. For once, Rhett remained silent and let him continue. "Like I had to compete with Rhett to get your attention."

His mom stopped blotting at the tears in her eyes. "That's ridiculous! We love you both."

"Why have you never come to watch me ride?" They'd never participated in what had been the most important thing in his life up until about twenty minutes ago when he learned he was going to be a father. "You've gone to most of Rhett's football games but you've never come to a competition. Even when I've asked."

His mom dissolved into tears again.

"That doesn't mean we don't care about you," his dad said, putting an arm around his mom. "It's never been a competition. You both can be boneheads sometimes but we still love you all the same."

That didn't answer his question. "But why haven't you come? I need to know why."

His parents shared a long look.

"Because it always felt to me like you didn't care," Ty continued. His parents were good people, but they had to understand how their absence made him feel. "I bought you tickets. And you never showed up. All I'd see from the arena were the empty seats I'd gotten you. Everyone else had family there, but I was alone." So he'd gotten used to being alone. He'd preferred it, even.

"You had friends there." His mom wouldn't look at him.

"Yeah. I had good friends. But I wanted my family there. I wanted you to be proud of me." Every emotion he'd shut out came rising back to the surface. "I needed you there. And you weren't."

"I'm sorry," his mom sobbed, reaching for his hand. "I couldn't. It's so dangerous. I can hardly watch those riders on TV and I don't even know them. I couldn't stand to see you get hurt like that, Ty. I don't think I'd ever recover. We'd always plan to go, but then I'd get to feeling so sick about it..."

"It's not that we think you're not good at it," his father added. "It's just...well, you'll understand soon enough, son. When you have a child of your own. You never want anything bad to happen. I used to be able to protect you, but I can't anymore."

"I know that has to be hard. And you're right—you can't protect me anymore." No one could. He couldn't guarantee nothing would go wrong. Hell, he'd had his fair share of close calls. "But you can be there for me. I need you to be there for me."

His mom nodded, sniffling and dabbing at her eyes.

"I got you the best seats in the house for the rodeo tomorrow night." That was all he wanted from them. Just one night of their support.

His dad took his mom's hand, holding it tightly in his. "Then we'll be there," he promised.

Chapter Twenty-One

Darla checked her phone for about the five hundredth time since she'd gotten to the Chocolate Therapist to do inventory an hour ago. One o'clock. They had three hours before the rodeo. Three hours before she had to watch Ty ride, and her hands were already shaking.

He'd called her the previous night to tell her about his conversation with his parents, and then he'd asked if he would see her at the rodeo. She'd planned to go but had toyed with the idea of going late. After he rode. She'd seen him ride, but that was before. Before she was carrying his baby. Before he'd kissed her like she had the power to save him. Before she'd slept with him and realized how hard she'd fallen for him.

Darla eased into a chair and set down her iPad. The inventory of her wine stock hadn't changed much since she'd done it last week, but she'd been hoping to find something to keep her busy. A distraction to take the edge off her anxiety. Ty had likely ridden at least a hundred times and nothing had ever happened to him. But that was the thing about anxiety. It wasn't rational. It was physical. She could tell herself over and over that he would be okay. That he wouldn't die on her like Gray had, but the fear came anyway—wedging itself into her throat, bearing down on her chest, palpitating through her heart.

I'll quit riding. She kept hearing his offer over and over. It told her everything. He would give up something he loved for her. For a second, she'd been so tempted to tell him yes, but it wouldn't matter. She would always find something else to fear, and that wasn't a life. She couldn't let him sacrifice his ambitions for her. It wasn't fair.

A knock sounded on the door. Once again, she checked her phone—1:03. The bar didn't typically didn't open for another four hours, and she'd planned on opening even later tonight because of the rodeo. She walked out of the wine cellar and stopped when she saw the door.

Nora Michaels, her dear mother-in-law, stood outside.

Tears flooded her eyes. "Oh my god." She ran for the door and fumbled with the lock before finally pulling the door open. "Nora." She all but fell into her mother-in-law's arms. "What are you doing here?"

The woman held on to her just as tightly. "Larry and I drove up for the day. He went on ahead to the hardware store, but I wanted to come right over to see you." She pulled back. "I had to check on you. I got the thank-you for the Christmas gifts I sent, but you didn't mention the letter." Her smile was so warm and familiar it made Darla cry harder. "I thought maybe you'd want to talk about it."

How did she know she needed to talk? Nora always seemed to know. Darla forced herself to let go of the woman so she could usher her fully into the bar. "Yes.

Let's talk." It had been months since she'd been to Denver to visit her in-laws, but Nora never seemed to change. She had plump cheeks and a welcoming smile. The fine lines around her eyes proved she laughed often. Oh, those eyes. They reminded Darla so much of Gray. After her recent trip to Hawaii her mother-in-law looked tan and healthy and happy.

Nora slipped off her coat and hung it on the back of her chair. "The whole time we were gone, I thought about you. About Gray's letter. And I wondered if I shouldn't have sent it."

"It was a shock," she admitted. "I mean, to see his handwriting. And those words…I could almost hear his voice." She reached into the pocket of her jeans and pulled out the letter, carefully unfolding it. Lately it had been a habit for her to read it in the morning and then tuck into her pocket as if it would somehow help guide her, as if it would give her the strength to do what Gray was asking. "What did he say when he gave it to you?"

Nora gazed at the paper with sadness in her eyes. "He said it was his last wish. But that you wouldn't be ready to hear it for a while." She smiled at the same time a single tear slipped down her cheek. "He told me to wait ten years. And if by that time you had a new family, he asked me to throw it out. But he said if you hadn't remarried, I had to send it to you." She shook her head and lowered her gaze to the table. "I honestly didn't know what to do. You've obviously built a family of sorts here. You've done so many wonderful things in the last ten years, Darla. And I'm so proud of you. He would be too."

Darla laid the letter where Nora could read it. "I miss having a family." She lowered her hands to her belly, holding them there like she so often did. Ty had offered her one and she'd been too afraid to accept it.

Nora read the letter, tracing each line with her finger as though she could feel a connection to Gray. When she'd finished, she knowingly held Darla's gaze. "You can build a new family. When is that baby due?"

Darla let her hands fall to her lap. "How did you know?"

Nora's eyes sparkled again. "No one touches their tummy like that unless they're pregnant, honey. And I can see it in your face. Your cheeks are a tiny bit fuller."

Reaching up, Darla touched her cheeks. "I just found out. About the baby. I'm due in late summer." She laughed but continued crying too. "It was a bit of a surprise."

"Such a happy surprise!" Nora rose from her chair to hug her over the table. "It's wonderful news, Darla," she said, sitting back down. "Especially hearing it on such a hard day."

A hard day . . .

Darla choked on a swallow. It was December 23. The ten-year anniversary of Gray's death. How could she have forgotten the date? She hadn't thought about him. Not once all morning. She'd been too busy thinking about Ty—

"You forgot, didn't you?" Nora asked, the words careful and kind.

"Yes." Guilt bore down on her. "I can't believe I didn't remember." She should've remembered this morning. Right when she woke up. But instead, Ty had been the first thing on her mind.

"You would have remembered eventually." Nora was always so gracious. "Even if I hadn't come." She squeezed her hands. "Darla, that's a good thing. Do you know that? It means you're letting go. And it's time, honey. It's time for you to love again."

"I don't know how." She closed her eyes, her heart caught in a violent tug-of-war. Part of her wanted to let go of the fear, but the other part wanted to hold on even tighter because it was her protection. It wouldn't let her get too close to someone she might lose...

"Do you regret marrying Gray?" his mom asked.

"No." Darla opened her eyes. "God, of course not. He taught me how to love. How to be loved." Yes, after he'd died, she'd gone through a phase of anger, of wishing she'd never met him so she didn't hurt, but she knew she wouldn't be who she was without him.

"So it was worth it then?" Nora prodded. "Love? The risks? The pain?"

No one had ever asked her that. "It was worth it." Every second she got to spend with Gray was worth it. Denying that would be denying the impact he'd had on her life.

"Do you love the father of your child?" her mother-in-law asked.

"Ty. His name is Ty." When she said his name, her heart filled with tenderness. "And yes. I think I do." It was the first time she'd admitted it out loud. Right on cue, the drumming in her heart started. It was that fear again, but anticipation flooded her too.

"And he loves you?"

"Yes." She didn't doubt his feelings. "But I'm so afraid. I can't go through that again. I can't love Ty. Not the way he deserves to be loved." She would always have this brokenness, this uncertainty.

"I think perhaps you have that backwards," Nora told her. "Maybe you're the best person to love him because you know what it costs. You know what it means to lose love and you've learned how short life is. Most people don't even find real love once. And you have a chance to find it twice. You have the chance to have the family you've always wanted."

"I don't know how." How could she let go? How could she stop panicking every time Ty got too close?

"Take it one step at a time," Nora murmured. "Tell the man how you feel. The only safe place in the world is with someone you love. With someone who loves you."

"I know." She'd had that once—a safe place, and she'd started to feel it again with Ty. "Maybe I could take it one step at a time." Without looking so far into the future. She had to focus on the present. On what was happening today. Today Ty was riding and she would go. Even though it scared her, she would take that one step so she could be there for him the way he'd been there for her.

* * *

"He looks even meaner up close." Ty's mom eyed Ball Buster from the other side of the fence around his pen.

"Who? Ball Buster?" Ty laughed. "Ha. If you think he's lethal you should see Man Eater. That bull tossed me off in less than a second and almost stepped on my head—"

His mother shot him a glare meant to shut him up. *Right.* She likely didn't want to hear about all of his close calls an hour before she watched him ride for the first time. "I mean...yep, Ball Buster is about as ornery as they come."

The bull in question gave him a long, lazy glance. The Cortez brothers had picked Ball Buster so the cowboys would have an actual shot at staying on for eight seconds to give the crowd a thrill.

Not that Ty's mother seemed to be in the mood for a thrill. He recognized the narrow slant to her eyes as the same worry that had emerged whenever he'd taken a spill off his bike or had fallen from one of the trees he used to climb growing up. "Truthfully, Ball Buster is on the verge of retirement." He gave his mom's shoulder what he hoped was a reassuring squeeze. "So you don't have much to worry about. He goes pretty easy on us these days." As easy as a bucking bull could go, anyway. "I guess that about concludes the behind-the-scenes tour." He led his family to the gates that opened out into the arena.

Earlier that morning, he'd caught on to his mother's anxiousness when she'd accidentally burned the pancakes she was making for breakfast. She hadn't burned pancakes a day in her life, and Ty knew she was dreading this afternoon. Earlier, he'd offered to let them off the hook so they could go to that show they'd gotten tickets for, but his mom had refused.

He'd offered to take them on a tour of the rodeo complex, hoping that once she saw all of the work and thought that went into ensuring the riders' and the animals' safety, she'd understand the sport a little better. He still couldn't tell if it had helped.

As they all walked away, Ty heard his mom tell off the bull behind them. "You be nice to my boy tonight, you understand?" She was trying to whisper but the woman's voice had always carried. "You hurt him, you'll have to answer to me," she went on.

Rhett busted up laughing. "I bet he's terrified."

Ty glanced over his shoulder. Ball Buster continued to stand there under the guise of being a gentle giant, but the minute the gate opened and he shot into the arena, he'd become a beast. Still, he'd likely still be no match for Maureen Forrester. "I don't know, Mom can be pretty intimidating when she wants to be."

"I'd listen up if I were that bull," their dad added. "You remember what your mom did when that principal wanted to suspend you two for fighting that bully?"

"She raised hell," Rhett said.

Oh, yeah. That was the day Ty had learned what the term *Mama Bear* had meant. She'd always been that way when they were young—standing up for them, fighting for them. And Ty would be the same way with his own child.

He paused in the corridor to wait for her to catch up. The crowd had started filing in through the main doors, and people were already finding their seats in the main arena.

"Rhett!" Sierra DeYoung waved and hurried over, leaving her group of friends behind.

"Hey." Ty assessed the entranced look on his brother's face. Oh, yeah. He had it bad.

"You must be Sierra." Their mom beelined down the corridor and nearly knocked Ty out of the way in her haste to meet Rhett's newest love interest.

"Yes." The woman gracefully held out her hand. "Sierra DeYoung. You must be Mrs. Forrester. It's wonderful to meet you."

"The pleasure is all ours, isn't it, Robert?" She nudged her husband forward to present him to Sierra. "This is Robert. Rhett's father."

"The one who gave him his good looks," their dad added.

Rhett looked like he wanted to face-palm. "Okay. You've met my parents. It looks like your friends are already finding seats. You'd better not keep them waiting."

Sierra seemed to hesitate. Ty watched the scene unfold with amusement.

"Actually, maybe I'll sit with your family," the woman finally said.

Oh, this was going to be good.

"Really?" A gaping frown gave away his brother's lack of enthusiasm at sharing Sierra with their parents. Rhett had never been good at disguising his feelings.

"Sure." Sierra gave off a charming smile. "I think it would be fun to sit with your folks. If it's all right, that is."

"It's more than all right," their mother answered for all of them. Rhett remained silent.

"Hello, Ty." Sierra turned to him.

"Sierra. It's nice to see you again." Nice to know she wasn't the diva he'd originally thought she might be.

"It's good to see you too. Is your fiancée here?"

A strangled sound came from his mom. She was still having trouble with him and Darla not being engaged.

"Actually, Darla should be here." At least he hoped she would.

"Oh, she's definitely here," his mother said. "I saw her walk in with Everly a while ago." His mother leaned a little closer. "She also said she had something important to tell you. After you ride. She didn't want to distract you, but I think that's a good sign, don't you?"

He was almost afraid to think. "Hope so." No matter what she had to say, it meant a lot to him, her fighting her fears to be here. He turned to Sierra. "By the way, she's not my fiancée." Might as well start getting the word out. "It's a long story. Rhett can explain it later." He'd have enough explaining to do when word got around town that they weren't engaged but Darla was pregnant. Scandalous news like that tended to travel like a wildfire. But he couldn't deal with it now. He'd already spent enough time chatting. "I should go get ready for my ride."

"Already?" his mom asked with a glance at her watch. "It's still early . . ."

"I have to warm up." Clear his mind, go through his pregame rituals. He leaned in to hug his mother. "Try not to worry. I'll be fine out there."

"Of course he will," his father said gruffly. "Look at him. He's tough as a two-dollar steak."

Their mother pouted. "Why did we have to raise two daredevil sons? Why couldn't one of you have become a librarian or something?"

"There you go." Ty clapped his brother's shoulder. "That's your next career. I could totally see you working in a library."

"I have about as much of a chance of becoming a librarian as you do of becoming a yoga instructor," Rhett shot back.

Right. That would be the day. He couldn't even touch his toes.

"Come on. Let's go find our seats." Ty's dad put his arm around his wife and started to lead her away.

"Good luck!" his mom called. "Be careful! Hold on tight!"

"I always do." For as long as he could anyway.

Rhett gave him a jab in the ribs. "This is probably the only time I'll ever tell you this, but you're a total badass and I'm proud of you."

"You're kind of a badass yourself," Ty said. He looked at Sierra. Couldn't resist. "Except when it comes to spiders. You want to hear Rhett scream, put a spider in front of him."

"Really?" She smiled teasingly at his brother. "Spiders, huh? Don't worry. I can kill them for you." She lifted her glittery cowgirl boot off the ground and stomped. "I'll protect you."

"Thanks for that. Both of you." Rhett slipped his hand into Sierra's. "We should go sit. Before he tells you more of my secrets."

"You can tell me later," Sierra said with a wave.

Ty waved back. "Oh, I will."

His brother flipped him off behind his back. Ty took it as a compliment. He'd missed this. The joking, the time with his family. He hadn't realized how much he'd missed it until they'd come.

Chapter Twenty-Two

Why had she eaten all that cotton candy? Darla followed Everly to their seats in the stands, sipping from a water bottle in an attempt to counteract the sugar she'd consumed over the course of the day.

Cotton candy proved to be the worst combination with the chocolate truffles she and Nora had eaten for lunch. When Larry had come to pick her up, Nora had hugged her tight, and Darla promised to come down for a visit next week. The woman had reminded her one more time to be brave, and she was really trying. She'd planned it all out—she'd catch Ty after his ride and tell him how she felt about him. How she wanted to work on her fears so they could have a future. But watching the first half of the rodeo hadn't exactly inspired courage. Rider after rider had gotten thrown, and though there hadn't been any serious injuries yet, she could see the potential for something catastrophic to happen.

That was her fear talking again. For the few hours after Nora had left, Darla had actually felt some peace, but the minute she pulled up at the rodeo grounds the anxiety had come barreling back in like one of those mean, angry bulls down there, and she couldn't seem to tame it with rational thoughts.

"Are you okay?" Everly asked. Somehow, she'd secured them seats in the very front row. She'd been so excited that Darla hadn't wanted to tell her she'd rather sit higher where she couldn't see as well. They were so close to the action she could almost feel the dirt flying into her face.

"I think I've eaten too much sugar today." That probably would not help her nerves. Maybe she should tell Everly she wasn't feeling well. It wouldn't be a lie. But then Ty would've known she hadn't stayed to watch him ride. And she wanted him to know she was here for him. Nora was right. It would take time and courage and honesty, but she wanted Ty to know how deep her feelings went. She wanted to be with him, and this would be part of their life.

"Popcorn?" Everly offered her the bag, but Darla shook her head.

"It's probably best if I don't eat anything right now."

"I've been craving everything salty." Her friend stuffed another handful into her mouth. "Of course, my mother insists that means I'm having a boy."

"Well that must mean I'm having a girl because I'm a total sugar fiend." A girl! She could picture a sweet little bundle all swaddled in a pink blanket.

"Ty would be so adorable with a girl," Everly said with a sigh. "So would Mateo for that matter. I have a feeling those big, tough cowboys would be reduced to teddy bears if they had a little girl."

"For sure." Her heart swelled thinking about Ty holding a little pink bundle. "Have you told anyone else you're pregnant yet?" Darla asked, wondering how she would go about making the announcement.

"Only our families. They're ecstatic, of course." Everly set down the popcorn. "Actually, if you're okay with it, we thought we would make the announcement tomorrow at the party you're having."

"What a great idea!" To celebrate their earnings from the festival, they had planned a big banquet at the rodeo grounds. Christmas Eve was the perfect day to celebrate how the town had come together to help two of their own. "That'll make the event extra special."

"That's what we thought. We're so appreciative of you and Ty for making all of this happen."

"We were happy to do it." Darla had to smile thinking about how much closer it had brought her and Ty. Just in time to have a baby together...

The arena lights dimmed again, signaling that the intermission was over. Mayor Hank Green barked another welcome into the microphone. Darla tried to settle in her seat as the mayor went over the order of events, but she couldn't seem to sit still. Ty was riding first. On the other side of the corral she could see the bull already in the chute. Her mouth started to go dry. There weren't enough water bottles in the world to douse the worry. "How do you do this?" she whispered to Everly. "How do you watch Mateo ride?"

"Honestly?" her friend whispered back. "I wish I could say I'm used to it, but I still hold my breath every time."

Darla wasn't sure she would have any breath left to hold. Her hands gripped the armrests at either side of her stadium seat. Nerves prickled deep inside her chest, giving rise to panic.

The crowd cheered as Ty climbed the fence, preparing

to slide onto the bull's back. Darla tried to clap, but her hands moved slow and clumsily, connecting only about every other time.

The crowd quieted into an awed concentration. The gate swung open and Darla lurched to the edge of her seat, gripping the fence railing in front of her.

Ball Buster flung Ty around, but the man held his ground, his arm whipping back and forth over his head. It was almost graceful how he moved, even with the bull getting madder and madder beneath him.

Ball Buster jackknifed and spun, forcing Darla to squeeze her eyes shut. When she opened them, she realized Ty had survived the maneuver, but now the bull arced his backend in a series of kicks that jerked Ty violently.

Cheers rang out from the crowd, but they sounded muted, like she was sinking underwater. Instead of holding her breath, she gasped air into her lungs and expelled it rapidly, trying not to hyperventilate.

The bull stampeded to the other side of the corral, kicking and bucking so hard it made *her* neck hurt. The seconds dragged by with the crowd noise competing against the loud thumps of her pulse in her ears.

Ball Buster kicked and spun, catapulting Ty into the air. He hit the ground hard on his back and Darla shot to her feet. "No. Oh no." She couldn't see anything past the blur of tears and fear.

"He's okay," Everly said next to her. "I think he's okay."

But Darla wasn't okay. She still couldn't manage to take a deep breath.

"He's up." Her friend dropped her arm over Darla's shoulders as though trying to offer her comfort. "Yep. He's waving to the crowd."

Darla staggered and fought for a full, deep breath.

"My stomach." Pains shot through her lower abdomen, stabbing through her. "Something's wrong." She doubled over, holding her stomach, twisting her lips to hold back a cry at the sudden discomfort.

"What?" Everly doubled over with her. "Oh no. Is it the baby?"

"I don't know." She could hardly speak. The pain seemed to radiate up the front of her lower abdomen and subside before gaining intensity again. It was what she'd imagined a contraction would feel like...

"I'll call an ambulance." Everly fumbled with her purse and found her phone.

"No." Darla stumbled over people's feet and purses, staggering to get to the edge of their row. "Just take me in. I don't want to make scene." No one except for Everly, Ty, and his family even knew she was pregnant.

"What about Ty?" Everly rushed over and supported her. "I can try to find him..."

"We don't have time." If something was wrong, they had to go. Now. Darla continued on down the walkway, trying to focus on breathing, trying to hold herself together.

"I'm sure everything is fine," her friend said as they ducked out the doors and hurried into the parking lot. "It's probably just your muscles adapting to the baby. I've read about it."

Darla had read a lot too. She'd read enough to know that cramping this early in a pregnancy was not a good sign. She'd read that fifteen to twenty percent of pregnancies ended in a miscarriage. She climbed into Everly's SUV and cradled her stomach in her hands. *Not this one. Please.* Silent tears slipped down her cheeks. She didn't bother to wipe them away.

"Everything will be okay," her friend murmured, but

Everly's voice shook too. She gunned the engine and ignored every speed limit sign all the way to the small county hospital. Instead of finding a spot in the parking lot, Everly pulled the SUV right up to the doors and ripped the keys out of the ignition. By the time Darla had opened the door, her friend stood there ready to help her out of the car.

She hunched over, trying to find a more comfortable position, and let Everly guide her into the ER.

"We need a wheelchair," her friend blurted to the woman behind the front desk. "She's pregnant and she's having cramps."

"I'll be right back." The woman disappeared behind a door.

Everly knelt next to Darla. "You okay?"

Darla poked and prodded her stomach. "I can't tell. It might be a little better." What did that mean? Did that mean she'd already lost the baby?

"You don't feel like there's blood or anything, do you?" Everly asked.

"I don't know. I don't think so." But she couldn't be sure.

The doors opened automatically and a nurse hurried through with a wheelchair. "Here we go." She guided Darla to sit down while the other woman behind the desk handed Everly a clipboard. "You can help her fill in her information after they get her in a room."

Not leaving her side, Everly took care of the paper-work while the nurse asked a bunch of questions and took Darla's vitals.

"Your blood pressure is elevated," she commented, writing it down on a chart.

"I think it's from the stress." Of watching Ty ride, of worrying about losing the baby.

"She's had a very stressful week," Everly added, taking ahold of Darla's hand.

"Any bleeding or spotting?" the nurse asked.

"Not that I've noticed." But had she been paying attention?

"All right. You two go ahead and finish up that paperwork." She pulled a gown out of a cabinet. "We'll have you change into one of our glamorous dresses here, and I'll be back in a few minutes."

"Thank you," Darla said weakly. Every part of her felt cold, like the worry had hollowed her out. She found her insurance card and handed it to Everly. While her friend finished filling in the forms for her, she shakily got herself undressed and put on the hospital gown.

"Have you ever been pregnant before?" Everly read from one of the forms.

"No. I didn't think I could get pregnant. Gray and I never used anything to prevent pregnancy, but it never happened." So maybe it was her. Maybe she couldn't carry a pregnancy. Fear roiled up through her chest, consuming everything in its path. "What if lose the baby?" The baby that she and Ty had made together. She'd seen the happiness radiate through him when he'd learned he was going to be a dad. "I don't know how I would tell Ty."

"You're not going to lose the baby," Everly said firmly. "Have faith, Darla."

She'd had faith once. Faith in a future that had been taken away from her. "I don't know how. I live under this fear that I won't be able to hold on to anything good. That some tragedy will ambush me again and steal the things I love the most."

"I understand." Everly sat on the gurney next to her. "I know you went through so much trauma when Gray died.

But I think this baby is a gift. I think this is the restoration of the dreams that were taken away from you. You might be afraid to believe it, but that's okay. Because I believe enough for both of us right now. Everything will be okay."

* * *

As was their custom, Ty stood with Mateo, Levi, and Charity at the fence, watching the last rider try his luck on Ball Buster.

"I think you've got the victory," Levi said, checking the standings on the scoreboard. As it stood, Ty was currently in first place, with Levi in second. For the barrel-racing portion of the competition, Charity held the title—no surprise there—and in bronc riding, Mateo had managed to secure a third-place spot.

"We'll see. Clay is good." He was newer on the circuit. Younger than Ty by at least eight years, and he'd already won a fair amount of prize money.

"He's done," Mateo estimated, watching the rider on the other side of the corral. "His grip is weak. It's only a matter of—"

Before he could finish, the bull tossed Clay into the dirt with a thud. Tucker McGrath, the Cortez's stable manager, lured the animal away while Clay staggered to his feet.

"Wait until you're over thirty, buddy," Levi muttered. "It'll hurt even worse."

"You got that right." Ty tried to stretch out his lower back. Seemed that part of him always took the brunt when he couldn't land on his feet.

"Over thirty and still winning." Levi offered Ty a high five. "Just so you know, I could've held out if I'd wanted to, but I knew your family was in town, so..."

"You never let me win," Ty said, searching the stands for his family. There they were. Easy to spot. Right in the middle, all crammed into the seats, with his mother sitting next to Sierra and chatting away. He had to laugh. Rhett was probably sweating. Their mother had a knack for telling embarrassing stories. Ty's gaze wandered away from his family, still searching for Darla's seat.

The arena speakers crackled. "We have a winner, ladies and gentlemen," Hank Green announced. "First place for the bull-riding competition goes to Ty Forrester."

The crowd got to their feet, cheering, and Levi pushed Ty toward the fence. "Go take your victory lap."

Nah. Back in his twenties, he used to trot around the arena when he won, showing off for the crowd. That was back when riding was the only thing that mattered to him. Still searching the stands for Darla, he opted to linger by the fence while he waved to the crowd.

Hank Green went on to announce the rest of the winners. "After a short intermission, we'll have the awards ceremony."

People in the stands began standing and mingling, but Ty still hadn't found the one person who mattered. Where was Darla? He scanned row after row searching for her.

"We have to go." Mateo grabbed his shoulder.

"What?" Ty spun, his lower back still threatening to give out.

His friend nudged him away from the others. "Everly just called. She took Darla to the hospital thirty minutes ago."

That got his heart going. "Hospital?" He jogged to keep up with Mateo as he crossed the corral. "Why? What's wrong?"

"She was having some cramping. They're running tests."

Ty stopped to catch his breath, but he couldn't seem to fill his lungs. Cramping?

"Hey!" Charity called behind them. "Where are you going? The awards ceremony is in ten minutes."

He got moving again. "I can't stay. Tell them I had an emergency." He and Mateo ducked out of the arena and sprinted down the corridor. His mind raced ahead. He had no idea what cramping meant. Was it bad? Would it hurt the baby?

"Are they okay?" he asked when they made it to the parking lot. "Darla? The baby? Are they okay?"

"I don't know." Mateo unlocked the truck and they both climbed in. His friend peeled out before Ty even had his seat belt on.

"What exactly did she say?" He didn't mean to sound so angry, but the adrenaline pounded through him and seemed to amplify everything, including his voice.

"She said Darla started having stomach cramps right after you rode," Mateo reported. "Everly took her to the hospital and they're doing some tests. That's all she said."

"What kind of tests?" Ty demanded. And why didn't Darla have Everly call *him*?

"Everly didn't say what tests." Mateo bounced his gaze back and forth between the road and Ty. "I'm sorry. I would assume they're checking on the baby."

A rip current of fear dragged him under. "What does cramping mean? Is she going to lose the baby?" He braced himself for the answer, for the possibility. Jesus, just yesterday he found out he was going to be a dad— that he'd been given the best and most important job in the world—and now...he couldn't even think about what it would be like if they lost the baby.

"I don't know." Mateo's voice was low and rough. He

almost sounded as angry as Ty. But he knew it wasn't anger plaguing either of them.

Ty let the silence drag on. Even though Mateo sped down the highway, the miles seemed to crawl by. He'd never felt so helpless.

"I'll drop you off." Mateo swerved the truck in front of the emergency room entrance. Ty hopped out before his friend had even hit the brakes. The hospital doors rolled open and he busted inside.

The place was deserted except for a woman behind the desk. "I'm here for Darla Michaels." All he could muster was a growl.

"Are you family?" the woman asked pleasantly. She seemed to have no clue that he would gladly dodge her and fight his way back into those exam rooms if that was what it would take.

"I'm the baby's father." He might not have held that child in his arms yet, but he was a dad. The jumble of emotions coursing through him tangled—fear and resolve and this powerful protective instinct he'd never experienced before. It didn't matter what he found back there. He would be strong. He would be what Darla needed him to be.

Apparently done asking questions, the nurse rose from her chair. "Right this way. I'll bring you back." She buzzed open a door and escorted him past room after room until she finally gestured for him to go inside one.

Ty rushed past her and found Darla sitting on an exam table. She was dressed in a hospital gown, her eyes red and swollen. Everly stood next to her holding her hand.

Ty couldn't bring himself to ask any questions, so he simply said, "I'm here."

"Oh Ty. Thank god." Everly backed away from Darla,

wiping her own tears. On her way past him, she gave his arm a squeeze. Whatever had happened, it didn't seem good.

"I'm here," he said again, approaching the exam table. Darla peered up at him. The tears running down her cheeks were enough to rip out his heart.

"They couldn't find the baby's heartbeat," she half whispered. "On the Doppler. The nurse couldn't find it."

Pain ripped through him, but he deflected it with resolve. He couldn't fall apart. She needed him. Darla needed him to stand strong. "Okay." He wrapped his arms around her, and brought her in close, holding her while he stroked her hair.

She leaned her cheek against his chest as though she'd been searching for that safe place to rest. "They're sending an ultrasound tech in." A sob broke through the words. "To see if..." Her voice trailed off.

To see if the baby was still alive. Pain wrenched his heart again, almost unbearable. Ty closed his eyes on his own tears and held her tighter. "It'll be okay," he murmured against her hair.

"I'm so sorry." She clung to him and sobbed against his shoulder. "What if the baby is gone? Oh God, Ty. What if our baby doesn't make it?"

Even with the anguish bearing down on him, he continued to hold her, finding strength and purpose in sheltering her. "Then I'll get you through it. I promise. We'll get each other through it." He brushed her hair away from her eyes and lifted her face to his. She wasn't alone anymore. He wasn't alone anymore. "Losing the baby won't change how I feel about you." The pain, this fear, only intensified his feelings for her. "I love you, Darla."

"I love you too." She rested her forehead gently against

his lips. "I chose you. Even though I'm terrified." She raised her face. Sadness clouded her eyes, but there was something else there too. Courage. "I don't want to be scared anymore," she murmured, bringing her hands to either side of his jaw. "I want to brave. For our baby."

Ty kissed her, letting his lips linger over hers, breathing her in, breathing in the hope and the anticipation of their future. "You are brave. No matter what happens, we'll be brave together."

Chapter Twenty-Three

Darla held Ty's face in line with hers, staring into those calming blue eyes. His eyes held tears too, but also so much love. When he had walked into the room, somehow he'd driven out all of her fears, all of the questions. *I'm here.* Those two simple words had raised her up. They'd rescued her from depths of a bottomless grief that threatened to drag her under.

He was there. He had been there so many times, and yet she'd been so afraid to hold on to him. Now, though, in the face of another devastating loss, he'd given her the strength to hold on. That was all she had to do, hold on to him, and he would hold on to her and they would get through this together.

"I'm sorry I pushed you away." She kissed him with tears running down her cheeks. "I was so afraid."

"I know. I would wait longer if that's what you need," Ty murmured. "I would wait until you're ready."

"I don't want to wait." Her heart seemed to pound harder

than it had in a long time. "We've already wasted too much time." Nora was right. Gray had given her so much, he'd taught her so much, and because of that she could move on. She could learn to let herself love someone again.

A knock on the door separated them. Only slightly though. Ty stayed close, hovering next to her.

"Hi there!" A scrub-clad woman poked her head into the room. "I'm Karen. I'll be doing your ultrasound today."

Saying nothing, Darla reached for Ty. He laced their fingers together and stroked her knuckles with his thumb.

"Will you be able to see the baby?" Ty asked. Concern had deepened his voice.

"We'll see." The woman likely didn't want to make any promises given the situation. She guided Darla to lay back, and then eased up the hospital gown, before placing a blanket over her hips and upper thighs.

"This is going to be cold." She squirted some gel onto Darla's stomach and took the wand from her machine, turning slightly to watch the small monitor. A swishing sound came over the speaker, and Darla held her breath, listening, listening, listening.

"Does that hurt the baby?" Ty asked eyeing the way the tech pressed the wand into Darla's abdomen.

The woman smiled as though she got that question from nervous dads all the time. "Not at all."

He gazed down at Darla, his eyes tender. "Does it hurt you?"

"No." She wouldn't care if it did. As long as it showed them a healthy baby, she would do anything, give everything.

"Ah. Here we go." The tech had zeroed in on a spot to the lower left side below Darla's belly button. "I think the little peanut was trying to hide before, but I'm good at this game."

"You see the baby?" Hope caught in her chest, sparking the tears in her eyes again.

"Yep." The tech pointed to the monitor. "Right now he or she is about the size of a raspberry." She turned a dial on the machine, and the swishing sound grew louder. But there was something else too. A thumping sound, so quiet she could only hear it if she strained her ears. "Is that—"

"It's the heartbeat!" Ty looked at the tech, his eyes five times wider than they normally were. "It's the baby's heartbeat, isn't it?"

The woman smiled and went back to moving the wand. "Yes. Your baby has quite the strong heartbeat."

Ty kissed her forehead, her temple, her cheek. "You're beautiful. The baby's beautiful."

Darla pressed her hands to her lips, watching that spot on the monitor, that beautiful, miraculous spot. "We couldn't hear the heartbeat earlier. On the Doppler."

"I'd guess it's a bit too early to be able to hear it on the Doppler." The tech typed something into the keyboard on the machine. "The ultrasound is much stronger. Based on the baby's size, I'd put you at about seven weeks along."

"Seven weeks!" Ty's laugh was so giddy it made Darla laugh too. "That means the baby'll be due sometime in August?" he guessed.

"Most likely." The tech moved the wand back. "But I'll let the doctor give you more specific information." She wiped the end of the wand with a rag, and then cleaned off Darla's belly. "Congratulations, you two. The doctor will be in to talk to you in a few minutes."

The woman had hardly cleared the door, when Ty planted a happy kiss on Darla's lips. "August. We're having a baby in August," he marveled, looking like a kid on Christmas morning. "This is everything I've ever wanted. *You* are everything I've ever wanted."

"I feel the same way." This was everything she'd wanted, and nothing she thought she could ever have again.

Another knock on the door interrupted their kiss. Everly crept in nervously. "Mateo and I are just out in the waiting room with your family, and I thought I would check in."

Ty sat on the gurney next to Darla. "My family's here?"

"Yeah. I guess when you left, word traveled fast about the emergency. Charity texted me and demanded to know what was going on, so I told her Darla was being checked out at the hospital." The woman looked back and forth between them. "She's been texting me ever since demanding to know what's going on, so I finally told her about the baby. You guys are smiling. And crying, but you're smiling too, so that's good, right?"

"We heard the baby's heartbeat." Darla would never forget that sound, not as long as she lived.

"The tech thinks he or she will be due in August," Ty added, his eyes shining. "That seems like forever away."

"It'll come faster than you can believe." The doctor stepped into the room to join them. "I hear congratulations are in order."

Everly let out a little squeal. "I knew it! I knew everything would be okay. I have to go tell the others." She slipped out of the room.

The doctor chuckled as he walked in. His white hair and friendly assortment of smile lines revealed he'd had plenty of experience with good news. "Based on the ultrasound results, we don't see any cause of concern," he informed them. "But you'll need to follow up with an OB as soon as you can get an appointment."

"We will," Ty assured him.

Darla wouldn't have been surprised if he made her an appointment before they left the hospital. "So what caused the pain?" she asked, doing her best to focus on the positives.

"There's no way to be sure." The doctor took as seat on the stool across from them. "Sometimes, even very early, a woman's body starts stretching, which can cause ligament pain. Or especially in early pregnancy, certain things you eat can irritate your digestive system."

"Things like cotton candy and chocolate?" she asked guiltily.

He smiled again. "Potentially. The nurse also noted that your blood pressure was elevated when you came in."

"Yeah." She snuck a sideways glance at Ty. "I was dealing with some nerves."

The man didn't seem too surprised by that either. "Well, you'll want to stay on top of that too. Anxiety can definitely affect your pregnancy."

"I will." She wouldn't hide anymore. Not from Ty, not from the fears. She'd face it all with him by her side.

"Sounds good." The doctor stood. "Once you get dressed, you're free to go."

"Thank you so much." Ty shook the man's hand and watched him leave before turning back to Darla. Concern had subdued his jovial expression. "How stressed were you watching me ride?"

She couldn't lie. Not if they were going to give this a shot. "I felt like I was having a heart attack." And she couldn't keep letting it happen. She didn't want to end up here again.

"That's why you were in pain?"

"It could've been the chocolate I had for lunch," she

said, trying to lighten the mood, to bring back that elated grin. "Or the cotton candy."

A smile flashed on his face but it was too brief. "I meant what I said before. I want to be with you, Darla. With you and with our baby. I want a family, a future with you. And I'll quit riding if that's what you need."

Darla gave the question serious consideration. "I want to be with you too." The relief of acknowledging that—of telling Ty the truth made her heart lighter. "But I don't want you to quit. Not until you're ready to quit. Not until your body is ready to quit." That alone was proof she loved him. If she didn't, she would have said, *Yes. Please quit.* But she couldn't be the reason. She couldn't take away something he loved—something that was so much a part of him. She couldn't continue to let her fears rule the direction of her life. Or her child's life. Or her and Ty's possible life together. "I don't want to live in the future anymore, worrying about what could happen. I want you now. Today. I want us."

He nodded, approaching her again. "I'm not far away from retirement. I'm not sure I'll be able to complete after next year."

She stood and eased her body up against his. "Then what're you going to do?"

"Maybe I'll be a bartender." His eyebrows bounced with a teasing look. "I've heard that wine bar in town is a nice place to work."

She played along with a frown. "I've heard the owner can be difficult sometimes."

"I've always liked a challenge," he insisted. "Speaking of challenges, do I get to help you get dressed?"

"In a minute." Darla pressed her palms into his chest and backed him up against the wall. "Do you remember how you kissed me the day of the calendar shoot?"

Ty slipped his arms around her. "Oh, I remember."

"Do it again. Only this time don't walk away so soon."

* * *

Hospital gowns weren't supposed to be sexy, but Darla had a knack for making everything sexy. Ty eased back, breaking off the kiss before it was too late. "Is there a reason you're trying to seduce me? Don't get me wrong, I'm happy to be seduced, but this tiny little hospital room can't accommodate all the things I want to do to you." And then there was the whole no-lock-on-the-door thing...

Darla kept her arms around him and gave him a repentant grin. "I might be stalling. It sounds like there're a lot of people out there in the waiting room."

Yeah, he'd thought about that too. Only a few of those people had known she was pregnant before now. "But they're all people who care." He brought her in closer, fastening his hands together at the small of her back. "My family. Not to mention Levi and Charity and whoever else they dragged along with them." His friends never let friends go to the hospital alone.

Darla inhaled deeply, her shoulders rising. "They probably all know I'm pregnant now, huh?"

"I'm guessing they do." He gazed down into Darla's eyes. "Are you okay with that?"

She didn't answer right away. As she continued to stare up at him, her smile grew until it finally reached her eyes. "Yeah. I just don't want to steal Mateo and Everly's thunder. They haven't told anyone they're expecting a baby yet. We could've kept it a secret longer."

"Well, given the hospital run, it might be a little late for that." In some ways that was a relief. Hell, he wasn't sure *he* could have kept it a secret. "Knowing our friends, everyone'll be ecstatic." He brushed a kiss across her lips. "*I'm* ecstatic."

"Me too." Darla pressed her lips into his, taking the kiss deep enough to ignite his body.

Ty let his arms fall to his sides. "We'd better leave before I start kissing you again." He dragged his gaze down her body. "Then we might never get out of here."

"I suppose." She stepped away from him and reached around her back to untie the string on the gown before letting it slip off her shoulders.

He took in the sight of her naked body, of her rounded breasts, the small swell of her stomach beneath her belly button, of the sexy curve of her hips. "On second thought, we don't have to rush out. I could brace a chair against the door."

Darla laughed as she slipped on her underwear and bra. "No, you're right. This isn't the time or the place."

"I'm never right," Ty said, moving in closer. He had to touch her. He rested his hands on her hips. "Everyone else can wait."

Shaking her head at him, Darla slipped on a pair of leggings that had been neatly folded on the chair. She tossed Ty her sweater. "You said you'd help me get dressed."

He was tempted to toss the sweater in the trash can. "I like helping you get undressed better. That's more my skill set."

"You're very good at it." Swaying her hips like she wanted to torture him, Darla approached and held her arms up, with her eyebrows raised in a silent command. *Put on the sweater.*

Ty pouted with a sigh, but he pulled it over her

head. "Shame to cover up all those perfect curves," he muttered.

Darla tugged the sweater into place. "You can uncover them later. Maybe you should stay at my place tonight."

"I'm planning on it." After what had just happened, it would be hard for him to let her out of his sight. "Since you're getting out of the hospital, we should probably go straight home." If it were up to him they'd skip all the inevitable conversations in the waiting room and break every traffic law they could on the way to her place.

"I don't know. I'm pretty hungry," she teased as they walked out the door together.

"Takeout doesn't require clothes." He draped an arm around her shoulders so he could nestle her against his side. "We'll stop for food—whatever you want—on the way home. Then we're not gonna leave your place for a real long time."

"Well at least not until the big party tomorrow night," she reminded him.

They walked through the doors and into a whole crowd of people. Whoa. Not only his parents and brother and Sierra, but also Charity and her husband Dev, Levi and Cassidy, and Mateo and Everly. Everyone swarmed them.

"Are you okay?" his mother asked, crying.

"Come on, Maureen," his dad said softly. "Give the kids a little space."

"I can't help it! I was so worried." She pressed a fisted Kleenex against her nose. "I mean, I know Everly said things were okay, but I had to see you for myself."

"We're okay, Mom." Ty gave her a hug. "All of us are okay. The baby looks great."

"Oh thank god!" His mother wriggled away from him and threw her arms around Darla.

As she hugged his mom back, Ty noticed a few tears in Darla's eyes too. "Thank you for coming, Maureen."

His mom finally let go, so Darla looked around. "Thank you all for coming. I know you're probably surprised—"

"Shocked," Charity corrected. "I can't believe Ty didn't spill the beans. He usually sucks at keeping secrets."

"Well, we didn't want to overshadow anyone else." He snuck a glance at Mateo and Everly, trying not to be too obvious. They both simply smiled and shook their heads. "We're so happy for you," Everly said, moving in to give them hugs.

"You had everyone pretty worried." His brother moved in next while Sierra politely congratulated Darla: "Glad everything turned out okay."

"Me too." Ty embraced his brother. Why the hell not? He was gonna be a dad. He'd hug just about anyone right now.

"The mayor was pretty pissed you weren't there to accept your award," Rhett told him.

"I couldn't care less about the award." Any award. "Darla and the baby are all that matter."

"That may be true, but you were great out there. I couldn't do what you do." Coming from Rhett, the statement was the equivalent of an Academy Award.

"Thanks. That means a lot."

"Oh, look at you two!" Their mother swooped in and snapped a picture. "It makes my heart happy to see you getting along."

Ty shot Rhett a smirk. "Yeah, well, I think you'll be seeing it a lot more."

His brother nodded, then moved off to talk to Sierra. Ty was looking for Darla when his mother snagged his elbow. "I need to talk to you."

Before he could respond, she was dragging him around the corner where no one could see them. "I know you two say you're not together, but—"

"That's changed. We're definitely together."

"Really?" A look of hope flared in her eyes. "You're engaged?"

"We're not engaged." Not yet anyway. "But we're going to give things a shot."

"Oh! I knew it! I knew she had feelings for you too!"

"It'll take time," he said before his mother got too carried away. "Maybe a really long time. We still have some stuff to work through, but there's hope."

"Of course there's hope! You two are meant to be! Everyone thinks so. I knew it the minute I saw her."

Ty gave her a look. "Easy. You have to keep this quiet. Let us do this our own way. On our own time."

She pressed her lips firmly together and gave him a solemn nod.

Before they walked back to the crowd, Ty gave his mom a hug "Thanks for coming to the hospital. It means a lot to her. That you're all here. That you were worried."

"She's part of our family now." His mom got all misty-eyed again. "No matter what happens between you and Darla. She and the baby will always be part of our family."

He'd forgotten that about his parents, how accepting they were, how they'd always opened their home and their hearts to whoever needed a place. "I'm glad you could come for Christmas."

"Me too." His mom stood on her tiptoes and reached up to pat his cheek. "And I'm so proud of you, son. I knew you were tough, but seeing you ride..." A few tears slipped down her cheeks. "It was really something. I only had to turn away twice."

"It meant a lot to have you there." It had felt like they were finally becoming part of his world.

"We'd like to come this summer," she said. "As often as we can."

"It looks like I'll be taking the second half of the summer off. The doctor thinks the baby will be due in August." But he'd change his schedule so he'd be home in July too. There was no way he'd miss the birth of his child.

"I can't wait." His mom did a little jig. "I'll start knitting right when I get home. Don't you worry, you and Darla won't have to buy a thing. Just let me know—"

"There you are." Darla careened around the corner.

"Yeah." Busted. Ty tugged Darla close. "We were just… Uh…"

"I was telling him how much we enjoyed watching him ride," his mother offered. "And we were so worried about you." She looked Darla over carefully. "Are you sure everything's all right?"

"I'm sure." Darla looked embarrassed. "It was only cramping. I probably overreacted."

"Pshaw." His mom waved her hand. "I had the same thing with both of my pregnancies. It's always a good idea to get it checked out. And you can call me. If you ever have questions about anything."

The words seemed to touch Darla. "Really?"

"Of course," his mom insisted. "We want to be there for you. And the baby. Anything you need, honey. You just let us know how we can help."

"We will," Darla said, brushing away tears. "Thank you."

Chapter Twenty-Four

Darla sat straight up on the couch. Crap. Had she fallen asleep? She threw off the fuzzy blanket Ty had tucked around her when he told her he was going to clean up the dishes. On the way home from the hospital, they'd picked up takeout and had enjoyed a nice romantic dinner in front of a warm fire in her living room. And then she'd proceeded to zonk out. Leave it to her to nod off when the cowboy of her dreams was within reach.

Across the room, she could see him rummaging around the kitchen, so she took a few seconds to smooth her hair and pinch her cheeks and try to make herself look as sexy as possible. Since he still seemed to be busy, she quietly stood and snuck over to the mirror hanging on the wall by the entryway.

So much for sexy. Sleep lines crisscrossed her right cheek, and her eyes had gotten red and puffy. That meant she'd have to draw the attention away from her face. Darla quickly unbuttoned the top four buttons on her shirt and hiked up her bra to make sure she had as much cleavage visible as possible. There. That should—

"I'd be happy to undo those buttons for you."

Great. She'd been caught. Darla turned around slowly, but instantly forgot her embarrassment when she laid eyes on Ty. He had that Santa hat on—the one he'd worn for the calendar shoot. The one she'd stuck in a box and stored in the laundry room behind the kitchen. No shirt though. He'd taken that off and had tossed it on a nearby chair. His jeans sat low on his chiseled hips, and he held out a tray with two mugs. And a can of whipped cream.

"Hot chocolate?" he asked with a naughty raise of his eyebrows.

"Yes please," she nearly whimpered. Desire raced through her hot and fast, pushing her over to him in a desperate rush.

Grinning, he backed to the coffee table and set down the tray. "Whipped cream?"

"Mm-hmm." She swiped the can off the tray and popped the lid. "But not on the hot chocolate." She pointed the spout at his chest and drew a long line of white foamy cream down to his waist. Then she lowered her head and followed the trail with her tongue. When she reached his stomach, Ty stole the can out of her hand. "Not so fast." He backed to the light switch and turned them off, darkening the room into a romantic glow from the fire and the white Christmas lights draped over the mantel.

Taking her hand, he snatched the plush blanket off the couch and laid it down on the floor in front of the fireplace. He set the whipped cream can on the mantel and slowly undressed her, taking his time with each of the remaining buttons on her shirt. Finally, he slipped it off her shoulders and touched his lips to the lace edge of her bra, tracing the lines while he reached around her back and unhooked the clasp.

Hunger and energy and a deep well of emotions all converged inside her with a force she hadn't experienced in a long time.

Moving his lips down to cover her shoulder with kisses, Ty slid off her bra and let it drop to the floor. He straightened back up, running his gaze over her body with a scorching heat. "You've never looked more beautiful than you do right now."

"And I've never wanted anyone the way I want you right now." There was so much power in this connection between them. It seemed to hold all of her—her heart, her body. She pulled him against her and they lowered to the floor that way, arms tangled around each other while his tongue explored her mouth, teasing, making her ache for his touch everywhere.

"I'll always be here for you, Darla. As long as you'll let me." Ty lay on his side next to her, his hand tugging her leggings and underwear down over her hip.

"I know." The promise had settled in her heart and she believed him. "And I'll be there for you too. Every time you ride. I'll be there to cheer you on." She shimmied her legs, working her pants and underwear the rest of the way off, then sat up so she could undo his belt and the buttons on his jeans.

Ty took over, pushing off the rest of his clothes before reaching up to snag the whipped cream off the mantel. Hovering over her, he pointed the can down and drew a heart over the lower half of her stomach. Right where their baby would be. "I meant what I said that night at the cookie exchange," he murmured, kissing away the whipped cream. "You make me happier. And I'll do everything I can to bring you and our child happiness every day."

Tears snuck out of the corners of her eyes and flowed down over her temples. She ran her hands lovingly through his hair while he kissed that heart-shaped pattern on her stomach. "I don't think I could be any happier than I am right now." Having him, having the baby.

A profound hope swelled through her. She and Ty were building the family she'd always desired.

* * *

Ty couldn't say he'd ever been to a fancy Christmas party. Judging from the monkey suit Darla had laid out for him to wear, it was the kind of event that went way above his pay grade.

A tux? He hadn't worn one of those since one of his friends had forced him into being a groomsman a few years ago. And he definitely hadn't been a fan. Still, if Darla wanted him in a tux, she would get him in a tux. He quickly dressed, though he decided to forego the tie and left the top few buttons of the crisp white shirt undone for good measure. A cowboy was a cowboy whether he wore a tux or jeans.

It was a shame Darla wasn't there to approve of his take on black tie. She'd gone over to Everly's to get ready, and probably to eat chocolate and giggle a lot or something, but she'd be back to meet him any minute and he wanted to be ready. He found his black cowboy boots in his closet and shoved them on his feet before walking out to the living room.

Rhett and Sierra were having a pregame drink at the dining room table while his dad paced the floor. "I swear, your mother has been in there getting ready for the last two hours and now she's saying she can't find the right lipstick."

"Oh! Take her this one." Sierra opened her little hand-held purse thing and produced a tube of lipstick. "It'll go with anything—and it's perfect for every complexion."

"I sure hope so," his dad muttered, already heading up the stairs.

Just when Ty looked at his watch to check the time, Darla walked in, and he swore the entire universe tilted on its axis. The woman was so smoking hot she seemed to suck all the gravity out of a room. "That dress should be outlawed." It was long and sleek and black with a plunging neckline and a slight shimmer to it. It showed off every curve. And somehow the fire-engine red heels she wore made the whole ensemble even more appealing.

He walked over to her.

"I like what you did with the tux." Darla reached out and fingered the buttons at his collar.

"I really like what you did with that dress." She'd taken a simple black number and kicked it up about five hundred notches.

"It's getting tight already." She pressed a hand into her abdomen.

"No. It's perfect. You're perfect." He leaned down to kiss her.

"Darla!" His mother always had impeccable timing. She hurried down the stairs as though she was afraid they'd leave before she could get out her camera. "You look lovely. Let me snap a picture."

Before the sentence had even finished both Ty and Darla were posing. "She has us conditioned," he said, holding his smile in place.

Darla gave his hand a squeeze. "I think it's sweet."

"Your turn." His mom moved on to capture Rhett and Sierra, while Ty prodded Darla to the door. It might be a little early for them to leave, but he wanted to sneak a few minutes alone with her.

"We'll see you at the party," he said, using his best James Bond voice.

His family bid them goodbye, and they stepped out onto the front porch.

"Are you sure the dress is okay?" Darla asked nervously.

He stopped and pretended to look her over carefully. "I don't know... maybe I should see what you're wearing underneath it and then decide."

"Ha." She whapped his shoulder. "Later. Don't forget I have to be up onstage to present the check to Mateo and Everly. I can't be looking all disheveled." She wrapped her arm around his and leaned on him as they navigated the bits of ice and snow on his driveway.

He walked her over to the passenger's side of the car and then paused before opening the door. Darla gazed up at him shyly. "What?"

"I just can't believe how lucky I am. You're radiant. And smart. And giving." He could keep going, but then he'd sound like a chum.

"And you are one sexy cowboy, Ty Forrester." She stole a kiss on his cheek, likely leaving a lipstick mark, but he didn't wipe it away.

"Just you wait." He helped her into the roadster and they drove over to the rodeo grounds.

Darla chatted about what the evening would be like. "It'll probably be long and drawn out and maybe a little stuffy," she said apologetically.

"I don't care." Ty parked the roadster and helped her

out. "As long as I'm with you, nothing about it is going to be boring."

They walked into the banquet room and were instantly greeted by their friends. "You look fabulous!" Everly gushed over Darla's dress.

"Where's your tie?" Charity demanded. "If I had to wear this getup"—she gestured to the fancy red dress she wore—"you should've had to wear a tie."

"I seem to have forgotten it," he said innocently, and then moved on to talk to Mateo before the woman could punch him.

The band started up, and they all moved to the dance floor. Ty held Darla as close as he could get away with. They didn't say much, just stared and smiled, and he couldn't believe how much they could communicate without saying a word.

After a few songs, the mayor invited Darla up to the stage. Ty escorted her to the stairs and then let her go. It was amazing how she never wobbled in those high heels.

After Hank thanked her for her efforts, Darla took the mic. "I can't take any credit for our success over the weekend. Without you all it wouldn't have been possible. Thank you for coming, and for all of your participation in the events over the last week. Because of your generosity, we were able to raise fifty-three thousand dollars to help Mateo and Everly Torres rebuild the Farm Café."

Cheers rose up from the crowd, and Ty didn't think he'd ever been as proud as he was in that moment. She might deflect all of the praise, but none of it would've been possible without her determination.

"Mateo and Everly, why don't you come on up?" She waited while they crossed the room and climbed the stairs to the stage. "You two have been such an integral part of this community, and it is with gratitude that we present you this check." She handed over the check and Everly broke down in tears.

Darla handed the mic to Mateo and hurried down the stairs to where Ty waited. He slipped his arm around her as they moved toward the center of the crowd for Mateo's speech.

"Thank you all so much," his friend started. "There's no way for us to express our gratitude." He glanced at Everly and they both got those secretive grins. Ty grinned too.

"This community means everything to us, and we're excited to share a secret we've been keeping."

A few whistles rang out. Suspicions of baby news had obviously been running high for quite a while.

"We'll be welcoming a new little buckaroo into our family come summer," Mateo said.

When the cheers quieted, he took Everly's hand. "After the fire, we weren't sure how things would work out, but you all have made sure we don't have to worry. We're so grateful to be part of this community, to be part of something bigger and stronger than ourselves. It's amazing what happens when we all come together."

Darla sniffled and then ducked away, quickly moving through the crowd. Ty caught up to her at the outskirts of the room.

"What's wrong? Are you okay?"

She nodded but continued to cry, which didn't make him feel any better.

"He's right," she finally managed. "About being stronger when you're part of something bigger. Like your family. It's still intact. After all these years. Even through the hard times. Your parents are still together."

"Yeah. They are." Things hadn't always been easy. As

ranchers, times were tight sometimes. There'd been plenty of ups and downs, but they'd weathered it all side by side. "I never thought about it like that. I took my family for granted." The last few years he'd been too busy feeding his own resentment to appreciate them.

"I want that," Darla said. "Something that will stay intact no matter what. I want that for me and I want that for the baby."

"Then that's what we'll build," he promised. "Starting tonight. Starting now." He held her in his arms, knowing that feeling would never get old. "We'll build a love that's strong enough to hold everything else together."

* * *

A clanging woke Darla out of a deep, tranquil sleep. She lay in her bed, listening, and smiled when she recognized the chaos happening in her kitchen. Given that she was alone in her bed, Ty must be making her breakfast—though from the sound of things, it wasn't going quite as smoothly as the day his mother had done the cooking.

She stacked her pillows and shimmied up to a sitting position, and then splayed her open hands across her tummy, feeling warm all over. Sunlight peeked in between the curtains, and she could see a snatch of the white glittering world outside.

"What a perfect Christmas morning," she murmured to the baby, pressing in her fingers slightly as though to knock in greeting. It was ridiculous, she knew. The baby was so tiny he or she likely couldn't hear or feel a thing, but that didn't stop her from wanting to connect with this new life growing inside of her. "Christmas is my favorite holiday," she said. She'd forgotten that. It had been her favorite holiday once upon a time. Especially after she'd married Gray. It had made the day so much more magical when she had someone to share it with. "And now I have two someones," she marveled. The thought filled her heart to brimming.

The last time Ty had made her breakfast in bed, it had triggered the flight instinct in her. *Don't get attached. Don't love. Don't hope.* She'd thought those mantras had been her salvation, but they'd only been shielding her from feeling anything.

She would always have memories of Gray—their lazy mornings together, their spontaneous weekend trips, their shared hopes that were forced to remain unfulfilled dreams. But instead of holding on to those memories in her white-knuckled grip, she was learning how to re-arrange them, to slide them over to make room for new ones. Somehow, ever since she'd learned she was pregnant her heart seemed to have tripled in size. There was more room for everything good—hope, love, joy. "We can't wait to meet you," she murmured, giving her tummy a pat. "Your daddy and I—"

The door creaked open and Ty stepped into the room carrying a tray. "Who are you talking to?"

"The baby," she said matter-of-factly.

"Oh yeah?" Ty set the tray on the nightstand and sat next to her on the bed. Darla folded her lips in a smile. The French toast was burned and crumbling at the edges, and the bacon was so charred it looked like he'd stuck it straight in the fire. She couldn't wait to dig in.

"What were you saying to the baby?" he asked, lying next to her.

"I was just telling our little bean how lucky he or she is

to have you for a daddy." Ty might have zero skills in the kitchen, but he had a big heart.

"I think I'm the lucky one." He eyed the breakfast tray. "Trust me. You are definitely not lucking out with a capable chef."

Darla laughed. "It looks great," she lied.

"I'm pretty sure you shouldn't eat it." He eased his body closer to hers. "I tried though. I'll always try." His hand moved to cover her stomach. "Hear that? You're going to learn to love burned French toast."

"And Eggo waffles," Darla added with a giggle. Luckily Ty laughed too.

"Merry Christmas," he said, suddenly looking very serious.

"Merry Christmas." She eased her body on top of his.

"Wait." He rolled away from her. I have something for you." He pushed off the bed and disappeared out the door. When he returned he had a huge package balanced in his arms.

"You want me to open it now?" Darla sat up taller. When was the last time a man had given her a Christmas gift? Not since Gray. The thought didn't sting. Instead it made her smile.

"Yes. Open it, open it, open it." He set it beside her and sat on the edge of the bed.

"Okay." She worked at the ribbon on top. "I'm impressed. I think you're better at wrapping gifts than I am."

"I had help," he said cryptically.

He offered no more explanation as she tore off the wrapping paper and opened an unassuming cardboard box only to reveal another wrapped package, this one in candy cane paper. "Clever," she said, starting all over on a new bow.

"I like to drag out opening presents as long as possible."

She opened eight more carefully wrapped boxes, each one smaller than the last, until finally she opened a miniature shoe box. Tiny cowboy boots fit for a toddler sat inside. Darla lifted them out and ran her fingers over the soft leather. "These have to be the most adorable boots I have ever seen. And I have a whole closet full."

"There's something else inside that one." Ty pointed at the one in her right hand.

She reached her hand in and pulled out a very familiar square-shaped box. Her heart seemed to swell, filling her chest, pressurizing her throat with emotion.

He gently took the last box from her and opened it, giving her a glimpse of that beautiful engagement ring she'd worn before. "Yes," she whispered, raising her eyes to his.

"Not so fast. I have a whole speech prepared." Still holding the open box, Ty dropped to one knee on the floor beside the bed. "I've been thinking about all of those things you said about family yesterday. I didn't tell you the whole story about the ring. My grandfather designed it and sold his prized Ford truck in order to have it made."

The bit of history brought even more meaning to the gift.

"He and my grandma were married for almost sixty years. And she still wore it every day after he passed away." Ty carefully took the ring out of the box. "I never want to rush you into anything, but I want to make this promise to you. I'll be here for you always. When you need someone to hold you, or to make you laugh, or to have your back, or to wipe away your tears." He took her hand and kissed her knuckles. "I will probably never be able to make good French toast, but I love you. I love our little baby. I want to marry you. I want to build a life with you. Whenever you're ready—"

"I'm ready." She threw off the covers and pulled him up to her. "I don't want to wait. It's already been too long. Too lonely. Until you reminded me how to feel something." She pulled him in for a kiss. "Let's get married. Let's go to Hawaii and get married on the beach with your family. Before I'm too fat to wear a bikini."

His hand cupped her butt. "You'll never be too fat to wear a bikini."

"I'm already getting a little rounder. But it's okay. I don't mind getting fat." It was for a good cause.

"You won't have to do it alone." Ty patted his own flat belly. "I've always wanted to get fatter."

He tried to stick out those washboard abs and all Darla could do was roll her eyes. "I'm pretty sure a six-pack is the exact opposite of fat." She pulled off her pajama shirt and tossed it aside. "See?" She patted the bulge that seemed to have doubled in size from the day before. "This is round."

"I love your body," Ty said, lowering his head to kiss her belly. "I'll always love your body." He started to slide her pajama bottoms down, but Darla stopped him. Only for a second. "This is the best Christmas morning I've ever had." She needed him to know that, needed him to know how much he meant to her.

"Me too." He kissed her lips. "And I promise to make each year even better than the one before."

Epilogue

Are you ready to go?" Darla hurried into the living room, but quickly stopped when she caught sight of Ty on the couch. His head had fallen back against the cushions and he was snoring loudly.

Awww...

Graycie Faith was nestled in the crook of his shoulder, looking even tinier than her eight pounds compared to her daddy. Not surprisingly, the baby had fallen asleep too. It didn't matter how fussy she was, the minute Ty lifted her into his arms everything in her world righted. Sometimes, little Graycie would stare up at Ty in wonder, but mostly she'd settle right against all of those strong muscles in his chest and fall into a deep, contented sleep.

Creeping across the rug, Darla pulled her phone out of her pocket and captured the moment, zooming in so everyone on her social media page would be able to see just how cute her daughter's bowed pink lips looked. In the previous two weeks Darla had come to understand

Maureen's picture habit. Seriously, she had run out of room on her cloud at least four times since they'd brought Graycie home from the hospital, but she'd had no idea how many pictures babies required. In two weeks, the baby had already changed so much, and she didn't want to miss out on any new little face she'd make—there were so many of them, even when the little doll was sleeping.

Doing her best not to wake either of them, Darla moved in closer and took the same picture from a different angle.

"Are you taking a picture?" Ty's eyes were still closed and he didn't raise his head. They'd both missed out on so much sleep between the feedings and the diaper changes and the new-parent worries. True to his promise, Ty had been by her side for all of it, never complaining or groaning when he heard the baby cry.

"I can't help it." Darla went to sit with him on the couch. "You two are the cutest thing I've ever seen." And she had about five hundred pictures to prove it.

Ty sat up straighter, but Graycie didn't even stir. Always so happy in her daddy's arms.

Darla could relate. Her husband had the best arms for holding a person, strong and tender and warm. In fact...she snuggled in closer to his side, and he slipped his free arm around her with a smile. "Is this your way of trying to tell me it's time to go?" A yawn broke through the words.

"I suppose we should." Though she wouldn't mind sitting here like this for another whole day, just her and the two loves of her life. "It's been two weeks since we've been out. I guess we shouldn't miss our own baby shower." Since Everly and Mateo had welcomed their new addition, Harper Rose, into the world only a week and a half before Graycie made her appearance, all of their friends had decided to throw them a joint baby shower. They'd insisted the party needed to happen after the babies were born so they could get their baby fix. For the first time in two weeks, Darla glanced at the clock that hung in their kitchen. "We're twenty minutes late already." She supposed that wasn't too bad, considering this was their first real outing since they'd brought Graycie home.

Cradling the baby in a football hold, Ty stood and then helped Darla up. She'd healed remarkably well, thanks to a fast delivery and all the prenatal yoga she and Everly had done over the previous few months, but that didn't stop her husband from doting on her every chance he got.

"You look gorgeous, babe." He admired the simple sundress she'd chosen for the event. That was one nice thing about having a baby in late summer—she could wear comfy cotton dresses without worrying about the postbaby belly.

"Thank you." She planted a kiss on Ty's cheek. "But I have to admit, I do miss my yoga pants." That had been her new mom uniform for the previous two weeks—yoga pants and a tank top.

"I miss them too." He stole a glance at her butt. "The dress looks really great on you though. Who am I kidding? Everything looks great on you." With Gracie nestled between them, he gave Darla a long lingering kiss that made her wish they weren't under the dreaded postbaby abstinence protocol. Talk about torture.

"All right, angel baby. Time to go." Ty carried their daughter to her car seat carrier, which had sat on a bench by the front door since they'd brought her home from the hospital. He buckled her in, checking all the straps at least three times. Graycie startled and did that adorable stretch, raising her tiny fists above her head, and immediately started to whimper.

"You can just never put her down," Darla told him, bringing over her pacifier.

"Shhh. It's okay, angel baby," he cooed, swinging the car seat lightly. "I've still got you. Your daddy's still holding you."

Yeah, she couldn't resist. Darla pulled out her phone again and snapped another picture.

"We're going to run out of space again," Ty teased.

"Then we'll buy more." She took another picture to show him she wouldn't back down. "In fact, we might have to buy more space before the party is over." She held open the door for him, and together they walked outside.

It was a perfect Colorado summer afternoon with a cloudless blue sky stretching over the small acreage they'd bought on the edge of town. To say the previous six months had been a whirlwind would be putting it mildly. In February, they had indeed invited Ty's family to join them on a trip to Hawaii, where they'd gotten married barefoot on the beach. They'd moved into Darla's house for a couple of months while they waited patiently for their dream house to go on the market. Finally, the Realtor called with a new listing—a modest three-bedroom ranch-style home situated on five acres where Ty could train riders after he retired.

"So who's going to be at the shower?" he asked once they'd all gotten situated in his truck.

"Definitely Mateo, Everly, and Harper Rose." Darla couldn't wait to see that sweet little baby girl again. They'd made a trip to the hospital right after she was born but hadn't seen her since. "Besides them, it will pretty much be the whole gang from what I've heard." The

Cortez brothers and their wives, Dev and Charity, Tucker McGrath and his wife Kenna. "Oh, and Josie, Ralph, Peter, and Norman will be there too, of course." After keeping them a secret for far too long, her two worlds in Topaz Falls and Glenwood Springs had officially collided, and she couldn't have been happier about it.

"I love those guys," Ty said, driving extra slowly and cautiously. Darla smiled to herself, wondering if he'd ever go the speed limit again when Graycie was in the car.

"They love you too." She and Ty had invited her bereaved spouses support group over for dinner at least once a month since the spring, and the six of them had gotten close. She couldn't wait for them to meet the baby—it would be like having four extra grandparents to spoil her.

"So what do you do at baby showers?" Ty asked, not taking his eyes off the road. "I've never been to one."

"Well…" She wasn't sure what to tell him without scaring him. "There's usually a lot of pregnancy talk. And everyone feels compelled to share their birthing story."

"Ew." He stopped at a stop sign and looked over at her. "Seriously?"

"Yes, but since this is a co-ed shower, I'm guessing it'll be a little more laid-back. We'll probably eat and hang out." God knew birthing talk would scare all the men out of the room. Ty had been a champ at her bedside when she'd delivered Graycie, but he'd told her later, he'd had to talk himself out of keeling over a few times.

"Eating and hanging out. I can handle that." He eased a foot back onto the gas, and they moseyed down Main Street all the way to the end, where they turned into the driveway that led to the brand-new Farm Café. Mateo and Everly had rebuilt an exact replica of the original farmhouse where Everly had started the café when she'd moved to town. Except now, everything was shiny and new. They'd gotten the business up and running again in time for the summer season, and had even hired extra help to run the place while Everly took some maternity leave.

"I can't wait to see everyone." As nice as it had been to have some alone time with Ty and the baby the last few weeks, she'd missed their friends. Most of them had dropped by at one point or another to bring them dinner and get a peek at the baby, but Darla had been so groggy she hadn't socialized much.

"I can't wait to show off our little girl." Ty parked the truck and they both carefully fussed over getting Graycie's car seat out of the base, and then the three of them walked into a party that had already started.

"You're here!" Everly was the first one to spot them. "Look at you, Graycie Faith." She leaned over the car seat. "Oh my goodness, she looks exactly like you with that beautiful dark hair."

Darla liked to think so too. Apparently, unruly dark hair was genetic. Graycie's usually stuck up all over her head, but today Darla had slicked it together in a miniature ponytail and added a bow.

"Where's Harper?" she asked her friend, already itching to get a picture of the two of them together.

Everly hiked a thumb over her shoulder in Mateo's direction. "He won't let anyone hold her yet. Can't seem to give her up."

"I get that." Ty set the car seat on a nearby table and lifted Graycie into his arms. Darla and Everly tagged behind as he crossed the room to introduce their daughter to her new best friend.

"Look who it is," Mateo said in his best baby voice.

"Your buddy." He held out Harper and Ty held out Graycie, and Darla took yet another picture.

The four of them caught up briefly—comparing sleeping and eating and pooping patterns until Josie, Ralph, Norman, and Peter arrived.

"Look at you!" Peter drew Darla in for a hug. "You're radiant!" He shot a sly smile at Ty. "Don't worry, I know she's taken."

"I'm not worried." Ty gave them all sidearm hugs too, showing off Graycie to each of them and getting the required *ahhh*s back in return.

"You comin' back to group next month?" Norman asked hopefully. "I sure have missed your truffles."

"I wouldn't miss it." Darla had managed to make it to every meeting except for the previous month's, when she'd been too tired to stay up past seven o'clock in the evening, and she'd even found herself opening up more to them too. She'd had her ups and downs with her anxiety issues during the pregnancy, but the doctor was able to help her find a low-dose medication that had helped. Her friends' support had helped too. And of course, she'd had Ty to walk through it with her.

"You could bring the baby if you want," Josie offered. "There are no rules against that or anything."

Darla stroked her daughter's soft head. "She would love to come."

The rest of their friends closed in, obviously getting restless for their turns to hold the babies. Ty and Mateo had no choice but to pass Graycie and Harper around, and the sight of all that love being showered on her daughter made Darla burst into tears.

Everly was in the same boat, it seemed. They looked at each other and said "Hormones" at the exact same time.

While Ty and Mateo kept a close watch on their baby girls, Darla and Everly answered all the typical questions about the birth.

"Was it awful?" Charity asked with a facial expression that declared she assumed it was.

"No," Darla said. "Not at all. It was hard and excruciating and exhausting, but it was the best thing I've ever done." She glanced over and watched Ty share their baby girl with the world. Their new little family was a dream that had been abandoned and then restored and fulfilled. The day they'd welcomed Graycie Faith into the world had felt like the start of a whole new adventure.

"Hey everyone." Ty clanked a spoon against his glass. "I'd like to make a toast." It took a few minutes but the room finally quieted. Darla scurried away from her friends and went to join her husband.

"Thank you all for coming out to celebrate our little girls." Ty secured Graycie in one arm and he wrapped his other arm around Darla. Being so close to him was still the best feeling in the world.

"I've moved around a lot and traveled to a lot of different places, and I've never seen a community like the one in Topaz Falls."

Murmurs of agreement went around the room. Darla looked out at all their friends, these people who had been there for her, who had helped her heal, who had helped her hold on to the courage to find love again.

"We couldn't ask for a better place to raise our daughter. We couldn't ask for better people to help shape her life." He glanced down at Darla and brushed a kiss on her head. "It's been a long time since I've felt like I had a home, but that all changed when I moved here. And I'm so grateful that Graycie and Harper will grow up knowing what 'home' means." He somehow managed to lift his glass from the table beside them. "To family and friends and a community that comes together."

Everyone raised their glasses and repeated the toast. That was when the celebration really began. The room erupted into a happy chaos. Darla held Ty's hand as they showed off their daughter and accepted advice and hugs from all her favorite people. It was all such a blur, but her heart had never felt so full.

No matter what the future held, as long as she had Ty and Graycie and this roomful of beautiful people, her life would be full of love and light.

About the Author

Sara Richardson grew up chasing adventure in Colorado's rugged mountains. She's climbed to the top of a fourteen-thousand-foot peak at midnight, swum through Class IV rapids, completed her wilderness first aid certification, and spent seven days at a time tromping through the wilderness with a thirty-pound backpack strapped to her shoulders.

Eventually Sara did the responsible thing and got an education in writing and journalism. After a brief stint in the corporate writing world, she stopped ignoring the voices in her head and started writing fiction. Now she uses her experience as a mountain adventure guide to write stories that incorporate adventure with romance. Still indulging her adventurous spirit, Sara lives and plays in Colorado with her saint of a husband and two young sons.

You can learn more at:
SaraRichardson.net
Twitter @SaraR_Books
Facebook.com/SaraRichardsonBooks
Instagram @SaraRichardsonBooks

KEEP READING FOR THE BONUS NOVELLA,

A Cowboy's Christmas Eve

by R. C. Ryan!

Colin Malloy enjoys spending
Christmas with his family at the Malloy
ranch. But this holiday, what he really
wants to do is to get closer to the
alluring Dr. Anita Cross. So when a
blizzard conspires to keep her from
joining the Malloy family's festivities,
neither snow, sleet, nor spun-out cars
will prevent Colin from reaching
her side.

Chapter One

Colin Malloy urged his big bay gelding through snowdrifts that were belly high in places along the trail. When the latest snowstorm had begun in earnest in the hills, he'd had half a mind to remain snug and warm in his mountain cabin retreat until it blew itself out. But he couldn't miss Christmas Eve supper at the ranch.

Colin peered through the curtain of snow toward the distant lights of the Malloy Ranch. He wasn't really bothered by the snowy trail or the bite in the wind. Having grown up on these thousand-plus acres here in Montana, he was as comfortable in a blizzard as he was sleeping under the stars on a warm summer night. Though he often enjoyed a quiet night up at the cabin, with a steak over the fire and a cold longneck, the thought of his family's special Christmas Eve guest had him thinking instead about a bottle of champagne and some roast goose. But only if it came with a certain pretty dark-haired woman who'd been sneaking into his thoughts lately.

Dr. Anita Cross, the beautiful new doctor who had come to Montana to join her uncle at the town's medical clinic. The only time they'd ever spoken was when his nephew, Matt, had been seriously injured and required a doctor's care. Anita had impressed him with not only her skill as a physician, but also with her radiant personality. Just the thought of her filled him with a sort of quiet joy. She had a smile that could light up the darkest night and a sweet nature that made him want to treat her with the greatest of care—that is, when he wasn't thinking about taking her into his arms and tasting those perfect lips and ravishing her until they were both sated.

He hadn't felt like this about a woman since Shelby Ross, whose father owned a ranch in Rock Creek. They'd been barely out of their teens, but it had felt a lot like love. Maybe that was because his older brother had married the great love of his life, Bernadette, when the two were just seventeen and Colin had assumed that was how life was and would always be. Watching Patrick and Bernie had made Colin believe in true love and happily-ever-after. But those beliefs were shattered when the two had been killed in a brutal accident on a snowy road one cold December night. It wasn't long after that that Colin learned Shelby had run off with one of her father's wranglers.

So much for true love and happy endings.

Now, all these years later, he was beginning to believe in such things all over again.

He swore softly.

Not that a doctor from a big city would ever give him a second look, and if she did, he stood no chance of being alone with her. With his big, noisy family, they probably wouldn't get a single word in edgewise tonight.

"Come on, Buddy." He leaned over to run a big,

work-roughened hand over his horse's snow-matted mane. "Time to get home and make sure Ma has a Merry Christmas. If I'm lucky, I can sit in the corner and stare to my heart's content at the prettiest girl in the whole world, even though she doesn't know I'm alive."

"Hey, Yancy." Reed Malloy shook snow from his hair as he looked around the kitchen of his family's ranch house, where the table was set with festive holiday plates, and the countertops were covered with serving dishes of every size and shape.

Yancy Martin, the short, boyish-looking cook for the Malloy family for over thirty years, looked up to grin at the youngest of the Malloy men. "Hey, Reed." He returned his attention to putting the finishing touches on an elegant holiday torte, making swirls of dark chocolate in the creamy white frosting.

"Something smells amazing." Luke Malloy, Reed's older brother, trailed behind, his arm around the waist of his bride, Ingrid. "Looks like you're going all out on the menu for Christmas Eve supper."

Yancy's head came up. "Miss Grace told me she wanted it to be extra special, because of our guests."

"Guests?" Matt Malloy, oldest of the three brothers, walked into the kitchen hand in hand with his wife, Vanessa, and tried to dip a finger in the frosting. It was quickly slapped away by Yancy's wooden spoon. "Are we having more than family here tonight?"

Yancy gave a conspiratorial grin. "Your grandma invited old Doc Cross and his niece, Dr. Anita."

Luke shared a look with his brother. "All this fuss for two extra people?"

"One of them is extra special, according to Miss Grace."

At their puzzled looks, Yancy shook his head, sharing a knowing smile with Vanessa and Ingrid. "Where've you three been? Don't you know your grandmother has had her eye on Anita Cross as a potential wife for your uncle Colin ever since that pretty young doctor came to town?"

The two women were nodding in agreement.

"Wife?" Reed started laughing. "Seems to me Gram Gracie's had every pretty girl in the town of Glacier Ridge paired with Colin since we were teenagers. None of them worked out. What makes her think this will be any different?"

Yancy shrugged.

It was the boys' great-grandfather, Nelson LaRou, called "Great One" by all of them, seated in his favorite chair across the room, who answered. "If I had to hazard a guess, I'd say it's the two family weddings this past year. First Matt to his Nessa and then"—he turned to fix Luke with a pointed stare—"Luke and Ingrid." He paused to sip the martini Yancy had learned to fix to his exact specifications and gave a nod of approval. "Now Grace Anne hopes all that romance rubs off on your uncle Colin. I swear, my daughter's bound and determined to get that poor man married off before, as she says, it's too late."

Reed reached for a gingerbread cookie cooling on a wire rack, until Yancy stopped him with a hairy eyeball. "Too late for what?"

"Too late for him to give me more grandchildren." Grace Malloy breezed into the kitchen, wearing her usual ankle-skimming denim skirt and a sky-blue blouse that matched her eyes, her white hair a cap of breeze-tossed curls.

She made a full circle in the room, staring around with satisfaction. "It all looks and smells wonderful, Yancy."

Reed put a hand on her arm. "Are you really setting up poor Colin on the pretext of a holiday dinner?"

"Setting up poor Colin?" Grace gave her grandson a withering look. "I'm merely being a good mother and a good neighbor. After all, Anita came to Glacier Ridge from Boston to give her aging uncle a hand at the clinic, and she hasn't had any time off since. She's young and beautiful and certainly deserves at least a bit of a social life. It's the same with Colin. He's spent so many years helping us with the ranch, not to mention helping your father and me with you three—a handful, I might add—he's forgotten there even is such a thing as a social life."

Reed merely shook his head. "Poor Colin. Being led to the slaughter like a lamb, without even a warning."

"Enough of that kind of talk. He'll thank me one day. And," Gracie added with a twinkle in her eye, "I'll expect you to be here to witness his eternal gratitude. Maybe, if you're lucky, I'll even steer you toward finding that one special woman for yourself."

Reed put his hand up to his ears and gave a mock shudder. "Now you're working overtime to ruin my Christmas, Gram Gracie. I've seen enough lovey-dovey stuff around here in the past year to give me a sugar buzz."

The others shared a laugh as Reed rushed from the kitchen and up the stairs to shower and dress for Christmas Eve supper.

Dr. Leonard Cross poked his head into the examining room, where his niece was busy soothing the mother of a crying five-year-old girl.

Anita Cross put her hand on the mother's shoulder. "The rapid strep test confirmed that it's strep throat,

Millie. I'll write a prescription. Agnes will have it at the reception area when you check out. Be sure to pick it up at Woodrow's Pharmacy before it closes tonight, and start Brittany on the medication right away. She won't be feeling 100 percent by tomorrow, but she'll feel a lot better than she does right now."

"Oh, thank you, Dr. Anita. She's been so worried that Santa wouldn't find her here at the clinic if she had to be admitted."

Turning on her megawatt smile that always put her patients at ease, Anita closed her hand over the little girl's tightly clenched fist. "You'll be home in plenty of time for Santa to visit, Brittany. You should know that Santa has no problem finding children who have to be in the clinic. He visits children on Christmas Eve no matter where they are."

Big blue eyes went even wider. "He does?"

"He does. Why, when I was working in the hospital in Boston, Santa visited every boy and girl there and left them exactly what they'd asked for."

"That's nice." The tears were replaced with a big smile. "But I'm glad I can go home."

"So am I. I can't think of a better place to be on Christmas Eve than with the people you love. Merry Christmas," Anita called as the mother and daughter walked out of the room and her uncle stepped inside.

Seeing that he'd changed from his white lab coat to a suit jacket, she arched a brow. "Is Dr. Miller here from Rock Creek yet?"

Her uncle shook his head. "Not yet. I expect he'll be here any minute. He's already half an hour late."

"Have you phoned him?"

"Twice. No service. But he gave me his word he'd take

care of things here while we're at the Malloy Ranch. I'm sure he'll be along any minute now."

Anita gave a sigh. "Is that the last of the patients?"

"According to Agnes. I told her to duck out of here as soon as she finishes with Millie Davis so she doesn't get stuck for another hour or two."

He glanced out the window at an approaching truck bearing the Malloy logo on the side. "There's our limousine. I promise you, you're going to love Christmas Eve dinner at the Malloy ranch. Nobody cooks like Yancy Martin. You're in for a fine feast."

Anita knew it wasn't the feast she was looking forward to as much as the chance to spend some time with a certain cowboy. From the first moment she'd met Colin Malloy, quietly taking charge of the chaos that always seemed to accompany his family during a crisis, he had become, in her mind, the personification of a real Montana cowboy. Tall and ruggedly handsome. A body sculpted with muscle from years of ranch chores. Dark hair always in need of a trim. A quiet man who didn't say much, but when he spoke in that low, easy drawl, she felt a hitch in her heart. And when he aimed those blue eyes her way and smiled, her whole world seemed to tilt.

She didn't need food. Colin Malloy was a feast for her eyes and heart and soul.

Until coming to Montana, she'd despaired of ever meeting a man who could check off every item on her wish list.

Of course, she thought, there had been men in the past, and one in particular, who had tempted her to believe they were special. Not one had ever lived up to the promise.

She thought about the bitter tears she'd shed over Dr. Jason Trask. At the time, she'd thought her heart would never mend. Now she realized she'd been too young and foolish to recognize that while she'd been spinning dreams of love and marriage, he'd been concerned only with himself and his career. It was only later, hearing the whispers and rumors, that she learned she'd been one of many naïve med students who had fallen for his tired line. As she followed her uncle along the hallway, she paused to greet Burke Cowley, the Malloy ranch foreman, who was heading toward them. "Hello, Burke."

"Miss Anita." The courtly old cowboy removed his wide-brimmed hat and gave her a smile.

"I'll just be a minute while I get my coat."

"I'll let you lock up." Her uncle picked up several handled bags, which contained the cookies she'd lovingly baked, along with gifts she'd insisted on wrapping for the entire Malloy family.

With his hands filled, he indicated several more bags, and Burke picked them up.

Over his shoulder, her uncle called, "We'll load these and wait for you in the truck. I'm sure Dr. Miller will be here any minute now."

Anita stepped into her office and was hanging up her lab coat when she heard voices calling from the reception area. She hurried out to find a rancher with his arm around a teen boy's shoulders.

The boy's arm was wrapped in a bloody towel.

"Ma'am." The rancher looked relieved. "I saw old Doc Cross getting into a truck outside. I called to him, but he couldn't hear me over the wind blowing, and I was afraid we were too late to get any help. My name's Huck Whitfield. This is my son Ben. He put his hand through a glass windowpane."

"Mr. Whitfield. Ben. I'm Dr. Anita Cross."

"I heard old Doc talked a niece into coming out from the big city to give him a hand with this place."

"That's me. And I assure you, I didn't need to be talked into coming. I'm loving this experience in your pretty town. Please come this way." She led them to an examining room and carefully removed the blood-soaked towel.

She looked up at the boy. "That's a nasty cut, Ben." She tried to put him at ease. "You must have been really mad at that window to hit it so hard."

Instead of the expected laugh, two bright spots of color bloomed on the boy's cheeks. "Oh no, ma'am. I was just giving my pa a hand trying to clear the snow."

His father nodded. "That's a fact."

"I was only teasing."

At that, the father and son realized her joke and shared a grin.

She indicated the table. "You can lie down here. I'll need to look at this closely under the lights to remove any glass fragments. From the looks of all that blood, you'll need a few stitches." She started toward the door. "I'll be right back."

Once in the hallway, she punched in the number of Dr. Rob Miller, praying he would tell her he'd be here any minute now. In reply, she got a notice of no service.

She retrieved her lab coat before going in search of her uncle and Burke. When she stepped outside, she was surprised to see that a heavy snow had begun falling, and even though it was early evening, the sky had grown as dark as night.

Burke lowered the window as she approached the truck.

"Sorry, Uncle Leonard. I tried Dr. Miller's number, with no response. I won't be able to go with you. This is an emergency. Huck Whitfield and his son, Ben, came in while you were loading the truck. Ben put his hand through a window, and the cut looks deep. I'd hoped to pass them along to Rob Miller, but since he's still not here, I have to stay. From the looks of that boy's arm, I'll be another hour or more."

Old Dr. Cross gave a sigh. "That's what I was afraid of. Even on Christmas Eve, we always seem to get slammed with one emergency or another. That's why I arranged for a doctor here, just in case."

Anita gave him a gentle smile. "Please don't worry, Uncle Leonard. You go ahead and have a lovely dinner with the Malloy family. I'll stay here and take care of business."

The two men exchanged a look before Burke said, "We'll wait for you."

"There could be complications. I don't want to hold up the entire Malloy family on Christmas Eve."

Burke considered before nodding. "All right. But don't you worry, ma'am. I'll take Dr. Cross out to the ranch now, and I'll head right back for you."

"That's awfully generous of you, Burke, but you could end up missing dinner."

"Wouldn't be the first time, ma'am."

She gave him a grateful smile. "All right. You'd better phone first, though. Like Uncle Leonard said, I could get slammed with more emergencies, and I can't leave until my replacement arrives."

Burke nodded. "Yes, ma'am. I'll call and, no matter how late it is, someone will be here to drive you to the ranch. When Miss Gracie issues an invitation, it's like a royal command."

"Please give Miss Grace my apologies for this hitch in

her plans." With a grin, Anita sprinted back to the door of the clinic.

As she stepped inside, she had to shake snow from her dark hair.

Squaring her shoulders, she headed toward the examining room. Even Christmas, she thought, couldn't stem the flow of emergencies. When she completed her medical studies, hadn't she known this would be her life? Not that she regretted it. Not a bit of it. Nor did she regret her move from a bustling city hospital to this sleepy little small-town clinic. Here, finally, she was doing what she'd always dreamed of. Seeing to every sort of medical emergency possible, from setting broken bones to removing tonsils. From dealing with preschool illnesses to arranging end-of-life care. As her uncle had promised, this place offered her the chance to follow her patients from childhood into old age. These strangers were no longer patients but were slowly becoming her neighbors and friends. Her family. She couldn't think of a more rewarding gift than the chance to live out her life in this sleepy little town of Glacier Ridge, with its fascinating assortment of characters, and this homey little clinic that had taken over her life.

If she felt a twinge of regret at missing her chance to spend more time with a handsome cowboy, she reluctantly pushed it aside. For now, she would give all her attention to Ben Whitfield and get him home in time for Christmas with his family.

Chapter Two

Colin led Buddy through the drifts that had begun piling up against the north side of the barn. Once inside, he unsaddled his horse and toweled him dry before turning him into the warm shelter of his stall and filling the troughs with feed and water.

As he crossed the snow-covered yard, the warm glow of lights spilled from every window of the big house. It brought a smile to his lips. There was no denying how much he loved this ranch and his family. From the time he was just a boy, he'd known this was the only place he ever wanted to be. Riding the range with his father and older brother, herding cattle, doing the million and one tedious chores that went with ranching. Like his father before him, Colin was a rancher to his core. He wouldn't trade places with the richest man in the world. In fact, he knew, without a doubt, that that particular title was already his. He was rich in family. Rich in contentment. Rich in all the ways that really mattered.

He stepped into the mudroom, shaking snow from his hat and parka before hanging them on pegs by the door. He sat on a bench, gratefully kicking off his frozen boots before crossing to the big sink to roll his sleeves and wash to his elbows. The hot water felt heavenly after the frigid cold of the trail.

Hearing a chorus of voices in the great room, he headed up the stairs to shower before joining his family. Of course, he admitted, his family took a backseat at the moment to the one he most wanted to see. But not until he did his best to make a good impression.

After stripping, he shaved away the growth of beard from the trail before stepping under the warm spray to soak up more heat. With a sigh, he toweled himself, grateful to be home. Though he loved the solitude of the hills, he had to admit there was comfort in being here. The tantalizing fragrance of Yancy's prime rib along with roast goose and the faint perfume of cinnamon from Yancy's snickerdoodles, the holiday cookies Yancy baked every Christmas, had his mouth watering. Judging by the laughter coming from the great room, the family and their guests were in full festive mode.

Colin buttoned his shirt and tucked it into the waistband of clean denims. Pulling on his best Sunday boots, he ran a brush through his shaggy hair and hurried down the stairs.

He stopped by the kitchen to snatch up a cold longneck before heading toward the great room.

In the doorway, he paused when he recognized old Dr. Cross telling a story to the family.

"...and I said to her, Martha, when I asked for a specimen, I didn't mean a sample of your Bundt cake."

The roar of laughter that followed had Colin grinning

from ear to ear. Only Doc Cross, who was everyone's friend, could spill secrets about a neighbor and never be offensive.

"Oh, Colin." Grace was out of her chair and hurrying across the room to wrap him in a quick embrace. "I was afraid with this blizzard you wouldn't make it."

"Buddy and I have been through enough storms that you don't ever have to worry, Ma." He turned to the others, his gaze moving quickly over all of them, seeking one special face. When he didn't see Anita, he schooled his features, hoping his disappointment didn't show. "Though I have to admit, this one was a challenge. I thought for a few minutes I might have to dismount and lead poor Buddy, who was up to his haunches in snowdrifts."

"We have a problem." Grace drew him aside to say in a soft voice, "I don't want to send Burke out in this weather."

"I agree. What do you need? I'm happy to fetch it."

"It's Doc's niece."

At the very mention, Colin struggled to keep his emotions banked. Not an easy task when the very mention of her had his heart doing crazy somersaults.

Grace blushed like a kid caught with her hand in the cookie jar. "I may have forgotten to mention that I invited both Leonard and his niece for Christmas Eve supper."

He fought to hold back his smile but lost the battle. It even showed in his quiet tone of voice. "I believe you mentioned it."

She looked away, avoiding his eyes. "The young doctor they'd hired to fill in for Christmas Eve never arrived. An emergency walked into the clinic just as they were preparing to leave, so Doc came alone. Burke said he'd be happy to drive back to town to pick up Anita, but he's been working with your father since dawn. It doesn't seem fair to send him out again."

Colin hoped his disappointment didn't show. "Anita Cross is a grown woman. I'm sure she'll be fine in town."

"Yes. Of course. I guess I just needed to hear it from you."

He waited a beat, searching his mind for any excuse to see her. "But then, this is her first Christmas in Glacier Ridge, far away from Boston and everything familiar. And now her only relative is here with us."

"That's what worries me. Still, you've been out in this snowstorm. What do you think? Would the roads still be passable?"

Colin chose his words carefully, knowing how his mother reacted all these years later about any family member traveling icy roads. The loss of his brother and his brother's wife had left its mark on her soul. "It does seem a shame for Doc's niece to be alone on her first Christmas in town. Why don't I give it a try?"

"Oh, Colin, would you mind?"

"You know I don't."

At the warmth in his tone, she looked up sharply. "Are you saying you don't mind that I really want Anita here?"

"Ma, we both want her here."

She sighed, trying to keep her delight from being too obvious. "You'll turn back if the roads are too icy? Promise me you won't take any foolish chances, Colin."

He brushed a kiss over her cheek. "Promise. But don't hold supper for us. Even if I manage to get through, with a storm like this you know we'll be late."

"We'll wait as long as we can. If we do eat without you,

no matter how late you two get here, I guarantee you'll find a feast."

Colin said his good-byes to the others before heading toward the mudroom. He chose his warmest winter parka before stepping outside. In the equipment barn he climbed into one of the ranch trucks and checked the gas gauge before driving along the curving ribbon of driveway that led to the highway.

A snowy road trip wasn't exactly how he'd planned on spending Christmas Eve, but the thought of Anita Cross waiting for him at the end of the drive had him smiling as he turned on the radio and hummed along with Willie, crooning an old holiday standard. With any luck, they could be back here in a few hours.

It just might turn out to be a holly, jolly Christmas after all.

Anita peered through the magnifier, picking out shards of glass from Ben Whitfield's wound before thoroughly cleansing it.

She noticed that his big, strong father had to look away from the bloody mess.

"You may want to take a seat over there, Huck. This is going to get worse before it gets better."

He didn't need any coaxing. His skin had already turned the color of putty.

"I'll give you something to deaden the pain before I start stitching you up, Ben."

The teen swallowed hard before nodding.

A short time later, assured that the lidocaine had taken effect, Anita began the task of stitching up the wound. While she worked, Ben watched with interest.

She looked up. "Can you feel this?"

He shook his head. "Even though I'm watching you, it's like you're working on someone else, Doc."

"That's good. But you'll have to endure some pain when the effects of this local anesthetic wear off." She tied off the last stitch. "I'll give you a prescription for pain. If you're lucky, you may be able to fill it at Woodrow's Pharmacy, if they haven't yet closed for the night. If they have, call and leave them a message so they have it ready for you first thing in the morning. And just in case, I'll find you a sample to take home so you won't have to spend the night in any discomfort."

Satisfied that the wound was neat and tidy, Huck Whitfield stepped up beside his son. "I'm so glad you were here, Dr. Cross."

"So am I." She gave him a warm smile.

"I hope we haven't spoiled your plans, Doc."

"Not at all."

The boy sat up and Anita braced a hand to his chest. "Hold on, Ben. You'll want to move slowly for a while and maybe lean on your father when you leave here."

He was about to argue when he suddenly went pale.

"Is the room spinning, Ben?"

He nodded.

Huck wrapped an arm around his son's shoulders and held on until the boy's normal color returned.

"Wait here and I'll get a wheelchair." Anita turned and was out of the room before father or son could say a word.

Minutes later she returned.

Huck eased his son from the gurney and helped him into the wheelchair.

At the reception desk, Anita wrote out a prescription and handed it to Huck, along with a sample pill from a drawer.

He hurried outside and drove his truck right up to the front door. With Anita pushing the chair, he managed to get his son into the passenger side.

"Thanks again, Dr. Cross."

"You're welcome, Huck. Merry Christmas."

He touched the brim of his hat in a salute before rounding the truck and climbing into the driver's side.

The snow, Anita noted, was nearly knee-high.

She gave a sigh of regret, thinking about the fine food her uncle had boasted about waiting for them at the Malloy Ranch. There was no way Burke would make it through this blizzard to fetch her and no way she could even make it back to her uncle's house across town.

It looked as though her first Christmas in Glacier Ridge would be spent in the sterile confines of the clinic.

Not that it mattered. She'd spent plenty of lonely nights while working at the hospital in Boston. Like every profession, there was a pecking order. The newest interns were assigned the hours that the established doctors managed to avoid. And though Anita had enjoyed the camaraderie and the spontaneous celebrations she and the others often gave to lift their spirits on their working holidays, she'd missed the warmth of family that had been lost along the way.

Tonight, it wasn't the loneliness or the lack of dinner that had her spirits plummeting. It was the fact that she'd allowed herself to spin way too many fantasies about a certain rugged cowboy. Now here she was, staring reality in the face once again.

Her sweet mother used to warn her that she was much too fanciful to endure the rigors of a medical career. Just thinking about the mother who died too young had Anita feeling the old twinge of regret. Her mother had always hoped her only child would follow her into a teaching career, but after spending time with her father at his medical practice in Boston, Anita had fallen completely under the spell of medicine. When she was just a little girl, she'd known that she would be a doctor like her father and her uncle. To that end, she'd worked doggedly through college and medical school, hoping to join her father in his practice. But when her father had remarried while Anita was fulfilling her internship and had moved across the country to begin a life with his new, much younger bride, Anita decided to make her own way and had stayed on in Boston.

Her uncle's need for an assistant had given her a lifeline when she'd most needed it. While she gave him the help he needed, he, in turn, filled her need for family.

And it had come at the lowest point of her life, when a selfish surgeon had trampled on her poor heart.

Shivering, she hurried inside, grateful for the warmth. At least she was warm and snug and safe from the storm. Hopefully Dr. Rob Miller would soon arrive from Rock Creek to share the work. Her uncle had assured her that Dr. Miller would take good care of their patients in their absence.

She gave a firm nod of her head.

What could possibly go wrong?

Chapter Three

The wind was howling like a beast, sending the snow into drifts that completely obliterated any trace of the road in places. As the ranch truck reached the end of the dirt track and inched onto the interstate, Colin could feel the wheels skidding as they tried to grab traction. A layer of ice on the pavement beneath the mounds of snow presented a real problem. For a moment the truck slid; then the wheels found a dry spot and Colin breathed a sigh of relief as he was able to guide his vehicle into a line of tracks dug deep into the snow. Apparently he wasn't the only fool trying to navigate this blizzard. Now all he needed to do was hope the fool whose tracks he was following knew where the road ended and the snowbanks began.

Even with the wipers at full speed, it was impossible to see more than a few feet through the blowing curtain of snow.

He spotted the headlights of an approaching vehicle. When the car suddenly swerved, he realized it was heading directly into his path.

To avoid the head-on collision, he turned the wheel as far as he could. He felt the rush of air rock his truck as the crazy driver roared past.

Though Colin had managed to avoid an accident, he couldn't stop the skid that suddenly turned into a wild spin as his truck careened off the road and landed backward in a deep gully.

For long moments he sat very still, feeling the rush of adrenaline when he thought of what could have happened. Finally he reached for his cell phone. He was halfway between the ranch and town. An impossible walk in either direction.

He studied his phone with a frown. There was no service. It was typical in a town ringed by so many hills and mountains.

Forcing his way out of the passenger side of the truck, he studied the crazy angle and knew, without a doubt, there was no way he would be able to drive out of this mess. His truck was stuck here until the blizzard passed and a tow truck could make it through the interstate. It could be days before that happened. And with no phone service, he couldn't hope for any help from the ranch.

Knowing he couldn't stay here, he turned up the collar of his parka and started walking. He had to choose between walking back to the ranch or toward Anita, and that was an easy decision to make.

With the storm swirling around him, Colin had no way of judging how long he'd been on the road or how far he'd come when he heard the sound of an approaching truck.

He turned and began waving his arms, hoping the driver could spot him in the blowing snow.

The snowplow slowed, then stopped.

"Hey." The driver shoved open the passenger door. "Not a night to be out in this mess. Where're you headed?"

"Glacier Ridge." Colin climbed inside, grateful for the blast of heat. His hands and feet had long ago gone numb.

"I won't be going in that far. Our job is to clear the interstate first. Probably won't hit the small towns until late tonight. But I can drop you a couple of miles from Glacier Ridge if you want to walk the rest of the way."

"Thanks. I appreciate it."

"I guess some guys will go through anything to get home for Christmas."

Colin didn't bother to correct him. It seemed too much effort to explain why he was going to all this trouble on Christmas Eve.

As the driver put the truck in gear and started forward, Colin gave a sigh. All this, and he had no way of knowing if Anita Cross would even be at the clinic by the time he reached it. If there were no emergencies or if the doctor they'd hired to handle their patients while they were away had finally arrived, she might have headed back to her uncle's place. Though he'd tried calling several times, there was still no service. He wouldn't know anything more until he got there.

When the snowplow finally came to a halt, the driver called, "This is as far as I go. Glad I could get you almost home for the holidays."

"Thanks. Merry Christmas."

Colin stepped from the truck and directly into the blowing, drifting snow.

It was too late to consider what he had gotten himself into. Like the gamblers at Clay's Pig Sty, the local saloon in Glacier Ridge, who thought of themselves as those big-time gamblers they saw on television, he was all in.

There was no turning back.

Colin trudged through drifts that in places were nearly to his waist. His dark Stetson was mounded with a layer of white. His breath plumed in the frigid air.

When he reached the town, it looked otherworldly, until he realized what was wrong. There were no lights. No blinking red and green on the gaudy tree in D and B's Diner. No sparkly gold lights at Gert and Teddy Gleason's new fancy spa next to their barbershop. And no winking welcome sign at Clay Olmsted's saloon.

He made his way to the clinic, which was in total darkness.

His heart dropped. With the power out and the roads too clogged with snow to drive her car, poor Anita would have had to walk in the darkness to her uncle's place across town, nearly a mile.

He gave a sigh of disgust. He'd come this far. There was no turning back now. Though the other side of town felt like the other side of the moon right now, he had no choice but to see this through.

He was about to turn away when he spotted some movement inside the glass doors of the clinic.

"Hello." He pounded on the heavy outer door with both fists. "Who's there?"

He pressed his face to the door and struggled to see through the frosty glass.

There was more movement, closer now. Suddenly the door was opened and Anita seemed as astonished to see him as he was to see her.

"Colin." Even in the darkness, her relief was evident.

Without a thought to what she was doing, she threw her arms around his neck, her fingers curling into the collar of his parka, as though holding on for dear life.

"Anita." At her embrace, he felt the quick curls of pleasure. Their faces were touching. He breathed her in, and the sweet smell of her perfume went straight to his heart. "I was afraid you might have left for your uncle's house." His breath feathered the hair at her temple.

She looked up, her lips brushing his cheek. "I couldn't leave the clinic without someone here to handle emergencies. Dr. Miller from Rock Creek was supposed to be here, but I guess he couldn't make it through the storm."

She seemed to realize what she was doing and made an awkward attempt to step back.

As she held the door, he moved past her, shaking snow from his hat.

His first thought had been to just keep on holding her out of pure relief that she was here and she was all right. Since he didn't feel free to do that, it was enough to just stand and look at her, all buttoned up in her white lab coat, her cheeks a bit flushed, her eyes a little too bright.

"I see you've lost power."

She nodded. "I guess the whole town did."

"This is a medical clinic. I'm sure your uncle would have had a generator installed for just such emergencies."

"I'm pretty sure you're right. When it didn't kick on, I tried phoning my uncle, and there was no service."

"Yeah. My cell phone is dead, too." He stood still, trying to get his bearings. "Got a flashlight?"

She shook her head. "I've been going through drawers and cabinets, but so far, nothing."

"That's all right." He started toward the inner rooms.

"You stay here. I wouldn't want you to trip on something. If I'm lucky and find the generator, there should be light and heat in a few minutes."

She put a hand on his arm. "Would you mind if I come along?"

He absorbed the warmth snaking through his veins at her simple touch and thought again about drawing her into his arms but didn't want to add to her alarm by being too bold. "You afraid of being alone?"

She sighed. "I guess I am. Just a little. I've been hearing noises, like the rattling of doors. Probably the wind. I was very close to panic just before you got here, thinking I'd be spending the night alone in a cold, dark place."

"It's okay. I don't blame you for feeling spooked."

Bold or not, it was the perfect excuse to draw an arm around her shoulders.

Oh, she felt so good tucked up by his side. He was tempted to linger here in the darkness, absorbing all the little sparks of heat that had his heartbeat revving.

"We'll be the blind leading the blind." His mouth brushed the hair at her temple as he added, "Just remember to move slowly and keep one hand out in front of you so you don't get smacked by a wall or door."

He felt her shiver as they made their way slowly and carefully along a hallway, touching half a dozen doors before Colin paused, his hand on the knob of the door at the end of a long hall. "If I'm right, this should be the utility room, where we'll find the furnace, air, and, hopefully, the generator."

"I hope so." Her warm breath teased his cheek, and he thought it the sweetest feeling in the world.

Colin left Anita just inside the door while he felt his way across the room before dropping to his knees. Minutes later a motor kicked on, and the room was flooded with faint light.

Anita couldn't keep from clapping her hands in relief. "Oh, how wonderful. I never thought I'd be this excited over such a simple thing as light."

Colin fiddled with dials and knobs before turning to her with a smile. "That'll do it. In no time this place will be warm as toast."

Her head tilted upward as he walked to her. "I'm so grateful."

"I'm happy to oblige." Her mouth was inches from his, and the thought of kissing her filled him with a quiet thrill.

"I was driving myself crazy wondering what I was going to do. By morning it was bound to be freezing in here. But seeing the power was out all over town, I knew it wouldn't be any better at Uncle Leonard's house. I'd pretty much decided I would just have to hunker down and stay the night. At least I knew I'd have plenty of blankets."

He kept an arm around her shoulders as he guided her across the room. As they stepped out into the hallway, a figure darted into the shadows.

All Colin's instincts sharpened. His only thought was Anita and her safety. Anyone wandering the halls of a darkened clinic on Christmas Eve had to be up to no good.

"Stay here." Colin pressed Anita back against the wall before rushing down the hall.

Despite Colin's words of caution, Anita raced after him.

Colin snagged the arm of the intruder before he could slip away through a back door that was standing slightly ajar.

"He has something in his hand," Anita shouted. "Oh, dear heaven, a gun."

Colin's hand connected with the intruder's, sending the object dropping heavily to the floor.

Colin kicked it aside before pressing both hands on the intruder's shoulders, slamming him up against the wall.

"Who are you and what are you doing in here?" Colin demanded.

Anita bent to the object the intruder had dropped. "Not a gun. A hammer." She looked up to study the intruder and realized he was just a boy. "At least now I know it wasn't the wind I'd been hearing. How did you get that door open?"

The boy clamped his mouth shut and shot her a look that was somewhere between sullen and terrified.

Colin tightened his grip on the boy's shoulders. "You'll answer Dr. Cross, or you can answer to Sheriff Graystoke."

At the mention of the law, the boy's face fell and he looked as though he would cry. "The guy outside pried it open and sent me in."

"This guy have a name?"

The boy shrugged. "I don't know him."

"You'd break into a medical clinic for a stranger?" Colin's face was inches from the boy's. "What did he offer you?"

The boy hung his head. "Ten dollars. I told him I needed twenty."

"And in return, what were you supposed to get for him?"

The boy wouldn't meet Colin's eyes. "He said to grab any medicine that wasn't locked up. Or, he said, if nothing else, a prescription notepad from the doctor's office. He said if I didn't come out with something he could use, he'd hurt me."

Colin's eyes narrowed with sudden fury. He turned to Anita. "Keep hold of that hammer. And stay here with the boy."

Before she could respond, he was out the back door.

She stood, frozen with fear.

The thought of Colin rushing into the path of a gun-toting criminal had her heart pounding in her chest and the blood throbbing in her temples.

A dozen thoughts and images crowded her mind, each one more horrible than the next. She stood rooted to the spot, terrified that she would hear a gunshot.

Colin was risking his life out there, and she was helpless to do anything except wait and wonder and worry.

And pray.

Chapter Four

After what seemed an eternity, the back door was shoved inward and Colin strode through, eyes fierce, his mouth a grim, tight line of anger. He leaned in to the door before locking it.

Without a word, he caught the boy by the arm and dragged him along the hallway until they were at the reception area, where, thanks to the generator, the lights of a gaily decorated Christmas tree and the soft strains of holiday music were in sharp contrast to his dark mood.

With a grip on the boy's chin, he forced his head up. "Look at me. The man's gone and he won't be coming back. Not if he values his life. Now, what's your name?"

"Chip. Chip Carter."

Anita gasped. "Is your mother Emily?"

He nodded.

"How old are you, Chip?" Colin fought to keep the anger from creeping into his voice.

"Fourteen."

"What in the hell is a fourteen-year-old doing breaking into a medical clinic on Christmas Eve? You'd better tell me the truth, because I already heard the other guy's story."

The boy closed his eyes. "I needed to get some money for my mom."

"You needed it so badly you'd resort to stealing?"

A tear slid from the boy's closed eyes.

Colin removed his hands from the boy. "Where's your father, Chip?"

"He's somewhere in Oklahoma. He...took a job driving a big rig to make enough money to keep our ranch going, and now he's caught in this storm. My mom spent her last twenty dollars buying my little brother a pair of used ice skates over at Anything Goes. She figured my dad would be home by now with his paycheck. I heard her talking on the phone with him. She said she doesn't even have enough left for Christmas supper."

"You ever think about earning money the old-fashioned way instead of stealing it?"

The boy looked away. "I tried. I offered to clean tables or wash dishes at D and B's Diner earlier today, but they said they didn't need me 'cause they were closing up early. I asked to work the counter at Woodrow's Pharmacy, but he said I was too young. I have to be sixteen before he can legally hire me. That's when that stranger heard us talking and led me outside before offering me money to just walk in here."

Colin's voice was low with fury. "He may have jimmied the door, but you were the one who was actually going to steal. Do you know how much trouble you could have been in if you'd succeeded in getting what that junkie wanted? Do you think he'd have calmly paid you the money he promised and let you walk away, knowing you'd be a witness against him later?"

"No, sir. I...wasn't thinking. It didn't seem like a big deal. It was just Dr. Cross's notepad."

"A notepad with her clinic's seal. Good enough in most towns to get a prescription filled." Colin fell silent for nearly a full minute before glancing at Anita. "Could you use some help around here?"

She arched a brow. "I...suppose so. What do you have in mind?"

He turned to Chip. "Are you serious about wanting to work?"

The boy swallowed hard before giving a nod.

"Can you come in every day after school and on the weekends to sweep the floors, clean the bathrooms, empty the trash, and do whatever Dr. Cross wants you to do?"

For the first time, the boy actually met his steely gaze. "Yes, sir. I'd like that. It would be a help to my mom and dad."

"All right, then." Colin flicked a glance at Anita. "Are you willing to trust him? He did, after all, try to rob you."

She never hesitated. "I'm willing to risk it."

Colin stared directly at the boy, gauging his reaction. "You can always file a report with Sheriff Graystoke if Chip doesn't live up to his part of the bargain."

Anita nodded. "I'll keep that in mind."

Reaching into his back pocket, Colin removed his wallet.

When he handed a bill to Chip, the boy's eyes went wide. "This is fifty dollars."

"Give it to your mom for Christmas dinner."

Chip was shaking his head, holding out the bill. "I can't take that. I have no right..."

Colin closed Chip's hand around the money and pro-
pelled him toward the front door. "You okay with walking
home through this storm?"

"Yes, sir. But—"

"Good." Colin put a hand on Chip's shoulder. "Now
you listen to me, son. If you want to give your
folks the best gift ever, remember to never again do
anything that would bring them shame. Soon enough
you'll be a man. Grow into one who will always make
them proud."

"Yes, sir." The boy's voice trembled with emotion.
"Thank you."

He looked past Colin to where Anita stood. "Thank
you, Dr. Cross. I won't let you down. I'll see you the day
after Christmas."

As the boy disappeared into the night, Anita fought
back tears.

"Hey." Colin laid a hand over hers. "It's okay now."

She wiped at her eyes. "You realize, don't you, that you
just saved that boy from making a horrible mistake."

"He strikes me as a good kid who was about to fall into
a deep hole."

"And you caught him before he fell. Oh, Colin. I was so
afraid when you rushed out into the dark. That man could
have been waiting with a gun."

"Don't think about that now."

"I can't help thinking that if you hadn't been here, this
could have ended so badly."

Colin's hand fisted just thinking about it. A lone
woman, in the dark, and a desperate junkie. He would be
forever grateful that he'd been here with her.

At his movement, Anita caught sight of his knuckles,
bloody and swollen. "I wondered how you got the stranger

to agree to just walk away. I should have known, from the fierce look of you, that it ended in a fight. I'd better get some ice. That looks pretty painful."

He straightened his hand and shook off the pain. "Don't bother. I've had worse. The guy had a chin like a block of concrete." Then he gave her one of those slow, devilish smiles. "I think I broke his jaw."

He looked around, pleased that the lights, though dimmer than usual, were working throughout the clinic. The dim glow of lights and the sound of music added a festive feeling. The hum of the furnace assured him that it would soon be comfortably warm inside.

Anita glanced at the darkness outside. "I didn't see your headlights before you knocked on the door."

He shook his head. "I didn't drive."

"How did you get here?"

"I hitched a ride with a snowplow driver and walked from the interstate."

"But that's miles from here."

He gave a lazy shrug of his shoulders. "What's a few miles on a pretty night like this?"

She was amazed that after what they'd just been through, she could laugh at his humor. "Of course. The perfect night for a walk in hip-deep snowdrifts."

"Waist-deep by now."

"Even worse. Especially with the temperature below freezing."

"Just a minor inconvenience."

She gave a shake of her head. "Colin Malloy, you're amazing."

He winked. "Why thank you, ma'am." He shrugged out of his parka and hung it on a coatrack near the reception desk before adding his hat as well.

Anita studied the ripple of muscle across his back and shoulders. "I hope you took time for dinner before coming all this way."

"No time. My mother has her mind set on having you there with the family."

"I don't see how it can happen now." Anita twisted her hands. "I feel terrible about spoiling all her plans."

He stepped closer to put a big palm on her shoulder and absorbed another jolt to his already-charged system. "From what I heard, you had no choice. Wasn't it an emergency that kept you here?"

"It was. Ben Whitfield put his hand through a window and needed stitches."

"I know Ben and his pa, Huck. I'm glad you were here to help."

"I'm glad, too." Her smile bloomed. "I know it was Ben who got hurt, but his poor father was suffering every bit as much as his son."

"Huck's a good man. If I were a father, I'd be worried sick if my son put a hand through glass."

"Have you ever been married, Colin?"

"No." He paused, almost afraid of the question and the answer. "You?"

She shook her head and he felt his heart begin to beat faster.

He seemed to realize that he was still touching her. He started to lift his hand away, then, thinking better of it, began running his hand across her shoulder, down her arm. "You warm enough?"

"Yes. Thanks." Anita shivered as her body strained toward his. "Oh, Colin, I'm so glad you're here. Not just because of the break-in, though that had me terrified. And not just because you got the generator going. But I was feeling..." She sighed. "I guess I was feeling sorry for myself. Alone. Afraid. And..."

"And in a strange new place." His voice lowered. Softened. "Don't beat yourself up. You had every right to those feelings. Nobody wants to be alone on Christmas Eve."

She felt the warmth of his breath, the strength of his hand as it moved along her arm.

He was staring at her in a way that had her heart speeding up.

Without meaning to, she moved closer to him, until their bodies were nearly touching.

His head dipped slightly.

Hers lifted in anticipation.

At a sudden knock on the outer door of the clinic, both heads came up sharply.

They stepped apart with matching looks of guilt.

When Anita started toward the door, Colin stopped her with a hand to her arm. "Wait. Let me check it out before you open the door."

They walked together to the entrance and peered into the darkness.

A young man stared back at them, his face pinched with worry. He was holding on to the rope of a toboggan. On it, wrapped in layers of quilts and blankets, was a girl, half-sitting, half-lying, her face mirroring her pain.

"Oh, Colin. Hurry and unlock the door," Anita called.

As soon as he did, she thrust the door open and the man lifted the young woman, blankets and all, from the toboggan and hurried inside.

"What's wrong?" Anita stood aside as the young man rushed past her, carrying his burden into the warmth. "What happened to her?"

Still holding her, the man turned to Anita, noting her white lab coat. "Are you the doctor?"

"I am."

"Thank goodness." In the light his face appeared even younger. Now that he was no longer frowning, he appeared dangerously close to tears. "We're having a baby."

Chapter Five

"Follow me." Anita led the way past the reception area and along a hallway toward an examining room, with Colin and the young man following.

When Colin offered to help with his burden, the boy refused, saying, "It's okay. She's not heavy. I've got her."

The girl clung firmly to the boy, burying her face in his neck.

Colin held the door and the young man carried her to a bed, setting her down with great care, as if to cushion any further pain.

Anita was busy washing her hands at the sink. "I'm Dr. Anita Cross, and this is Colin Malloy."

"I'm Scott Kelly. This is Carly."

"Do you have a last name, Carly?"

At Anita's question, the girl glanced hesitantly at Scott before giving a nod. "Carly Jennings."

"Carly, I'll need to examine you to see how far the baby has progressed." Anita turned to Scott. "If you two gentlemen would step out, I'll do my exam and you can return and hear the results."

Colin led the way out the door and into the hallway before turning to the boy, who was leaning nervously against the wall. "Are you two from around here?"

Scott shook his head. "We're both from Timberline."

Colin gave the boy a steady look. "That's a couple of hours from here."

"Yes, sir."

"Where were you headed?"

"To my grandfather's cabin up in the hills."

"Your family having a holiday reunion up there?"

He shook his head. "We just...thought we'd settle in there for a while."

"That's a pretty remote area. You figured on delivering this baby by yourself?"

Scott looked down at the floor. "We thought we had a few more weeks before the baby would be here. By then, we'd figure out where we wanted it to be born."

"All right, gentlemen. I've completed my exam. You can come back now."

At Anita's words, Scott's head came up sharply and he hurried into the room, with Colin trailing.

Anita was smiling as she covered her young patient, now wearing a cotton gown, with a blanket. "It's a good thing you got here when you did, Scott. The baby's made good progress and is on its way."

"On its way?" Scott tensed. "How soon?"

"I'd say no more than an hour." She turned to Carly. "While I get a birthing room ready, you have two choices. You can stay here in bed, or if it feels better, you can walk the halls, as long as Scott stays right beside you."

"I can walk?" Carly started to swing her legs over the edge of the bed.

"Hold on." Anita put a hand on her shoulder and slipped a second gown over the other, to cover her back from neck to ankles. "You can walk only if it relieves some of the pain. And, as I said, only if Scott is right beside you. Any distress, and you get right back to bed and send for me. Agreed?"

The girl nodded, and Scott hurried over to take her hand.

With great tenderness, he helped her ease off the edge of the bed. Though her movements were clumsy, she looped an arm through his and walked beside him from the room.

When they were gone, Anita hurried to a second room and began preparing it for delivery.

Colin followed behind her. "You okay with this?"

She arched a brow. "Delivering a baby?"

"It could get complicated. She's hardly more than a kid herself."

"Seventeen."

"She told you that?"

Anita nodded. "She and Scott are both seventeen and seniors in high school."

"And they're running."

Anita slanted him a glance. "He admitted that?"

"Not in so many words, but it's pretty easy to figure out."

She sighed. "We'll have plenty of time to get to know them and, hopefully, to hear their story."

"I thought you said an hour."

She smiled. "Babies have their own particular time-tables. They come into this world when they're ready. Since this is a first and the mother is young, it could be quick and easy or slow and plodding. Until we see how it progresses, all bets are off."

She touched a hand to the frown that creased Colin's forehead. "Getting nervous, cowboy?"

"You bet. Walking miles through a blizzard is a piece of cake. Birthing a baby isn't something I'm prepared for."

She patted his cheek. "Fortunately for you, I can handle this. And so can that young mother, whether she's ready or not. All you and Scott have to do is stand on the sidelines and be the cheering section."

"If you say so." When she started to turn away, he drew her back and tilted her face up to his. "I just hope, when all this is over, you'll remember where we were before we were interrupted."

She gave him a smoldering look. "I'm not about to forget."

He placed a big, callused hand to her cheek.

The flare of heat was so stunning, they both looked startled by the unexpected flow of emotions.

Anita felt her heart take a sudden hard dip before shifting into high gear. There was such an incredible rush wherever he touched her. What would it be like if he kissed her? The thought of his mouth on hers had little fires starting deep inside.

How was it possible that right now, when all her thoughts should be centered on the pending birth, the only thing she could think about was Colin and the way he made her feel?

Maybe because he was so much more than any man she'd ever known. The fact that he was here, in a driving blizzard, proved that he was steady as a rock. The sort of man she would trust in time of need. Still, there was something raw and earthy about him that had her heart stuttering with barely contained excitement. He was so cool. So self-contained. A man's man, accustomed to forging his own trails. And here he was, making her feel as if she were the only woman in the world, and he was thrilled to spend his Christmas Eve in a medical clinic.

"If we were alone..."

His words had her breath backing up in her throat and her heart hammering in her temples. "Why don't you tell me what you'd do if we were alone."

"For openers, I'd do this." He lowered his face to hers and covered her lips with a kiss that had her heart stuttering.

Oh, the man knew how to kiss. How to make a woman feel special, cherished. She was enveloped in those strong arms while his mouth moved over hers in the most delicious kiss that had all the breath backing up in her throat as a fire began deep inside.

"And then I'd..." His hands moved along her sides, causing the heat to build as his thumbs encountered the soft swell of her breasts. Her nipples hardened instantly, and she couldn't stop the little gasp that escaped her lips.

"If we were alone, I'd already have you out of these clothes so I could just take my time looking at you. You're so beautiful, you take my breath away. I'm thinking a lifetime wouldn't be long enough to get my fill of looking at you."

She ran her palms up his arms, across his shoulders. "You're easy on the eye, too, cowboy. I think I like hearing all the things you'd do if we were alone."

"That's just the start of it. Next I'd—"

"Dr. Cross!"

At Scott's cry, Anita touched a finger to his lips. "You've certainly got my attention. Hold that thought, cowboy. I can't wait to hear how this will end."

She hurried out the door, leaving Colin frowning in frustration.

He felt trapped by his own words. Hot as hell. While he'd been thinking he was seducing her, he was the one who'd been seduced. By the mere look of her. The touch of her. And now there was nothing to do but wait and hope this latest emergency didn't take all night.

My fault, he thought with a sudden wry laugh. *That's just what comes of trying to get time alone with a busy doctor while she's being hit with one emergency after another.*

Sooner or later, they'd find their moment, he vowed as he trailed slowly behind.

"Carly's hurting, Doc." Scott hovered over the girl, who was leaning heavily against the wall.

"Are the pains worse?" Anita drew an arm around the girl.

"Uh-huh." Her breath was coming in short huffs. "Really bad now."

"On a scale of one to ten, ten being the worst, what number would you give your pains?"

"Eleven." Carly's voice shook.

"Then I'd say it's time we get you to bed." Anita signaled for Scott to take Carly's arm as she led the way toward the sterile birthing room.

While Scott got Carly settled in the bed, Anita bustled about preparing the instruments, many of which would be used only in case of an emergency.

She wheeled a tiny bassinet next to the bed and prepared the items necessary for a possible premature birth. Heat. Light. Oxygen. From her calculations, the baby seemed a safe size, but she had to be prepared for any emergency.

Colin stepped up beside her. "Can I do anything to help?"

She shot him a brilliant smile. "Just having you here is a help to me."

She turned away, all brisk business now. "All right, gentlemen. Make yourselves scarce for a few minutes while I do another check on mama and baby."

Colin stood quietly watching as Scott paced the length of the hall and back, his face a mask of intense concern. It seemed a lot for a high school kid to handle, but this young man struck him as up to the task.

Hoping to distract the boy, he asked, "You play any sports?"

Scott paused. "Football. Soccer. Baseball."

"A man for every season, I see."

The boy managed a weak smile. "I guess so. It just comes natural to me."

"Varsity?"

Scott nodded. "I'm captain of all three teams."

"That means you're good."

He shrugged. "I try."

"And it means your teammates trust you to lead them."

Another shrug of his shoulders as he stared nervously at the closed door of the birthing room.

Recognizing the boy's fear, Colin plunged ahead, determined to keep Scott's mind on anything except the coming event. "All that popularity with your classmates. You class president, too?"

The boy shook his head. "That's Carly. She's the smartest and most popular girl in our class."

"Really? Is she into sports, too?"

The boy brightened. "She's a mean soccer player. I think if she put her mind to it, she could beat me. We've practiced together a lot. She's the captain of her team, too."

"Either of you thinking about using it as a springboard for a college scholarship?"

"That was the plan." His smile faded. "I've got a job lined up right after graduation."

"Doing what?"

"Ranching. My uncle Rick needs more wranglers. It's all I know. All I want to know. I've been ranching with my dad since I was old enough to hold a shovel."

"Your dad doesn't need you?"

Scott looked away, but not before Colin saw the pain in his eyes. "My dad said he expects me to be the first one in our family to graduate from college. He won't let me work our ranch unless I promise to go."

"You can do both. Work as a wrangler and take classes online at night. Ranchers around these parts have done it for years. That's how I managed both."

Scott shook his head. "That's what I'm hoping. But not for a while. Carly's going to need some help with a new baby and all..."

"Yeah. But babies grow. You two could take a class each semester. Before you know it, the baby is in school and the two of you are college graduates."

Scott looked thoughtful. "Maybe. We'll just have to—"

"You two can come back in." Anita's voice from the doorway had Scott racing toward the side of Carly's bed and grabbing her hand.

Colin lifted a brow in question and Anita merely smiled. "Our baby's making progress. It should be any time now."

"Would you like me to wait outside?"

She shook her head. "You can stand behind Scott and be his backup." In a whisper she added, "Be sure and catch him if he starts to drop."

Colin reminded himself to breathe as he followed her into the room and took up a position beside Scott, ready to catch the boy if the entire process proved too much for him. Of course, he had no way of knowing how he himself would survive if anything should go wrong. He hoped he could remain upright and not embarrass himself.

In these past years he'd helped raise three nephews, had stepped in as his father had aged to shoulder more of the responsibilities of their huge ranch, and had assisted in thousands of animal births. He knew the whims of nature and had never felt overwhelmed by the blood and gore and brutality of it. But right now, as this scene was about to unfold before him, he couldn't actively participate. He had no choice but to stand by and be nothing more than an observer.

Or, as Anita had called it, a cheerleader. Something alien to his very nature.

All his life he'd been in the center of all the action going on around him at the ranch. He had always assumed he would one day marry and have a family. It was the way of things. Living in such a loving, nurturing family, he'd taken for granted that he would follow his parents' example. Theirs was such an amazing love story. But after the death of Patrick and Bernie, his dreams had taken a sharp turn. At first because of the pain his family was enduring and the need to try his best to be father and mother to his nephews.

When had the years slipped away? One minute he was a fearless young man, sowing his wild oats. The next he was forty and still single.

The seasons had come and gone in a flurry of ranch chores and family dramas, and he'd been content to deal with one thing after another. Now, suddenly, the arrival of Anita Cross in his world had changed everything.

And right this minute, he wanted, more than anything, to carry her off to somewhere so isolated, they were the only two people in the universe. If that happened—when that happened, he mentally corrected—he would show her in every way possible just how much she had begun to mean to him.

For now, caught up in this latest emergency, he would have to practice patience and step back to be nothing more than a bit player in a drama that was absolutely breathless to witness.

That fact left him feeling, for the first time in his life, helpless and completely out of his element.

Chapter Six

Carly was struggling not to cry out each time a new pain rolled through her, but sometimes, when a particularly painful contraction began, she couldn't contain herself.

Beside her, Scott, wide-eyed and manfully fighting to maintain his control, kept murmuring words meant to soothe while reminding her to breathe.

Colin appeared stoic, his eyes focused on the young couple. The girl in the bed was gripping Scott's hand so tightly, her nails were drawing blood. To his credit, Scott, though clearly suffering every pain right along with her, kept up a continuous stream of loving words meant to comfort.

Through it all, Dr. Anita Cross was the calm in the center of a storm.

"You're doing really well, Carly. Everything is moving along like textbook."

The girl gave her a grateful smile before the next pain rose up and she squeezed Scott's hand.

"Did your doctor tell you if you're having a boy or girl?"

Scott answered for both of them. "We didn't want to know." He smiled down at Carly. "We wanted to be surprised."

"Interesting. And rare these days. Well, you'll know soon enough. We'll all know."

Just as Carly let out a piercing cry, Anita pressed a hand on the girl's engorged tummy and smiled. "Any minute now, in fact. This is the big one."

At the startled gasp from both Scott and Carly, she said, "I'm going to ask you to push and not stop until I say so. Starting . . . right . . . now."

Carly's hands fisted in the bed linens as she did as she'd been told.

Standing at the head of the bed, Scott placed both hands on her shoulders, kneading, caressing as he breathed for both of them.

Standing behind him, Colin placed a big hand on the boy's shoulder and squeezed.

With a sudden rush of fluid, the baby slid free into Anita's waiting hands.

"Carly and Scott, you have a beautiful baby boy."

She laid the infant, its umbilical cord still attached, on Carly's chest.

The baby gave a lusty cry.

"With a very healthy set of lungs," Anita added with a laugh before handing Scott a pair of sterile scissors. "Would you like to do the honors?"

For a single moment, Scott looked terrified and astounded. Then, gathering himself, he walked to the side of the bed, accepted the scissors, and cut where the doctor indicated.

"Good job. Have you decided on a name?"

At Anita's question, the two shared a secret smile.

"Jesse," they said in unison. The name was uttered on a whisper, as though in prayer.

Anita's composure slipped for just an instant as her eyes filled. "What a perfect name for a baby born on this day." She wiped away her tears before glancing at the clock on the wall.

Her gaze fell on Colin, whose own eyes were moist. They shared a tender look before Anita said to the young couple, "In case you were a little too preoccupied to notice, it's twelve-oh-five. Your little Jesse is a Christmas baby."

In an instant, the pain and fear were forgotten as Scott and Carly slipped into the very private world of new parenthood, huddling over this beautiful new creature they'd helped create, crying together, then laughing through their tears as they cooed and cuddled.

Anita went about the work of finalizing the delivery, cleaning up the mother, and disposing of the soiled linens.

With Carly tucked up beneath a warming blanket, Anita reached for baby Jesse. "I'll weigh him, clean him up, and bring him right back. Promise," she added when she saw their looks of alarm. "Jesse and I will only be a few minutes."

Scott clutched Carly's hand. "You're shaking. You warm enough?"

"I am now, thanks to this blanket Dr. Cross put over me." She held out a corner. "Feel it. It's heated."

"That's good." He brushed tear-damp hair from her eyes. "You were amazing."

"So were you. I couldn't have done it without you, Scott."

The two stared into each other's eyes.

Carly was the first to look away. "I wish my mom could have been here."

"Yeah. Mine too."

Colin stood to one side, feeling like a voyeur. "I'll leave now. You two deserve some alone time."

Scott turned. "No. Stay." He stuck out his hand. "Thanks for being here. I could feel your hand on my shoulder. It felt good. Like my dad's."

Colin accepted his handshake. "You two were great." He paused before asking, "You plan on phoning your folks as soon as we get service?"

Scott shook his head. "There's no reason to contact them. They'll never forgive us for this."

"*Never* is a pretty strong word."

The boy took Carly's hands in his. "Our folks got together and had a family meeting. They agreed that the best thing for everyone was to give up our baby for adoption and finish school. They said if we wanted to get married after we finish college, they would give us their blessing."

Colin saw the way Carly's eyes filled with tears. "Did they include you in this family meeting?"

The two nodded.

"Did you tell them what you wanted?"

Scott cleared his throat. "We tried. They weren't hearing us. They said two kids our age don't really know what love is and that they were just sparing us a lot of pain and heartache."

"That's what good parents try to do, son. They figure they've lived long enough to know all the pitfalls, and it's their job to save their kids from falling into them."

"Yes, sir." Scott's voice lowered with feeling. "But Carly and I know what we're feeling is real. We'll do whatever it takes to stay together and keep our baby. You saw him. Jesse is ours. Nobody has the right to take him away from us. As soon as this storm blows over, we'll be heading out as planned."

"I guess if you think it's best for the two of you, you have the right to follow your hearts."

The two young people looked up at him with surprise. "You agree with us?"

Colin chose his words carefully. "It's not a matter for me to agree or disagree. I've got no stake in this. It's up to the people involved, and the two of you more than anyone. Some people in this world just seem to know, from a very early age, that they're right for each other. I don't believe anybody can tell us what we're feeling."

Scott looked at Carly while saying to Colin, "You're the first adult to say that."

Colin cleared his throat. "I had an older brother, Patrick. He was my hero. The only thing I ever wanted was to be like him. Patrick married the love of his life, Bernadette, when they were both just seventeen. You two remind me of them."

Scott looked intrigued. "Did their parents object?"

Colin chuckled. "At first. Like all parents, they didn't want to see their children hurt. But when my brother let them know that he was going to marry his Bernie with or without their permission, they did what they could to make it work. Pat and Bernie lived with our family on our ranch and had three boys—Matt, Luke, and Reed. Through the years, every time my brother and his wife looked at each other, everyone could see the love in their eyes for each other and for their three sons."

Carly sounded doubtful. "What about Bernadette's parents? How did they feel?"

"As you can imagine, they weren't happy to not only lose their daughter to a brash rancher but to also have her move in with his family. After the birth of their first son, though, her parents fell in love with their first grandson and with their daughter's husband. They came to love Pat as much as Bernie did."

Scott exchanged a hopeful smile with Carly. "Are they still happily married?"

Colin had to swallow twice. "They're...dead."

At Colin's words, the two young people fell silent.

It was Scott who finally asked, "How did they...die?"

Colin cleared his throat before he could continue. "They were celebrating their thirteenth anniversary right here in town. In honor of the event, my grandfather had loaned them his fancy Rolls-Royce, a car he'd never allowed anyone to drive. It was a snowy night, much like this one, and on the way home they went off the road and hit a tree. They both died at the scene."

Carly put a hand to her throat. "I'm so sorry."

"Thank you, Carly. It was a terrible loss for our family. Their three young sons lost devoted parents. My folks and grandfather lost their firstborn. I lost my hero." His tone lowered. Softened. "But think about this. Even though they died young, they'd managed to live a rich, full life. A life filled making so many happy memories. All because they bravely followed their hearts. Maybe, if they'd been persuaded not to marry, they wouldn't have given us those three wonderful sons who've helped fill the hole in our hearts when their parents were taken too soon."

His voice rose with passion. "So I suggest that as soon as there's phone service after the storm, you two phone your parents. By now they must be worried sick. Tell them where you are and ask them to join you here so that, together, you can all deal with the here and now and whatever is to come."

He winked at Carly. "I do believe, once they see that beautiful little grandson, their anger and fear may well be forgotten and overcome by a blazing love. You might very well see them have a true change of heart. It happens, you know. Especially when there's a baby involved. Jessie isn't just yours now. He belongs to them, too, in a very special way. I've watched my parents with their grandsons. They've been given a chance to relive those early days of parenthood, as well as the joys of being grandparents. It's a really special bond. One you shouldn't deny your own parents."

The two young people fell silent just as Anita stepped into the room. From the flush on her cheeks and the hitch in her voice, it was obvious that she'd overheard Colin's impassioned speech.

"Here we are. Just as I promised. Jesse weighed in at six pounds even." She smiled at Carly. "You may have miscalculated the due date, or he may have decided to come a bit early. Either way, he's perfectly healthy in every way."

She set the swaddled baby in a bassinet beside Carly's bed before indicating a recliner across the room. "Scott, if you'd roll that here beside Carly, I'll place Jesse's bassinet between the two of you. I think you should try to catch a little rest. This day has been quite an adventure for you both. A wild ride through a storm. A trip on a toboggan. And now a beautiful new life that's in your care."

After setting them up so they were as close as possible, she handed a control to Carly. "If you need anything at all, just press this."

The two new parents seemed not to hear her as they gratefully snuggled under the warm blankets and turned toward each other, heads bent to the tiny bundle in the clear bassinette.

With a smile, Anita signaled for Colin to follow her from the room.

"I think, after all they've been through, they'll sleep now."

She paused at a door marked STAFF and opened it to reveal a simple sitting room with several leather chairs and a cot in one corner. There was a sink and several cabinets, as well as a refrigerator and a coffeemaker.

As she started in, Colin placed a hand on her shoulder. "What you did back there..." He shook his head. "It left me speechless. You were amazing. In the midst of all that storm of pain and fear and confusion, you were so calm. So professional."

She gave him a gentle smile. "That's what I'm trained to be."

"Maybe. But I found it incredibly sexy to watch the way you calmly took charge. Each time they started to panic, you knew exactly what to say to bring them back from the edge. Despite all that was happening, you led them forward without a pause."

She arched a brow. "If you think that was sexy, remind me to invite you to my next surgery."

He chuckled. "No thanks. I'll just leave that to my imagination."

She closed a hand over his. "I didn't mean to eavesdrop, but I overheard what you told those two. I'm so sorry, Colin. I had no idea you lost your brother and his wife."

"It was a long time ago, but in truth, the loss still haunts our family."

"I can tell. Sharing it with Scott and Carly was extremely generous of you. Standing there, listening to you,

I couldn't help hearing the emotion in your voice. Seeing a man open his heart to strangers is also"—she sighed—"incredibly sexy."

He arched a brow, unable to hide his surprise at her admission.

She put a hand on his arm. "I think your honesty may be the one thing that could persuade those two sweet young people to contact their families."

He absorbed the heat of her touch, enjoying the way it charged through his system. "I hope they do. They're going to need all the love and support they can get."

She nodded.

As she started to turn away, he leaned close to whisper, "I think we were speaking of sexy..." He lifted a hand to her hair and gathered her close before glancing at the cot across the room.

Seeing the direction of his gaze, she burst into laughter, even while she shivered at his touch. "Your timing couldn't be worse. In case you've forgotten, you walked miles through a blizzard and I've just come through a storm of sorts myself. Why don't we see if there's anything to eat in this fridge and treat ourselves to a Christmas meal before we think about"—she shrugged—"anything else."

"You're not going to make this easy, are you? The only thing I'm hungry for is you." His smile slowly returned. "I guess I could be persuaded to eat something. Especially since it will fuel us for"—he mimicked her shrug—"anything else."

Still laughing, she crossed the room and opened the small refrigerator before turning with a teasing look. "I do like the way you think, cowboy. Food first. And then, hopefully, a little time all to ourselves to indulge...other hungers."

Chapter Seven

There's a plate of cheese and some tuna salad." Anita turned from the fridge. "My uncle's favorite snack. Also a longneck he stashed behind the jar of mayo."

"Sounds perfect."

"There's bread up there." She pointed to a cupboard. "And plates and mugs up here."

He reached over her head at the same moment she turned.

Their faces were mere inches apart, and Colin nearly bobbled the plates in his hand. The need to touch his lips to hers had him sweating.

He stepped back and carefully set the dishes on the small table, cursing his bad timing and wishing for a replay of the moment. He'd gladly sacrifice a few plates for a chance to kiss that tempting mouth.

With a wicked smile he muttered, "Can I get a do-over?"

She arched a brow.

"That missed opportunity." He gathered her close and

covered her mouth with his, drawing out the kiss until they were both struggling for breath.

He drew a little away. "Thank you, ma'am."

"Anytime." She drew in a deep draft of air. "Would you like another?"

Without a word, she lifted her face to his and he kissed her with a thoroughness that left them both trembling.

Anita was the first to step back. With a hand on her heart, she sent him a smoldering look. "If we're not careful, we could starve to death."

"It would never happen." He caught her shoulders, running his hands up and down her arms. At her questioning look, he grinned. "All of a sudden, I believe in the old expression of living on love."

"I believe in food first."

"Spoilsport." He released her.

They worked companionably together, spreading tuna salad on bread, cutting slices of cheese. Minutes later they sat across from each other, enjoying a snack while sharing her uncle's longneck.

"I'm sorry you have to eat such plain food on Christmas. Uncle Leonard said your family's meal would be a feast."

"There's no doubt of that. With Yancy in the kitchen, it'll be fancy." Colin sat back. "What were your holidays like in Boston?"

She smiled. "When my mother was alive, they were really special. She always cooked a turkey and made a special oyster stew for my father."

"When did she die?"

"Just as I started college."

"Was she a doctor?"

Anita shook her head. "She was a high school teacher. She always hoped I'd follow in her footsteps, but I've been drawn to medicine since I was a girl going with my father to his clinic."

"Your dad's a doctor?" He paused before asking, "Why aren't you working with him?"

"I always thought I would. But while I was doing my internship, he met someone and married again. They moved across the country to be closer to her family."

Colin saw a hint of pain in her eyes. "You didn't want to join them?"

"I didn't really know what I wanted. While I was trying to figure out where I fit in, Uncle Leonard called to ask me if I would help him here in Montana, and I honestly felt he'd thrown me a lifeline. I had no idea what to expect, but I knew I had to give it a try."

"And now that you're here? Are you glad you came, or is a part of you wishing you'd stayed in the big city?"

Colin didn't even realize he was holding his breath until she smiled. "I'm so glad I was given this choice. I love it here. I'm never going back."

She glanced at his unfinished sandwich. "Is it that bad?"

He chuckled. "I guess I just forgot to eat. I'd rather listen to the sound of your voice. In truth, I can't remember the last time a tuna sandwich tasted like heaven."

"When did you last eat?"

He thought a minute. "This morning, or rather yesterday morning, up in the hills."

"Oh, Colin." Alarmed, she placed a hand over his. "Here you are, after walking miles in a blizzard, your last meal a day ago, and I never thought to offer you anything to eat until now. It's a wonder you're still standing."

He went perfectly still, absorbing the thrill of her touch through his entire system. "I told you I believe in living on love."

He gave her one of those famous Malloy smiles. "If I'd known you were going to fuss over me like this, I'd have told you sooner."

"I have juice and cookies I keep in the cupboard for our patients. If you'd like—"

They both looked up at the sound of a buzzer.

Anita was on her feet in an instant. "That's Carly."

With a sigh, Colin pushed away from the table to follow her to the birthing room.

Scott and Carly were huddled around the bassinet, their faces wreathed in smiles.

Scott held up his cell phone. "I got service and decided to take your advice and call my folks. They're with Carly's folks, driving together, on the road somewhere trying to find us. They've been out all night and were relieved to hear that we were all right."

"*Relieved* is probably an understatement." Anita's smile was quick. "I'm glad you called them. Did you tell them about Jesse?"

Carly nodded. "Our moms were screaming in the background. Our dads said they'd try to make it to Glacier Ridge if the roads are passable."

"That's just grand. Now, how about some food?"

The two shrugged, more concerned with staring at their baby than with thinking about food.

A short time later, Anita and Colin brought in a tray bearing the last of the tuna sandwiches, along with cans of apple juice and several sugar cookies.

While Scott and Carly ate, Colin dug out his cell phone. Finding service, he phoned the ranch to report that he was safely in town at the clinic. He could hear the relief in his mother's voice when she heard the news.

In a soft voice he added, "I know how you worry about

snowy roads, Ma, but without service, there was no way
to assure you until now. All's well here, though. I guess I
won't be seeing you until morning."

He disconnected and took hold of Anita's hand, leading
her toward the privacy of the staff lounge. Once inside, he
drew her close.

"Now that the new parents are content and my family
can relax knowing I'm safe, maybe the two of us can
have some quiet time and really get acquainted...or
something."

She lifted her face to him with a smile of delight. "Now
that sounds heavenly. Especially that 'or something.'"

"I was hoping you'd say that." Wrapping his arms
around her, he ran soft kisses over her upturned face,
brushing his lips over the curve of her brow, the corner of
her eye, before pausing to tug on her lobe.

She shivered as his mouth continued its exploration.
With his tongue, he traced the outline of her lips before
dipping lower, to the softness of her throat.

She trembled. "You're teasing me."

"I am. Is it working?"

"You know exactly what you're doing." With a sigh,
she caught his face between her hands and pressed her
mouth to his.

On a moan of pleasure, he gathered her firmly against
him and kissed her with a thoroughness that had them
nearly crawling inside each other's skin. And still it wasn't
enough.

They both looked up at the sound of snowplows heading through the main street of Glacier Ridge. Headlights
glared through the glass doors of the clinic as one of the
plows swung into their parking lot.

Minutes later there was a pounding on the door. Anita

gave a sigh of frustration as she hurried over to admit two men bundled to their chins in winter gear.

"You the doc?" one of the men asked.

She nodded. "Dr. Anita Cross."

A second man, his face contorted in pain, was moving slowly behind.

"My name's Blake, Doc. Rusty here tried to adjust one of the plow's blades, and it slipped. I think his shoulder is dislocated."

She was suddenly all business. "Follow me."

Once in an examining room, she and Blake helped Rusty out of his heavy parka. Each movement had Rusty moaning.

His face, Anita noted, was bathed in sweat.

It took no more than a quick examination to concur with Blake's assessment. She nodded. "Definitely dislocated." She turned to Rusty. "The solution is pretty quick, but I have to warn you that the pain will be much worse before you find any relief."

His teeth were chattering. "I know, Doc. I've been through this once before."

She walked to a locked cabinet and returned with a hypodermic needle. "Sit here, Rusty. I'll give you something to ease the pain a little."

"No need, Doc. Just do what you got to do."

She set aside the needle and called Colin to join them.

Once he was there, she said, "The two of you will get on either side of Rusty. When I tell you to pull, you'll pull in opposite directions while I manipulate the shoulder back into its socket."

She looked into Rusty's eyes. "I really recommend you take that sedative first."

He shook his head. "I need to be clearheaded enough to drive tonight, Doc. We've got miles of roads to clear."

"Rusty, even without a sedative, you'll be in too much pain to do any more driving. When this is over, I recommend your friend take you home."

After a few moments of discussion, with Blake forcefully insisting there were enough drivers to handle the snow, Rusty nodded. "Okay, Doc. Give me the shot and let's get this over with."

She picked up the needle and plunged it into his arm before he had a chance to change his mind.

She indicated his arms, and Blake and Colin each took hold.

"Now," Anita said, and the two men pulled.

Rusty let out a holler that could be heard blocks away while Anita quickly and efficiently maneuvered the shoulder back into the socket.

Moments later, Rusty sat, his breathing labored, sweat pouring from his face, before a smile creased his brow. "You're good, Doc. That's the fastest I've ever been lifted out of that kind of hell. I thank you kindly."

"You're welcome." She put a hand to his forehead. "You may want to lie over there on that table for an hour, until your strength returns."

He gave a shake of his head and motioned for his friend to help him into his shirt and parka. "Blake here has to get to work. There's a mountain of snow to move so the folks in town can get back to their routine."

"But not you, Rusty." Anita trailed behind him as he and his partner started from the room.

At the front door he said, "Mind if I come in tomorrow to settle my bill?"

"No need. It's on the house. Call it an early Christmas present."

He shook her hand. "That's a first. Thanks, Doc."

"You're welcome."

As he and Blake headed for the entrance door, she called, "And, Rusty."

"Yeah, Doc?"

"Enjoy your night with your family."

He was grinning broadly. "My wife is going to be so happy. She was having fits when I got the call to start plowing. We've got two little boys at home who are still waiting for Santa."

"I hope Santa is good to them. To all of you. Merry Christmas," Anita called.

He flashed her a gleaming smile. "Merry Christmas, Doc."

When she turned, Colin was standing behind her with a look of admiration.

"You did it again."

"Did what?"

"Worked a miracle without even trying."

She flushed. "I'm sure you've seen a dislocated shoulder a time or two."

He nodded. "I've even had one myself. It's not something I'd ever like to go through again."

"How long did you have to suffer before it was made right?"

"Long enough that I agree with Rusty. It's like being in hell. Unlike Rusty, I wasn't lucky enough to have a compassionate doctor to help. I was up in the hills, too far to go for help. I had to tie my arm to a fence post and pull in the opposite direction until I heard that pop telling me the shoulder had gone back into the socket."

Anita could only stare in amazement at this rugged rancher. In her years of practice, she'd seen grown men close to hysteria because of the pain of dislocation. Yet he'd calmly gone about doing what needed to be done.

Not that she was surprised. There was something so strong and sure about Colin Malloy. She suspected he could always be counted on to do whatever necessary to see a job done.

It was one more in a growing list of things about this cowboy that she found absolutely fascinating.

Colin carried the tray of empty juice cans from the birthing room to the staff room. Once there, he walked up behind Anita, who was busy at the sink.

"Alone at last." He set aside the tray and turned to her.

"How are Scott and Carly getting on?"

"Good. As far as I could tell, they were starting to wind down from their adrenaline high." He shot her one of those sexy smiles. "If we're lucky, they may even sleep for a while."

She laid a hand on his cheek. "Mmm. That would be lovely."

He closed a hand over hers. "I was thinking..."

They both looked up at a pounding on the entrance doors.

Colin muttered, "Next time you have maintenance on the generator, remember to have those doors part of the extended power so they can open and close without doing it manually."

She merely laughed. "If they were working properly, we could be surprised and embarrassed by people crowding in here without warning."

"Yeah, but at least I'd have a few more minutes alone with you."

They started down the hall and paused at the front doors to see a man with his arm around the shoulder of a frail-looking older woman.

"Hello." Anita pushed open the heavy door and held it as the two started in.

"Dr. Cross?"

She nodded.

"I'm Rafe Thompkins. I know your uncle, Dr. Leonard. This is my mother, Verna. She's having trouble breathing."

"Rafe. Verna." She gave them both a smile before saying, "Follow me."

Once inside an examining room, she indicated the reclining chair. "I think this might be more comfortable for your mother than the bed." She moved efficiently across the room, helping the older woman remove her coat before helping her into the chair.

With just a few quick questions, she learned that the woman had suffered from asthma for most of her life and that this episode had begun shortly after the power went off and the ranch house grew cold, even though she'd used her inhaler.

"Cold can be a trigger." She smiled gently at the woman. "And so can fear. A storm of this size is bound to make us fearful, especially once the heat and lights go out."

She removed a vial from a cabinet and filled a syringe. "A shot of this epinephrine should bring you relief within minutes."

"Yes, ma'am." Rafe Thompkins visibly relaxed. "That's exactly what your uncle always does to bring Ma around."

At his words, Anita realized she'd just garnered this man's approval. He'd been watching and listening, comparing her care of his mother to that of her uncle. Not that she minded. She recognized that she was new to town, and many of her uncle's regular patients would be uncomfortable until they came to know her better and to trust her.

After injecting the shot, she covered the woman with a warming blanket and elevated the footrest on the recliner.

Within minutes, Verna Thompkins was resting and breathing comfortably.

"How'd you get here, Rafe?" Colin asked.

"Drove my truck as far as I could, then carried Ma the rest of the way."

"That's quite a feat through all that snow."

The man shrugged, clearly embarrassed at being singled out for courage. "She's my ma."

Colin nodded. "I hear you. I know I'd do the same."

Overhearing them, Anita turned to study these two good men.

In an instant, she was thrust back to her younger days in Boston, recalling the millions of tears she'd shed. Tears over a brilliant surgeon who had cruelly trampled her poor heart. At the time, she'd thought she might never recover from the pain of her loss. Now, looking back, she realized her tears had been wasted on a vain, self-centered peacock, so full of himself he was incapable of caring for anyone except himself and his career. He would never be faithful to any woman. There had been no room in his heart for anyone except himself and his own selfish desire.

Seeing her looking his way, Colin winked.

She could barely swallow because of the way her poor heart was lodged in her throat.

All Colin Malloy had to do was look at her and she felt drawn to him in a way she'd never been drawn to any man. Without a word, with nothing more than a wink of his eye, this quiet, courtly cowboy touched her in a very special way.

The words *solid*, *dependable*, and *honorable* filled her mind.

Colin Malloy was all that.

And sexy as hell.

Chapter Eight

The night air was filled with the welcome sound of snowplows rumbling through the town, stopping to clear the mountains of snow that littered parking lots and side streets.

Shortly after the last of the plows echoed off into the distance, headlights danced across the glass doors of the clinic, announcing the arrival of yet another visitor.

Colin summoned Anita. "Brace yourself. Looks like you're about to get a new patient."

As she started toward the entrance, she said with a laugh, "More than one. I count"—she paused—"four people."

Before the new arrivals could knock on the door, she held it open and they streamed past her.

Two men and two women wore looks ranging from worry to eager anticipation.

"Doctor?"

"Yes. I'm Dr. Anita Cross. Which of you is the patient?"

They looked from one to the other, before the truth dawned.

While the others smiled, a tall, balding man stuck out his hand. "I'm Clark Kelly. This is my wife, Bev. And these are Mary Lee and Curtis Jennings. My son Scott said he and Carly were here."

"Oh, yes." Anita's smile widened. "I'm so glad you were able to make it through this storm. Congratulations to all of you. I'm sure you can't wait to have your first look at your beautiful new grandson, Jesse."

The two women returned her smiles, while the two men looked positively grim.

"If you'll follow me, I'll take you to them."

Seeing the mixed reactions of these four, Colin fell into step beside Anita.

She paused to say, "This is Colin Malloy, a rancher in this area."

Though they acknowledged the introduction, it was obvious they had more important things on their minds. They made no attempt at small talk.

Anita paused outside the birthing room. "If you'll wait here a moment."

When she stepped inside, closing the door behind her, it looked as though Clark Kelly intended to push through. Colin positioned himself in front of the closed door and crossed his arms over his chest.

His determined, imposing presence had the four stepping back a pace.

Moments later Anita opened the door and stood aside. "Scott and Carly are eager to see you."

When they stepped around her, Colin whispered, "I don't think it's safe to leave them alone. From the looks of these two angry fathers, those kids might need us."

Anita smiled. "Scott and Carly will be fine. They have a secret weapon."

Colin shook his head. "Let's just wait a minute, in case they start a war."

The four parents made a quick dash inside. While Anita and Colin watched, the two women hurried across the room to embrace their children, while the two men seemed undecided just how to proceed.

Finally, at the urging of their wives, the two fathers crossed to their children. Curtis Jennings hugged his daughter. Clark Kelly offered Scott a brief handshake, before suddenly drawing his son close and giving him an awkward hug and a pat on the shoulder.

Then the four new grandparents circled the bassinet. Carly picked up the tiny bundle and offered it to her mother, who promptly burst into tears. After a few minutes, Mary Lee Jennings handed the baby over to Bev Kelly, who was already shedding a bucket of tears. By the time each of the new grandfathers was given the chance to hold his new grandson, the tears had become a gusher.

Anita touched a hand to Colin's. "All right. Let's leave them to their privacy. I think it's safe to say that peace will reign."

As they closed the door and started down the hall, he shook his head in amazement. "How did you know?"

She chuckled. "I told you the new parents had a secret weapon. A beautiful new baby has the amazing ability to soften even the most hardened hearts."

Anita and Colin headed toward the staff room, hoping for a quiet moment. Once inside, Colin drew her into his arms and kissed her soundly.

When at last he lifted his head, she found enough breath to ask, "What was that for?"

"Do I need a reason?"

She dimpled. "No, thank heaven. Would you mind if we did that again?"

He needed no coaxing as he gathered her firmly against him. As her lips softened against his, the rush of heat was so intense they both paused before his mouth crushed hers with a fierceness that left her gasping. His fingers dug into the tender flesh of her upper arms as he dragged her close. He feasted on her lips like a starving man. Later, he promised himself, he would take the time to taste, to savor. For now, he was a glutton, ready to devour her.

With his mouth on hers, he drove her back against the open door. His lips left hers to nuzzle her throat. Impatient, he unbuttoned the front of her lab coat to nibble hot, wet kisses along the sensitive hollow of her neck and throat.

"All these clothes." His muttered curse had her attempting to laugh. Instead it came out as a soft sigh.

"Do you think we could lock ourselves in here for an hour, Dr. Cross?"

"The way I'm feeling right now, you have me so hot we'd need only minutes."

He shot her a dark look. "Woman, for what I have in mind, an entire night wouldn't be nearly enough."

He dragged her so close, she could feel his heartbeat inside her own chest. With a sigh of approval, she wrapped her arms around his waist and gave herself up to the most intense pleasure. She knew, without a doubt, that this was what she wanted.

Colin Malloy was what she wanted.

Wrapped around each other, lost in their newly discovered feelings, they almost missed the string of headlights that flickered across the windows of the clinic.

Two heads came up sharply.

Two figures reluctantly stepped apart once more.

Colin caught Anita's hand and, with a moan of frustration, led her toward the entrance.

"More patients," he muttered. "I'm beginning to think it's some sort of conspiracy to keep us apart."

As they watched, a convoy of trucks, all bearing the logo of the Malloy Ranch, circled the parking lot and came to rest just outside the doors.

When the truck doors opened, Colin's family streamed out, each of them carrying something.

Leading the way was Grace, on the arm of her husband, Frank.

"It's my family." Colin turned to Anita. "They must have left the ranch as soon as the roads were plowed. Brace yourself."

Colin pulled open the heavy front door and bent to kiss his mother's cheek.

She patted his shoulder before pausing in front of Anita, who was quick with an apology.

"I'm so sorry I didn't make it to your Christmas Eve dinner, Miss Grace."

"Hush, now. Not a word about it. You're a doctor, doing what doctors do. We can't expect people in need to just wait patiently while you celebrate."

"Oh, Grace, I'm so glad you understand." She kissed Grace's cheek and was rewarded by an embrace from the older woman, followed by a hard, rib-cracking hug from Frank.

Trailing behind them was the Great One, supported by Burke.

The old man gave his grandson a punch to the shoulder. "Aren't you the sly one? You offer to pick up a dinner guest and then get snowed in. Not a bad excuse to spend alone time with the pretty doctor."

Burke leaned close to whisper, "I saw your truck in a snowbank. I don't think the others noticed, with all the snow swirling around the windshield. That had to be some walk here."

Colin gave a grunt of amusement. "I hitched a ride with a snowplow driver along the interstate. I only had to walk in from there."

"What's a few miles in a blizzard when you get the chance to spend it with your lady?"

"Yeah. That's what I figured." Colin looked beyond him, to the parade of family bearing covered dishes. "What's all this?"

Hearing him, Yancy had a grin from ear to ear. "Miss Grace figured if you and the good doctor couldn't make it to the feast, we'd bring the feast to the two of you now that the roads are plowed."

Anita clapped her hands in delight. "Oh my. All this food."

"And these are the leftovers," Yancy said with a chuckle.

As the others streamed past, they gathered around the reception area until old Dr. Cross stepped in and directed them toward the staff lounge.

Inside, under Yancy's direction, they began setting out a buffet on the long countertop.

Matt and Luke were put in charge of unloading a box of dishes and silverware, while Matt's wife, Nessa, and Luke's bride, Ingrid, arranged them in some sort of order.

Soon the entire clinic was perfumed with the wonderful fragrance of prime rib, roast goose, garlic mashed potatoes, an assortment of rolls and vegetables, and even a tray of sweets.

After a quick peek in the other rooms, Dr. Leonard Cross returned to confront his niece.

"So many patients here. I finally managed to get through to Dr. Miller. He was stuck in a snowbank somewhere between Rock Creek and here. How did you manage alone?"

She smiled at Colin. "Thank heaven I wasn't alone. I don't know what I would have done without Colin here. When he arrived, the clinic was in darkness, and I didn't know how to get the generator working. As soon as Colin got heat and light, we found a young couple on our doorstep about to deliver a baby."

"A baby?" Grace's head came up, sensing drama. "However did they get through the blizzard?"

"Believe it or not, the young husband pulled her on a toboggan he had stored in the back of his truck. She delivered a baby boy they've named Jesse, and their parents just got here to celebrate with them."

"Then we'll invite them to join us in our feast." Grace turned away, eager to handle the invitation personally. "It's the perfect night for the celebration of a baby's birth. I should think that will make our little party extra special."

While the family commented over that, Anita added, "Then one of the snowplow drivers arrived with a dislocated shoulder. After he left, we were visited by a rancher in the area, Rafe Thompkins, and his mother, Verna, who was having an asthma attack. In fact, they're still here, staying warm in room two."

Frank looked pleased. "I know Rafe Thompkins and his mother, Verna. If they're feeling up to it, I'll go and invite them to join us, too."

Within minutes, the room was filled to overflowing with all the patients and their families.

Reed popped the cork on several bottles of champagne and was soon passing among them with a tray of fluted glasses.

Scott and Carly stood within the circle of their parents, beaming with pride.

Rafe Thompkins and his mother, now completely recovered, looked surprised and pleased to be included in such a lovely celebration.

The Great One, accustomed to directing important events, took charge.

Getting slowly to his feet, he lifted his champagne flute and used his dramatic voice to its full effect. "We came here tonight to celebrate Christmas with one of our family who was missing. But now we feel truly blessed to celebrate with all of you as well. For this night, unto you"—he turned to bow slightly toward Scott and Carly— "a child has been born. Instead of a donkey, the young mother arrived on a toboggan. Instead of an overcrowded inn, you came to our little clinic and found a welcome. However it happens, wherever it happens, the birth of a baby is always cause for celebration. Let us hope, as we pray at the beginning of all new life, that this child will bring love to all whose lives he touches."

For the space of a heartbeat, there was an awed silence, as though they were in some grand cathedral. Then, as one, they lifted their flutes and called out in agreement.

From his vantage point, Colin saw Scott's parents and Carly's parents draw closer to their son and daughter, before placing their hands on the tiny bundle in Carly's arms.

Rafe and Verna Thompkins were smiling and nodding, Verna's earlier discomfort completely forgotten.

Then Colin glanced around at his family, noisily laughing and teasing, filling the air with the sound of so much energy and love. He experienced a deep sense of pride at the determination of his family to bridge the miles that had kept one of their own from this very special Christmas celebration.

The knowledge of the sacrifice they'd made to be here with him filled him with a sense of wonder and delight.

"To family." Colin lifted his glass.

"To family," the others called.

Colin caught Anita's eye as she stood beside her uncle, drinking a toast to his family. When he winked, her smile grew until it rivaled the sun.

They may not have had much time to themselves, and wasn't it a shame? he thought. But they had something even better. Right now, this minute, they were sharing something life-affirming. Sharing something truly amazing, with all the people who mattered most to them.

Christmas Eve supper had never before tasted so sweet.

Chapter Nine

"Oh, Yancy." Anita looked over at the ranch cook after her first taste of prime rib. "This is amazing. I swear it melts in my mouth."

Yancy couldn't hide his pleasure. "I'm glad, Dr. Anita. I wanted your Christmas Eve supper to be perfect."

"It is. Thank you."

The cook was soon flanked by Bev Kelly and Mary Lee Jennings, who were begging for his recipes. He looked proud and happy as he wrote down their addresses, with a promise to send them all the information.

"Have I told you lately how much I love your family?" Nessa pressed a kiss to her husband Matt's mouth.

"They're your family, too."

"Yes, they are." She touched a hand to his cheek. "And if you ever do me wrong, I'm keeping them."

"There's not a chance in heaven I'll ever let you go, woman."

Her smile could have melted all the snow in town

as she began passing around a tray of homemade cookies.

"Try these." She indicated the small, round disks. "They're Yancy's snickerdoodles. I dare anybody to eat just one."

Amid sighs and words of praise, the tray was soon empty. As were most of the platters of prime rib, roast goose, potatoes, vegetables, and rolls.

Luke grabbed the last roll and offered it to his wife, Ingrid, tucked up against his side. She bit into it with a sigh of pleasure.

Luke shook his head in disbelief. "You'd think a swarm of locusts passed through here. Look at this place. Picked clean."

The others merely smiled and sipped their coffee or champagne, too content to move.

At last Rafe Thompkins started toward the door. "I'll just walk a couple of blocks and see if my truck is still stuck in a snowdrift or if the snowplows were able to free it."

Burke eased himself from a chair. "I'll drive you, Rafe. If it's stuck, I'll give you a push."

"Thanks, Burke." Rafe moved around the room, shaking hands, thanking the Malloy family for the feast and thanking Anita for her help. "I should be back soon to pick up my mother."

He and Burke left, returning less than half an hour later. Rafe helped his mother into her coat, and the two thanked everyone again before taking their leave.

Rafe turned to Dr. Leonard. "Your niece, Dr. Anita, is a welcome addition to the clinic, Doc. She treated Ma just the way you always do. I can tell you it wouldn't have been much of a Christmas if Ma had to spend the whole night suffering."

Old Dr. Cross merely beamed at the praise heaped on his niece.

After a brief consultation with Anita, to assure themselves that it was all right for Carly to leave the clinic, the two families packed up Scott, Carly, and baby Jesse, and crowded into their SUV for the long drive back to retrieve Scott's truck and return to Timberline.

The Malloy family and the two doctors crowded around the entrance to wave good-bye to the new family.

Carly rushed over to throw her arms around Anita's neck. "Thank you, Dr. Cross. You'll never know what your kindness meant to me."

"You're welcome, Carly. Take care of yourself. And take care of that sweet baby boy."

"I will."

Scott stood solemnly beside her and shook Colin's hand. "Thanks again for sharing your family's story with us. Even though I wasn't sure it could happen, you were right about our parents. They've already fallen in love with Jesse."

"That's just a hint of the love you're all going to feel as the years go by, son. Take care. And make wise choices."

"Yes, sir."

When the vehicle disappeared, Colin and Anita fell silent as they trailed the Malloy family back to the staff room, where they began packing up their supplies in preparation for the long drive home.

The family members made endless trips back and forth from the clinic to the trucks parked outside as they loaded up an assortment of roasting pans, containers, and fancy platters.

As they finished up, Grace took Anita's hands. "I'm glad Colin was able to get through the storm to be here with you. I know your uncle was fretting all through supper that you might be here alone."

"Poor Uncle Leonard. With the service out, there was no way to reach him." Anita pressed Grace's hands. "I know Colin was wishing he could let you know he was safe, too. Now that I've learned of your loss on a night like this, I can understand how much you must have worried."

Grace gave her a gentle smile. "Colin gave me his word he'd be safe. That was enough for me. All my men pride themselves on the fact that their word is their bond." She paused before adding, "I hope you'll come to dinner at the ranch another time."

"I'd love to."

"Good." Grace leaned close to brush a kiss on the young doctor's cheek. "Merry Christmas, Anita."

"Merry Christmas, Grace."

Frank shook old Dr. Cross's hand and kissed Dr. Anita before offering his arm to his wife.

He and Grace led the procession of family members who paused to offer their wishes to Anita and her uncle before trailing out to their waiting trucks.

Reed picked up a final serving dish and tucked it under his arm before pausing to say good night to the two doctors.

He turned to Colin. "After all the walking you did tonight, I'm sure you'll be happy to ride home. Come on. You can go with me."

"Thanks. I'll be there in a minute."

Colin stood beside Anita and her uncle at the entrance to the clinic as they called their thanks and good-byes to his family.

One by one, the Malloy family climbed into their trucks for the long ride home.

Colin was doing his best not to stare at Anita, but he couldn't help it. These were their last moments together, and despite the presence of her uncle, he wanted to just fill himself with her before he left.

A horn honked in the stillness of the night, and Reed lowered his window to wave Colin over.

At that moment, the phone began ringing at the reception desk. Before Anita could turn toward it, her uncle walked away to answer the call.

Colin stood, hat in hand, twirling it around and around and trying to think of something, anything to keep her beside him for just a minute more.

"I guess all this must seem pretty different from the celebrations you were used to in Boston."

For a moment she went silent, and he regretted his question.

Then she seemed to positively glow with happiness.

"In truth I'd rather be here than anywhere I can think of."

That brought the smile back to his eyes.

Eyes, she thought, that mirrored his soul. Here was goodness. Here was a solid, dependable, honorable man who would always be as good as his word. This quiet, good man touched her soul in a way that no other man ever could.

"Anita, I'm sorry my big, noisy family came charging in here uninvited. They—"

"Colin." She put a hand on his. "I'm absolutely delighted they came. This will go down as one of the most memorable Christmas Eves I've ever celebrated."

"You mean it?"

"I do."

His smile grew. "That's nice. But I wish we could have had more time alone."

"That would have made it perfect."

He cleared his throat. "I have a cabin up in the hills. It's not fancy. In fact, it's pretty ordinary, but it's set in some of the prettiest countryside you'll ever see. The view of the surrounding hills and valleys, and the most amazing sunsets, takes my breath away. I go there sometimes when the world gets to be too much. Or when I just want to take some alone time. I'd love to take you there sometime."

Anita glanced across the reception area to where her uncle was talking on the phone. "How about next week? For New Year's Eve? Uncle Leonard owes me a weekend off. And," she added softly, "I'd love to spend New Year's Eve with you at your cabin, Colin."

For the space of several seconds, he simply stared. Then it seemed the most natural thing in the world for him to wrap a big arm around her waist and draw her firmly against him, lifting her off her feet. "It's a date, then."

He captured her mouth and kissed her long and slow and deep.

Stunned and deeply moved, Anita felt the room start to spin, or was that her head spinning? She wrapped her arms around his neck and held on, diving into the kiss with a passion that caught them both by surprise.

The horn outside honked again.

Colin lowered her ever so slowly, feeling her in every pore of his body. At last he released her, backing up a step, then seemed to think better of it and caught her to him and kissed her one more time. Just a hard, quick, solid kiss that went straight to his heart and started a smoldering fire deep in his soul.

"Merry Christmas, Anita."

"Merry Christmas, Colin."

Without another word, he sauntered out to Reed's waiting truck.

At that moment, the lights inside the clinic flickered before becoming brighter.

A check of the entrance showed the lights blazing and the sign announcing the Glacier Ridge Clinic open for business.

All through the town the lights came on, blinking red and green in D and B's Diner and glowing gold against the layer of snow at the spa.

As Reed put the truck in gear and started away, he turned to his uncle. "Sorry you got stuck in town in the middle of a blizzard on Christmas Eve. I guess this will be one for the books, huh?"

Colin watched Anita's reflection in the side-view mirror, seeing her standing in a spill of bright light at the entrance of the clinic, looking like an angel in her white lab coat, her dark hair spilling around that gorgeous face in a silken cloud.

Wonder of wonders, she wanted to be with him.

He could hardly wait until next week. New Year's Eve. Alone together. Nobody around for miles. In his cabin in the hills.

Merry Christmas, indeed.

He already knew, without a doubt, Anita Cross was the one.

The only one who would ever own his heart and soul.

His very own Christmas angel.

He leaned his head back and closed his eyes before placing his wide-brimmed hat over his face to hide the grin that split his lips.

"Yeah. One for the books."

Yancy's Snickerdoodles

Mix thoroughly:

- ½ cup softened butter
- ½ cup soft shortening
- 1½ cups sugar
- 2 eggs

Sift together and stir in:

- 2¼ cups flour
- 2 teaspoons cream of tartar
- 1 teaspoon baking soda
- ¼ teaspoon salt

Roll into balls the size of small walnuts.

Roll in mixture of 2 tablespoons granulated sugar and 2 teaspoons cinnamon.

Place 2 inches apart on baking sheet lined with parchment. Bake until lightly browned but still soft. These cookies puff up at first, then flatten out.

Baking Temperature: 400 degrees

Time: Bake 8 to 9 minutes

Amount: Approx. 5 dozen 2-inch cookies

Note: A favorite of the Malloy family and cowboys everywhere.

About the Author

New York Times bestselling author R. C. Ryan has written more than a hundred novels, both contemporary and historical. Quite an accomplishment for someone who, after her fifth child started school, gave herself the gift of an hour a day to follow her dream to become a writer.

In a career spanning more than thirty years, Ms. Ryan has given hundreds of radio, television, and print interviews across the country and Canada and has been quoted in such diverse publications as the *Wall Street Journal* and *Cosmopolitan*. She has also appeared on CNN and *Good Morning America*.

R. C. Ryan is a pseudonym of *New York Times* bestselling author Ruth Ryan Langan.

You can learn more about R. C. Ryan and her alter ego Ruth Ryan Langan at:

RyanLangan.com
Twitter @RuthRyanLangan
Facebook.com/RuthRyanLangan

DON'T MISS A MOMENT OF LIFE ON THE MALLOY RANCH!